A Suitable
VENGEANCE

Also by Elizabeth George

A GREAT DELIVERANCE
PAYMENT IN BLOOD
WELL-SCHOOLED IN MURDER

A Suitable
VENGEANCE

ELIZABETH GEORGE

BANTAM BOOKS
NEW YORK · TORONTO · LONDON · SYDNEY · AUCKLAND

A SUITABLE VENGEANCE
A Bantam Book / July 1991

Library of Congress Cataloging-in-Publication Data

George, Elizabeth.
    A suitable vengeance / Elizabeth George.
        p.   cm.
    ISBN 0-553-07407-5
    I. Title.
PS3557.E478S85   1991
813'.54—dc20   91-10575
                                                         CIP

Published simultaneously in the United States and Canada

Bantam Books are published by Bantam Books, a division of Bantam Double-
day Dell Publishing Group, Inc. Its trademark, consisting of the words ''Ban-
tam Books'' and the portrayal of a rooster, is Registered in U.S. Patent and
Trademark Office and in other countries. Marca Registrada. Bantam Books,
666 Fifth Avenue, New York, New York 10103.

PRINTED IN THE UNITED STATES OF AMERICA

BVG   0 9 8 7 6 5 4 3 2 1

*For my husband, Ira Toibin,
in gratitude for twenty years of
patience, support, and devotion.*

*And for my cousin,
David Silvestri*

Contents

Acknowledgements

A certain amount of research goes into the creation of any novel, but I am particularly indebted to several people who assisted me with incalculably valuable background information for this book:

Dr. Daniel Vallera—Professor and Director of the Section of Experimental Cancer Immunology, Department of Therapeutic Radiology —at the University of Minnesota fielded countless lengthy telephone calls on countless aspects of medical research. I deeply appreciate his good-humored ability to explain the inexplicable in a hundred different and creative ways.

Dr. L. L. Houston of CETUS Corporation in San Francisco, California, spent a patient and thorough conversation walking me through all the steps of the development of a drug, from its initial "discovery" to its final marketing.

Inspector Michael Stephany generously provided me with information which he gleaned from the Orange County Narcotics Squad.

And Virginia Bergman first made me aware of the potential uses of a drug called ergotamine.

Beyond those people, I thank Julie Mayer, my finest and most devoted critic; Vivienne Schuster, Tony Mott, and Georgina Morley who make valiant attempts to keep me true to my subject; Deborah Schneider, the most supportive literary agent I could possibly hope for; and Kate Miciak, my editor and advocate at Bantam.

Of all affliction taught a lover yet,
'Tis sure the hardest science to forget!
How shall I lose the sin, yet keep the sense,
And love the offender, yet detest th' offence?
How the dear object from the crime remove,
Or how distinguish penitence from love?

ALEXANDER POPE

Part I

SOHO NIGHTS

Prologue

Tina Cogin knew how to make the most of what little she had. She liked to believe it was a natural talent.

Some floors above the rumble of nighttime traffic, her naked silhouette gargoyled against the wall of her half-darkened room, and she smiled as her movements made the shadow shift, creating ever new forms of black upon white like a Rorschach test. And what a test, she thought, practising a gesture of come-hither quality. What a sight for some psycho!

Chuckling at her talent for self-deprecation, she went to the chest of drawers and affectionately appraised her collection of underwear. She pretended hesitation to prolong her enjoyment before reaching for an appealing arrangement of black silk and lace. Bra and briefs, they'd been made in France, cleverly designed with unobtrusive padding. She donned them both. Her fingers felt clumsy, largely unused to such delicate clothing.

She began to hum quietly, a throaty sound without identifiable melody. It served as a paean to the evening, to three days and nights of unrestricted freedom, to the excitement of venturing out into the streets of London without knowing precisely what would come of the night's mild summertime promise. She slid a long, painted fingernail under the sealed flap of a package of stockings, but when she shook them out, they caught against skin that was more work-hardened than she liked to admit. The material snagged. She allowed herself a single-word curse, freed the stocking from her skin, and examined the damage, an incipient ladder high on the inner thigh. She would have to be more careful.

As she pulled on the stockings, her eyelids lowered, and she sighed with pleasure. The material slid so easily against her skin. She savoured the sensation—it felt just like a lover's caress—and heightened her own pleasure by running her hands from ankles to calves to thighs to hips. Firm, she thought, nice. And she paused to admire her shape in the cheval glass before removing a black silk petticoat from the chest of drawers.

The gown that she took from the wardrobe was black. The neck high, the sleeves long, she had purchased it solely for the manner in which it clung to her body like a midnight liquid. A belt cinched in its waist; a profusion of jet beadwork decorated its bodice. It was a Knightsbridge creation whose cost—mounting on all the other calls upon her finances—had finally precluded the indulgence of travel by taxi for the rest of the summer. But that inconvenience was no matter, really. Tina knew that some things ultimately pay for themselves.

She slid her feet into black high-heeled pumps before finally switching on the lamp next to the daybed to illuminate a simple bed-sitting-room with the sole delicious luxury of a private bath. On her first trip to London all those months ago—newly married and looking for a haven of escape—she had made the mistake of taking a room in the Edgware Road where she'd shared the bath with a floor of smiling Greeks, all eager to observe the ins and outs of her personal hygiene. After that experience, sharing so much as a wash basin with another human being had been inconceivable to her, and although the additional cost of a private bath had presented something of a challenge at first, she had managed to surmount it in a competent fashion.

She made a final assessment of her makeup and gave approval to eyes correctly shadowed in order to accentuate their colour and correct their shape, to brows darkened and brushed into an arch, to cheekbones shaded artfully to soften what would otherwise be a rectangular face, to lips defined by both pencil and colour to express sensuality and invite attention. She shook back her hair—as black as her dress—and fingered the wispy fringe that fell across her brow. She smiled. She would do. By God, she would do.

With a final glance round the room, she picked up the black handbag she had tossed on the bed, checking to make sure she carried only money, her keys, and two small plastic bags which contained the drug. That done, her preparations complete, she left.

A few moments in the lift and she was out of the building, breathing in the mixed perfumes of the city night, that teeming blend of machinery and humanity peculiar to this corner of London. As always, before heading towards Praed Street, she glanced fondly at the smooth stone exterior of her own building, her eyes gliding over the words *Shrewsbury Court Apartments* which served as epigraph above the double front doors. They opened upon her hideaway and harbour, the only place on earth where she could be herself.

She turned away, walking towards the lights of Paddington Station where she took the District line to Nottinghill Gate, and from there the Central to Tottenham Court Road with its heady miasma of exhaust fumes and its pushing crowds of a Friday night.

She made her way quickly to Soho Square. Here, the patrons of nearby peepshows were milling about, their voices ringing with every possible accent as they exchanged lewd evaluations of the titillating sights they'd had of breasts and thighs and more. They were a surging mass of prurient thrill seekers, and Tina knew that on another night she might have considered one or more of them as possibilities for an amusing encounter of her own. But tonight was different. Everything was in place.

On Bateman Street, a short distance from the square, she saw the sign she was looking for, swinging above a malodorous Italian restaurant. Kat's Kradle, it announced, with an arrow pointing into an unlit alleyway next door. The spelling was absurd, an attempt to be clever that Tina always found especially repellent. But she had not been the one to select the rendezvous, so she made her way to the door and descended the stairs which, like the alley in which the club was housed, were gritty and smelled of liquor and vomit and plumbing gone bad.

In nightclub hours, it was early yet, so the crowd in Kat's Kradle was small, confined to a scattering of tables that surrounded a postage stamp dance floor. At one side of this, musicians were taking up a melancholy piece of jazz on saxophone, piano, and drums while their singer leaned against a wooden stool, smoking moodily and looking largely bored as she waited for the appropriate moment to make some sort of noise into a nearby microphone.

The room was quite dark, lit by one weak, bluish spotlight on the band, candles on the tables, and a light at the bar. Tina made her way to this, slid onto a stool, ordered a gin and tonic from the barman, and admitted to herself that, for all its grime, the location was truly inspired, the best Soho had to offer for a liaison meant to go unobserved.

Drink in hand, she began to survey the crowd, a first viewing that gleaned nothing but an impression of bodies, a heavy cloud of cigarette smoke, the occasional glitter of jewellery, the flash of a lighter or a match. Conversation, laughter, the exchange of money, couples swaying on a dance floor. And then she saw him, a young man seated alone at the table farthest from the light. She smiled at the sight.

It was so like Peter to select this sort of place where he would be safe from the mischance of being seen by his family or any of his posh friends. He ran no risk of condemnation in Kat's Kradle. He faced no fear of trouble, of being misunderstood. He had chosen well.

Tina watched him. Anticipation curled in her stomach as she waited for the moment when he would see her through the smoke and the dancers. Oblivious of her presence, however, he looked only at the door, running his fingers through close-cropped blond hair in nervous agitation. For several minutes Tina studied him with interest, seeing him order and down two drinks in rapid succession, noting how his mouth became harder as he glanced at his watch and his need expanded. From what she could see, he was dressed quite badly for the brother of an earl, wearing a tattered leather jacket, jeans, and a T-shirt bearing the faded inscription *Hard Rock Cafe*. A gold earring dangled from one pierced earlobe, and from time to time he reached for this as if it were a talisman. He gnawed continually at the fingers of his left hand. His right fist jumped in spasms against his hip.

He stood abruptly as a group of boisterous Germans entered the club, but he fell back into his chair when it became apparent that the person he sought was not with them. Shaking a cigarette from a pack that he removed from his jacket, he felt in his pockets but brought forth neither lighter nor matches. A moment later, he shoved back his chair, stood, and approached the bar.

Right to mama, Tina thought with an inward smile. Some things in life are absolutely meant to be.

By the time her companion nosed the Triumph into a parking space in Soho Square, Sidney St. James could see for herself how finely strung his nerves had become. His whole body was taut. Even his hands gripped the steering wheel with a telling control which was inches short of snapping altogether. He was trying to hide it from her, however. Admitting need would be a step towards admitting addiction. And he wasn't addicted. Not Justin Brooke, scientist, *bon vivant,* director of projects, writer of proposals, recipient of awards.

"You've left the lights on," Sidney said to him stonily. He didn't respond. "I said the lights, Justin."

He switched them off. Sidney sensed—rather than saw—him turn in her direction, and a moment later she felt his fingers on her cheek. She wanted to move away as they slid down her neck to trace the small swell of her breasts. But instead she felt her body's quick response to his touch, readying itself for him as if it were a creature beyond her control.

Then a slight tremor in his hand, child of anxiety, told her that his caress was spurious, an instant's placation of her feelings prior to making his nasty little purchase. She pushed him away.

"Sid." Justin managed a respectable degree of sensual provocation, but Sidney knew that his mind and body were taken up with the ill-lit alleyway at the south end of the square. He would want to be careful to hide that from her. Even now he leaned towards her as if to demonstrate that foremost in his life at the moment was not his need for the drug but his desire to have her. She steeled herself to his touch.

His lips, then his tongue moved on her neck and shoulders. His hand cupped her breast. His thumb brushed her nipple in deliberate strokes. His voice murmured her name. He turned her to him. And as always, it was like fire, like loss, like a searing abdication of all common sense. Sidney wanted his kiss. Her mouth opened to receive it.

He groaned and pressed closer to her, touching her, kissing her. She snaked her hand up his thigh to caress him in turn. And then she knew.

It was an abrupt descent to reality. She pushed herself away, glaring at him in the dim light from the streetlamps.

"That's wonderful, Justin. Or did you think I wouldn't notice?"

He looked away. Her wrath increased.

"Just go buy your bloody dope. That's why we've come, isn't it? Or was I supposed to think it was for something else?"

"You want me to go to this party, don't you?" Justin demanded.

It was an age-old attempt to shift blame and responsibility, but this time Sidney refused to play along. "Don't you hit me with that. I can go alone."

"Then why don't you? Why did you phone me, Sid? Or wasn't that you on the line this afternoon, honey-tongued and hot to get yourself laid at the evening's end?"

She let his words hang there, knowing they were true. Time after time, when she swore she'd had enough of him, she went back for more, hating him, despising herself, yet returning all the same. It was as if she had no will that was not tied to his.

And for God's sake, what was he? Not warm. Not handsome. Not easy to know. Not anything she once dreamed she'd be taking into her bed. He was merely an interesting face on which every single feature seemed to argue with all the others to dominate the bony skull beneath it. He was dark, olive skin. He was hooded eyes. He was a thin scar running along the line of his jaw. He was nothing, *nothing* . . . except a way of looking at her, of touching her, of making her thin boyish body sensual and beautiful and flaming with life.

She felt defeated. The air in the car seemed stiflingly hot.

"Sometimes I think of telling them," she said. "They say that's the only way to cure it, you know."

"What the hell are you talking about?" She saw his fingers curl.

"Important people in the user's life find out. His family. His employers. So he bottoms out. Then he—"

Justin's hand flashed, caught her wrist, twisted her hand. "Don't even think of telling anyone. Don't even think of it. I swear if you do, Sid . . . if you do . . ."

"Stop it. Look, you can't go on like this. What are you spending on it now? Fifty pounds a day? One hundred? More? Justin, we can't even go to a party without you—"

He dropped her wrist abruptly. "Then get out. Find someone else. Leave me bloody well alone."

It was the only answer. But Sidney knew she couldn't do it and she hated the fact that she probably never would.

"I only want to help."

"Then shut up, all right? Let me go down that sodding alley, make the buy and get out of here." He shoved open the door and slammed it behind him.

Sidney watched him walk halfway across the square before she opened her own door. "Justin—"

"Stay there." He sounded calmer, not so much because he was feeling any calmer, she knew, but because the square was peopled with Soho's usual Friday night throng and Justin Brooke was not a man who generally cared for making public scenes.

She ignored his admonition, striding to join him, disregarding the certain knowledge that the last thing she ought to be doing was helping him get more supplies for his habit. She told herself instead that if she weren't there, sharply on the lookout, he might be arrested or duped or worse.

"I'm coming," she said when she reached him.

The whipcord of tension in his features told her he had moved beyond caring.

"As you like." He headed towards the gaping darkness of the alley across the square.

Construction was underway there, making the alley mouth darker and narrower than usual. Sidney made a moue of distaste at the smell of urine. It was worse than she had expected it to be.

Buildings loomed up on either side, unlit and unmarked. Grills covered their windows and their entryways housed shrouded, moaning figures who conducted the sort of illicit business which the nightclubs of the district seemed eager to promote.

"Justin, where're you planning to—"

Brooke raised a cautionary hand. Up ahead, a man's hoarse cursing had begun to fill the air. It came from the far end of the alley where a brick wall curved round the side of a nightclub to form a sheltered alcove. Two figures writhed upon the ground there. But this was no love tryst. This was assault, and the bottom figure was a black-clad woman who appeared to be no match in either size or strength for her furious assailant.

"You *filthy* . . ." The man—blond by the appearance of him and wildly angry by the sound of his voice—pounded his fists against the woman's face, ground them into her arms, slammed them into her stomach.

At this, Sidney moved, and when Brooke tried to stop her, she cried out, "No! It's a woman," and ran towards the alley's end.

She heard Justin's sharp oath behind her. He overtook her less than three yards away from the couple on the ground. "Keep back. Let me see to it," he said roughly.

Brooke grabbed the man by his shoulders, digging into the leather jacket he wore. The action of pulling him upward freed his victim's arms, and she instinctively brought them up to protect her face. Brooke flung the man backwards.

"You idiots! Do you want the police after you?"

Sidney pushed past him. "Peter!" she cried. "Justin, it's Peter Lynley!"

Brooke looked from the young man to the woman who lay on her side, her dress dishevelled and her stockings in tatters. He squatted and grabbed her face as if to examine the extent of her injuries.

"My God," he muttered. Releasing her, he stood, shook his head, and gave a short bark of laughter.

Below him, the woman drew herself to her knees. She reached for her handbag, retching momentarily.

Then—most oddly—she began to laugh as well.

Part II

LONDON AFTERNOONS

1

Lady Helen Clyde was surrounded by the trappings of death. Crime scene exhibits lay upon tables; photographs of corpses hung on the walls; grisly specimens sat in glass-fronted cupboards, among them one particularly gruesome memento consisting of a tuft of hair with part of the victim's scalp still attached. Yet despite the macabre nature of the environment, Lady Helen's thoughts kept drifting to food.

As a form of distraction, she consulted the copy of a police report that lay on the worktable before her. "It all matches up, Simon." She switched off her microscope. "B negative, AB positive, O positive. Won't the Met be happy about that?"

"Hmmm," was her companion's only response.

Monosyllables were typical of him when he was involved in work, but his reply was rather aggravating at the moment since it was after four o'clock and for the last quarter hour Lady Helen's body had been longing for tea. Oblivious of this, Simon Allcourt-St. James began uncapping a collection of bottles that sat in a row before him. These contained minute fibres which he would analyse, staking his growing reputation as a forensic scientist upon his ability to weave a set of facts out of infinitesimal, blood-soaked threads.

Recognising the preliminary stages of a fabric analysis, Lady Helen sighed and walked to the laboratory window. On the top floor of St. James' house, it was open to the late June afternoon, and it overlooked a pleasant brick-walled garden. There, a vivid tangle of flowers made a pattern of undisciplined colour. Walkways and lawn had become overgrown.

"You ought to hire someone to see to the garden," Lady Helen said. She knew very well that it hadn't been properly tended in the last three years.

"Yes." St. James took out a pair of tweezers and a box of slides. Somewhere below them in the house, a door opened and shut.

At last, Lady Helen thought, and allowed herself to imagine Joseph Cotter mounting the stairs from the basement kitchen, in his hands a tray covered by fresh scones, clotted cream, strawberry tarts, and tea. Unfortunately, the sounds that began drifting upward—a thumping and bumping, accompanied by a low grunt of endeavour—did not suggest that refreshments were imminent. Lady Helen sidestepped one of St. James' computers and peered into the panelled hall.

"What's going on?" St. James asked as a sharp *thwack* resounded through the house, metal against wood, a noise boding ill for the stairway banisters. He got down awkwardly from his stool, his braced left leg landing unceremoniously on the floor with an ugly thud.

"It's Cotter. He's struggling with a trunk and some sort of package. Shall I help you, Cotter? What are you bringing up?"

"Managing quite well," was Cotter's oblique reply from three floors below.

"But what on earth—?" Next to her, Lady Helen felt St. James move sharply away from the door. He returned to his work as if the interruption had not occurred and Cotter were not in need of assistance.

And then she was given the explanation. As Cotter manoeuvred his burdens across the first landing, a shaft of light from the window illuminated a broad sticker affixed to the trunk. Even from the top floor, Lady Helen could read the black print across it: *D. Cotter/U.S.A.* Deborah was returning, and quite soon by the look of it. Yet as if this all were not occurring, St. James devoted himself to his fibres and slides. He bent over a microscope, adjusting its focus.

Lady Helen descended the stairs. Cotter waved her off.

"I c'n manage," he said. "Don't trouble yourself."

"I want the trouble. As much as do you."

Cotter smiled at her reply, for his labours were born of a father's love for his returning child, and Lady Helen knew it. He handed over the broad flat package which he had been attempting to carry under his arm. His hold on the trunk he would not relinquish.

"Deborah's coming home?" Lady Helen kept her voice low. Cotter did likewise.

"She is. Tonight."

"Simon never said a word."

Cotter readjusted his grip on the trunk. "Not likely to, is 'e?" he responded grimly.

They climbed the remaining flights of stairs. Cotter shouldered the trunk into his daughter's bedroom to the left of the landing, while Lady Helen paused at the door to the lab. She leaned the package against the wall, tapping her fingers against it thoughtfully as she observed her friend. St. James did not look up from his work.

That had always been his most effective defence. Worktables and microscopes became ramparts which no one could scale, incessant labour a narcotic that dulled the pain of loss. Lady Helen surveyed the lab, seeing it for once not as the centre of St. James' professional life, but as the refuge which it had become. It was a large room scented faintly by formaldehyde; walled by anatomy charts and graphs and shelves; floored by old, creaking hardwood; ceilinged by a skylight through which milky sun provided an impersonal warmth. Scarred tables furnished it, as did tall stools, microscopes, computers, and a variety of equipment for studying everything from blood to bullets. To one side, a door led into Deborah Cotter's darkroom. But that door had been closed for all the years of her absence. Lady Helen wondered what St. James would do if she opened it now, flinging it back like an unavoidable invasion into the reaches of his heart.

"Deborah's coming home tonight, Simon? Why didn't you tell me?"

St. James removed one slide from the microscope and replaced it with another, adjusting the dials for a higher degree of magnification. After a moment of studying this new specimen, he jotted down a few notes.

Lady Helen leaned across the worktable and clicked off the microscope's light. "She's coming home," she said. "You've not said a word about it all day. Why, Simon? Tell me."

Instead of answering, St. James looked past her shoulder. "What is it, Cotter?"

Lady Helen swung around. Cotter was standing in the doorway, frowning, wiping his brow with a white linen handkerchief. "You've no need to fetch Deb from the airport tonight, Mr. St. James," he said in a rush. "Lord Asherton's to do it. I'm to go as well. He rang me not an hour ago. It's all arranged."

The ticking of the wall clock made the only immediate response to Cotter's announcement until somewhere outside, a child's frantic weeping—rife with outrage—rose on the air.

St. James stirred to say, "Good. That's just as well. I've a mountain of work to get through here."

Lady Helen felt the sort of confusion that requires an accompanying cry of protest. The world as she knew it was taking on a new shape. Longing to ask the obvious question, she looked from St. James to Cotter, but their reserve warned her off. Still, she could tell that Cotter was willing to say more. He appeared to be waiting for the other man to make some additional comment that would allow him to do so. But instead, St. James merely ran a hand through his unruly black hair. Cotter shifted on his feet.

"I'll be about my business, then." With a nod, he left the room, but his shoulders looked burdened and his steps were heavy.

"Let me understand this," Lady Helen said. "Tommy's fetching Deborah from the airport. Tommy. Not you?"

It was a reasonable enough question. Thomas Lynley, Lord Asherton, was an old friend to both St. James and Lady Helen, something of a colleague as well since for the past ten years he had worked in the Criminal Investigations Department of New Scotland Yard. In both capacities, he had been a frequent visitor to St. James' Cheyne Row house. But when on earth, Lady Helen wondered, had he come to know Deborah Cotter well enough to be the one to meet her at the airport after her time away at school? To phone her father coolly with the arrangements every bit as if he were . . . what on earth *was* Tommy to Deborah?

"He's been to America to see her," St. James replied. "A number of times. He never told you that, Helen?"

"Good heavens." Lady Helen was nonplussed. "How do you know that? Surely Deborah didn't tell you. As for Tommy, he *knows* that you've always—"

"Cotter told me last year. I suppose he'd spent some time wondering about Tommy's intentions, as any father might."

His dry, factual tone spoke volumes more than any telling comment he might have chosen to make. Her heart went out to him.

"It's been dreadful for you, hasn't it, these last three years without her?"

St. James drew another microscope across the table and gave his attention to the removal of a speck of dust that seemed to be adhering stubbornly to its eyepiece.

Lady Helen watched him, seeing clearly how the passage of time, in conjunction with his wretched disability, was doing its best to make him every year less of a man in his own eyes. She wanted to tell him how untrue and unfair such an assessment was. She wanted to tell him how little difference it made. But to do so bordered too closely upon pity, and she would not hurt him by a display of compassion he did not want.

The front door slamming far below saved her from having to speak at all. Rapid footsteps followed. They flew up three flights of stairs without a pause for breath and served as harbinger of the only person with sufficient energy to make so steep a climb in so little time.

"That sounds like Sidney," St. James said moments before his younger sister burst into the room.

"I knew I'd find you in here," Sidney St. James announced, brushing a kiss against his cheek. She flopped onto a stool and said by way of greeting her brother's companion, "I do love that dress, Helen. Is it new? How can you manage to look so put together at a quarter past four in the afternoon?"

"While we're talking of being put together . . ." St. James eyed his sister's unusual attire.

Sidney laughed. "Leather pants. What d'you think? There's a fur as well, but I left it with the photographer."

"Rather a warm combination for summer," Lady Helen said.

"Isn't it beastly?" Sidney agreed happily. "They've had me on Albert Bridge since ten o'clock this morning in leather pants, a fur coat, and nothing else. Perched on top of a 1951 taxi with the driver—I wish someone would tell me where they get these male mannequins—leering up at me like a pervert. Oh yes, and a bit of au naturel showing here and there. My au naturel, if it comes to that. All the driver has to do is look like Jack the Ripper. I borrowed this shirt from one of the technicians. We're breaking for now, so I thought I'd pop over for a visit." She looked round the room curiously. "So. It's past four. Where's tea?"

St. James nodded towards the package which Lady Helen had left leaning against the wall. "You've caught us in disarray this afternoon."

"Deborah's coming home tonight, Sid," Lady Helen said. "Did you know?"

Sidney's face lit. "Is she at last? Then those must be some of her snaps. Wonderful! Let's have a peek." She hopped off her stool, shook the package as if it were an early Christmas gift, and blithely proceeded to remove its outer wrapping.

"Sidney," St. James admonished her.

"Pooh. You know she wouldn't mind." Sidney tossed away the sturdy brown paper, untied the cords of a black portfolio, and picked up the top portrait from the stack within. She looked it over, whistling between her teeth. "Lord, the girl's handier with a camera than she's ever been.'' She passed the photograph to Lady Helen and went on with her perusal of the others in the stack.

Self and Bath. The three words were scrawled in haphazard script across the bottom edge of the picture. It was a nude study of Deborah herself, arranged in three-quarter profile to the camera. She had composed the piece cleverly: a shallow tub of water; the delicate arch of her spine; a table nearby on which sat a pitcher, hair brushes, and comb; filtered light striking her left arm, her left foot, the curve of her shoulder. With a camera and using herself as a model, she had copied *The Tub* by Degas. It was lovely.

Lady Helen looked up to see St. James nod as if in appreciation of it. He walked back to his equipment and started sorting through a stack of reports.

''*Did* you? Did you know it?'' Sidney was asking them impatiently.

''Know what?'' Lady Helen said.

''That Deborah's involved with Tommy. Tommy Lynley! Mummy's cook told me, believe it or not. From what she said, Cotter's quite up in arms about it. Honestly, Simon, you must talk some sense into Cotter. For that matter, talk some sense into Tommy. I think it's completely unfair of him to choose Deb over me.'' She resumed her stool. ''That reminds me. I've got to tell you about Peter.''

Lady Helen felt a margin of relief at this welcome change of subject. ''Peter?'' she said helpfully.

''Imagine this.'' Sidney used her hands to dramatise the scene. ''Peter Lynley and a lady of the night—dressed all in black with flowing black hair like a tourist from Transylvania—caught in *flagrante delicto* in an alley in Soho!''

''Tommy's brother Peter?'' Lady Helen clarified, knowing Sidney's proclivity for overlooking pertinent details. ''That can't be right. He's in Oxford for the summer, isn't he?''

''He looked involved in things far more interesting than his studies. History and literature and art be damned.''

''What are you talking about, Sidney?'' St. James asked as she hopped off the stool and began to prowl round the lab like a puppy.

She switched on Lady Helen's microscope and had a look through it. ''Crikey! What is this?''

''Blood,'' Lady Helen said. ''And Peter Lynley?''

Sidney adjusted the focus. ''It was . . . let me see. Friday night. Yes, that's right because I'd a grim little drinks party to attend in the West End on Friday and that was the night I saw Peter. On the ground in an alley. Scuffling with a prostitute! Wouldn't Tommy be pleased if he heard about that?"

"Tommy's not been happy with Peter all year," Lady Helen said.

"Doesn't Peter know it!" Sidney looked at her brother plaintively. "What about tea? Is there hope?"

"Always. Finish your saga."

Sidney grimaced. "There's not much else to tell. Justin and I came upon Peter grappling with this woman in the dark. He was punching her in the face, as a matter of fact, and Justin pulled him off. The woman— now this was a bit odd—began to laugh and laugh. Of course, she must have been hysterical. But before we had a chance to see if she was fit, she ran off. We drove Peter home. Squalid little flat in Whitechapel, Simon, with a yellow-eyed girl in filthy blue jeans waiting for Peter on the front steps." Sidney shuddered. "Anyway, Peter wouldn't say a word to me about Tommy or Oxford or anything. Embarrassed, I suppose. I'm sure the last thing on earth he expected was to have a friend stumble upon him as he rolled round an alley."

"What were you doing there?" St. James asked. "Or was Soho Justin's idea?"

Sidney avoided his gaze. "D'you think Deb'll take a set of photos of me? I ought to start work on a new portfolio now my hair's cut off. You've not said a word about it, Simon, and it's shorter than yours."

St. James was not to be so easily diverted. "Haven't you had enough of Justin Brooke?"

"Helen, what do you think of my hair?"

"What about Brooke, Sid?"

Sidney directed a wordless apology towards Lady Helen before she faced her brother down. The resemblance between them was remarkable, a sharing of the same curly black hair, the same spare aquiline features, the same blue eyes. They looked like skewed mirror images: the liveliness of one was replaced by resigned repose in the other. They were before-and-after pictures, the past and the present, joined by an undeniable bond of blood.

Sidney's words, however, seemed an effort to deny this. "Don't mother-hen me, Simon," she said.

The sound of a clock chiming in the room startled St. James out of sleep. It was three A.M. For a dazed moment—half sleeping, half waking—he wondered where he was until a knotted muscle, cramping painfully in his neck, brought him fully awake. He stirred in his chair and got up, his movements slow, his body feeling bent. Stretching tentatively, he walked to the study window and looked out on Cheyne Row.

Moonlight lit tree leaves with silver, touching upon the restored houses opposite his own, the Carlyle Museum, and the corner church. In the past few years, a renaissance had come to the riverside neighbourhood, taking it from its Bohemian past into an unknown future. St. James loved it.

He went back to his chair. On the table next to it, a balloon glass still held a half inch of brandy. He drained it, switched off the lamp, and left the study, making his way down the narrow hallway to the stairs.

These he mounted slowly, pulling his bad leg up next to him, gripping the handrail against the strain of dead weight. He shook his head in weary denigration at his solitary, fanciful dance of attendance upon Deborah's return.

Cotter had been back from the airport for some hours, but his daughter had stopped in only briefly, remaining for the entire time in the kitchen. From his study, St. James could hear Deborah's laughter, her father's voice, the barking of the dog. He could even imagine the household cat jumping down from the windowsill to greet her. This reunion among them had gone on for half an hour. Then, instead of Deborah coming up to bid him hello, Cotter had stepped into the study with the uneasy announcement that Deborah had left again with Lord Asherton. Thomas Lynley. St. James' oldest friend.

Cotter's embarrassment at Deborah's behaviour only promised to worsen an already uncomfortable situation.

"Said she'd only be a while," Cotter had stammered. "Said she'd be back directly. Said she'd—"

St. James wanted to stop the words but couldn't think how to do it. He resolved the situation by noting the time and declaring his intention of going to bed. Cotter left him in peace.

Knowing sleep would elude him, he remained in the study, trying to occupy himself with reading a scientific journal as the hours passed and he waited for her to return. The wiser part of him insisted there was no point to a meeting between them now. The fool longed for it, in a welter of nerves.

What idiocy, he thought, and continued climbing the stairs. But as if his body wished to contradict what his intellect was telling him, he made his way not to his own bedroom but to Deborah's on the top floor of the house. The door stood open.

It was a small room with a jumble of furnishings. An old oak ward-robe, lovingly refinished, leaned on uneven legs against the wall. A sim-ilar dressing table held a solitary, pink-edged Belleek vase. A once colourful rug, handmade by Deborah's mother just ten months before her death, formed an oval on the floor. The narrow brass bed that had been hers from childhood stood near the window.

St. James had not entered this room for the three years of Deborah's absence. He did so now reluctantly, crossing to the open window where a soft breeze rustled white curtains. Even at this height, he could catch the perfume of the flowers planted in the garden below. It was faint, like an unobtrusive background on the canvas of night.

As he enjoyed the subtle fragrance, a silver car glided round the corner from Cheyne Row onto Lordship Place and halted next to the old garden gate. St. James recognised the Bentley and its driver, who turned to the young woman next to him and took her into his arms.

The moonlight that earlier had served to illumine the street did as much for the interior of the car. As St. James watched, unable to move from the window even if he had wanted to—which he did not—Lynley's blond head bent to Deborah. She raised her arm, fingers seeking first his hair, then his face before drawing him nearer to her neck, to her breast.

St. James forced his gaze from the car to the garden. Hyacinth, larkspur, alyssum, he thought. Kaffir lilies that wanted clearing out. There was work to be done. He needed to see it. But he couldn't use the garden to avoid his heart.

He had known Deborah from the day of her birth. She had grown up, a member of his small Chelsea household, the child of a man who was to St. James part nurse, part servant, part valet, part friend. During the darkest time of his life, she'd been a constant companion whose presence had saved him from the worst of his despair. But now . . .

She's chosen, he thought, and tried to convince himself in the face of this knowledge that he felt nothing, that he could accept it, that he could be the loser, that he could go on.

He crossed the landing and entered his laboratory where he turned on a high intensity lamp that cast a circle of light upon a toxicology report. He spent the next few minutes attempting to read the document—a pitiful endeavour to put his house in order—before he heard the car's engine start, a sound that was shortly followed by Deborah's footsteps in the lower hall.

He put on another light in the room and walked to the door, feeling a rush of trepidation, a need to find something to say, an excuse for being up and about, fully dressed, at three in the morning. But there was no time to think, for Deborah came up the stairs nearly as quickly as Sidney had done, bringing their separation to an end.

She stepped onto the final landing and started when she saw him. "Simon!"

Acceptance be damned. He held out a hand and she came into his arms. It was natural. She belonged there. Both of them knew it. Without another thought, St. James bent his head, seeking her mouth but finding instead her mane of hair. The unmistakable smell of Lynley's cigarettes clung to it, a bitter reminder of who she had been and who she had become.

The odour brought him to his senses, and he released her. He saw that time and distance had caused him to magnify her beauty, attributing physical qualities to her that she didn't possess. He admitted to himself what he had always known. Deborah was not beautiful in any conventional way. She didn't have Helen's sleek, aristocratic lines. Nor had she Sidney's provocative features. Instead, she was a compilation of warmth and affection, perception and wit, qualities whose definition rose from her liveliness of expression, from the chaos of her coppery hair, from the freckles that dashed across the bridge of her nose.

But there were changes in her. She was too thin, and inexplicable, illusory veins of regret seemed to lie just beneath the surface of her composure. Nonetheless, she spoke to him much as she always had done.

"Have you been working late? You've not waited up for me, have you?"

"It was the only way I could get your father to go to bed. He thought Tommy might spirit you away this very night."

Deborah laughed. "How like Dad. Did you think that as well?"

"Tommy was a fool not to."

St. James marvelled at the rank duplicity behind their words. With one quick embrace they had neatly sidestepped Deborah's reasons for having left England in the first place, as if they had agreed to play at their old relationship, one to which they could never return. For the moment, however, even spurious friendship was better than disjunction.

"I have something for you."

He led her through the laboratory and opened the door of her darkroom. Her hand went out for the light, and St. James heard her gasp of surprise as she saw the new colour enlarger standing in place of her old black and white one.

"Simon!" She was biting the inside of her lip. "This is . . . How very kind of you. Truly . . . it's not as if you had to . . . and you've even waited up for me." Colour smudged across her face like unattractive thumbprints, a reminder that Deborah had never possessed any skills of artifice to fall back upon when she was distressed.

In his grasp, the doorknob felt inordinately cold. In spite of the past, St. James had assumed she would be pleased by the gift. She was not. Somehow, his purchase of it represented the inadvertent crossing of an unspoken boundary between them.

"I wanted to welcome you home somehow," he said. She didn't respond. "We've missed you."

Deborah ran her hand over the enlarger's surface. "I had a showing of my work in Santa Barbara before I left. Did you know that? Did Tommy tell you about it? I phoned him because, well, it's the sort of thing that one dreams of happening, isn't it? People coming, liking what they see. Even buying . . . I was so excited. I'd used one of the enlargers at school to do all the prints and I remember wondering how I'd ever afford the new cameras I wanted as well as . . . And now you've done it for me." She inspected the darkroom, the bottles of chemicals, the boxes of supplies, the new pans for the stop bath and the fixer. She raised her fingers to her lips. "You've stocked it as well. Oh, Simon, this is more than . . . Really, I didn't expect this. Everything is . . . it's exactly what I need. Thank you. So much. I promise I'll come back every day to use it."

"Come back?" Abruptly, St. James stopped himself, realising that he should have had the common sense to know what was coming when he saw them in the car together.

"Don't you know?" Deborah switched off the light and returned to the lab. "I've a flat in Paddington. Tommy found it for me in April. He didn't tell you? Dad didn't? I'm moving there tomorrow."

"Tomorrow? You mean already? Today?"

"I suppose I do mean today, don't I? And we'll be in poor shape, the both of us, if we don't get some sleep. So I'll say good night, then. And thank you, Simon. Thank you." She briefly pressed her cheek to his, squeezed his hand, and left.

So that's that, St. James thought, staring woodenly after her.

He headed for the stairs.

In her room, she heard him go. No more than two steps from the closed door, Deborah listened to his progress. It was a sound etched into her memory, one that would follow her right to her grave. The light drop of healthy leg, the heavy thump of dead one. The movement of his hand on the handrail, clenched into a tight, white grip. The catch of his breath as precarious balance was maintained. And all of it done with a face that betrayed nothing.

She waited until hearing his door close on the floor below before she moved away from her own and went—as she could not know he had done himself only minutes before—to the window.

Three years, she thought. How could he possibly be thinner, more gaunt and ill, an utterly unhandsome face of battling lines and angles on which was engraved a history of suffering. Hair, always too long. She remembered its softness between her fingers. Haunted eyes that spoke to her even when he said nothing himself. Mouth that tenderly covered her own. Sensitive hands, artist's hands, that traced the line of her jaw, that drew her into his arms.

"No. No more."

Deborah whispered the words calmly into the coming dawn. Turning from the window, she tugged the counterpane off the bed and, fully clothed, lay down.

Don't think of it, she told herself. Don't think of anything.

2

Always, it was the same miserable dream, a hike from Buckbarrow to Greendale Tarn in a rain so refreshing and pure it could only be phantasmagorical. Scaling outcroppings of rock, running effortlessly across the open moor, sliding helter-skelter down the fell to arrive, breathless and laughing, at the water below. The exhilaration of it all, the pounding of activity, the rush of blood through his limbs that he felt—he would swear it—even as he slept.

And then awakening, with a sickening jolt, to the nightmare. Lying in bed, staring at the ceiling, willing desolation to fade into disregard. But never quite able to disregard the pain.

The bedroom door opened, and Cotter entered, carrying a tray of morning tea. He placed this on the table next to the bed, eyeing St. James guardedly before he went to open the curtains.

The morning light was like an electrical current jolting directly through his eyeballs to his brain. St. James felt his body jerk.

"Let me get your medicine," Cotter said. He paused by the bed long enough to pour St. James a cup of tea before he disappeared into the adjoining bathroom.

Alone, St. James dragged himself into a sitting position, wincing at the degree to which sounds were magnified by the pounding in his skull. The closing of the medicine cabinet was a rifle shot, water running into the bath a locomotive roar. Cotter returned, bottle in hand.

"Two of these'll do it." He administered the tablets and said nothing more until St. James had swallowed them. Then, casually he asked, "See Deb last night?"

As if the answer didn't really matter to him, Cotter returned to the bathroom where, St. James knew, he would test the heat of the water pouring into the tub. This was a completely unnecessary civility, an act giving credence to the manner in which Cotter had asked his question in the first place. He was playing the servant-and-master game, his words and actions implying a disinterest which he didn't feel.

St. James sugared his tea heavily and swallowed several mouthfuls. He leaned back against the pillows, waiting for the medicine to take effect.

Cotter reappeared at the bathroom door.

"Yes. I saw her."

"A bit different, wouldn't you say?"

"That's to be expected. She's been gone a long time." St. James added more tea to his cup. He forced himself to meet the other man's eyes. The determination written across Cotter's face told him that if he said anything more, he would be extending a blanket invitation to the sort of revelations he would rather not hear.

But Cotter didn't move from the doorway. It was a conversational impasse. St. James surrendered. "What is it?"

"Lord Asherton and Deb." Cotter smoothed back his sparse hair. "I knew that Deb would give 'erself to a man one day, Mr. St. James. I'm no fool about the ways of the world. But knowing 'ow she always felt about . . . well, I suppose I'd thought that . . ." Cotter's confidence seemed to dwindle momentarily. He picked at a speck of lint on his sleeve. "I'm that worried about 'er. What's a man like Lord Asherton want with Deb?"

To marry her, of course. The response came like a reflex, but St. James didn't voice it even though he knew that doing so would give Cotter the peace of mind he sought. Instead, he found himself wanting to voice warnings of Lynley's character. How amusing it would be to limn his old friend as a Dorian Gray. The desire disgusted him. He settled on saying, "It's probably not what you think."

Cotter ran his finger down the doorjamb as if testing for dust. He nodded, but his face remained unconvinced.

St. James reached for his crutches and swung himself to his feet. He headed across the room, hoping Cotter would see this activity as a conclusion to their discussion. But his design was foiled.

"Deb's got 'erself a flat in Paddington. Did she tell you that? Lord Asherton's keeping the girl like she was some tart."

"Surely not," St. James replied and belted on the dressing gown that Cotter handed him.

"What money's she got, then?" Cotter demanded. "How else is it paid for, if not by 'im?"

St. James made his way to the bathroom where the rush of water told him that Cotter—in his agitation—had forgotten that the tub was rapidly filling. He turned off the taps and sought a way to put the discussion to an end.

"Then you must talk to her, Cotter, if that's what you think. Set your mind at rest."

"What *I* think? It's what you think as well and there's no denying it. I c'n see it plain as plain on your face." Cotter warmed to his topic. "I tried talking with the girl. But that was no good. She was off with 'im last night before I'd the chance. And off again this morning as well."

"Already? With Tommy?"

"No. Alone this time. To Paddington."

"Go to see her, then. Talk to her. She might welcome the chance to have some time alone with you."

Cotter moved past him and began setting out his shaving equipment with unnecessary care. St. James watched warily, his intuition telling him the worst was on its way.

"A solid, good talk. Just what I'm thinking. But it's not for me to talk to the girl. A dad's too close. You know what I mean."

He did indeed. "You can't possibly be suggesting—"

"Deb's fond of you. That's always been the case." Cotter's face spoke the challenge beneath the words. He was not a man to avoid emotional blackmail if it took him in the direction which he believed that he—and St. James—ought to be travelling. "If you'd caution the girl. That's all I'd ask."

Caution her? How would it run? *Don't have anything to do with Tommy, Deborah. If you do, God knows you may end up his wife.* It was beyond consideration.

"Just a word," Cotter said. "She trusts you. As do I."

St. James fought back a sigh of resignation. Damn Cotter's unquestioning loyalty throughout the years of his illness. Blast the fact that he owed him so very much. There is always a day of accounting.

"Very well," St. James said. "Perhaps I can manage some time today if you have her address."

"I do," Cotter said. "And you'll see. Deb'll be glad of what you say."

Right, St. James thought sardonically.

*   *   *

The building that housed Deborah's flat was called Shrewsbury Court Apartments. St. James found it easily enough in Sussex Gardens, sandwiched in between two seedy rooming houses. Recently restored, it was a tall building faced with unblemished Portland stone, iron-fenced in the front, its door gained by passing across a narrow concrete walkway that bridged the cavernous entrance to additional flats below the level of the street.

St. James pressed the button next to the name Cotter. An answering buzz admitted him into a small lobby with a floor covered by black and white tile. Like the outside of the building, it was scrupulously clean, and a faint odour of disinfectant announced the fact that it intended to stay that way. There was no furniture, just a hallway leading to the ground floor flats, a door discreetly hung with a hand-lettered sign reading *concierge*—as if a foreign word might attest to the building's respectability—and a lift.

Deborah's flat was on the top floor. Riding up to it, St. James reflected upon the absurdity of the position into which Cotter had placed him. Deborah was an adult now. She would hardly welcome anyone's intrusion into her life. Least of all would she welcome his.

She opened the door at once to his knock, as if she'd spent the afternoon doing nothing save awaiting his arrival. Her expression shifted quickly from welcome to surprise, however, and it was only after a fractional hesitation that she stepped back from the door to admit him.

"Simon! I'd no idea . . ." She offered her hand in greeting, seemed to think better of the gesture, and dropped it to her side. "You've quite surprised me. I was expecting . . . this is really . . . you've only . . . Oh, why am I babbling? Please. Come in."

The word *flat* turned out to be a euphemism, for her new home was little more than a cramped bed-sitting-room. Still, much had been done to fill it with comfort. Pale green paint, refreshing and springlike, coated the walls. Against one of them, a rattan day bed was covered with a bright, multicolored counterpane and embroidered pillows. On another, a collection of Deborah's photographs hung, pieces which St. James had never seen before and realised must represent the result of her years of training in America. Music played softly from a stereo near the window. Debussy. *Afternoon of a Faun.*

St. James turned to comment upon the room—what a far cry it was from the adolescent eclecticism of her bedroom at home—and caught sight of a small alcove to the left of the door. It comprised a kitchen where an undersized table was set with a china tea service. Two places were laid.

He should have realised the moment he saw her. It was hardly in character for her to be lolling around in the middle of the day, wearing a soft summer dress in place of her usual blue jeans.

"You've someone coming. I'm sorry. I should have phoned."

"I'm not connected yet. It doesn't matter. Really." She extended her arm to encompass the room. "What do you think? Do you like it?"

The entire bed-sit was, he thought, pretty much what it was intended to be: a room of peace and femininity in which a man would want to lie at her side, throwing off the day's burdens for the pleasure of making love. But that was hardly the response Deborah wanted from him. To avoid having to give one, he walked to her pictures.

Although more than a dozen hung on the wall, they were grouped in such a way that his eyes were drawn to a striking black and white portrait of a man standing with his back to the camera, his head turned in profile, his hair and skin—both lit with a shimmering cast of water—acting as contrast to an ebony background.

"Tommy photographs well."

Deborah joined him. "He does, doesn't he? I was trying to give some definition to his musculature. I'm not at all sure about it, though. The lighting seems off. I don't know. One minute I like it and the next I think it's about as subtle as a mug shot."

St. James smiled. "You're as hard on yourself as you ever were, Deborah."

"I suppose I am. Never satisfied with anything. That's always been my story."

"I'd say a piece was fine. Your father would agree. We'd bring in Helen for a third opinion. Then you'd celebrate your success by throwing it away and claiming we all were hopeless judges."

She laughed. "At least I didn't fish for compliments."

"No. You didn't do that." He turned back to the wall. The brief pleasure of their exchange withered to nothing.

A different sort of study had been placed next to the black and white portrait. It too was of Lynley, seated nude in an old iron bed, rumpled bed linen thrown over the lower part of his torso. With one leg raised, an arm resting on his knee, he gazed towards a window where Deborah stood, her back to the camera, sunlight gleaming along the swell of her right hip. Yellow curtains billowed back frothily, no doubt serving to hide the cable release that had allowed her to take the picture. The photograph looked completely spontaneous, as if she had awakened at Lynley's side and found an opportunity in a chance of light, in the contrast of curtains and morning sky.

St. James stared at the picture, trying to pretend he could evaluate it as a piece of art, knowing all the time it was affirmation that Cotter had guessed the entire truth about Deborah's relationship with Lynley. In spite of the sight of them together in his car last night, St. James knew that he had been holding on to an insubstantial thread of hope. It snapped before his eyes. He looked at Deborah.

Two spots of colour had appeared high on her cheeks. "Heavens, I'm not a very good hostess, am I? Would you like something to drink? Gin and tonic? Or there's whisky. And tea. There's tea. I've lots of tea. I was about to—"

"No. Nothing. You've someone coming. I'll not stay long."

"Stay for tea. I can set another place." She went to the tiny kitchen.

"Please, Deborah. Don't," St. James said quickly, imagining the awkward civility of getting through tea and three or four digestive biscuits while Deborah and Lynley made polite conversation with him, all the time wishing he would be on his way. "It's really not right."

Deborah paused at the kitchen cupboard, a cup and saucer in her hand. "Not right? What d'you mean? It'll just be—"

"Listen, little bird." He wanted only to get everything said, do his miserable duty, keep his promise to her father, and be gone. "Your father's worried about you."

With studied precision, Deborah put down the saucer, and then, even more carefully, the cup on top of it. She lined them up with the edge of the work top. "I see. You're here as his emissary, aren't you? It's hardly the role I'd expect you to play."

"I told him I'd speak to you, Deborah."

At that—perhaps it was the change in his tone—he saw the spots of colour on her cheeks deepen. Her lips pressed together. She walked to the day bed, sat down, and folded her hands.

"All right. Go ahead."

St. James saw the unmistakable flicker of passion cross her face. He heard the first stirring of temper in her voice. But he chose to ignore both, deciding to go on with what he had come to say. He assured himself that his motivation was his promise to Cotter. His given word meant commitment, and he could not leave without making certain Cotter's concerns were explained to his daughter in the most explicit terms.

"Your father's worried about you and Tommy," he began, in what he deemed a reasonable manner.

She countered adroitly. "And what about you? Are you worried as well?"

"It has nothing to do with me."

"Ah. I should have known. Well, now that you've seen me—and the flat as well—are you going to report back and justify Dad's worries? Or do I need to do something to pass your inspection?"

"You've misunderstood."

"You've come snooping around to check up on my behaviour. What is it exactly I've misunderstood?"

"It isn't a question of your behaviour, Deborah." He was feeling defensive, decidedly uncomfortable. Their interview wasn't supposed to take this course. "It's only that your relationship with Tommy—"

She pushed herself to her feet. "I'm afraid that's none of your business, Simon. My father may be little more than a servant in your life, but I'm not. I never was. Where did you get the idea you could come round here and pry into my life? Who do you think you are?"

"Someone who cares about you. You know that very well."

"Someone who . . ." Deborah faltered. Her hands clenched in front of her as if she wished to stop herself from saying more. The effort failed. "Someone who *cares*? You call yourself someone who cares about me? You, who never bothered to write so much as a single letter all the years I was gone. I was seventeen years old. Do you know what that was like? Have you any idea since you *care* so much?" She walked unevenly to the other side of the room and swung to face him again. "Every day for months on end, there I was, waiting like an idiot—a stupid little fool—hoping for word from you. An answer to my letters. Anything! A note. A card. A message sent through my father. It didn't matter what as long as it was from you. But nothing came. I didn't know why. I couldn't understand. And in the end, when I could face it, I just waited for the news that you'd finally married Helen."

"Married *Helen*?" St. James demanded incredulously. He didn't stop to consider how or why their conversation was escalating so rapidly into an argument. "How in God's name could you even think that?"

"What else was I to think?"

"You might have had the sense to start out with what existed between the two of us before you left England."

Tears sprang into her eyes, but she blinked them back furiously. "Oh, I thought of that, all right. Every night, every morning, I thought of that, Simon. Lying in my bed, trying to come up with a single good reason to get on in my life. Living in a void. Living in hell. Are you pleased to know it? Are you satisfied now? Missing you. Wanting you. It was torture. A disease."

"With Tommy the cure."

"Absolutely. Thank God. With Tommy the cure. So get out of here. Now. Leave me alone."

"I'll leave, all right. It would hardly do to have me here in the love nest when Tommy arrives to claim what he's paid for." He pointed crudely at each object as he spoke. "Tea laid out nicely. Soft music playing. And the lady herself, ready and waiting. I can see I'd get just a bit in the way. Especially if he's in a rush."

Deborah backed away from him. "What he's *paid* for? Is that why you're here? Is that what you think? That I'm too worthless and stupid to support myself? That this is Tommy's flat? Who am I then, Simon? Who bloody well am I? His bauble? Some scrubber? His tart?" She didn't wait for the answer. "Get out of my flat."

Not yet, he decided. By God, not yet. "You talk a pretty piece about torture, don't you? So what the hell do you think these three years have been like for me? And how do you imagine I felt waiting to see you, last night, hour after hour—after three goddamned years—and knowing now you were here all that time with him?"

"I don't care how you felt! Whatever it was, it couldn't come close to the misery you foisted on me."

"What a compliment to your lover! Are you sure *misery* is the word you want to use?"

"It comes back to that, doesn't it? Sex is the issue. Who's screwing Deb. Well, here's your chance, Simon. Go ahead. Have me. Make up for lost time. There's the bed. Go on." He didn't reply. "Come on. Screw me. Have me for a quickie. That's what you want, isn't it? Damn you, isn't it?"

When still he was silent, she reached in a fury for the first available object that came into her hand. She threw it at him with all her strength, and it crashed and splintered against the wall near his head. They both saw too late that in her rage she had destroyed his gift to a long ago childhood birthday, a porcelain swan.

The act ended anger.

Deborah started to speak, a fist at her lips, as if she were seeking the first horrified words of apology. But St. James felt beyond hearing another word. He looked down at the broken fragments on the floor and crushed them into powder beneath his foot, a single sharp movement with which he demonstrated that love, like clay, can be pitiably friable.

With a cry, Deborah rushed across the room to where a few pieces lay beyond his reach. She picked them up.

"I hate you!" Tears finally coursed down her cheeks. "I hate you!

This is just the sort of thing I'd expect you to do. And why not when everything about you is crippled. You think it's just your stupid leg, don't you, but you're crippled inside, and by God, that's worse.''

Her words knifed the air, every nightmare come to life. St. James flinched from their strength and moved towards the door. He felt numb, weak, and primarily conscious of the terrible awkwardness of his gait, as if it were magnified a thousand times for her to see.

"Simon! No! I'm sorry!''

She was reaching towards him and he noted with interest that she'd cut herself on the edge of one of the pieces of porcelain. A hairline of blood ran from palm to wrist.

"I didn't mean it. Simon, you know I didn't mean it.''

He marvelled at the fact that all previous passion was quite dead in him. Nothing mattered at all, save the need to escape.

"I know that, Deborah.''

He opened the door. It was a mercy to be gone.

The blood felt like rising floodwaters within his skull, the usual precursor of an intolerable pain. Sitting in his old MG outside the Shrewsbury Court Apartments, St. James fought it, knowing that if he gave it even a moment's sway, the agony would be so excruciating that finding his way back to Chelsea without assistance would be impossible.

The situation was ludicrous. Would he actually have to telephone Cotter for assistance? And from what? From a fifteen-minute conversation with a girl just twenty-one years old? Surely he, eleven years her senior with a world of experience behind him, ought to have emerged the victor from their encounter, rather than what he was at the moment, shattered, weak-kneed, and ill. How rich.

He closed his eyes against the sunlight, an incandescence that seared his nerves, one that he knew did not really exist but was only the product of his heat-oppressed brain. He laughed derisively at the tortured convolution of muscle, bone, and sinew that for eight years had been his bar of justice, prison, and final retribution for the crime of being young and being drunk on a winding road in Surrey long ago.

The air he drew in was hot, fetid with the scent of diesel fuel. Still, he sucked it in deeply. To master pain in its infancy was everything, and he did not pause to consider that doing so would then give him leave to examine the charges which Deborah had hurled against him and, worse, to admit to the truth of every one.

For three years, he had indeed not sent her a message, not a single letter, not a sign of any kind. And the damnable fact behind his behaviour was that he could not excuse it or explain it in a way she might ever come to understand. Even if she did, what point would it serve for her to know now that every day without her he had felt himself growing just a bit more towards nothing? For while he had allowed himself to die by inches and degrees, Lynley had taken up position within the sweet circumference of her life, and there he had moved in his usual fashion, gracious and calm, completely self-assured.

At the thought of the other man, St. James made himself stir and felt for the car keys in his pocket, determined not to be found—looking like a puling schoolboy—in front of Deborah's apartment building when Lynley arrived. He pulled away from the kerb and joined the rush-hour traffic that was hurtling down Sussex Gardens.

As the light changed on the corner of Praed and London Streets, St. James braked the car and let his glance wander forlornly with a heaviness that matched the condition of his spirit. Without registering any of them, his eyes took in the multifarious business establishments that tumbled one upon the other down the Paddington street, like children eager to grab one's attention on the pathway to the tube. A short distance away, beneath the blue and white underground sign, a woman stood. She was making a purchase of flowers from a vendor whose cart stood precariously, one wheel hanging over the kerb. She shook back her head of close-cropped black hair, scooped up a spray of summer flowers, and laughed at something the vendor said.

Seeing her, St. James cursed his unforgivable stupidity. For here was Deborah's afternoon guest. Not Lynley at all, but his very own sister.

The knocking began at her door just moments after Simon left, but Deborah ignored it. Crouched near the window, she held the broken fragment of a fluted wing in her hand, and she drove it into her palm so that it drew fresh blood. Just a drop here and there where the edges were sharpest, then a more determined flow as she increased the pressure.

Let me tell you about swans, he had said. *When they choose a mate, they choose once and for life. They learn to live in harmony together, little bird, accepting each other just the way they are. There's a lesson in that for us all, isn't there?*

Deborah ran her fingers over the delicate moulding that was left of Simon's gift and wondered how she had possibly come to engage in such an act of betrayal. What possible triumph had she managed to achieve beyond a brief and blinding vengeance that had as its fountainhead his complete humiliation? And what, after all, had the frightful scene between them managed to prove at the heart of the matter? Merely that her adolescent philosophy—spouted to him so confidently at the age of seventeen—had been incapable of standing the test of a separation. *I love you,* she had told him. *Nothing changes that. Nothing ever will.* But the words hadn't proved true. People weren't like swans. Least of all was she.

Deborah got to her feet, wiping at her cheeks roughly with the sleeve of her frock, uncaring if the three buttons at the wrist abraded her skin, rather hoping they would. She stumbled into the kitchen where she found a cloth to wrap round her hand. The fragment of wing she placed in a drawer. This latter she knew was fruitless activity, carried out in the ridiculous belief that the swan itself might someday be mended.

Wondering what excuse she could make to Sidney St. James for her appearance, she went to the door where the knocking continued. Wiping her cheeks a second time, she turned the knob, trying to smile, but managing only a grimace.

"What a mess. I'm perfectly—" Deborah faltered.

A bizarrely clad, but nonetheless attractive, black-haired woman stood on the threshold. She held a glass of milky green liquid in her hand, and she extended it without a prefatory remark. Nonplussed, Deborah took it from her. The woman nodded sharply and walked into the flat.

"Men are all the same." Her voice was husky, with a regional accent she seemed to be trying to shed. She padded on bare feet to the centre of the room and continued to speak as if she and Deborah had known each other for years. "Drink it up. I go through at least five a day. It'll make you feel a new woman, I swear it. And Christ knows, these days *I* need to feel like new after every—" She stopped herself and laughed, showing teeth that were extraordinarily white and even. "You know what I mean."

It was hard to avoid knowing exactly what the woman did mean. In a black satin negligee with voluminous folds and flounces, she was a walking advertisement for her calling in life.

Deborah held up the glass which had been pressed upon her. "What is this?"

A buzzer sounded, indicating the presence of someone on the street below. The woman walked to the wall and pressed the reciprocal bell for entry.

"This place is as busy as Victoria Station."

She nodded to the drink, removed a card from the pocket of her

dressing gown and handed it to Deborah. "Nothing but juices and vita-
mins, that. A few veggies thrown in. A little pick-me-up. I've written it
all down for you. Hope you don't mind the liberty but from the sound
of today, you'll be needing a lot of it. Drink it. Go on." She waited
until Deborah had raised the glass to her lips before sauntering to her
photographs. "Very nice. This your stuff?"

"Yes." Deborah read the list of ingredients on the card. Nothing
more harmful than cabbage, which she'd always loathed. She placed the
glass on the work top and smoothed her fingers across the cloth that was
wrapped round her palm. She lifted her hand to her tangled mess of hair.
"I must look a sight."

The woman smiled. "I'm a wreck myself until after nightfall. I
never bother much in the light of day. What's the point, I say. Anyway,
you're a perfect vision as far as I'm concerned. How d'you like the
drink?"

"It's not quite like anything I've ever tasted."

"Special, isn't it? I ought to bottle the stuff."

"Yes. Well, it's good. Very good. Thank you. I'm terribly sorry
about the row."

"It was a great one. I couldn't help overhearing most of it—walls
being what they are—and for a bit I thought it might come to blows.
I'm just next door." She cocked her thumb to the left. "Tina Cogin."

"Deborah Cotter. I moved in last night."

"Is that what all the thumping and pounding was about?" Tina
grinned. "And to think I was imagining some competition. Well, none
of that talk. You don't look the type to be on the game, do you?"

Deborah felt herself colouring. Thank you hardly seemed an appropriate response.

Apparently finding reply unnecessary, Tina busied herself looking
at her reflection in the glass that covered one of Deborah's photographs.
She rearranged her hair, examined her teeth, and ran a long fingernail
between the front two. "I'm a ruin. Makeup just can't do it all, can
it? Ten years ago, a bit of blusher was all it took. And now? Hours in
front of a mirror and I still look like hell when I'm done."

A knock sounded on the door. Sidney, Deborah decided. She wondered what Simon's sister would say about this unexpected visitor to her
flat who was currently studying the photograph of Lynley as if she were
considering him a source of future income.

"Would you like to stay for tea?" Deborah asked her.

Tina swung from the picture. One eyebrow lifted. "Tea?" She said
the word as if the substance had not passed her lips for the better part of

her adult life. "Sweet of you, Deb, but no. Three in this kind of situation is a bit of a crowd. Take it from me. I've tried it."

"Three?" Deborah stammered. "It's a woman."

"Oh, no!" Tina laughed. "I was talking of the table, love. It's a bit small, you see, and I'm all elbows and thumbs when it comes to tea. You just finish that drink and return the glass later. Right?"

"Yes. Thank you. All right."

"And we'll have a nice little chat when you do."

With a wave of her hand, Tina opened the door, swept past Sidney St. James with an electric smile, and disappeared down the hall.

3

Peter Lynley hadn't chosen his Whitechapel flat for either amenities or location. Of the former, there were none, unless one could call four walls and two windows—both painted shut—a strong selling feature. As to the latter, the flat indeed had ease of access to an underground station, but the building itself was of pre-Victorian vintage, surrounded by others of a similar age, and nothing had been done to clean or renovate either buildings or neighbourhood in at least thirty years. However, both the flat and its location served Peter's needs, which were few. And more importantly, his wallet, which as of today was nearly empty.

The way he had it worked out, they could make it another fortnight if they played it conservatively and held themselves to just five lines a night. All right, perhaps six. Then during the day, they'd start looking for work in earnest. A job in sales for him. New performances for Sasha. He had the brains and the personality for sales. And Sasha still had her art. She could use it in Soho. They'd want her there. Hell, they'd probably never seen anything like her in Soho. It would be just like Oxford, with a bare stage, a single spotlight, and Sasha on a chair, letting the audience cut her clothes off, daring them to cut off everything. "Get in touch with yourself. Know what you feel. Say what you want." All the time she'd be smiling, all the time superior, all the time the only person in the room who knew how to be proud of who and what she was. Head high, held confidently, arms at her sides. *I am,* her posture declared. *I am. I am.*

Where was she, Peter wondered.

He checked the time. His watch was an unattractive, second-hand Timex that managed to exude an air of unreliability simply by existing. He'd sold his Rolex some time ago and had quickly discovered that relying on this current piece for accuracy was just about as ridiculous as relying on Sasha to make a score on her own without latching onto a copper's nark by mistake.

He avoided dwelling upon that thought by shaking his wrist anxiously and peering at the watch. Had its blasted hands even moved in the last half hour? He held it to his ear, swore in disbelief at the gentle ticking. Could it only have been two hours since she'd left? It seemed like ages.

Restlessly, he got up from the sagging sofa, one of the room's three pieces of fourth-hand furniture, if one didn't count the cardboard cartons in which they kept their clothes or the overturned vegetable crate that held their only lamp. The sofa unfolded into a lumpy bed. Sasha griped about it daily, saying it was doing in her back, saying she hadn't had a decent hour's sleep in at least a month.

Where *was* she? Peter went to one of the windows and flicked back its covering, a bedsheet crudely fashioned into a curtain by shoving a rusting rod through its hem. He gazed through the pane. It was grimy inside as well as out.

As Peter searched the street for Sasha's familiar form—for a glimpse of the old carpetbag satchel she always carried—he took a dirty handkerchief from the hip pocket of his blue jeans and wiped his nose. It was an automatic reaction, done without thought. And the brief spurt of pain that accompanied it was gone in an instant and thus easily ignored as inconsequential. Without looking at the linen or examining the new, rust-coloured stains upon it, he replaced the handkerchief and chewed with rabbit bites on the side of his index finger.

In the distance, at the mouth of the narrow street in which they lived, pedestrians passed in Brick Lane, commuters on their way home for the day. Peter tried to focus upon them, making a deliberate exercise of attempting to pick Sasha out of the bobbing heads on their way to or from Aldgate East Station. She'd come on the Northern, he told himself, make a switch to the Metropolitan and home. So where was she? What was so hard about one buy, after all? Give over the money. Get the stuff. What was taking so long?

He mulled over the question. What *was* taking Sasha so long? For that matter, what was to prevent the little bitch from taking off with his cash, making the score on her own, and never coming back to the flat at all? In fact, why should she bother to return? She'd have what she wanted. That's why she continued to hang about.

Peter rejected the idea as completely impossible. Sasha wouldn't leave. Not now, not ever. She said only last week that she'd never had it as good as she had it from him. Didn't she beg for it practically every night?

Pensively, Peter wiped his nose on the back of his hand. When *had* they last done it? Last night, wasn't it? She was laughing like crazy and he'd caught her up against the wall and . . . wasn't that last night? Sammy from across the hall pounding on the door and telling them to hold it down and Sasha shrieking and scratching and gasping for breath— only she wasn't shrieking, she was laughing—and her head kept bouncing back against the wall and he didn't finish with her, couldn't finish, but it didn't matter at the time because both of them were up in the clouds.

That was it. Last night. And she'd be back when she scored.

With his teeth, he pulled at the rough edge of a fingernail.

So. What if she couldn't make the buy? She'd talked big enough this afternoon about Hampstead, a house near the heath where deals went down if the money was right so where was she how long could it take to get there and back where the hell *was* she?

Peter grinned, tasted blood where he'd bitten through the skin. It was time for control. He inhaled. He stretched. He touched his toes.

It didn't matter, anyway. He had no real need of it. He could stop any time. Everyone knew that. One could stop any time. Still and all, he was something with it. Master manipulator, king of the world.

The door opened behind him and he spun to see that Sasha was back. In the doorway, she pushed her lank hair off her face and watched him warily. Her stance reminded him of a cornered hare.

"Where is it?" he asked.

An emotion flickered across her features. She kicked the door closed and went to the sofa where she sat on its threadbare brown cushions, her back to him, her head dropped forward. Peter felt the skeletal fingers of warning dance against his skin.

"Where is it?"

"I didn't . . . I couldn't . . ." Her shoulders started shaking.

Control disintegrated in an instant.

"You couldn't *what?* What in hell's going on?" He dashed to the window and inched back the curtain. Christ, had she blown it? Had she been followed by the cops? He peered at the street. There was nothing out of the ordinary there. No unmarked police car held occupants busily observing the building. No van stood illegally against the kerb. No plain-clothes policeman loitered beneath the streetlamp. There was nothing.

He turned back to her. She was watching him over her shoulder. Her eyes—like a dog's curious shade of yellow and brown—were watery, red-rimmed. Her lips trembled with defeat. He knew.

"Jesus Christ!" He flew across the room, shoved her to one side, and grabbed the carpetbag. He dumped its contents onto the sofa and sifted through them. His hands were clumsy, his frantic search useless. "Where the hell. . . ? Where's the stuff, Sasha? Where is it? Where?"

"I didn't—"

"Then where's the cash?" Sirens shrieked in his head. The walls tilted in. "Sasha, what the fuck have you done with the cash?"

Sasha reared up at that, right off the sofa and across the room. "That's it?" she shouted. " 'Where the fuck is the cash?' Not 'Where've you been?' Not 'I've been worried.' But 'Where the fuck is the cash?' " She whipped back the sleeve of her stained, purple jersey. Deep scratches covered her jaundiced skin. Bruises were rising to the surface there. "Look for yourself! I was mugged, you little bastard!"

"You were *mugged*?" The question climbed a scale of disbelief. "Don't you give me that crap. What've you done with my cash?"

"I told you! Your sodding wad of cash was pinched on the bloody platform of the bloody station. I've spent the last two hours socialising with the bloody Hampstead police. Ring them yourself if you don't believe me." And she began to sob.

He couldn't believe it. He wouldn't. "Christ, you can't do anything, can you?"

"No, I can't. And neither can you. If you'd got it yourself last Friday like you said you would—"

"I told you, goddamn it. How many times do I have to repeat it? It didn't work out."

"So you got *me* to do it, didn't you?"

"I got *you*?"

"You did. You bloody well did!" Her face worked bitterly. "You were too flipping terrified that you'd get busted, weren't you? So you left it to me. Don't harp on it now when it didn't work out."

Peter felt his palm itch with the need to strike her, to see the red rush of blood on her skin. He walked away from her, buying time, seeking calm, trying to think what to do. "You've got them, Sash. All the facts. All in order."

"It was all right, wasn't it, if I took the fall? What difference would that make? Sasha Nifford. Nobody. Nothing in the newspapers about her, right? But what would it look like if the Honourable Peter got his little hands slapped?"

"Shut up about that."

"Making smelly little messes on the family name?"

"Shut up!"

"Upsetting the applecarts of three hundred years of law-abiding Lynleys? Upsetting Mummy? Upsetting big brother at Scotland Yard CID?"

"Goddamn you, shut up!"

Someone below them pounded on the ceiling, shouting for peace. Still, Sasha glared at him, her posture and expression daring him to disprove what she'd said. He couldn't.

"Let's just think this out," he muttered. He noticed that his hands were shaking—every joint had begun to sweat as well—and he shoved them into his pockets. "There's always Cornwall."

"Cornwall?" Sasha sounded incredulous. "Why the hell—"

"I don't have enough money here."

"I don't believe it. If you're out of money, ask your brother for a cheque. He's rolling in cash. Everyone knows that."

Peter went back to the window, gnawing his thumb.

"But you won't do that, will you?" Sasha continued. "You wouldn't dare ask your brother for a loan. We're going to traipse all the way to Cornwall because you're scared to death of him. You're absolutely petrified at the thought of Thomas Lynley's getting wise to you. And what if he does? What is he, your keeper? Just some big toff holding an Oxford degree? Are you such a little pansy that—"

"Stow it!"

"I won't. What the hell's in Cornwall that we've got to go there?"

"Howenstow," he snapped.

Her jaw dropped. "Howenstow? A little visit with Mummy? Jesus, that's just about what I'd expect of you next. Either that or sucking your thumb. Or playing with yourself."

"Fucking bitch!"

"Go ahead! Hit me, you pathetic little twit. You've been aching to do it ever since I walked in the door."

His fist clenched and unclenched. God, how he wanted to. Years of upbringing and codes of behaviour to hell. He wanted to pound on her face, see blood pour from her mouth, break her teeth and her nose, to blacken both of her eyes.

Instead, he fled the room.

Sasha Nifford smiled. She watched the closed door, meticulously counting the seconds that it would take Peter to crash down the stairs. When a sufficient amount of time had elapsed, she cracked the bedsheet back from the window and waited for him to fling himself from the building and stumble down the street towards the corner pub. He did not disappoint her.

She chuckled. Getting rid of Peter hadn't been difficult at all. His behaviour was as predictable as a trained chimpanzee's.

She went back to the sofa. From the spilled contents of her carpetbag, she took a chipped compact and flipped it open. A pound note was folded into the mirror. She removed it, rolled it, and reached into the V neck of her jersey.

Brassieres, she thought dryly, have such varied uses. She removed a plastic bag which held the cocaine she'd bought for them in Hampstead. Cornwall be damned, she smiled.

Her mouth watered as she poured a small quantity of the drug onto the compact's mirror, hastily using a fingernail to chop it into dust. Using the rolled pound note, she inhaled it greedily.

Heaven, she thought, leaning back against the sofa. Unutterable ecstasy. Better than sex. Better than anything. Bliss.

Thomas Lynley was on the telephone when Dorothea Harriman entered his office, a sheet of memo paper in her hand. She gave the paper a meaningful shake and winked at him like a fellow conspirator. Seeing this, Lynley brought his conversation with the fingerprint officer to a conclusion.

Harriman waited until he had hung up the phone. "You've got it, Detective Inspector," she announced, using his full, organisational title in her cheerfully perverse fashion. Harriman never referred to anyone by mister, miss, or ms when she had the opportunity to string six or ten syllables together as if she were making introductions at the Court of St. James. "Either the stars are in the right position, or Superintendent Webberly's won the football pools. He signed without a second glance. I should be so lucky when I want time off.''

Lynley took the memo from her. His superior officer's name was scrawled in approval across the bottom along with the barely legible note, "Have a care if you're flying, lad," seven words that telegraphed Webberly's accurate guess that he planned upon heading to Cornwall for a long weekend. Lynley had no doubt that the superintendent had also deduced his reason for the trip. Webberly had, after all, seen and remarked upon the photograph of Deborah on Lynley's desk, and although he was not himself uxorious, the superintendent was always first with congratulations when one of his men got married.

The superintendent's secretary was examining this picture herself at the moment. She squinted to bring it into focus, once again eschewing the spectacles which Lynley knew were in her desk. Wearing spectacles detracted from the marked resemblance Harriman bore to the Princess of Wales, a resemblance which she did much to promote. Today, Lynley noted, Harriman was wearing a reproduction of the black-sashed blue dress which the Princess had worn to the Tomb of the Unknown Soldier in America. Royalty had looked quite svelte with it on. Harriman, however, was given over just a bit too much to hips.

"Rumour has Deb back in London," Harriman said, replacing the picture and frowning at the unorganised clutter of his desktop. She gathered up a fan of telephone messages, clipped them together, and straightened five files.

"She's been back for more than a week," Lynley answered.

"That's the change in you, then. Grist for the marriage mill, Detective Inspector. You've been grinning like a fool these last three days."

"Have I?"

"Walking on bubbles with not a trouble in the world. If this is love, I'll take a double portion, thank you."

He smiled, sorted through the files, and handed two of them to her. "Take these instead, will you? Webberly's waiting for them."

Harriman sighed. "I want love and he gives me"—she examined them—"fibre optic reports from a killing in Bayswater. How romantic. I'm in the wrong line of work."

"But it's noble work, Harriman."

"Just what I need to hear." She left him, calling out to someone to answer a phone that was ringing in an unmanned office nearby.

Lynley folded the memo and flipped open his pocket watch. It was half past five. He'd been on duty since seven. There were at least three more reports on his desk waiting for comment, but his concentration was dwindling. It was time to join her, Lynley decided. They needed to talk.

He left his office, making his way down to the lobby and out the revolving doors onto Broadway. He walked along the side of the building—such an unprepossessing combination of glass, grey stone, and protective scaffolding—towards the green.

Deborah still stood where he had seen her from his office window, in the corner of that misshapen trapezoid of lawn and trees. She appeared to be alternating between studying the top of the Suffragette Scroll and gazing at it through her camera, which she had mounted on its tripod perhaps ten feet away.

Whatever she hoped to capture through the lens seemed to elude her, however. For as Lynley watched, she scrunched up her nose, dropped her shoulders in disappointment, and began disassembling her equipment, packing it away in a sturdy metal case.

Lynley prolonged the moment before he crossed the green to join her, taking pleasure in a study of her movements. He savoured her presence. Even more, he savoured the fact that she was home. He had no fondness for the tender angst of being in love with a woman who was six thousand miles away. So Deborah's absence had created anything but an easy time for him. Most of it he had spent with his mind fixed upon when he would next see her in one or another of his quick trips to California. But now she was back. She was with him. He was fully determined to keep it that way.

He crossed the lawn, scattering pigeons who were pecking about in search of crumbs from afternoon lunches. They took hasty flight, and Deborah looked up. Her hair, which had been pulled back with a haphazard arrangement of combs, tumbled towards freedom. She muttered in exasperation and began to fuss with it.

"You know," she said by way of greeting him, "I always wanted to be one of those women who're described as having hair like silk. You know what I mean. An Estella Havisham type."

"Did Estella Havisham have hair like silk?" He pushed her hand away and saw to the snarls himself.

"She must have. Can you imagine poor Pip falling for someone who didn't have hair like silk? *Ouch!*"

"Pulling?"

"A bit. Honestly, isn't it pathetic? I lead one life and my hair leads another."

"Well, it's fixed now. Sort of."

"That's encouraging."

They laughed together and began gathering her belongings which were scattered on the lawn. She'd come with tripod, camera case, a shopping bag containing three pieces of fruit, a comfortable old pullover, and her shoulder bag.

"I saw you from my office," Lynley told her. "What are you working on? A tribute to Mrs. Pankhurst?"

"Actually, I was waiting for the light to strike the top of the scroll. I thought to create some diffraction with the lens. Utterly defeated by the clouds, I'm afraid. By the time they decided to drift away, the sun had done so as well." She paused reflectively and scratched her head. "What an appalling display of ignorance. I think I mean the earth." She fished in her shoulder bag and brought out a mint which she unwrapped and popped into her mouth.

They strolled back towards Scotland Yard.

"I've managed to get Friday off," Lynley told her. "Monday as well. So we're free to go to Cornwall. I'm free, that is. And if you've nothing planned, I thought we might . . ." He stopped, wondering why he was adding the verbal apologia.

"Cornwall, Tommy?" Deborah's voice was no different when she asked the question, but her head was turned away from him so he couldn't see her expression.

"Yes. Cornwall. Howenstow. I think it's time, don't you? I know you've only just come back and perhaps this is rushing things. But after all, you've never met my mother."

Deborah said only, "Ah. Yes."

"Your coming to Cornwall would give your father an opportunity to meet her as well. And it's time they met."

She frowned at her scuffed shoes and made no reply.

"Deb, it can't be avoided forever. I know what you're thinking. They're worlds apart. They'll have nothing to say to each other. But that isn't the case. They'll get on. Believe me."

"He won't want to do this, Tommy."

"I've already thought of that. And of a way to manage it. I've asked Simon to come along. It's all arranged, in fact."

He did not include in the information the details of his brief encounter with St. James and Lady Helen Clyde at the Ritz, they on their way to a business dinner and he en route to a reception at Clarence House. He also didn't mention St. James' ill-concealed reluctance nor Lady Helen's quick excuse. An enormous backlog of work, she'd said, promising to keep them busy for every weekend over the next month.

Helen's declining the invitation had been too quick to be believable, and the speed of her refusal, in combination with the effort she made not to look at St. James, told Lynley how important absence from Cornwall was to them both. Even if he had wanted to lie to himself, he couldn't do so in the face of their behaviour. He knew what it meant. But he needed them in Cornwall for Cotter's sake, and the mention of the older man's possible discomfort was what won them over. For St. James would never send Cotter alone to be wretchedly enthroned as a weekend visitor to Howenstow. And Helen would never abandon St. James to what she clearly visualised as four days of unmitigated misery. So Lynley had used them. It was all for Cotter's sake, he told himself, and refused to examine the secondary reasons he had—even more compelling than Cotter's comfort—for arriving at Howenstow with a surfeit of companions.

Deborah was inspecting the silver letters on the Yard's revolving sign. She said, "Simon's to go?"

"And Helen. Sidney as well." Lynley waited for her further reaction. When there was none other than the smallest of nods, he decided they were finally close enough to the single area of discussion which they had long avoided. It lay between them, unspoken, putting down roots of potential doubt which needed to be extirpated once and for all.

"Have you seen him, Deb?"

"Yes." She shifted her tripod from one hand to the other. She said nothing else, leaving everything up to him.

Lynley felt in his pocket for cigarette case and lighter. He lit up before she had a chance to admonish him. Feeling weighted down by a burden he did not wish to define, he sighed.

"I want to get us through this, Deb. No, that's not quite true, is it? We need to get through it."

"I saw him the night I got home, Tommy. He was waiting up for me in the lab. With a homecoming present. An enlarger. He wanted me to see it. And then the next afternoon, he came to Paddington. We spoke."

That's all was left unsaid.

Lynley tossed his cigarette to one side, angry with himself. He wondered what it was that he really wanted Deborah to say and why he expected her to account for a relationship with another man that had spanned her entire life, and how on earth she could ever begin to do so. He disliked the belief that was eating at his confidence, a gnawing conviction that somehow Deborah's return to London had the power to nullify every word and act of love that had passed between them in the last several years. Perhaps, hidden beneath the most troubling of his feelings, was the real reason he was determined to have St. James with them in Cornwall: to prove to the other man once and for all that Deborah was his. It was a contemptible thought.

"Tommy."

He roused himself to find that Deborah was watching him. He wanted to touch her. He wanted to tell her how he loved the way her green eyes were flecked with bits of gold, the way her skin and hair reminded him of autumn. But all of that seemed ridiculous right now.

"I love you, Tommy. I want to be your wife."

That, Lynley decided, didn't seem ridiculous at all.

Part III

BLOOD SCORE

4

Nancy Cambrey scuffed her feet along the gravel drive that wound from the Howenstow lodge to the great house. She sent up delicate puffs of dust like miniature brown rain clouds. It had been an unusually dry summer thus far, so a greyish patina of grime dressed the leaves of the rhododendrons that lined the roadway, and the trees arching overhead seemed not so much there to provide shade as to trap the heavy, dry air beneath their boughs. Out from under the trees the wind whipped round from Gwennap Head on its way into Mount's Bay from the Atlantic. But where Nancy walked, the air was still as death, and it smelled of foliage burnt to cinders by the sun.

Perhaps, she thought, the heaviness pressing so uneasily upon her lungs was not really born of the air at all, but was instead a child of her dread. For she had promised herself that she would speak to Lord Asherton the first time he came on one of his rare visits to Cornwall. Now he was coming.

She ran her fingers through her hair. It felt limp, its ends brittle. In the last few months she had taken to wearing it pulled back with a piece of plain elastic at the nape of her neck, but today she had given herself a shampoo and left her hair to dry, hanging straight and simple, bluntly cut round her face and shoulders. It didn't feel right. She knew it didn't look right, unattractive and unflattering when once it had been a source of bashful pride.

How your hair shines, Nance. Yes. How it had.

The sound of voices up ahead made her pause and squint myopically through the trees. Vague figures moved near a table set out on the lawn where an old oak provided a substantial area of shade. Two of the Howenstow dailies were at work there.

Nancy recognised their voices. They were girls she had known from childhood, acquaintances who had never quite become her friends. They belonged to that collection of humanity who lived behind the barrier which she had erected between herself and others on the estate, barring her from intimacy with the Lynley children as effectively as with the children of the tenants, the farmers, the day workers, and the servants.

Nowhere Nancy, she had labelled herself, and her life had been an effort to carve out a singular place where she might belong. She had that place now, nominal at best, but decidedly her own, a world circumscribed by a five-month-old baby daughter, Gull Cottage, and Mick.

Mick. Michael Cambrey. University graduate. Journalist. World traveller. Man of ideas. And husband of Nancy.

She had wanted him from the first, eager to bask in his charm, to relish his looks, to hear his conversation and his easy laughter, to feel his eyes upon her and hope to be the cause of their animation. So when she went on her weekly visit to his father's newspaper to check over the bookkeeping as she'd done for two years, when she found Mick there in place of his father, his invitation to linger and chat for a bit had been welcome.

How he loved to talk. How she loved to listen. With little to contribute save her admiration, however, how simple it had been to arrive at the belief that she needed somehow to contribute more to their relationship. And she had done so—on the mattress in the old Howenstow mill where they'd spent an entire April making love, starting January's baby.

She'd given little thought to how her life might change. She'd given less thought to how Mick himself might change. Only the moment existed, only sensation mattered. His hands and mouth, his hard, male body insistent and eager, the faint salt on his skin, his groan of pleasure as he took her. The knowledge that he wanted her superseded any reflection upon the possible consequences. They were insubstantial.

How different it was now.

"Can we talk about it, Roderick?" she'd heard Mick say. "With our money situation being what it is, I hate to see you make a decision like this. Let's talk about it when I get back from London."

He'd listened, laughed once, replaced the telephone receiver, and turned to find her shrinking back from the doorway, a flame-faced eavesdropper. But he wasn't concerned by her presence. He merely ignored her and returned to his work while above them in the bedroom little Molly wailed.

Nancy had watched as he tapped on the keys of his new word processor. She heard him mutter and saw him pick up the manual to read a few pages. She didn't cross the room to speak to him. Instead, she wrung her hands.

With our money situation being what it is . . . They didn't own Gull Cottage. It was merely a rental, let to them on a monthly basis. But money was tight. Mick spent it too freely. The last two rental payments hadn't been made. If Dr. Trenarrow intended an increase now, if that increase were added to what they already owed, they would sink. And if that happened, where on earth could they go? Certainly not to Howenstow where they would have to live in the lodge on her father's angry charity.

"Linen's gotter 'ole in it, Mary. Brought another?"

"Not with. Set a plate down on't."

" 'Oo the 'ell's gonna sit squat in the middle of the table, Mar?"

Laughter drifted Nancy's way as the dailies shook out a crisp white table cloth. It billowed from their hands, caught in a sudden gust of wind that managed to find its way through the armour of the trees. Nancy raised her own face to it, but it captured a patch of dead leaves and dust and flung them up at her so that she tasted fine grit.

She lifted a hand to brush at her face, but the effort drained her of strength. Sighing, she trudged on towards the house.

It was one thing, of course, to talk of love and marriage in London. It was another to feel the full range of implications behind those easy words when she saw them spread out before her in Cornwall. By the time she got out of the limousine that had met them at the Land's End air strip, Deborah Cotter was feeling decidedly light-headed. Her stomach was churning as well.

Because she had never known Lynley in any way other than in her own environment and upon her own terms, she hadn't thought about what it would mean to marry into his family. She knew he was an earl, of course. She'd ridden in his Bentley, been to his London house, even met his valet. She'd eaten off his china, drunk from his crystal, and watched him dress himself in his hand-tailored clothes. But all of that had somehow fallen into a category of behaviour which she had conveniently labelled How Tommy Lives. None of it had ever affected her own life in any way. However, seeing Howenstow from the air, as Lynley circled the plane twice over the estate, had served as the first indication to Deborah that life as she had known it for twenty-one years faced potential—and radical—alteration.

The house was an enormous Jacobean structure built in the shape of a variegated E with its central leg missing. A large secondary wing grew in reverse direction from the building's west leg and to the northeast, just beyond its spine, stood a church. Beyond the house clustered a scattering of outbuildings and stables, and beyond these the Howenstow park spread out in the direction of the sea. Cows grazed on this parkland amid towering sycamore trees that grew in abundance, protected from the sometimes inclement southwestern weather by a fortuitous, natural slope of land. At the perimeter of all this, the skillfully crafted Cornish wall marked the boundary of the estate proper, but not the end of the Asherton property which was, Deborah knew, divided among dairy farms, agriculture, and abandoned mines that had once provided the district with tin.

Faced with the concrete, undeniable reality that was Tommy's home —no longer an illusory setting for the weekend house parties she had overheard discussed by St. James and Lady Helen for so many years— Deborah's mind became taken up with the risible notion of herself— Deborah Cotter, the child of a servant—moving blithely into the life of this estate as if it were Manderley with Max de Winter brooding somewhere within its walls, waiting to be rejuvenated by the love of a simple woman. Hardly an act in her line, she thought.

What on earth am I doing here? The entire situation felt like a dream, with chimerical elements stacking one upon the other. The flight down in the plane, the first viewing of Howenstow, the limousine and uniformed chauffeur waiting on the air strip. Even Lady Helen's lighthearted greeting of this man—"Jasper, my God! So sartorially splendid! The last time I was here, you hadn't even bothered to shave."—did little to allay Deborah's qualms.

At least nothing was expected of her on the drive to Howenstow other than to admire Cornwall, and she had. It was a wild part of the country, comprising desolate moors, stony hillsides, sandy coves whose hidden caves had long been used as smugglers' caches, sudden lush woodlands where the countryside dipped into a combe, and everywhere tangles of celandine, poppy, and periwinkle that dominated the narrow lanes.

The main drive to Howenstow shot off from one of these, canopied by sycamores and edged by rhododendrons. It passed a lodge, skirted the park, dipped beneath an ornate Tudor gatehouse, circled a rose garden, and ended before a massive front door above which a hound and a lion battled resplendently in the Asherton coat of arms.

They got out of the car with the usual jumble that accompanies an arrival. Deborah favoured the building with a single, fleeting look. It appeared to be deserted. She wished that were the case.

"Ah. Here's Mother," Lynley said.

Turning, Deborah found him looking not towards the front door, where she had expected to see an excessively well-dressed Countess of Asherton standing with one white hand extended limply in welcome, but towards the southeast corner of the house where a tall, slender woman was striding towards them through the shrubbery.

Deborah could not have been more surprised at the sight of Lady Asherton. She was wearing old tennis clothes, with a faded blue towel flung round her shoulders. This she used vigorously to wipe perspiration from her face, arms, and neck. Three large wolfhounds and a gangling young retriever bounded at her heels, and she paused, wrested a ball from one of them, and threw it with the skill of a bowler to the far side of the garden. She laughed as they disappeared in frantic chase after it, watching them for a moment before joining the party by the front door.

"Tommy." She spoke pleasantly. "You've had your hair cut a bit differently, haven't you? I like it. Very much." She didn't touch him. Instead, she gave her embraces to Lady Helen and St. James before turning to Deborah and continuing to speak with a rueful gesture at her tennis clothes. "Forgive my appearance, Deborah. I don't always greet guests so decidedly un-turned out, but frankly, I'm lazy, and if I don't take my exercise at the same hour every day, I manage to find a thousand excuses for not taking it at all. Tell me you're not one of those dreadful health fiends who jog every morning at dawn."

It was certainly not a welcome-to-our-family salutation. But on the other hand, it wasn't the sort of clever greeting that managed to mix requisite courtesy with unmistakable disapproval. Deborah wasn't sure what to make of it.

As if she understood and wanted to get them through the first moments as smoothly as possible, Lady Asherton merely smiled, squeezed Deborah's hand, and turned to her father. Throughout the exchange Cotter had been standing to one side. In the heat, sweat sheened his face. He was managing to make his clothes look as if they'd been made for a man several inches taller and much heavier than he.

"Mr. Cotter," Lady Asherton said. "May I call you Joseph? I'm only too delighted that you and Deborah shall be part of our family."

So here was the standard welcome. Wisely, Lynley's mother had saved it for the person she had intuitively known would most need to hear it.

"Thank you, m'lady." Cotter clasped his hands behind him as if in the fear that one might jump out and begin pumping Lady Asherton's arm of its own volition.

Lady Asherton smiled. It was a duplicate of Tommy's crooked smile. "It's Dorothy, actually, although for some reason that I've never quite understood, my family and friends have always called me Daze. Which is better than Diz, I suppose, since that suggests *dizzy,* and I'm afraid I should have to draw the line at something that comes so perilously close to describing my personality."

Cotter looked rather dumbfounded at what was clearly an invitation to address the widow of an earl by her Christian name. Nonetheless, after a moment for thought, he nodded sharply and replied, "Daze it is."

"Good," Lady Asherton responded. "Lovely. We've a beautiful weekend for a visit, haven't we? It's been a bit hot, of course—today's quite warm, isn't it?—but I expect we'll have a breeze this afternoon. Sidney's already arrived, by the way. And she's brought the most interesting young man with her. Rather dark and melancholy."

"Brooke?" St. James asked sharply. He didn't look pleased.

"Yes. Justin Brooke. Do you know him, Simon?"

"Rather better than he'd like, if the truth be told," Lady Helen said. "But he promises to behave himself, don't you, Simon darling? No poison in the porridge. No duelling at dawn. No brawls on the drawing room floor. Just utter civility for seventy-two hours. What perfect teeth-gritting bliss."

"I'll treasure each moment," St. James replied.

Lady Asherton laughed. "Of course you will. What house party could possibly be complete without skeletons swinging out of every closet and tempers on the boil? It makes me feel quite a young girl again." She took Cotter's arm and led the way into the house. "Let me show you something I'm absurdly proud of, Joseph," they could hear her saying as she pointed to the elaborate tessellated entry. "This was put in just after our great fire of 1849 by some local workmen. Now, don't you believe this for an instant, but legend has it the fire . . ." Her voice drifted out of their hearing. In a moment, Cotter's laughter rang out in response.

At that, the churning in Deborah's stomach lessened. Relief shot through her muscles like a spring releasing tension and told her how nervous she had really been about this first meeting of their parents. It could have been disastrous. It would have been disastrous, had Tommy's mother been any other sort of woman save the kind who swept away the diffidence of strangers with a few amiable words.

She's wonderful. Deborah felt the need to say it aloud to someone and without thinking, she turned to St. James.

All the signs of approval were on his face. The lines round his eyes crinkled more deeply. Briefly, he smiled.

"Welcome to Howenstow, Deb darling." Lynley put his arm round her shoulders and led her into the house where a high ceiling and a mosaic floor made the air cool and moist, a refreshing change from the heat outside.

They found Lady Asherton and Cotter in the great hall to the right of the entry. It was an elongated room, dominated by a fireplace whose chimneypiece of unadorned granite was surmounted by the head of a wild gazelle. Pendant plasterwork decorated the ceiling, and drop-moulded panelling covered the walls. Upon these hung life-sized portraits of the lords and ladies of Asherton, representatives from each generation, who gazed upon their descendants in every kind of pose and every kind of dress.

Deborah paused before an eighteenth-century portrait of a man in cream breeches and red coat, leaning against a half-broken urn with a riding crop in his hand and a spaniel at his feet. "Tommy, good heavens. He looks exactly like you."

"He's certainly what Tommy would look like if we could only talk him into wearing those delicious trousers," Lady Helen remarked.

Deborah felt Lynley's arm tighten round her shoulders. She thought at first it was in response to the laughter that greeted Lady Helen's comment. But she saw that a door had opened at the north end of the hall and a tall young man wearing threadbare blue jeans was padding in his bare feet across the parquet floor. A hollow-cheeked girl followed him. She too was shoeless.

This would be Peter, Deborah decided. Aside from his emaciated appearance, he possessed the same blond hair, the same brown eyes, and the same fine cheekbones, nose, and jaw of many of the portraits that lined the walls. Unlike his ancestors on canvas, however, Peter Lynley wore an earring through one pierced ear. It was a swastika dangling from a slender gold chain and it grazed the top of his shoulder.

"Peter. You're not in Oxford?" Lynley asked the question smoothly enough—a demonstration of good breeding before the weekend guests— but Deborah felt the tension in his body.

Peter flashed a smile, shrugged his shoulders, and said, "We came down for some sun only to discover you had the same idea. All we need is Judy here for a sibling reunion, right?''

Fingering the clasp that held earring to earlobe, he nodded at St. James and Lady Helen and drew his companion forward. In a gesture that duplicated Lynley's own, he put his arm round her shoulders.

''This is Sasha.'' Her arm encircled his waist. Her fingers slid beneath his grimy T-shirt and into his blue jeans. ''Sasha Nifford.'' Without waiting for his brother to make a similar introduction, Peter nodded at Deborah. ''And this is your bride-to-be, I take it. You've always had excellent taste in women. But we've seen that demonstrated well enough through the years.''

Lady Asherton came forward. She looked from one son to the other and extended her hand as if she would join them together in some way. ''I was so surprised when Hodge told me Peter and Sasha had arrived. And then I thought what a lovely idea it was to have Peter here for your engagement weekend.''

Lynley replied evenly. ''My thought exactly. Will you show our guests to their rooms, Mother? I'd like a few minutes with Peter. To catch up.''

''We've lunch planned in just an hour. The day's so fine that we thought we'd have it outdoors.''

''Good. In an hour. If you'll see to everyone . . .'' It was far more an order than a request.

Hearing his cool tone, Deborah felt surprise. She looked at the others to gauge their reactions, but saw in their faces only a determination to ignore the unmistakable current of hostility that crackled through the air. Lady Helen was examining a silver-framed photograph of the Prince of Wales. St. James was admiring the lid of an oriental tea case. Cotter was standing in a bay window gazing out at the garden.

''Darling,'' Lynley was saying to her. ''If you'll excuse me for a bit . . .''

''Tommy—''

''If you'll excuse me, Deb.''

''It's just this way, my dear.'' Lady Asherton touched her lightly.

Deborah didn't want to move.

Lady Helen spoke. ''Tell me you've given me that darling green room overlooking the west courtyard, Daze. You know the one. Above the gun room. I've been longing to spend a night there for years. Sleeping with that thrilling fear that someone might accidentally blast away at the ceiling below with a shotgun.''

She took Lady Asherton's arm. They headed for the door. There was nothing left to do but to follow. Deborah did so. But as she reached the inner hall, she looked back at Lynley and his brother. They faced each other warily, squaring off, poised to fight.

And whatever warmth the weekend had earlier promised iced over into nothing at the sight of them and at the sudden recognition of the great gaps in her knowledge of Tommy's relationship with his family.

Lynley closed the music room door and watched Peter walk—with a step that was much too careful and precise—to the window. He sat down on the window seat, curving his lengthy frame into a comfortable position on the green brocade cushion. The walls in the room were papered in a print of yellow chrysanthemums on a field of green, and that combination of colours in conjunction with the high sunlight of noon served to make Peter look even more haggard than he had in the great hall. Tracing a pattern against a distortion in the glass, he was doing his best to ignore Lynley altogether.

"What are you doing in Cornwall? You're supposed to be in Oxford. We'd made arrangements for a tutor for the summer. We'd agreed you'd stay there." Lynley knew that his voice was both cold and unfriendly, but he could do nothing to modulate it. The sight of his brother had shaken him. Peter was skeletally thin. His eyes looked yellow. The skin round his nostrils was excoriated and scabbed.

Peter shrugged, looking sullen. "It's just a visit, for God's sake. I'm not here to stay. I'm going back. All right?"

"What are you doing here? And don't give me that business about the weekend sun because I'm not going to buy it."

"I don't care what you buy. But just think how fortuitous my arrival is, Tommy. If I hadn't shown up unexpectedly this morning, I'd have missed the festivities altogether. Or was that your intention? Did you want to keep me away? Another nasty family secret kept under wraps so that your little redhead doesn't learn too many of them all at once?"

Lynley strode across the room and whipped his brother out of the window seat.

"I'll ask you again what you're doing here, Peter."

Peter shook him off. "I've chucked it, all right? Is that what you want to hear? I've dropped out. Okay?"

"Have you gone completely mad? Where are you living?"

"I've digs of my own in London. And don't worry. I've no intention of asking you for money. I've plenty of my own." He shouldered his way past Lynley and went to the old Broadwood piano. He fingered its keys in a light, staccato tapping, dissonant and irritating.

"This is nonsense." Lynley tried to speak reasonably, but he felt disheartened as he read the meaning behind Peter's words. "And who is that girl? Where did she come from? How did you meet her? Peter, she's not even clean. She looks like—"

Peter spun around. "Shut up about her. She's the best thing that's ever happened in my life and don't you forget it. She's the only decent thing that's happened to me in years."

That strained credibility. It also revealed the worst. Lynley crossed the room. "You're on drugs again. I thought you were clean. I thought we'd straightened you out in that programme last January. But you're back to it. You haven't chucked Oxford at all, have you? They've chucked you. That's it, isn't it? Isn't it, Peter?"

Peter didn't answer. Lynley grasped his brother's chin with thumb and index finger and turned Peter's head so that it was inches away from his own.

"What is it now? Are we trying heroin yet? Or are we still wrapped up in our devotion to cocaine? Have you tried mixing them? What about smoking them? Or that religious experience of mainlining the whole mess?"

Peter said nothing. Lynley pushed him for an answer.

"You're still after that ultimate high, aren't you? After all, drugs are what life's all about. And what about Sasha? Are you two developing a fine, meaningful relationship? Cocaine must be a great foundation for love. You can really bond to an addict, can't you?"

Still, Peter refused to respond. Lynley pulled his brother to a mirror that hung on a wall behind the harp and shoved him towards it so that he would have to look at his unshaven face. It was pasty. His lips were cracked. His nose was running onto his upper lip.

"Pretty sight, aren't you?" Lynley demanded. "What are you telling Mother? That you're not using any longer? That you just have a cold?"

Released, Peter rubbed his face where his brother's fingers had dug in and bruised the unhealthy flesh. "You can even talk about Mother," he whispered. "You can even *talk*. God, Tommy, I wish you'd just die."

5

Neither Peter nor Sasha showed up for lunch, and as if an appropriate response to this had been agreed upon in advance, no one mentioned the fact. Instead, everyone concentrated on passing round platters of prawn salad, cold chicken, asparagus, and artichokes *gribiche* while completely overlooking the two empty chairs that faced one another at the far end of the table.

Lynley welcomed his brother's absence. He wanted distractions.

One presented itself less than five minutes into the meal when Lynley's estate manager came round the south wing of the house and strode directly towards the oak tree. His attention, however, did not seem given to the party gathered beneath it. Instead, his gaze was fixed on the distant stables where a young man jumped nimbly over the dry stone wall and came across the park at a jog. The sun wove streaks of colour against him as he passed in and out of the shade of the trees.

From the table, Sidney St. James called out happily, "What a fine horseman your son is, Mr. Penellin. He took us out for a ride this morning, but Justin and I could hardly keep him in sight."

John Penellin flicked her a cursory nod of acknowledgement, but his dark, Celtic features were rigid. Lynley had known Penellin long enough to recognise when he was hard put keeping a tight rein on fury.

"And Justin generally rides quite well—don't you, darling? But Mark dazzled us both."

Brooke said only, "He's good, all right," and went back to his chicken. Faint beads of perspiration stood out on his swarthy skin.

Mark Penellin came under the oak in time to hear the last two comments. "I've just had lots of practice," he said generously. "You both did great.'' He ran the back of his hand across his damp forehead. A smudge of dirt discoloured his cheek. He was a softer, lighter version of his father. Penellin's grey-streaked black hair was brown in Mark, his craggy features unscored in Mark's youth. The father was sapped by age and anxiety. The boy looked energetic, healthy, alive. ''Peter's not here?'' he asked, looking the length of the table. ''That's odd. He phoned me at the lodge just a bit ago, said I was to come up.''

''To join us for lunch, no doubt,'' Lady Asherton said. ''How very good of Peter. We were in such a rush this morning that I didn't think to phone you myself. I'm so sorry, Mark. Sometimes I think my mind is splintering away altogether. Do join us. Mark. John. Please.'' She indicated the places that had been intended for Sasha and Peter.

It was obvious that John Penellin did not intend to brush off what was bothering him by sitting down to lunch with his employers and their weekend guests. This was a workday for him, like any other. And he had not come out of the house in order to signal his displeasure at being excluded from a luncheon to which he had no desire to be invited in the first place. Plainly, he had come to intercept his son.

Fast childhood friends, Mark and Peter were of an age. They had spent long years in each other's company, sharing games and toys and adventures along the Cornish coast. They had played together, swum together, sailed together, grown up together. Only their schooling had been different, with Peter attending Eton as had every male in the family before him and Mark attending a day school in Nanrunnel and from there a secondary school in Penzance. But the separation of their school days had not been enough to divide them. They had maintained their old friendship over time and distance.

But obviously not any longer, if Penellin could prevent it. Lynley felt the regret of a loss even before John Penellin spoke. Yet it was only reasonable to expect the man to protect his only son, seeking any way possible to keep him from becoming influenced by the changes that had come over Peter.

''Nancy's wanting you at the lodge,'' Penellin said to Mark. ''You've no need of Peter at the moment.''

''But he phoned and—''

''I've no interest in who phoned. Get back to the lodge.''

''Surely a quick lunch, John—'' Lady Asherton began.

''Thank you, my lady. We've no need of it.'' He looked at his son, black eyes unreadable in an inflexible mask. But his arms—bared because he wore the sleeves of his work shirt rolled up—showed veins like cords. "Come with me, boy." And then to Lynley, with a nod to the others, "Sorry."

John Penellin turned on his heel and walked back towards the house. After casting a look round the table—part supplication and part apology—his son followed him. They left behind that sort of uneasy reserve in which members of a party must decide whether to discuss what has just occurred or to ignore it altogether. They held true to their previous unspoken agreement to overlook anything which held the promise of blighting a weekend of bliss. Lady Helen led the way.

"Have you any idea," she said as she speared a fat prawn, "what a compliment it is to be enthroned—there's simply no other word for it, Deborah—in Great-Grandmama Asherton's bedroom for your engagement weekend? Considering the manner in which everyone's tiptoed reverentially by it when I've been here in the past, I've always got the distinct impression they've been saving that room for the Queen should she ever pop in for a visit."

"That's the room with the terrifying bed," Sidney put in. "Draperies and geegaws. Ghoulies and banshees carved right into the headboard like a Grinling Gibbons nightmare. This must be the test of true love, Deb."

"Like the princess and the pea," Lady Helen said. "Did you ever have to sleep there, Daze?"

"Great-Grandmama was alive when I first came here for a visit. So instead of sleeping in the bed, one had to spend several hours sitting next to it, reading from the Bible. She was quite a devotee of some of the more lurid passages in the Old Testament, as I recall. Extensive explorations into Sodom and Gomorrah. Sexual misbehaviour. Lust and salacity. She wasn't very interested in how God punished the sinners, however. 'Leave 'em to the Lord,' she'd say and wave a hand at me. 'Get on with it, girl.' "

"Did you get on with it?" Sidney asked.

"Of course. I was only sixteen. I don't think I'd ever read anything so delicious in my life." She laughed engagingly. "I count the Bible as largely responsible for the sinful life—" Her eyes suddenly dropped. Her quick smile faded, then reappeared in a determined fashion. "Do you remember your great-grandmother, Tommy?"

Lynley was concentrating on his wine glass, on his inability to define colour in a liquid that existed somewhere between green and amber. He made no reply.

Deborah's hand touched his, a contact so fleeting it might not have happened at all. "When I saw that bed, I wondered how gauche it would be if I slept on the floor," she said.

"One does somehow expect the entire affair to come creeping to life directly after nightfall," Lady Helen said. "But I long to sleep there anyway. I always have. Why have I never been allowed to spend the night in that terrifying bed?"

"It wouldn't be too horrible if one didn't have to sleep there alone." Sidney raised an eyebrow at Justin Brooke. "A second body to comfort one. A warm body, that is. Even more preferably a live one. If Great-Grandmama Asherton's taking to wandering the halls, I'd prefer she not drop in to keep me warm, thank you. But as for any of the rest of you, just knock twice."

"Some more welcome than others, I hope," Justin Brooke said.

"Only if they behave themselves," Sidney replied.

St. James looked from his sister to her lover, saying nothing. He reached for a roll, broke it neatly in half.

"This is obviously what comes of discussing the Old Testament over lunch," Lady Helen said. "A mere mention of Genesis and we become a group of reprobates."

The company's answering laughter got them through the moment.

Lynley watched them walk off in separate directions. Sidney and Deborah went towards the house where the former, learning that Deborah had brought her cameras, had announced she would change into something seductive to inspire Deborah to new photographic heights; St. James and Lady Helen sauntered towards the gatehouse and the open park beyond it; Lady Asherton and Cotter headed off together towards the northeast side of the house where, sheltered by a grove of beech and lime trees, the little chapel of St. Petroc housed Lynley's father and the rest of the Asherton dead; and Justin Brooke murmured vaguely about finding a tree under which to doze, a statement that Sidney pooh-poohed with a wave of her hand.

Within moments, Lynley was alone. A fresh breeze caught the edge of the tablecloth. He fingered the linen, moved a plate to one side, and regarded the ruins of the meal.

He had an obligation to see John Penellin after such a long absence. The estate manager would expect it of him. He would no doubt be waiting for him in the office, ready to go over the books and examine the accounts. Lynley dreaded their meeting. The dread had nothing to do with the possibility that Penellin might bring up Peter's condition and

Lynley's own responsibility to do something about it. Nor did the dread reflect a lack of interest in the life of the estate. The true difficulty lay in what both concern and interest implied: a return, however brief, to Howenstow.

Lynley's absence this time had been inordinately long, nearly six months. He was honest enough with himself to know what it was that he was avoiding by coming to Howenstow so seldom. It was exactly what he had been avoiding for so many years either by not coming at all or by bringing with him a troop of friends, as if life in Cornwall were a 1930 garden party with himself at the centre, laughing and talking and pouring champagne. This engagement weekend was no different in design from any trip he had made to Cornwall in the last fifteen years. He had merely used the excuse of surrounding Deborah and her father with familiar faces so that he himself would not have to meet alone the one face in his own life that he couldn't bear to see. He hated that thought at the very same time as he knew that his stormy relationship with his mother somehow had to be laid to rest during this weekend.

He didn't know how to do it. Every word she said—no matter how innocuous she intended it to be—merely served as a dredge, uprooting emotions he did not want to feel, producing memories he wanted to avoid, demanding actions he did not possess the humility or the courage to take. Pride was at issue between them, along with anger and guilt and the need to blame. Intellectually, he knew that his father would have died anyway. But he had never been able to accept that simple maxim. Far easier to believe that a person and not a disease had killed him. For one could blame a person. And he needed to blame.

Sighing, he pushed himself to his feet. From where he was on the lawn, he could see that the blinds in the estate office had been drawn against the afternoon sun. But he had no doubt John Penellin was waiting behind them, expecting him to act out the role of eighth Asherton Earl, no matter how little it was to his liking. He walked towards the house.

The estate office had been placed with an eye to its purpose. Situated on the ground floor across from the smoking room and abutting the billiard room, its location made it accessible to members of the household as well as to tenants come to pay their rent.

In no way did the room suggest ostentation. Green-edged hemp matting, rather than carpet, did duty as surface upon the floor. Paint, not panelling or paper, covered the walls upon which hung old estate photographs and maps. From a plain ceiling, iron chains supported two white-shaded light fixtures. Beneath them, simple pine shelves held decades of record books, a few atlases, half a dozen journals. The filing cabinets in the corner were oak, battered from generations of use, as were the desk and the swivel chair behind it. In this chair at the moment, however, sat not John Penellin, who conducted much of his business from the estate office. Instead a thin figure occupied his accustomed place, huddling as if cold, her cheek resting upon her palm.

As Lynley reached the open door, he saw that it was Nancy Cambrey in her father's chair. She was playing restlessly with a container of pencils, and although her presence instead of her father's gave Lynley the excuse he needed to be on his way and to put off his meeting with Penellin indefinitely, he found that he hesitated at the sight of the man's daughter.

Nancy was very much changed. Her hair, once a brown streaked with gold that shimmered in the light, had lost most of its shine and all of its beauty. It hung drearily round her face without style, grazing the tops of her shoulders. Her skin, once blushing and smooth with a cast of freckles making an endearing bandit's mask across nose and on cheeks, had become quite pallid. It looked thicker somehow, the way skin in a portrait looks if an artist adds an unnecessary layer of varnish and in doing so destroys the effect of youth and beauty he was trying to create. Everything about Nancy Cambrey suggested just that sort of destruction. She looked faded, used up, overwashed, overworn.

This extended to her clothes. A shapeless housedress replaced the trendy skirts, jerseys, and boots she once had worn. But even the dress was several sizes too large and it hung upon her loosely, much like a smock but without a smock's style. It was too old to be a piece of modern fashion, and together with Nancy's appearance, the dress made Lynley hesitate, made him frown. Although he was seven years her senior, he'd known Nancy Cambrey all of her life, liked her as well. The change was troubling.

She'd been pregnant. He knew that. There had been a forced marriage with Mick Cambrey from Nanrunnel. But that was the end of it, or so his mother's letter had informed him. And then a few months later, he received the birth announcement from Nancy herself. He responded with a duty gift and thought nothing more about her. Until now, when he wondered if having a baby could have brought about such a change.

Another wish granted, he thought wryly, another distraction. He entered the office.

She was looking through a crack in the blinds that covered the bank of office windows. As she did so, she chewed on the knuckles of her right hand, something she obviously did habitually for they were red and raw, too raw to have arrived at that condition through housework.

Lynley said her name. She jumped to her feet, hands thrust behind her back. "You've come to see Dad," she said. "I thought you might. After lunch. I thought—hoped—to catch you ahead of him. My lord."

Lynley felt his customary rush of embarrassment at her final two words. It sometimes seemed that he had spent most of the last ten years of his life avoiding every situation in which he might have to hear someone say them.

"You've been waiting to see me? Not your father?"

"I have. Yes." She moved from behind the desk and went to a ladder-back chair that stood beneath a wall map of the estate. Here she sat, her hands curled into tight balls in her lap.

At the end of the corridor, the outer door banged against the wall as someone shoved it open too recklessly. Footsteps sounded against the tiled floor. Nancy braced herself against the back of her chair, as if in the hope of hiding from whoever had come into the house. Instead of approaching the estate office, however, the footsteps turned left at the stillroom and faded on their way. Nancy exhaled in a nearly imperceptible sigh.

Lynley went to sit in her father's chair. "It's good to see you. I'm glad you came by."

She moved her large grey eyes to the windows, speaking to them rather than to him. "I need to ask you something. It's difficult for me. How to begin."

"Have you been ill? You've got awfully thin, Nancy. The baby. Has it—" He was mortified to realise that he had no idea of the baby's sex.

"No. Molly's fine." Still, she would not look at him. "But I'm eaten by worry."

"What is it?"

"It's why I've come. But . . . ." Tears rose to her eyes without spilling over. Humiliation mottled her skin. "Dad mustn't know. He can't."

"Then it's between us, whatever we say." Lynley fished out his handkerchief and passed it across the desk. She pressed it between her hands but did not use it, controlling the tears instead. "Are you at odds with your father?"

"Not I. Mick. Things've never been right between them. Because of the baby. And me. And how we married. But it's worse now than before."

"Is there some way I can help? Because if you don't want me to intercede with your father, I'm not sure what else . . ." He let his voice drift off, waiting for her to complete the sentence. He saw her draw her body in, as if she were garnering courage before a wild leap into the abyss.

"You can help. Yes. With money." She flinched involuntarily as she said the words but then went bravely on with the rest. "I'm still doing my bookkeeping in Penzance. And Nanrunnel. And I'm working nights at the Anchor and Rose. But it's not been enough. The costs . . ."

"What sort of costs?"

"The newspaper, you see. Mick's dad had heart surgery a year ago last winter—did you know?—and Mick's been running the paper for him ever since. But he wants to update. He wants equipment. He couldn't see how he'd be spending the rest of his life in Nanrunnel on a weekly paper with broken-down presses and manual typewriters. He has plans. Good plans. But it's money. He spends it. There's never enough."

"I'd no idea Mick was running the *Spokesman*."

"It's not what he wanted. He only meant to be here a few months last winter. Just till his dad got back on his feet. But his dad didn't recover as quick as they thought. And then I . . ."

Lynley could see the picture well enough. What had probably begun as a diversion for Mick Cambrey—a way to make the time at his father's newspaper in Nanrunnel less boring and onerous—had evolved into a lifelong commitment to a wife and child in whom he no doubt had little more than a passing interest.

"We're in the worst possible state," Nancy was continuing. "He's bought word processors. Two different printers. Equipment for home. Equipment for work. All sorts of things. But there's not enough money. We've taken Gull Cottage and now the rent's been raised. We can't pay it. We've missed the last two months as it is, and if we lose the cottage"—she faltered but again drew herself together—"I don't know what we'll do."

"Gull Cottage?" It was the last thing he had expected her to say. "Are you talking about Roderick Trenarrow's old place in Nanrunnel?"

She smoothed the handkerchief out along the length of her leg, plucking at a loose thread on the *A* embroidered at one corner. "Mick and Dad never got on, did they? And we needed to move once the baby came. So Mick made arrangements with Dr. Trenarrow for us to take Gull Cottage."

"And you find yourselves overextended."

"We're to pay each month. But these last two months, Mick hasn't paid. Dr. Trenarrow's phoned him, but Mick isn't bothered a bit. He says money's tight and they'll talk about it when he gets back from London.''

"London?"

"A story he's been working on there. The one he's been waiting for, he says. To set him up as a journalist. The kind he wants to be. He thinks he can sell it as a free-lance piece the way he used to. Maybe even get a television documentary made. And then there'll be money. But for now there's nothing. I'm so afraid we'll end up on the streets. Or living in the newspaper office. That tiny room in the back with a single cot. We can't come back here. Dad wouldn't have it.''

"I take it your father knows nothing about all this?''

"Oh no! If he knew . . .'' She raised a hand to her mouth.

"Money's not a problem, Nancy,'' Lynley said. He was relieved, in fact, that it was only money she wanted from him and not an understanding little chat with her landlord. "I'll lend you what you want. Take whatever time you need to pay me back. But I don't understand why your father mustn't know. Mick's expenditures seem reasonable if he's trying to modernise the paper. Any bank would—''

"She'll not tell you everything,'' John Penellin said grimly from the doorway. "Shame alone will stop her from telling it all. Shame, pure and simple. The best she's got from Mick Cambrey.''

With a cry, Nancy jumped to her feet, body arched for flight. Lynley rose to intervene.

"Dad.'' She reached out towards him. Voice and gesture both offered placation.

"Tell him the rest,'' her father said. He advanced into the room, but he shut the door behind him to prevent Nancy's escape. "Since you've aired half your dirty linen for his lordship, tell him the rest. You've asked for money, haven't you? Then tell him the rest so he understands what kind of man's on the receiving end of his investment.''

"It's not what you think.''

"Isn't it?'' Penellin looked at Lynley. "Mick Cambrey spends money on that newspaper, all right. There's truth in that. But the rest he spends on his lady friends. And it's Nancy's own money, isn't it, girl? Earned at her jobs. How many jobs, Nance? All the bookkeeping jobs in Penzance and Nanrunnel. And then every night at the Anchor and Rose. With little Molly in a basket on the floor of the pub kitchen because her father can't be bothered away from his writing to see to her while Nancy works to support them all. Only it's not his writing he's taken up with, is it? It's his women. How many are there now, Nance?''

"It isn't true," Nancy said. "That's all in the past. It's the newspaper costs, Dad. Nothing else."

"Don't make your shame worse by colouring it with a lie. Mick Cambrey's no good. Never was. Never will be. Oh, perhaps good enough to get the clothes off an inexperienced girl and plant his baby inside her. But not good enough to do a thing about it without being forced. And look at yourself, Nance, a shining example of the man's affection for you. Look at your clothes. Look at your face."

"It's not his fault."

"See what he's helped you become."

"He doesn't know I'm here. He'd never let me ask—"

"But he'll take the money, won't he? And never question how you came by it. Just as long as it meets his needs. And what are his needs this time, Nancy? Has he another lady? Perhaps two or three?"

"No!" Nancy looked desperately at Lynley. "I just . . . I . . ." She shook her head, her face dissolving into misery.

Penellin moved heavily to the wall map of the estate. His skin was grey. "Look at what he's done to you," he said dully. And then to Lynley, "See what Mick Cambrey's done to my girl."

6

"Simon and Helen shall come with us as well," Sidney announced. Only moments before, she had pulled a coral-coloured dress from the jumble of clothing scattered across her room. The colour should have been all wrong on her, but in this case fashion triumphed over hue. She was swirls of crepe from shoulder to midcalf, like a cloud at sunset.

She and Deborah were heading through the garden towards the park where St. James and Lady Helen walked together beneath the trees. Sidney shouted at them.

"Come and watch Deb snap away at me. At the cove. Half in and half out of a ruined dinghy. A seductive mermaid. Will you come?"

Neither responded until Deborah and Sidney reached them. Then St. James said, "Considering the volume of your invitation, no doubt you can expect quite a crowd, with everyone ready to see just the sort of mermaid you have in mind."

Sidney laughed. "That's right. Mermaids *don't* wear clothes, do they? Oh well. Pooh. You're just jealous that I'm to be Deb's subject for once and not you. However," she admitted, twirling in the breeze, "I did have to make her swear she'd take no snaps of you. Not that she needs any more, if you ask me. She must have a thousand in her collection already. A veritable history of Simon-on-the-stairs, Simon-in-the-garden, Simon-in-the-lab."

"I don't recall being given much choice about posing."

Sidney tossed her head and set off across the park with the others in her wake. "Poor excuse, that. You've had your chance for immortality, Simon. So don't you dare step in front of the camera today and take away mine.''

''I think I can restrain myself,'' St. James replied drily.

''I'm afraid I can't promise the same thing, darlings,'' Lady Helen said. ''I plan to compete ruthlessly with Sidney to be in the foreground of every picture Deborah takes. Surely I've a future as a mannequin just waiting to be discovered on the Howenstow lawn.''

Ahead of them, Sidney laughed and marched southeast, in the direction of the sea. Under the enormous park trees, where the air was rich with the fertile smell of humus, she found myriad sources of inspiration. Perched on a massive branch struck down by the winter storm, she was an impish Ariel, freed from captivity. Holding a cluster of larkspur, she became Persephone, newly delivered from Hades. Against the trunk of a tree with a crown of leaves in her hair, she was Rosalind, dreaming of Orlando's love.

After she had explored all the permutations of antic posturing for Deborah's camera, Sidney ran on, reaching the edge of the park and disappearing through an old gate in the rough stone wall. In a moment, the breeze brought her cry of pleasure back to the others.

''She's reached the mill,'' Lady Helen said. ''I'll see that she doesn't fall into the water.''

Without waiting for a response, without giving the other two a passing glance, she hurried off. In a moment, she too was through the gate and out of the park.

Deborah welcomed the opportunity to be alone with Simon. There was much to say. She hadn't seen him since the day of their quarrel, and once Tommy had informed her that he would be part of their weekend party, she had known she would have to say or do something to serve as apology and to make amends.

But now that a chance for conversation had presented itself, Deborah found that anything other than the most impersonal comment was unthinkable. She knew quite well that she had severed the final ties to Simon in Paddington, and there was no way she could unsay the words that had effected the surgical cut between them.

They continued in the direction that Lady Helen had taken, their slow pace dictated by St. James' gait. In the silence that grew, broken only by the ceaseless calling of the gulls, the sound of his footsteps seemed an amplified deformity. Deborah finally spoke in the need to drive that sound from her ears, reaching aimlessly back into the past for a memory they shared.

''When my mother died, you opened the house in Chelsea.''

St. James looked at her curiously. "That was a long time ago."

"You didn't have to do it. I didn't know that then. It all seemed so reasonable to my seven-year-old mind. But you didn't have to do it. I don't know why I never realised till today."

He brushed a tangle of Dutch clover from his trouser leg. "There's no real easing a loss like that, is there? I did what I could. Your father needed a place to forget. Or if not to forget, at least to go on."

"But *you* didn't have to do it. We could have gone to one of your brothers. They were both in Southampton. They were so much older. It would have been reasonable. You were . . . were you really only eighteen? What on earth were you thinking about, saddling yourself with a household when you were just eighteen? Why did you do it? Why on earth did your parents agree to let you do it?" She felt each question increase in intensity.

"It was right."

"Why?"

"Your father needed something to take the place of the loss. He needed to heal. Your mother had only been dead two months. He was devastated. We were afraid for him, Deborah. None of us had ever seen him like that. If he did something to harm himself . . . You'd already lost your mother. We none of us wanted you to lose your father as well. Of course, you'd have had us to take care of you. There's no question of that. But it's not the same as a real parent, is it?"

"But your brothers. Southampton."

"If he'd gone to Southampton, he'd just have been a spare wheel in an established household, at loose ends and feeling everyone's pity. But in Chelsea, the old house gave him something to do." St. James shot her a smile. "You've forgotten what a condition the house was in, haven't you? It took all his energy—mine as well—to make the place habitable. He didn't have time to keep agonising over your mother the way he had been. He had to start letting the worst part of the sorrow go. He had to get on with his life. With yours and mine as well."

Deborah played with the shoulder strap of her camera. It was stiff and new, not like the comfortably frayed strap on the old, dented Nikon she had used for so many years before she had gone to America.

"That's why you came this weekend, isn't it?" she said. "For Dad."

St. James didn't reply. A gull swept across the park, so close to them that Deborah could feel the wild rush of its wings beat the air. She went on.

"I saw that this morning. How thoughtful you are, Simon. I've been wanting to tell you that ever since we arrived."

St. James thrust his hands into his trouser pockets, a gesture that momentarily emphasised the distortion which his brace brought to his left leg. "It has nothing to do with thoughtfulness, Deborah."

"Why not?"

"It just doesn't."

They walked on, passing through the heavy birch gate, and entering the woodland of a combe that fell down to the sea. Sidney shouted unintelligibly up ahead, her words bubbling with laughter.

Deborah spoke again. "You've always hated the thought that someone might see you as a fine man, haven't you? As if sensitivity were a sort of leprosy. If it isn't thoughtfulness that brought you with Dad, what is it, then?"

"Loyalty."

She gaped at him. "To a servant?"

His eyes became dark. How funny that she had completely forgotten the sudden changes their colour could take on when an emotion struck him. "To a cripple?" he replied.

His words defeated her, bringing them full circle to a beginning and an end that would never alter.

From her perch on a rock above the river, Lady Helen saw St. James coming slowly through the trees. She'd been watching for him since Deborah had come hurrying down the path a few minutes before. As he walked, he flung to one side a heavy-leafed stalk that he'd broken from one of the tropical plants that grew in profusion in the woodland.

Below her, Sidney gambolled in the water, her shoes hanging from one hand and the hem of her dress dangling, disregarded, in the river. Nearby with her camera poised, Deborah examined the disused mill wheel that stood motionless beneath a growth of ivy and lilies. She clambered among the rocks on the river bank, camera in one hand, the other outstretched to maintain her balance.

Although the photographic qualities of the old stone structure were apparent even to Lady Helen's untutored eye, there was an unnecessary intensity to Deborah's study of the building, as if she had made a deliberate decision to devote all her energy to the task of determining appropriate camera angles and depth of field. She was obviously angry.

When St. James joined her on the rock, Lady Helen observed him curiously. Shadowed by the trees, his face betrayed nothing, but his eyes followed Deborah along the bank of the river and every movement he made was abrupt. *Of course*, Lady Helen thought, and not for the first time she wondered what inner resources of fine breeding they would have to call upon to get them through the interminable weekend.

Their walk finally ended at an irregularly shaped clearing which rose to a promontory. Perhaps fifty feet below, gained by a steep path that wound through scrub foliage and boulders, the Howenstow cove glittered in the steamy sun, the perfect destination on a summer afternoon. Fine sand cast up visible waves of heat on the narrow beach. Limestone and granite at the water's edge held tide pools animated by tiny crustaceans. The water itself was so perfectly crystalline that, had not the waves declared it otherwise, a sheet of glass might have been placed on its surface. It was a place not safe enough for boating—with its rocky bottom and its distant, reef-guarded outlet to the sea—but it was a fine location for sunbathing. Three people below them were using it for this purpose.

Sasha Nifford, Peter Lynley, and Justin Brooke sat on a crescent band of rocks at the water's edge. Brooke was shirtless. The other two were nude. Peter was skin stretched over a rib cage with neither sinews nor fat as buffer between them. Sasha consisted of a bit more mass, but it hung upon her with neither tone nor definition, particularly her breasts, which dangled pendulously when she moved.

"Of course, it's a lovely day for a lie in the sun," Lady Helen said hesitantly.

St. James looked at his sister. "Perhaps we'd—"

"Wait," Sidney said.

As they watched, Brooke handed Peter Lynley a small container from which Peter tapped powder onto the flat of his hand. He bent to it, hovered over it with such a passion to possess that even from the clifftop the others could see his chest heave with the effort to ingest every particle. He licked his hand, sucked it, and at the last, raised his face to the sky as if in thanksgiving to an unseen god. He handed the container back to Brooke.

At that, Sidney exploded. "You promised! Damn you to hell. You promised!"

"Sid!" St. James grabbed his sister's arm. He felt the tensility of her insubstantial muscles as adrenaline shot through her body. "Sidney, don't!"

"No!" Sidney tore herself away from him. She kicked off her shoes and began to descend the cliff, sliding in the dust, catching her frock against a rock, and all the time cursing Brooke foully with one imprecation after another.

"Oh, God," Deborah murmured. *"Sidney!"*

At the cliff bottom, Sidney hurtled across the narrow strip of sand to the rock where the three sunbathers were watching her in dazed surprise. She threw herself on Brooke. Her momentum dragged him down off the rocks and onto the sand. She fell upon him, punching his face.

"You told me you wouldn't! You liar! You bleeding, rotten, filthy little liar! Give it to me, Justin. Give it to me. Now!"

She grappled with him, her fingers gouging at his eyes. Brooke put up his arms to fend her off and thus exposed the cocaine. She bit his wrist and ripped the container from his hand.

Brooke shouted as she rose to her feet. He grabbed her legs and toppled her to the ground. But not before she had staggered to the water, uncapped the container, and thrown it—with a tomboy's sure strength—into the sea.

"There's your drug," she shrieked. "Go after it. Kill yourself. Drown."

Above them on the rock, Peter and Sasha laughed idly as Justin surged to his feet, pulled Sidney to hers, and began to drag her into the water. She clawed at his face and neck. Her nails drew a vicious four-pronged trail of blood on his skin.

"I'll tell them," she screamed.

Brooke struggled to hold on to her. He caught her arms and pinned them savagely behind her. She cried out. He smiled and forced her to her knees. He shoved her forward. Putting one foot on her shoulder, he plunged her head beneath the water. When she fought for air, he shoved her back down.

St. James felt rather than saw Lady Helen turn to him. His entire body had gone icy.

"Simon!" Never had his own name sounded so dreadful.

Below them, Brooke dragged Sidney to her feet. But her arms now released, she fell upon him, undaunted.

"Kill . . . you . . ." She was sobbing for breath. She aimed an ineffective blow at his face, attempted to smash her knee into his groin.

He filled his hand with her short, wet hair, hauled her head back sharply, and punched her. The blow and those that followed it resounded hollowly against the cliff. In defence, she lashed out at him, succeeding in getting her hands round his throat. Her fingers dug into his knotted veins and twisted. He ripped her hands away, catching her arms once again. But she was too quick for him this time. She turned her head and sank her teeth into the side of his neck.

"Jesus!" Brooke released her, stumbled back up onto the beach and sank into the sand. He held his hand to the spot where Sidney had bitten him. When he brought his hand away, it showed red with his blood.

Freed, Sidney struggled out of the water. Her dress hung on her body like a sodden second skin. She was coughing, wiping at her cheeks and her eyes. Her strength was spent.

It was then that Brooke moved. With a ragged curse, he leaped to his feet, grabbed her, and threw her to the ground. He straddled her body. He filled his fist with sand and ground it into her hair and across her face. On the rock above, Peter and Sasha watched curiously.

Sidney squirmed beneath him, coughing, crying, trying ineffectually to push him away.

"You want physical," he grunted, pressing one arm down against her neck. "You really want physical. Let's have it, hmm?"

He fumbled with his trousers. He began to tear at her clothes.

"Simon!" Deborah cried. She turned to St. James. She said nothing else.

St. James understood why. He was incapable of movement. Enraged. Unafraid. But most of all crippled.

"It's the cliff," he said. "Helen. For the love of God. I can't manage the cliff."

7

Lady Helen cast only one look at St. James before she reached for Deborah's arm.

"Hurry!"

Deborah didn't move. She stood with her eyes fixed powerlessly on St. James' face. When he began to turn from them both, she put out her hand as if she would touch him.

"Deborah!" Lady Helen grabbed Deborah's camera, dropped it to the ground. "There's no time. Hurry!"

"But—"

"Now!"

The panicked words spurred Deborah to action. She ran with Lady Helen for the path. They began the steep descent to the cove, mindless of the dirt and the dust that rose round them like smoke.

Beneath them on the sand, Sidney fought off Justin Brooke with the kind of renewed strength that is born of terror. But he was getting the better of her, and his previous fury was fast developing into sexual arousal and sadistic pleasure. Clearly, in his mind, Sidney was about to get what she had wanted all along.

Lady Helen and Deborah reached him simultaneously. He was a good-sized man but no match for the two of them. Especially since Lady Helen was driven by a fair amount of rage herself. They threw themselves upon him, and their confrontation was over in less than a minute, leaving Brooke splayed out on the ground, panting for breath and groaning from several furious kicks to his kidneys. Sidney, weeping, dragged herself away from him. She cursed and pulled at her shredded dress.

"Whoa. Oh, wow," Peter Lynley murmured. He took a new position with his head pillowed on Sasha's stomach. "Some rescue. Huh, Sash? Just when things were getting good."

Lady Helen flung her head up. She was out of breath. She was streaked with dirt. Her entire body was trembling so badly she wasn't sure if she would be able to walk.

"What's the matter with you, Peter?" she whispered hoarsely. "What's happened to you? This is Sidney. *Sidney!*"

Peter laughed. Sasha smiled. They settled themselves more comfortably to enjoy the sun.

Lady Helen listened at the heavy panels of St. James' bedroom door, hearing nothing. She wasn't quite certain what she had expected from him. Anything beyond brooding solitude would have been out of character, and St. James was not a man who generally acted out of character. He wasn't doing so now. The stillness behind the door was so complete that had she not seen him to this very room two hours before, Lady Helen would have sworn it was unoccupied. But she knew he was in there, damning himself to isolation.

Well, she thought, he's had enough time to flagellate himself. Time to rout him out.

She raised her hand to knock, but before she could do so, Cotter opened the door, saw her, and stepped into the corridor. He gave a quick, backward glance into the room—Lady Helen could see that the curtains had been drawn—and shut the door behind him. He folded his arms across his chest.

Had she been given to mythological allusions, Lady Helen would have dubbed Cotter Cerberus then and there. Since this was not her bent, she merely squared her shoulders and promised herself that St. James would not avoid her by posting Cotter to guard the gates.

"He's up by now, isn't he?" She spoke casually, an enquiry from a friend, deliberately overlooking the fact that the room's darkness indicated St. James was not up at all and had no intention of getting up any time soon. "Tommy has a Nanrunnel adventure planned for us tonight. Simon won't want to miss it."

Cotter tightened his arms. "He asked me to make 'is excuses. Bit of pain this afternoon. The 'eadaches. You know what it's like."

"No!"

Cotter blinked. Taking his arm, Lady Helen pulled him away from the door, across the corridor to a line of quarry windows which over-looked the pantry court. "Cotter, please. Don't let him do this."

"Lady Helen, we got to . . ." Cotter paused. His patient manner of address indicated that he wished to reason with her. Lady Helen wanted none of that.

"You know what happened, don't you?"

Cotter avoided answering by taking a handkerchief from his pocket, blowing his nose, and then studying the cobblestones and fountain in the courtyard below.

"Cotter," Lady Helen insisted. "You do know what happened?"

"I do. From Deb."

"Then you know he can't be allowed to brood any longer."

"But 'is orders were—"

"Damn his orders to hell. A thousand and one times you've ignored them and done exactly as you please if it's for his own good. And you know this is for his own good now." Lady Helen paused to consider a plan he'd accept. "So. You're wanted in the drawing room. Everyone's meeting there for sherry. You haven't seen me the entire afternoon, so you weren't here to stop me from barging in on Mr. St. James and taking charge of him after my own fashion. All right?"

Although no smile touched Cotter's lips, his nod signalled approval. "Right."

Lady Helen watched him walk off in the direction of the main body of the house before she returned to the door and entered the room. She could see St. James' form on the bed, but he stirred when she closed the door so she knew he wasn't asleep.

"Simon, darling," she announced, "if you'll pardon the ghastly use of alliteration, we're to have our collective cultural consciousness raised with a Nanrunnel adventure tonight. God knows we'll have to fortify ourselves with seven or eight stiff sherries—*can* a sherry be stiff?—if we're going to survive. I think Tommy and Deborah are well ahead of us in their drinking, so you'll have to be quick if we're ever to catch up. What will you wear?"

She walked across the room as she was speaking, going to the windows to pull back the curtains. She arranged them neatly—more to stall for time than to see to their proper hanging—and when she could find no reason to continue fussing with them, she turned to the bed to find St. James observing her. He looked amused.

"You're so obvious, Helen."

She sighed in relief. Pitying himself had never really been the question, of course. Hating himself was more likely. But she saw even that may have spent itself after their moments alone on the cliff when Deborah had taken Sidney back to the house.

Would Brooke have killed her or just raped her, St. James had demanded, *while I watched from up here like a useless voyeur? Quite safe, uninvolved. No risk incurred, right? It sounds like my whole life.*

There had been no anger contained in his words, only humiliation, which was infinitely worse.

She had shouted at him. *No one cares about it! No one ever has but you!*

She spoke only the truth, but that truth did nothing to mitigate the fact that his own caring about it so unforgivingly was a permanent scar on the fragile surface of his self-esteem.

"What is it?" he was asking her now. "A darts tournament at the Anchor and Rose?"

"No. Something better. A sure-to-be-dreadful performance of *Much Ado About Nothing,* put on by the village players on the grounds of the primary school. In fact, it's a special performance tonight in honour of Tommy's engagement. Or so, according to Daze, the rector said when he came to call today, complimentary tickets in hand."

"Isn't that the same group—"

"Who did *The Importance of Being Earnest* two summers ago? Darling Simon, yes. The very same."

"Lord. How could this current production match Nanrunnel's gallant bow to Oscar Wilde? The Reverend Mr. Sweeney waxing eloquent as Algernon with cucumber sandwiches sticking to the roof of his mouth. Not to mention the muffins."

"Then what do you say to Mr. Sweeney as Benedick?"

"Only a fool would pass that up." St. James reached for his crutches, swung himself to his feet, balanced, and adjusted his long dressing gown.

Lady Helen averted her eyes as he did so, using as an excuse the need to pick up three rose petals which had fallen from an arrangement that sat on the shelf of a cheveret to one side of the window. They felt like small pieces of down-covered satin against her palm. She looked for a rubbish basket and thus circumvented an open acknowledgement of St. James' primary vanity, a need to hide his bad leg in an attempt to appear as normal as possible.

"Has anyone seen Tommy?"

Lady Helen read the meaning underlying St. James' question. "He doesn't know what happened. We've managed to avoid him."

"Deborah's managed as well?"

"She's been with Sidney. She saw to her bath, got her to lie down, took her some tea." She gave a brief, humourless laugh. "The tea was my profound contribution. I'm not sure what effect it was supposed to have."

"What about Brooke?"

"Can we be so lucky as to hope he's taken himself back to London?"

"I doubt it. Don't you?"

"Rather. Yes."

St. James was standing next to the bed. Lady Helen knew she should leave the room to give him privacy to dress, but something in his manner—a meticulous control too brittle to be believed—compelled her to stay. Too much remained unsaid.

She knew St. James well, better than she had known any other man. She had spent the last decade becoming acquainted with his blind devotion to forensic science and his determination to stake out ground upon which he could build a reputation as an expert. She had come to terms with his relentless introspection as well as with his desire for perfection and his self-castigation if he fell short of a goal. They talked about all of this, over lunch and dinner, in his study while the rain beat against the windows, on their way to the Old Bailey, on the stairs, in the lab. But what they did not talk about was his disability. It had always represented a polar region of his psyche that brooked no one's intrusion. Until today on the clifftop. Even then, when he had finally given her the opening she had long awaited, her words had been inadequate.

What, then, could she say to him now? She didn't know. Not for the first time did she wonder what sort of bond might have developed between them had she not left his hospital room eight years ago simply because he asked her to do so. And to obey him then had been so much easier than taking the chance of walking into the unknown.

Still, she couldn't leave him now without attempting to say something that gave him—even in small measure—back to himself.

"Simon."

"My medication is on the counter above the wash basin, Helen," St. James said. "Will you fetch me two tablets?"

"Medication?" Lady Helen felt a quick surge of concern. She didn't think she had misread his reasons for locking himself away in his room for the afternoon. He hadn't been acting as if he was having any pain at all, despite Cotter's admonition to her earlier.

"It's just a precaution. Above the wash basin." He smiled, a flicker that passed across his face and was gone in an instant. "I take it that way sometimes. Before instead of during. It works just as well. And if I'm to put up with Mr. Sweeney as a thespian for an evening, I ought to be prepared."

She laughed and went to get it for him, calling back into the bedroom, "Actually, this isn't a bad idea. If tonight's production is anything like the other we saw, we'll all be popping pain killers before the evening's through. Perhaps we should take the bottle along with us."

She brought the tablets back into the bedroom. He had gone to the window where he was leaning forward on his crutches, looking out at the southern view of the grounds. But she could tell from his profile that his eyes registered nothing.

The sight of him like this negated his words, his polite cooperation, and the lightness of his tone. She realised that even his smile had been a device to cut her off completely, while all along he existed, as he always had done, alone.

She would not accept it. "You might have fallen," she said. "Please. Simon darling, the path was too steep. You might have been killed."

"Indeed," he answered.

The cavernous Howenstow drawing room did not possess the sort of qualities that made one feel at home wandering through it. The size of an over-large tennis court, its furniture—an aggregation of antiques positioned in conversational groupings—was scattered across a fine chenille carpet. Walled with Constables and Turners and displaying an array of fine porcelains, it was the sort of room that made one afraid of moving precipitately in any direction. Alone, Deborah carefully picked her way down its length to the grand piano, intent upon examining the photographs that stood on top of it.

They comprised a pictorial history of the Lynleys' tenure as the Earls of Asherton. The stiff-backed fifth Countess stared at her with that unfriendly expression so predominant in the photographs of the nineteenth century; the sixth Earl sat astride a large bay and looked down at an unruly pack of hounds; the present Lady was robed and gowned for the Queen's coronation; Tommy and his siblings frolicked through a youth of wealth and privilege.

Only Tommy's father, the seventh Earl, was missing. As she noticed this, Deborah realised that she had seen his likeness nowhere in the house, in either photograph or portrait, a circumstance she found decidedly odd, for she had seen several pictures of the man in the townhouse Tommy occupied in London.

"When you're photographed to join them, you must promise me you'll smile." Lady Asherton came to meet her, a glass of sherry in her hand. She looked cool and lovely in a cloudy white dress. "I wanted to smile, but Tommy's father insisted that it wasn't done and I'm afraid I caved in quite spinelessly. I was like that in my youth. Most appallingly malleable." She smiled at Deborah, sipping her sherry and moving from the piano to sit in the embrasure of a window behind it.

"I've so enjoyed my afternoon with your father, Deborah. I talked incessantly, but he was quite gracious about it, acting as if everything I said was the height of wit and sense." She turned her glass upon her palm and seemed to be watching how the light struck the design cut into the crystal. "You're very close to your father."

"Yes," she answered.

"That's sometimes the way when a child loses one parent, isn't it? It's the mixed blessing of a death."

"Of course, I was very young when my mother died," Deborah said in an attempt to explain away the distance she had not been able to ignore between Tommy and his mother. "So I suppose it was natural that I would develop a deeper relationship with Dad. He was doing double duty, after all. Father and mother to a seven-year-old. And I had no brothers or sisters. Well, Simon was there, but he was more like . . . I'm not sure. An uncle? A cousin? Most of my upbringing fell to Dad."

"And you became a unit as a result, the two of you. How lucky you are."

Deborah wouldn't have called her relationship with her father the product of luck. Rather it was the outcome of time, paternal patience, and willing communication. Saddled with a child whose impetuous personality was nothing like his own, Cotter had managed to adjust his own thinking in a constant attempt to understand hers. If devotion existed between them now, it was only due to years in which the seeds of a future relationship had been planted and cultivated.

"You're estranged from Tommy, aren't you?" Deborah said impulsively.

Lady Asherton smiled, but she looked very tired. For a moment Deborah thought that exhaustion might wear at her guard and prompt her to say something about what was at the root of the trouble between herself and her son. But instead, she said, "Has Tommy mentioned the play tonight? Shakespeare under the stars. In Nanrunnel." Voices drifted to them from the corridor. "I'll let him tell you about it, shall I?" That said, she gave her attention to the window behind her where a light breeze carried into the room the salty fragrance of the Cornish sea.

"If we fortify ourselves enough, we should be able to survive this with some semblance of sanity." Lynley was saying as he entered the room. He went directly to a cabinet and began pouring three sherries from one of the decanters that stood in a semicircle upon it. He gave one to Lady Helen, another to St. James, and tossed back his own drink before catching sight of Deborah and his mother at the far end of the room. He said, "Have you told Deborah about our Theseus and Hippolyta roles this evening?"

Lady Asherton raised her hand fractionally from her lap. Like her smile, the movement seemed weighted by fatigue. "I thought that was best left to you."

Lynley poured himself a second drink. "Right. Yes. Well"—this to Deborah with a smile—"we've a duty play, darling. I'd like to tell you that we'll go late and bow out at the interval, but the Reverend Mr. Sweeney is an old family friend. He'd be crushed if we weren't there for the entire production."

"Dreadful though the production will certainly be," Lady Helen added.

"Shall I take photographs while we're there?" Deborah offered. "After the play, I mean. If Mr. Sweeney's an especial friend, perhaps he'd like that."

"Tommy with the cast," Lady Helen said. "Mr. Sweeney will burst. What a wonderful idea! I've always said you belong on the stage, haven't I, Tommy?"

Lynley laughed, made a response. Lady Helen chatted on. As she did so, St. James took his drink and wandered towards two large Chinese vases that stood at either side of the doorway into the long Elizabethan gallery that opened off the east end of the drawing room. He ran his fingers over the smooth porcelain surface of one of them, tracing a particularly intricate pattern made by the glaze. Deborah noted that although twice he lifted his glass of sherry to his lips, he drank neither time. He seemed intent upon looking at no one.

Deborah hardly expected anything else after the afternoon. In fact, if not acknowledging anyone's presence helped him to forget about it all, she felt quite as if she would like to indulge in the same behaviour even though she knew that, for herself, forgetting would not occur any time soon.

It had been bad enough tearing Brooke away from Sidney, knowing his behaviour was the product of neither love nor lust but violence and a need to hammer her into submission. It was even worse helping Sidney climb the cliff, hearing her hysterical weeping, catching hold of her so that she wouldn't fall. Her face was bleeding and beginning to swell. The words she sobbed out were incoherent. Three times she stopped, wouldn't move, merely wept. All that had been a living nightmare. But then at the top, there was Simon, standing against a tree, watching for them. His face was half hidden. His right hand dug into the tree's bark so hard that the bones stood out.

Deborah had wanted to go to him. For what reason, to what possible end, she could not have said. Her only rational thought at the moment was that she couldn't leave him alone. But Helen stopped her when she took a step in his direction, pushing her with Sidney towards the path to the house.

That stumbling trip back had been the second nightmare. Each part stood out vividly in her mind. Coming upon Mark Penellin in the woods; making inarticulate excuses for Sidney's appearance and her distraught condition; approaching the house with an ever rising sense of trepidation that someone might see them; slipping by the gun room and the old servants' hall to look for the northwest stairway that Helen had insisted was near the pantry; taking a wrong turn at the top of those stairs and ending up in the disused west wing of the house; and all the time terrified that Tommy would come upon them and begin asking questions. Through it all, Sidney had gone from hysteria to rage to despair and finally to silence. But this last was dazed, and it frightened Deborah more than Sidney's earlier unrestrained agitation.

The entire experience had far exceeded dreadful, and when Justin Brooke walked into the drawing room, dressed casually for the evening as if he had not tried to rape a woman in front of five witnesses that afternoon, it was all Deborah could do to look at the man without screaming and flying into the attack.

8

"Good God, what happened to you?" Lynley sounded so surprised that St. James turned from his perusal of the Kang H'si porcelain to see Justin Brooke taking the proffered glass of sherry with complete nonchalance.

Christ, St. James thought, Brooke was actually going to join them, smugly confident that they were all too self-servingly well-bred to say anything about the afternoon while Lynley and his mother were in the room.

"Took a fall in the woods." Brooke looked around as he spoke, making eye contact with each of them, challenging one person after another to expose him as a liar.

At this, St. James felt his jaw clench automatically to bite back what he wanted to say. With an atavistic satisfaction which he did not deny himself, he noted the considerable damage that his sister had managed to do to Brooke's face Claw marks scored his cheeks. A bruise rose on his jaw. His lower lip was swollen.

"A fall?" Lynley's attention was on the inflamed teethmarks on Brooke's neck, barely obscured by the collar of his shirt. He looked at the others sharply. "Where's Sidney?" he asked.

No one replied. A glass clinked against the top of a table. Someone coughed. Outside, at some distance from the house, an engine roared to life. Footsteps sounded in the hall and Cotter entered the drawing room. He stopped barely two feet inside the door, as if he'd taken a quick reading of the ambience and was having second thoughts about exposing himself to it. He looked at St. James, a reflex reaction that sought direction and found it in the other man's detachment from the scene. He made no other move.

"Where's Sidney?" Lynley repeated.

At her end of the room, Lady Asherton rose to her feet. "Has something—"

Deborah spoke quickly. "I saw her half an hour ago, Tommy." Her face flushed. Its colour did battle with the fire of her hair. "She spent too much time in the sun this afternoon and thought . . . well, she's asked for . . . a rest. Yes. She said she needed a bit of a rest. She did send her apologies and . . . you know Sidney. She goes at such a pace, doesn't she? She wears herself out as if nothing at all . . . It's no wonder to me she's exhausted." Her fingers wandered to her throat as she spoke, as if her hand wanted to cover her mouth to prevent the lie from becoming even more obvious.

In spite of himself, St. James smiled. He looked at Deborah's father who shook his head weakly in affectionate recognition of a fact they both knew only too well. Helen might have been able to carry it off. Casual prevarication to smooth over troubled waters was more in her line. But Deborah was hopeless at this particular form of conversational legerdemain.

The rest of the party was saved from having to embellish upon Deborah's story by the entrance of Peter Lynley. His feet bare and a clean gauze shirt his only bow to dressing for dinner, he was trailed by Sasha whose glaucous-hued dress made her complexion seem more sallow than ever. As if she would speak to them or attempt to intercede in what she saw as a coming conflict, Lady Asherton started to walk in their direction.

Peter gave no indication that he saw his mother or anyone else. He merely wiped his nose on the back of his hand and went to the drinks tray. He poured himself a whisky, which he gulped down quickly, then poured himself another and Sasha some of the same.

They stood, an isolated little unit apart from the others, with the spirit decanters within easy reach. As she took a sip of her drink, Sasha slipped her hand under Peter's loose shirt and pulled him towards her.

"Nice stuff, Sash," Peter murmured and kissed her.

Lynley set his glass down. Lady Asherton spoke quickly. "I saw Nancy Cambrey on the grounds this afternoon, Tommy. I'm rather concerned about her. She's lost a great deal of weight. Did you happen to see her?"

"I saw her." Lynley watched his brother and Sasha. His face was unreadable.

"She seems terribly worried about something. I think it's to do with Mick. He's working on a story that's taken him away from home so much these last few months. Did she talk to you about it?"

"We talked."

"And did she mention a story, Tommy? Because—"

"She mentioned it. Yes."

Lady Helen attacked the issue of diversion from a new angle. "What a lovely dress that is, Sasha. I envy your ability to wear those wonderful Indian prints. I look like a cross between Jemima Puddleduck and a charwoman whenever I try them. Did Mark Penellin find the two of you? Simon and I saw him in the woods seeking you out."

"Mark Penellin?" Peter reached out to caress a length of Sasha's thin hair. "No, we never saw him."

In some confusion, Lady Helen looked towards St. James. "But we saw him. He didn't find you in the cove? This afternoon?"

Peter smiled a lazy, satisfied smile. "We weren't in the cove this afternoon."

"You weren't . . ."

"I mean, I suppose we were, but we weren't. So if he wanted to find us, he would have seen us but not seen us. Or maybe it was after we went in the water. And then he wouldn't have seen us at all. Not where we were. And I don't think I'd have wanted him to. What about you, Sash?"

He chuckled and traced the bridge of Sasha's nose. He ran his fingers across her mouth. Catlike, she licked them.

Wonderful, St. James thought. It's only Friday.

Nanrunnel was a successful combination of two disparate environments: a centuries-old fishing village and a modern tourist haunt. Built in a semicircular fashion round a natural harbour, its structures twisted up a hillside dotted with cedar, cypress, and pine, their exteriors hewn from rocks quarried in the district, some whitewashed and others left a natural, weather-streaked mixture of grey and brown. Streets were narrow—wide enough to allow only the passage of a single car—and they followed a strangely convoluted pattern which met the demands of the hills rather than the requirements of automobiles.

Fishing boats filled the harbour itself, bobbing rhythmically on the incoming tide and protected by two long crescent-shaped quays. Curiously shaped buildings perched on the harbour's edge—cottages, shops, inns, and restaurants—and an uneven, cobbled walkway running along the embankment gave their inhabitants access to the water below. Above, hundreds of seabirds cried from chimneys and slate roofs while hundreds more took to the air, circled the harbour, and flew from there into the bay where, in the distance, St. Michael's Mount rose in the failing evening light.

A considerable crowd had gathered at the primary school grounds on the lower part of Paul Lane. There, a humble open-air theatre had been created by the Reverend Mr. Sweeney and his wife. It consisted of only three elements. A sturdily crafted platform served as stage. Accommodation for the audience comprised folding wooden chairs of prewar vintage. And at the far side of the grounds, next to the street, a refreshment booth was already doing a respectable business with libations supplied by the village's largest pub, the Anchor and Rose. Nancy Cambrey, Lynley saw, was working the taps.

The rector himself met Lynley's party at the entrance to the school grounds, his portly face beaming with a rapturous smile of welcome. He wore a heavy layer of theatrical make-up through which he was perspiring heavily. In costume already, he was an incongruous sight in doublet and stockings, his bald head aglow under the strands of lights which crisscrossed the school yard.

"I shall wear a wig for Benedick, of course," Mr. Sweeney mocked himself gently. He greeted St. James and Lady Helen with the fondness of an old friend and then presented himself eagerly to be introduced to Deborah, a social nicety which he brushed aside almost as soon as he adopted it by bursting out with, "My dear, we are so *pleased* to have you here tonight. Both of you. It's grand," before Lynley could say a word. He might well have gone on to bow with a flourish had not the precarious position of his codpiece precluded any sudden movement. "We've put you right in front so you won't miss a thing. Come, it's just this way."

Missing a thing, missing several things, missing the entire play would have been too much blessing to hope for since the Nanrunnel Players had long been known for the stentorian nature of their performances rather than for their histrionic flare. However, led by Mr. Sweeney— with his wife as a short, plump Beatrice who managed to display a remarkably heaving bosom during speeches far more impassioned than required by the role—the drama proceeded with fiery enthusiasm to the interval. At this point, the audience rose to its feet as one and headed towards the refreshment booth to make the most of a respite filled with lager and ale.

The sole advantage to being the guests of honour showed itself in the quick progress Lynley and his party made to the booth. The crowd, which moments before had been surging forward towards the blessed salvation of Watney's and Bass, parted in a cooperative fashion, giving Lynley and the others quick access to relief.

The only other person to take advantage of this break in the mass of pushing and shoving humanity was a tall, middle-aged man who had managed to reach the refreshment booth first. He turned with a tray of glasses in his hands and presented it to Lynley.

"Have these, Tommy," he said.

Incredulously, Lynley stared at Roderick Trenarrow and at the tray of glasses he held. His intention was both unmistakable and unavoidable, a public meeting, a display of good cheer. As always, Trenarrow had chosen his moment like a master.

"Roderick," Lynley said. "How very good of you."

Trenarrow smiled. "I have the advantage of a seat near the booth."

"Strange. I hardly thought Shakespeare would be in your line."

"Other than *Hamlet,* you mean?" Trenarrow asked pleasantly. He directed his attention to Lynley's party, clearly expecting to be introduced. Lynley did so, mustering the good grace to appear unaffected by this unexpected encounter.

Trenarrow pushed his gold-rimmed spectacles up the bridge of his nose and directed his words to Lynley's friends. "I'm afraid Mrs. Sweeney caught me on the bus from Penzance, and before I knew it, I'd purchased a ticket to tonight's performance and sworn I'd attend. But there's mercy involved. Since I'm near the drinks booth, if the production gets any more appalling, I can swozzle down six or seven more lagers and pickle myself properly."

"Our very thought," Lady Helen said.

"One gets more experienced with the Nanrunnel productions every summer," Trenarrow went on. "I expect the rest of the audience will try sitting with me at the back next year. Eventually no one will be willing to fill up the front seats and Mrs. Sweeney will be forced to put on her play from inside the refreshment booth just to hold our attention."

The others laughed. Lynley did not. Instead he found himself annoyed at their willingness to succumb to Trenarrow, and he scrutinised the other man, as if an analysis of his physical properties would somehow reveal the source of his charm. As always, Lynley noticed not the whole but the details. Rich brown hair finally showing the signs of his age, weaving fine strands of silver back from his brow; a linen suit that was old but well-tailored, spotlessly clean and fitted to his figure; a jawline sharp and hard, carrying no spare flesh in spite of the fact that he was nearing fifty; warm laughter bursting out of him unrestrained; the webbing of flesh at his eyes; and the eyes themselves which were dark and quick to assess and understand.

Lynley catalogued all this with no system for observation, just a series of fleeting impressions. There was no way to avoid them, not with Trenarrow so close, standing—as he always had—so much larger than life.

"I see Nancy Cambrey's gone to work at the Anchor and Rose in addition to her other jobs," Lynley said to Trenarrow.

The other man looked over his shoulder to the refreshment booth. "It looks that way. I'm surprised she'd take it on with the baby and all. It can't be easy for her."

"It'll do something to ease their money troubles, though, won't it?" Lynley took a gulp of his lager. It was too warm for his liking and he would have preferred to dump it out onto the base of a convenient palm nearby. But Trenarrow would have read animosity in that action, so he continued sipping the drink. "Look, Roderick," he said brusquely, "I'm going to make good whatever money they owe you."

Both the statement and his manner of saying it put an end to conversation among the others. Lynley became aware of Lady Helen's hand coming to rest on St. James' arm, of Deborah's uneasy stirring at his own side, of Trenarrow's look of perplexity as if he hadn't an idea in the world what Lynley was referring to.

"Make good the money?" Trenarrow repeated.

"I'm not about to let Nancy go begging. They can't afford a rise in rent at the moment and—"

"Rent?"

Lynley found his gentle repetitions aggravating. Trenarrow was manoeuvring him into the bully's role. "She's afraid of losing Gull Cottage. I told her I'd make good the money. Now I'm telling you."

"The cottage. I see." Trenarrow lifted his drink slowly and observed Lynley over the rim of the glass. He gazed reflectively at the drinks booth. "Nancy doesn't need to worry about the cottage. Mick and I shall work it out. She needn't have bothered you for the money."

How absolutely like the man, Lynley thought. How insufferably noble he was. How far-sighted as well. He knew what he was doing. The entire conversation was the sort of parry and thrust that they had engaged in innumerable times over the years, filled with double-edged words and hidden meanings.

"I said I'd take care of it and I will." Lynley attempted to alter the tone if not the intention behind his words. "There's absolutely no need for you to—"

"Suffer?" Trenarrow regarded Lynley evenly for a moment before he offered a cool smile. He finished the rest of his drink. "How very kind of you. If you'll excuse me now, I seem to have been dominating your time long enough. There appear to be others here who'd like to be introduced." He nodded and left them.

Lynley watched him go, recognising as always Trenarrow's skill at seizing the moment. He'd done it again, leaving Lynley feeling like nothing more than a rough-edged lout. He was seventeen again. Over and over in Trenarrow's presence, he would always be seventeen.

Lady Helen's animated words filled the void created by Trenarrow's departure. "Good heavens, what a gorgeous man he is, Tommy. Did you say he's a doctor? Every woman in the village must line up at his surgery on a daily basis."

"He's not that kind of doctor," Lynley replied automatically. He poured out the rest of his lager along the trunk of a palm and watched the liquid pool onto the dry, unyielding earth. "He does medical research in Penzance."

Which is why he'd come to Howenstow in the first place, a man only thirty years old, called upon as an act of desperation to see to the dying earl. It was hopeless. He'd explained in that earnest fashion of his that there was nothing more to be done besides adhering to the current chemotherapy. There was no cure in spite of what they read and wanted to believe in the tabloids, he said there were dozens of different kinds of cancer, it was a catch-all term. The body was dying of its own inability to call a halt to the production of cells, and scientists didn't know enough, that they were working and striving but it would be years, decades . . . He spoke with quiet apologies. With profound understanding and compassion.

And so the earl had lingered and dwindled and suffered and died. The family had mourned him. The region had mourned him. Everyone save Roderick Trenarrow.

9

Nancy Cambrey packed the last of the pint glasses into a carton for the short trip down the hill to the Anchor and Rose. She was extremely weary. In order to be at the school in time to do the setting up that evening, she'd gone without her dinner, so she was feeling light-headed as well. She crisscrossed the carton flaps and secured the package, relieved that the evening's labour was done.

Nearby, her employer—the formidable Mrs. Swann—fingered through the night's taking with her usual passion for things pecuniary. Her lips moved soundlessly as she counted the coins and notes, jotting figures into her dog-eared red ledger. She nodded in satisfaction. The booth had done well.

"I'm off then," Nancy said with some hesitation. She never knew exactly what kind of reaction to expect from Mrs. Swann, who was notorious for her mood swings. No barmaid had ever lasted more than seven months in her employ. Nancy was determined to be the first. Money's the point, she whispered inwardly whenever she found herself on the receiving end of one of Mrs. Swann's violent outbursts. You can bear anything, so long as you're paid.

"Fine, Nance," Mrs. Swann muttered with a wave of her hand. "Off with you, then."

"Sorry about the call box."

The woman snorted and poked at her scalp with the stub of a pencil. "From now on, phone your dad on your own time, girl. Not on the pub's time. And not on mine."

"Yes. I will. I'll remember." Placation was paramount. Nancy held tightly to the booth in order to manage unruffling Mrs. Swann's feathers while betraying nothing of the aversion she actually felt for her employer. "I learn quick, Mrs. Swann. You'll see. People never do have to tell me anything twice."

Mrs. Swann looked up sharply. Her rat's eyes glittered in evaluation. "Learning things quick enough from that man of yours, girl? All sorts of new things, I expect. That right?"

Nancy rubbed at a smudge on her faded pink blouse. "I'm off," she said in answer and ducked under the booth.

Although the lights were still on, the yard was empty of everyone save Lynley's party and the Nanrunnel Players. Nancy watched them at the front of the theatre. While St. James and Lady Helen waited among the empty seats, Lynley posed with the cast as his fiancée took their pictures. Each flash lit one delighted face after another, catching their antic posturing on film. Lynley bore it all with his usual good grace, chatting away with the rector and his wife, laughing at cheerful remarks made by Lady Helen Clyde.

Life comes so easily to him, Nancy thought.

"It's no different, my dear, being one of them. It only looks that way."

Nancy started at the words, at their stabbing acuity. She whirled to see Dr. Trenarrow sitting in the shadows, against a wall of the school yard.

Nancy had avoided him for the entire evening, always keeping out of his reach or his line of vision when he came to the booth for a drink. Now, however, she could not avoid the contact, for he got to his feet and walked into the light.

"You're worried about the cottage," he said. "Don't. I shan't be putting you out on the street. We'll work things out, Mick and I."

She felt sweat break out on the back of her neck in spite of his gentle declaration. It was the nightmare she feared, coming face to face with him, having to discuss the situation, having to create excuses. Worse, just ten feet away, Mrs. Swann had raised her head from the money box, her interest no doubt piqued by the mention of Mick's name.

"I'll have the money," she stammered. "I'll get it. I will."

"You're not to worry, Nancy," Trenarrow said, more insistently. "And you've no need at all to go begging Lord Asherton for help. You should have spoken to me."

"No. You see . . ." She couldn't explain without giving offence. He would not understand why she could go hat in hand to Lynley but not to him. He wouldn't realise that a loan from Lynley carried no burden of unwelcome charity because he gave without judgement, in friendship and concern. And nowhere else in Nancy's life could she expect that sort of help without a companion assessment of the failure of her marriage. Even now she could feel the manner in which Dr. Trenarrow was evaluating her situation. Even now she could sense his pity.

"Because a rise in the rent isn't—"

"Please." With a small cry, she brushed past him, hurrying out of the school yard and into the street. She heard Dr. Trenarrow call her name once, but she kept going.

Rubbing arms that were sore from heaving pint glasses and working the taps all night, she scurried down Paul Lane towards the mouth of Ivy Street which led into the twisting collection of alleys and passageways that comprised the heart of the village. These were narrow inclines, cobbled and tortuous little streets too cramped for cars. During the day, summer holiday makers came here to photograph the picturesque old buildings with their colourful front gardens and crooked slate roofs. At night, however, the entire area was illuminated only by oblongs of light from cottage windows. Darkly shadowed and inhabited by generations of cats who bred in the hillside above the village and fed by night in rubbish bins, it was not a place for lingering.

Gull Cottage was some distance into the maze of streets. It sat on the corner of Virgin Place, looking like a whitewashed matchbox, with bright blue trim on its windows and a lavishly blooming fuchsia growing next to its front door. Blood-red flowers blown from this plant covered the ground nearby.

As Nancy approached the cottage, her steps faltered. She could hear the noise from three houses away. Molly was crying, screaming, in fact.

She looked at her watch. It was nearly midnight. Molly should have been fed, should have been fast asleep by now. Why on earth was Mick not seeing to the child?

Exasperated that her husband could be so selfishly deaf to his own daughter's cries, Nancy ran the remaining distance to the cottage, threw open the garden gate, and hurried to the door.

"Mick!" she called. Above her, in the only bedroom, she could hear Molly's screaming. She felt an edge of panic, picturing the baby's face, red with rage, feeling her small body tense with fright. She shoved open the door.

"Molly!"

Inside, she ran for the stairs, took them two at a time. It was insufferably hot.

"Molly-girl! Pet!" She flew to the baby's cot and picked her daughter up to find that she was wet to the skin, reeking of urine. Her body was feverish. Tendrils of auburn hair curled limply on her skull. "Love, lovely girl. What's happened to you?" she murmured as she sponged her off and changed her and then cried out, "Michael! Mick!"

With Molly against her shoulder, Nancy went back down the stairs, her feet striking the bare wood noisily as she headed for the kitchen at the rear of the cottage. Feeding the baby was foremost on her mind. Still, she allowed herself to give vent to a small eruption of anger.

"I want to speak with you," she snapped at the closed sitting room door. "Michael! D'you hear? I want a word. Now!"

As she spoke, she saw that the door was neither latched nor locked. She pushed it open with her foot.

"Michael, you can damn well answer me when—"

She felt the hairs bristling along the length of her arms. He was lying on the floor. Or someone was lying there, for she could just see a leg. Only one. Not two. Which was curious unless he was sleeping with one leg drawn up and the other splayed out in complete abandon. Except, how could he be asleep? It was hot. So hot. And the noise which Molly had been making . . .

"Mick, are you playing some pawky joke on me?"

There was no reply. Molly's crying had faded to an exhausted whimper, so Nancy took a step into the room.

"That's you, isn't it, Mick?"

Nothing. But, she could see it was Mick. She recognised his shoe, a frivolous high-topped red plimsole with a strip of metallic silver round the ankle. It was a new purchase of his, something that he didn't need. It costs too much money, she'd say to him. It bleeds off the chequebook. It takes away from the baby . . . Yes, it *was* Mick on the floor. And she knew what he was up to at the moment, pretending to be asleep so that she couldn't rant at him for ignoring the baby.

Still, it didn't seem like him not to hop to his feet, laughing at his ability to frighten her with another one of his practical jokes. And she *was* frightened. Because something wasn't right. Papers blanketed the floor, far more than represented Mick's usual mess. The desk drawers were open. The curtains were drawn. A cat yowled outside, but in the cottage, there was no sound, and the heavy, hot air was foul with the smell of faeces and sweat.

"Mickey?"

Her hands, her armpits, the back of her knees, the inside of her elbows. She was sticky and wet. Molly stirred in her arms. Nancy forced herself forward. An inch. Then another. Then an entire foot. Six inches after that. And then she saw why her husband had not heard Molly's cries.

Although he lay motionless on the floor, he was not pretending to be asleep at all. His eyes were open. But they were glazed and fixed and as Nancy watched, a fly walked across the surface of one blue iris.

Before her, his image seemed to swim in the heat, animated by a force external to his body. He should move, she thought. How can he be that still? Is it some sort of trick? Can't he feel the fly?

Then she saw the other flies. Six or eight. No more. They usually kept residence in the kitchen and pestered her while she cooked their meals. But now they buzzed and circled round her husband's hips where Mick's trousers were torn, where they were open at the waist, where they were jerked down brutally to give someone access . . . to allow someone to carve . . .

She was running with no sense of direction and no clear purpose. Her only thought was to get away.

She flung herself out of the cottage, through the gate, and into Virgin Place, the baby once again wailing in her arms. Her foot caught on a cobblestone and she nearly fell, but she staggered three steps, crashed against a rubbish bin, and righted herself by grabbing onto a cottage rainspout.

The darkness was complete. Moonlight struck the roofs and the sides of buildings, but these cast long shadows into the street, creating yawning ebony pools into which she dashed, heedless of the uneven pavement, of the small scurrying rodents who foraged in the night. The mouth of Ivy Street was up ahead, and she lunged for it and for the safety of Paul Lane which lay just beyond it.

"Please." Her mouth formed the word. She couldn't hear herself say it. And then, breaking through the rasping noise of her lungs, came voices and laughter, joking on Paul Lane.

"All right, I believe you. So find Cassiopeia," a man's pleasant voice said. Then he added, "Oh, for God's sake, at least you can manage the Big Dipper, Helen."

"Really, Tommy, I'm only trying to get my bearings. You've all the patience of a two-year-old. I can—"

Blessing. She reached them, crashed into them, fell to her knees.

"Nancy!" Someone took her arm, helped her back to her feet. Molly was howling. "What is it? What's wrong?"

It was Lynley's voice, Lynley's arm round her shoulders. He seemed like salvation.

"Mick!" she cried and pulled violently on the front of Lynley's jacket. Having said at last what needed to be said, she began to scream. "It's Mick! It's Mick!"

Lights went on in the cottages round them.

St. James and Lynley entered together, leaving the three women standing just inside the garden gate. Mick Cambrey's body was on the sitting room floor, not more than twenty feet from the front door. The two men went to it and stood staring down, frozen momentarily into inaction by horror.

"Good God," St. James murmured.

He had seen many grisly sights during his time on the scenes-of-crime team at New Scotland Yard, but the mutilation of Cambrey's body struck him forcefully, the sort of maiming that lay at the heart of every man's fear. Averting his eyes, he saw that someone had thoroughly searched the sitting room, for all the drawers had been pulled from the desk, correspondence and envelopes and stationery and countless other papers had been tossed round the room, broken picture frames had their backings torn off, and near a worn blue sofa, a tattered five-pound note lay on the floor.

It was an automatic reaction, born of his brief career with the police, fostered by his devotion to forensic science. Later, he would wonder why he even gave it sway, considering the disunity it provoked among them. "We're going to need Deborah," he said.

Lynley was squatting by the body. He jumped to his feet and intercepted St. James at the front door. "Are you out of your mind? You can't be thinking of asking her . . . That's madness. We need the police. You know that as well as I do."

St. James pulled open the door. "Deborah, would you—"

"Stay where you are, Deborah," Lynley interposed. He turned back to his friend. "I won't have it. I mean that, St. James."

"What is it, Tommy?" Deborah took a single step.

"Nothing."

St. James regarded the other man curiously, trying and failing to understand the nature of his admonition to Deborah. "It'll take only a moment, Tommy," he explained. "I think it's best. Who knows what the local CID are like. They may ask for your help anyway. So let's get some pictures in advance. Then you can phone." He called over his shoulder. "Will you bring your camera, Deborah?"

She began to come forward. "Of course. Here—"

"Deborah, stay there."

His explanation had seemed rational enough to St. James' own ears. But, rife with urgency, Lynley's response to it did not.

"But the camera?" Deborah asked.

"I said stay there!"

They were at an impasse. Deborah raised a querying hand, looked from Lynley to St. James.

"Tommy, is there something . . . ?"

Touching her arm lightly, Lady Helen stopped her and came to join the two men. "What's happened?" she asked.

St. James replied. "Helen, get me Deborah's camera. Mick Cambrey's been murdered and I want to photograph the room before we telephone the police."

He said nothing more until he held the camera in his hands. Even then, he looked it over thoroughly, studying its mechanism in a silence that he knew was growing more tense and unpleasant with every moment he allowed it to continue. He told himself that Lynley's main concern was that Deborah not be allowed to see the body or do the photographing herself. Indeed, he was sure that had been his friend's original intention when he insisted that she stay outside. He had misunderstood St. James' asking for Deborah. He had thought St. James wanted her to take the pictures herself. But that misunderstanding had dissolved into dispute. And no matter that much of the dispute remained unspoken, the fact that it had occurred at all charged the atmosphere with elements bleak and nasty.

"Perhaps you might wait out here until I'm done," St. James said to his friend. He walked back into the house.

St. James took the photographs from every angle, working his way carefully round the body, stopping only when he had run out of film. Then he left the sitting room, pulled the door partially closed behind him, and returned to the others outside. They had been joined by a small crowd of neighbours who stood in a hushed group a short distance from the garden gate, heads bent together, voices murmuring in speculation.

"Bring Nancy inside," St. James said.

Lady Helen led her across the front garden and into the cottage where she hesitated only a moment before directing Nancy towards the kitchen, an oblong room with an odd, sloping ceiling and a grey lino-leum floor sporting great black patches of wear. She sat her down on a chair that stood at one side of a stained pine table. Kneeling by her side, she looked closely at her face, reached for her arm and held her thin wrist between her own fingers. She frowned, touching the back of her hand to Nancy's cheek.

"Tommy," Lady Helen said with a remarkable degree of calm, "ring Dr. Trenarrow. I think she's going into shock. He can deal with that, can't he?" She prised the baby from Nancy's grasp and handed her to Deborah. "There must be baby milk in the refrigerator. Will you see to warming some?"

"Molly . . ." Nancy whispered. "Hungry. I . . . feed."

"Yes," Lady Helen said gently. "We're seeing to her, dear."

In the other room, Lynley was speaking into the telephone. He placed a second call and spoke even more briefly, but the altered formal sound of his voice was enough to tell the others that he was speaking to the Penzance police. After a few minutes, he returned to the kitchen with a blanket which he wrapped round Nancy in spite of the heat.

"Can you hear me?" he asked her.

Nancy's eyelids fluttered, showing nothing but white. "Molly . . . feed."

"I've got her right here," Deborah said. She was crooning to the baby in a far corner of the kitchen. "The milk's warming. I expect she likes it warm, doesn't she? She's a pretty baby, Nancy. I can't imagine a prettier one."

It was the right thing to say. Nancy relaxed in her chair. St. James nodded gratefully to Deborah and went back to the sitting room door. He pushed it open and stood on the threshold. He spent several minutes studying, thinking, evaluating what he saw. Lady Helen finally joined him. Even from the doorway, they could see the nature of the material that lay in disorder across the floor, upon the desk, against the legs of furniture. Notebooks, documents, pages of manuscripts, photographs. At the back of his mind, St. James heard Lady Asherton's words about Mick Cambrey. But the nature of the crime did not support the conclusion he otherwise might have naturally drawn from a consideration of those words.

"What do you think?" Lady Helen asked him.

"He was a journalist. He's dead. Somehow those two facts ought to hang together. But the body says no a thousand times."

"Why?"

"He's been castrated, Helen."

"Heavens. Is that how he died?"

"No."

"Then how?"

A knock at the door precluded reply. Lynley came from the kitchen to admit Roderick Trenarrow. The doctor entered wordlessly. He looked from Lynley to St. James and Lady Helen, and then beyond them to the sitting room floor where, even from where he stood, Mick Cambrey's body was partially visible. For a moment, it appeared that he might step forward and attempt to save a man who was beyond all rescue.

He said to the others, "Are you certain?"

"Quite," St. James replied.

"Where's Nancy?" Without waiting for an answer, he went on to the kitchen where the lights shone brightly and Deborah chatted about babies as if in the hope that doing so would keep Nancy anchored in the here and now. Trenarrow tilted Nancy's head and looked at her eyes. He said, "Help me get her upstairs. Quickly. Has anyone telephoned her father?"

Lynley moved to do so. Lady Helen helped Nancy to her feet and urged her out of the kitchen as Dr. Trenarrow led the way. Still carrying the baby, Deborah followed them. In a moment, Trenarrow's voice began asking gentle questions in the bedroom upstairs. These were followed by Nancy's querulous replies. Bed springs creaked. A window was opened. The dry wood of the sash grated and shrieked.

"There's no answer at the lodge," Lynley said from the telephone. "I'll ring on to Howenstow. Perhaps he's gone there." But after a conversation with Lady Asherton, John Penellin was still unaccounted for. Lynley frowned at his watch. "It's half past twelve. Where can he possibly be at this time of night?"

"He wasn't at the play, was he?"

"John? No. I can't say the Nanrunnel Players hold any charms for him."

Above them, Nancy cried out. As if in response to this single demonstration of anguish, another knock thudded against the front door. Lynley opened it to admit the local police, represented in the person of a plump, curly-haired constable in a uniform that took its distinction from large crescents of sweat beneath the arms and a coffee stain on the trousers. He looked about twenty-three years old. He didn't bother with any immediate introductions nor with any of the formalities inherent to a murder investigation. It was obvious within seconds that, in the presence of a corpse, he was in over his head and delighted to be there.

"Gotcherself a murder?" he asked conversationally, as if murders were a daily affair in Nanrunnel. Perhaps to give credence to nonchalance, he unwrapped a piece of chewing gum and folded it into his mouth. "Where's the victim?"

"Who are you?" Lynley demanded. "You aren't CID."

The constable grinned. "T.J. Parker," he announced. "Thomas Jefferson. Mum liked the Yanks." He elbowed his way into the sitting room.

"*Are* you CID?" Lynley asked as the constable kicked a notebook to one side. "Christ almighty, man. Leave the scene alone."

"Don't getcher knickers in a twist," the constable replied. "Inspector Boscowan sent me ahead to secure the scene. He'll be along soon 's he's dressed. Not to worry. Now. What d'we have?" He took his first look at the corpse and chewed more rapidly upon his gum. "Someone had it in for this bloke, all right."

That said, he began to saunter round the room. Gloveless, he fingered several items on Cambrey's desk.

"For God's sake," Lynley said hotly. "Don't touch anything. Leave it for your crime team."

"Robbery," Parker announced as if Lynley had not spoken. "Caught in the act, I'd say. A fight. Some fun afterwards with the secateurs."

"Listen, damn you. You can't—"

Parker cocked a finger at him. "This is police work, mister. I'll thank you to step back into the hall."

"Have you your warrant card?" St. James asked Lynley quietly. "He's liable to make a mess of that room if you don't do something to stop him."

"I can't, St. James. I have no jurisdiction."

As they were speaking, Dr. Trenarrow came back down the stairs. Inside the sitting room, Parker turned to the door, caught a glimpse of Trenarrow's medical bag, and smiled.

"We got quite a mess here, Doc," he announced. "Ever seen anything like it? Have a look, if you like."

"Constable." Lynley's voice attempted reason and patience.

Trenarrow seemed to realise how inappropriate the constable's suggestion was. He said softly to Lynley, "Perhaps I can do something to fend off disaster," and walked to the body. Kneeling, he examined it quickly, feeling for pulse, gauging for temperature, moving an arm to check the extent of rigor. He changed his position to the other side and bent to study the extensive wounds.

"Butchered," he muttered, looked up, and asked, "Have you found any weapon?" He looked round the room, feeling among the papers and debris that were nearest to the body.

St. James shuddered at the disruption of the crime scene. Lynley cursed. The constable did nothing.

Trenarrow nodded towards a poker that lay on its side by the fire-place. "Could that be your weapon?" he asked.

Constable Parker grinned. His chewing gum popped. He chuckled as Trenarrow got to his feet. "To do that business?" he asked. "I don't think it's near sharp enough, do you?"

Trenarrow didn't look amused. "I meant as a murder weapon," he said. "Cambrey didn't die from the castration, Constable. Any fool can see that."

Parker seemed unoffended by Trenarrow's implied rebuke. "Didn't kill him. Right. Just put an end to things, wouldn't you say?"

Trenarrow looked as if he were biting off an angry retort.

"How long's he been gone in your opinion?" the constable asked genially.

"Two or three hours, I'd guess. But surely you've someone coming to tell you that."

"Oh, aye. When she gets here," the constable said. "With the rest of CID." He rocked back on his heels, popped his gum once more, and studied his watch. "Two or three hours, you say? That takes us to . . . half nine or half ten. Well"—he sighed and rubbed his hands together with obvious pleasure—"it's a starting place, i'n' it? And you've got to start somewhere in police work."

Part IV

INVESTIGATION

10

From the moment they pulled up in front of the Howenstow lodge at a quarter past two in the morning, events began to tumble one upon the other. Not that events had not already been accumulating into an aggregate of experience too complicated to be readily assimilated. Inspector Edward Boscowan had seen to that, only moments after his arrival at Gull Cottage with the scenes-of-crime team from Penzance CID.

He'd taken one look at Constable Parker, who was lounging in an armchair not four feet from Mick Cambrey's body; he'd taken a second look at St. James, Trenarrow, and Lynley in the small entry foyer, at Deborah in the kitchen, at Lady Helen and Nancy Cambrey upstairs, at the baby in the cot. His face went from white to crimson. Then he finally spoke, but only to the constable. With such studied control that no other demonstration of his fury was even necessary.

"A tea party, Constable? Despite what you may think, you are not the Mad Hatter. Or has no one yet informed you of that?" The constable grinned uneasily in response. He shoved himself to his feet and scratched one armpit, nodding as if in agreement. "This is a murder scene," Boscowan snapped. "What in hell's name are all these people doing here?"

"They 'as inside when I got here," Parker said.

"Were they?" Boscowan asked with a thin smile. When Parker returned it, momentarily relieved by what he mistakenly perceived as bonhomie in his superior, Boscowan snarled, "Well, get them out now! Which is bloody well what you should have done in the first place!"

Lynley was aware of that fact himself. He knew that St. James was aware of it as well. Yet in the confusion engendered by Nancy's hysteria, the chaos of the sitting room, and the sight of Cambrey's body, both of them had disregarded or forgotten or developed an uncharacteristic indifference to that most basic tenet of police work. They had not sealed the crime scene. While they had not touched anything, they had been in the room, Trenarrow had been in the room, not to mention Helen and Deborah and Nancy in the kitchen and then upstairs. With all of them leaving fibres and hairs and fingerprints everywhere. What a nightmare for the forensic team. And he himself—a policeman—had been responsible for creating it, or at least for doing nothing productive to stop it. His behaviour had been unforgivably incompetent, and he could not excuse it by telling himself that he hadn't been thinking straight due to his being acquainted with the principals involved in the crime itself. For he'd known the principals involved in crimes before and had always kept his head. But not this time. He'd lost his grip the moment St. James involved Deborah.

Boscowan had said nothing more in condemnation of anyone. He had merely taken their fingerprints and sent them to stand in the kitchen while he and a sergeant went upstairs to talk to Nancy and the crime scene team began their work in the sitting room. He spent nearly an hour with Nancy, patiently taking her back and forth over the facts. Having gleaned from her what little he could, he sent her home with Lynley, home to her father.

Now, Lynley looked up at the lodge. The front door was closed. The windows were shut, the curtains drawn. Darkness enfolded it, and the trellised red roses that walled in the porch and encircled the windows on the ground floor looked like feather-edged smudges of ink in the shadows.

"I'll come in with you," Lynley said, "just in case your father's not yet home."

Nancy stirred in the rear seat where, between Lady Helen and St. James, she held her sleeping baby. Dr. Trenarrow had given her a mild sedative, and for the time being the drug shielded her from shock.

"Dad's only sleeping," she murmured, resting her cheek on Molly's head. "I spoke with him on the phone after the interval. At the play. He's gone to bed."

"He wasn't home when I phoned at half past twelve," Lynley said. "So he may not be home now. If he isn't, I'd rather you and Molly came on to the house with us and not stay here alone. We can leave him a note."

"He's only sleeping. The phone's in the sitting room. His bedroom's upstairs. He mightn't have heard it."

"Wouldn't Mark have heard it then?"

"Mark?" Nancy hesitated. Obviously, she hadn't yet considered her brother. "No. Mark sleeps heavy, doesn't he? Plays his music sometimes as well. He'd not have heard. But they're both upstairs asleep. For certain." She moved on the seat, preparatory to getting out. St. James opened the door. "I'll just go on in. I do thank you. I can't think what would've happened if I hadn't found you on Paul Lane."

Her words were growing progressively drowsier. Lynley got out, and with St. James he helped her from the car. Despite Nancy's declaration that both father and brother were sleeping soundly in the lodge, Lynley had no intention of leaving her without making sure that this was the case.

Beneath her words he had heard the unmistakable note of urgency which generally accompanies a lie. It was not inconceivable that she had spoken to her father by telephone during the evening. But he had not been home when Lynley had phoned from Gull Cottage just ninety minutes ago, and Nancy's protestations that he—as well as her brother— would sleep through the noise of the telephone were not only improbable but also indicative of a need to conceal.

Taking Nancy's arm, he led her up the uneven flagstone path and onto the porch where the climbing roses cast a sweet fragrance on the warm night air. Once inside the house, a quick look in the rooms affirmed his suspicions. The lodge was empty. As Nancy drifted into the sitting room and sat in a cane-backed rocking chair where she sang tonelessly to her daughter, he went back to the front door.

"No one's here," he said to the others. "But I think I'd rather wait for John than take Nancy up to the house. Do you want to go on yourselves?"

St. James made the decision for them all. "We'll come in."

They joined Nancy in the sitting room, taking places among and upon the overstuffed furniture. No one spoke. Instead they each attended to the Penellin personal effects which crammed the walls, the table tops, and the floor, attesting to the lives and personalities of the family who had occupied the lodge for twenty-five years. Spanish porcelains—the passion of Nancy's mother—collected dust upon a spinet piano. Mounted butterflies in a dozen frames hung on one wall and these, along with a quantity of aging tennis trophies, spoke of the wide swings which Mark Penellin's interests took. A broad bay window displayed a mass of Nan-

cy's poorly executed petit point pillows, faded and looking in their ser-
ried line as if they'd been placed there to get them out of the way. In
one corner, a television set held the room's only photograph, one taken
of Nancy, Mark, and their mother at Christmastime shortly before the
railway disaster that ended Mrs. Penellin's life.

After a few minutes of listening to the sounds of crickets and a
nightingale drifting in the window which Lynley had opened, Nancy
Cambrey stood. She said, "Molly's dropped off. I'll just pop her upstairs," and left them.

When they heard her movement on the floor above, it was Lady
Helen who put into words what had been playing in the back of Lynley's
mind. She spoke in her usual, forthright manner.

"Tommy, where do you suppose John Penellin is? Do you think
Nancy really spoke to him during the play? Because it seems to me that
there's something decidedly odd in the way she insisted that she'd talked
to him."

Lynley was sitting on the piano bench, and he pushed softly against
three of the keys, producing a barely audible discordance. "I don't know,"
he replied. But even if he could ignore Helen's intuitive remark, he
could not forget his conversation with Nancy that afternoon or the aversion with which her father had spoken of Nancy's husband.

The clock struck the half hour. Nancy returned to them. "I can't
think where Dad is," she said. "You've no need to stay. I'll be fine
now."

"We'll stay," Lynley said.

She pushed her hair behind her ears and rubbed her hands down the
sides of her dress. "He must've just gone out a bit ago. He does that
sometimes when he can't sleep. He walks on the grounds. Often he does
that before he goes to bed at night. On the grounds. I'm sure that's
where he's gone."

No one mentioned the wild improbability of John Penellin's taking
a walk on the grounds at half past two in the morning. No one even had
to, for events conspired to prove Nancy a liar. Even as she made her
final declaration, a car's lights swept across the sitting room windows.
An engine coughed once. A door opened and shut. Footsteps rang against
the flagstones and, a moment later, on the porch. She hurried to the
door.

Penellin's voice came to the others clearly. It sounded sharp. "Nancy?
What're you doing here? It's not Mark, is it? Nancy, where's Mark?"

She reached out a hand to him as he came in the door. He took it.
"Dad." Nancy's voice wavered.

At this, Penellin suddenly saw the others gathered in the sitting room. Alarm shot across his face. "What's happened?" he demanded. "By God, you tell me what that bastard's done to you now."

"He's dead," Nancy said. "Someone . . ." She faltered at the rest of it, as if those few words reminded her of the horror that the sedative had allowed her to escape for a short time.

Penellin stared. He brushed past his daughter and took a step towards the stairway. "Nancy, where's your brother?"

Nancy said nothing. In the sitting room, Lynley slowly got to his feet.

Penellin spoke again. "Tell me what happened."

"Nancy found Mick's body in the cottage after the play," Lynley said. "The sitting room looked as if it had been searched. Mick may well have surprised someone in the act of going through his papers. Or in the act of robbery. Although," he added, "that latter seems unlikely."

Nancy grasped this idea. "It *was* robbery," she said. "That's what it was and no mistake. Mick was doing the pay envelopes for the newspaper staff when I left him this evening." She tossed a look back over her shoulder at Lynley. "Was the money still there?"

"I saw only a five-pound note on the floor," St. James answered.

"But surely Mick didn't pay the staff in cash," Lynley said.

"He did," Nancy said. "It was always done that way on the newspaper. More convenient. There's no bank in Nanrunnel."

"But if it was robbery—"

"It *was*," Nancy said.

Lady Helen spoke gently, bringing up the single point that obviated robbery as a motive. "But Nancy, his body . . ."

"The body?" Penellin asked.

"He'd been castrated," Lynley said.

"Good God."

The front doorbell rang shrilly. All of them jumped, a testimony to the state of their nerves. Still in the hallway, Penellin answered the door. Inspector Boscowan stood on the porch. Beyond him, a dusty car was parked behind the estate Rover that Lynley had earlier driven to and from Nanrunnel.

"John," Boscowan said by way of greeting Penellin.

The use of Penellin's given name reminded Lynley all at once that not only were Boscowan and Penellin of an age, but like so many others who lived in this remote area of Cornwall, they were also former schoolmates and lifelong friends.

Penellin said, "Edward, you've heard about Mick?"

"I've come to talk to you about it."

Nancy gripped the newel post of the stairway. "To Dad? Why? He knows nothing about this."

"I've a few questions, John," Boscowan said.

"I don't understand." But Penellin's tone was an admission that he understood only too well.

"May I come in?"

Penellin glanced into the sitting room, and Boscowan followed his gaze to see the others gathered there.

"Still here, my lord?" he asked.

"Yes. We were . . ." Lynley hesitated. *Waiting for John to come home* asked to be spoken, an inadvertent accusation he would not make.

"Dad knows nothing," Nancy repeated. "Dad, tell him you know nothing about Mick."

"May I come in?" Boscowan asked once more.

"Nancy and the baby," Penellin said. "They're both here. May we talk in Penzance? At the station house?"

Requesting a different location wasn't a suspect's right. And that John Penellin was a suspect was illustrated in Boscowan's next words.

"Have you a solicitor you'd like to ring?"

"A solicitor?" Nancy shrilled.

"Nance. Girl. Don't."

Although Penellin reached for his daughter, she flinched away. "Dad was *here*."

Boscowan shifted his weight uneasily from one foot to the other. "I'm sorry, Nancy. Neighbours saw him at your cottage at half past nine. Others heard an argument as well."

"He was here. I spoke to him after the interval. Dad, tell him I spoke to you after the interval." She grabbed her father's arm, shaking it doggedly.

Her father loosened her fingers. "Let me go, lass. Stay here. Take care of Molly. Nancy, wait for Mark."

Boscowan didn't miss the exigent quality of Penellin's final direction to his daughter. "Mark's not here?"

Penellin replied, "I expect he's out with friends. In St. Ives or St. Just. You know how young men are." He patted Nancy's hand. "I'm ready then, Edward. Let's be off."

He nodded to the others and left the lodge. A moment later, Boscowan's car purred to life. The sound amplified briefly as he reversed down the main drive, then faded altogether as they headed towards Penzance.

Nancy spun towards the sitting room. "Help him!" she cried to Lynley. "He didn't kill Mick. You're a policeman. You can help. You must." Uselessly she twisted the front of her housedress in her hands.

Even as he went to her side, Lynley reflected upon how little he could actually do to help. He had no jurisdiction in Cornwall. Boscowan seemed a highly capable man, one unlikely ever to need assistance from New Scotland Yard. Had Constable Parker been in charge of the case, the Met's ultimate involvement would not have been long in doubt. But Parker wasn't in charge. And since Penzance CID looked perfectly competent, the investigation had to remain in their hands. However, he still wanted to say something, even if the only possible result was that form of purgation which comes from reliving the worst part of a nightmare.

"Tell me what happened tonight." He led her back to the rocking chair. Deborah rose from her place and covered Nancy's shoulders with a blanket that lay on the back of the couch.

Nancy stumbled through the story. She'd gone to do the drinks for the play, leaving the baby with Mick. Mick had been working at the sitting room desk, getting ready to do the pay envelopes for the newspaper staff. She'd placed Molly in a playpen nearby. She'd left them at seven o'clock.

"When I got back to the cottage, I could hear Molly crying. I was angry that Mick would let her go ignored. I shouted at him as I opened the door."

"The door was unlocked?" St. James asked.

It was, she told them.

"You didn't notice Mick's body?"

She shook her head and clutched the blanket closer round her thin shoulders. One elbow stuck out. It was bony and red. "The sitting room door was closed."

"And when you opened it, what did you notice at first?"

"Him. Mick. Lying . . ." She gulped for a breath. "Then all round him, the papers and notebooks and such."

"As if the room had been searched," St. James said. "Did Mick ever work on stories at home?"

Nancy rubbed her hand along the nap of the blanket and nodded a bit too eagerly. "Often, yes. At the computer. He wouldn't want to go back to the office after dinner, so he'd work a bit at home. He kept lots of notes for his stories at the cottage. Sort through this lot, Mickey, I'd tell him. We must throw some things away. But he didn't like to because he never knew when he'd need to look up some little detail in a notebook or a journal or his diary. Can't toss it out, Nance, he'd tell me. The first thing I throw away will be exactly what I need. So there were always papers. Scraps of this and that. Notes on paper napkins and on matchbook covers. It was his way. Lots of notes. Someone must have wanted . . . or the money. The money. We mustn't forget that.''

It was a difficult recital to listen to. Although the facts seemed relevant—the presence of material on the floor, the evidence of a hasty search—it did not appear that their connection to Mick Cambrey's profession was foremost on his wife's mind, no matter her attempt to make it seem so. Rather, she appeared to be concerned with an entirely different matter connected to the search.

She verified this by concluding with, "You know, I did talk to Dad after the interval. Perhaps at half past ten. From a call box.''

No one replied. Despite the room's warmth, Nancy's legs shook, causing the blanket that covered them to tremble. "I telephoned. I spoke to Dad. He was here. Lots of people must've seen me make the call. Ask Mrs. Swann. She knows I spoke to Dad. He was here. He said he'd not been out all evening.''

"But Nancy,'' Lynley said, "your father was out. He wasn't here when I phoned. He only just walked in a few minutes after we did. Why are you lying? Are you afraid of something?''

"Ask Mrs. Swann. She saw me. In the call box. She can tell you—''

A blast of rock and roll music shattered the mild night noises outside the house. Nancy leaped to her feet.

The front door opened and Mark Penellin entered. A large portable stereo rode upon his shoulder, blaring out "My Generation,'' nighttime nostalgia with a vengeance. Mark was singing along, but he stopped in midphrase when he saw the group in the sitting room. He fumbled incompetently with the knobs. Roger Daltrey roared even louder for an instant before Mark mastered the volume and switched the stereo off.

"Sorry.'' He placed the unit on the floor. It had left an indentation in the soft calfskin jacket he wore, and as if he knew this without looking, he brushed his fingers against the material to rejuvenate it. "What's going on? What're you doing here, Nance? Where's Dad?''

In conjunction with everything that had gone before, both her brother's sudden appearance at the lodge and his questions seemed to destroy the inadequate defences which Nancy had raised to avoid the reality of her father's behaviour that night. She fell back into the rocking chair.

"It's your fault!" she cried. "The police have come for Dad. They've taken him and he'll say nothing because of *you*." She began to cry, reaching for her handbag which lay on the floor. "What're you going to do to him next, Mark? What'll it be? Tell me." She opened her handbag and began fumbling through it, pulling out a crumpled tissue as she sobbed, "Mickey. Oh, Mick."

Still at the doorway to the sitting room, Mark Penellin swallowed, looking at each of them in turn before returning his gaze to his sister. "Has something happened to Mick?"

Nancy continued to weep.

Mark brushed back his hair. He ran his knuckles down his jawline. He brought their worst fears to light. "Nancy, has Dad done something to Mick?"

She was out of the chair, her handbag flying, its contents spraying across the floor.

"Don't you say that! Don't you dare. You're at the bottom of this. We know it. Dad and I."

Mark backed into the stairway. His head struck a banister. "*Me?* What're you talking about? This is crazy. You're crazy. What the hell's happened?"

"Mick's been murdered," Lynley said.

Blood flooded Mark's face. He spun from Lynley to his sister. "And you think I did it? Is that what you think? That I killed your husband?" He gave a wild shriek of laughter. "Why would I bother, with Dad looking for a way to put him under for a year?"

"Don't you say that! Don't you dare! It was you!"

"Right. Believe what you want."

"What I *know*. What Dad knows."

"Dad knows everything all right. Lucky for him to be so bloody wise."

He grabbed his stereo and flung himself up five stairs. Lynley's words stopped him.

"Mark, we need to talk."

"No!" And then as he finished the climb, "I'll save what I have to say for the flaming police. As soon as my sister turns me in."

A door crashed shut.

Molly began to wail.

11

"How much do you really know about Mark Penellin?" St. James asked, looking up from the paper on which he had been jotting their collective thoughts for the last quarter of an hour.

He and Lynley were alone in the small alcove that opened off the Howenstow drawing room, directly over the front entry to the house. Two lamps were lit, one on the undersized mahogany desk where St. James sat and the other on a marquetry side table beneath the windows where it cast a golden glow against the darkness-backed panes. Lynley handed St. James a glass of brandy and cupped his own in the palm of his hand, meditatively swirling the liquid. He sank into a wing chair next to the desk, stretched out his legs, and loosened his tie. He drank before answering.

"Not much in any detail. He's Peter's age. From what little's been said about him in the past few years, I gather he's been a disappointment to his family. To his father mostly."

"In what way?"

"The usual way young men disappoint their fathers. John wanted Mark to go to university. Mark did one term at Reading but then dropped out."

"Rusticated?"

"Not interested. He went from Reading to a job as a barman in Maidenhead. Then Exeter, as I recall. I think he was playing drums with a band. That didn't pan out as he would have liked—no fame, no fortune, and most particularly no lucrative contract with a recording studio—and he's been working here on the estate ever since, at least for the last eighteen months. I'm not quite sure why. Estate management never seemed to interest Mark in the past. But perhaps now he's thinking along the lines of taking over as Howenstow land manager when his father retires.''

"Is that a possibility?''

"It's possible, but not without Mark's developing some background and a great deal more expertise than would come from the sort of work he's been doing round here.''

"Does Penellin expect his son to succeed him?''

"I shouldn't think so. John's university-educated himself. When he retires—which is a good time away in the future—he wouldn't expect me to give his job to someone whose sole experience at Howenstow has been mucking out the stables.''

"And that's been the extent of Mark's experience?''

"Oh, he's done some time in one or two of the dairies. Out on several of the farms as well. But there's more to managing an estate than that.''

"Is he paid well?''

Lynley twirled the stem of his brandy glass between his fingers. "No, not particularly. But that's John's decision. I've got the impression from him in the past that Mark doesn't work well enough to be paid well. In fact, the whole issue of Mark's salary has been a sore spot between them ever since Mark returned from Exeter.''

"If he keeps him short of cash, wouldn't the money in Gull Cottage be a lure for him? Could he have known his brother-in-law's habits well enough to know that tonight he'd be doing the pay for the newspaper staff? After all, it looks as if he's living a bit above his means, if his salary here is as low as you indicate.''

"Above his means? How?''

"That stereo he was carrying must have set him back a few quid. The jacket looked fairly new as well. I couldn't see his boots clearly, but they looked like snakeskin.''

Lynley crossed the alcove to one of the windows and opened it. The early morning air felt damp and cool at last, and the stillness of night amplified the distant sound of the sea.

"I can't think that Mark would kill his brother-in-law in order to steal that money, St. James, although it's not hard to picture him coming upon Mick's body, seeing the money on the desk, helping himself to it. Murder doesn't sound like Mark. Opportunism does.''

St. James looked at his notes for a moment and read his summary of their conversation with Nancy Cambrey at the lodge. "So he'd go to the cottage for another reason, only to discover Mick dead? And finding him dead, he'd help himself to the cash?''

"Perhaps. I don't think Mark would plan out a robbery. Surely he knows what that would do to his sister, and despite how they acted tonight, Mark and Nancy have always been close.''

"Yet he probably knew about the pay envelopes, Tommy.''

"Everyone else probably knew as well. Not only the employees of the newspaper, but also the villagers. Nanrunnel's not large. I doubt it's changed much since I was a boy. And then, believe me, there were few enough secrets that the entire population didn't know.''

"If that's the case, would others have known about the notes Mick kept in the cottage?''

"I imagine the employees of the newspaper knew. Mick's father, no doubt, and if he knew, why not everyone else? The *Spokesman* doesn't employ that many people, after all.''

"Who are they?''

Lynley returned to his chair. "Aside from Mick, I didn't know any of them, except Julianna Vendale. If she's still employed there. She was the copy and wire service editor.''

Something in his voice made St. James look up. "Julianna Vendale?''

"Right. A nice woman. Divorced. Two children. About thirty-seven.''

"Attractive to Mick?''

"Probably. But I doubt that Mick would have interested Julianna. She's not thought much of men since her husband left her for another woman some ten years ago. No one's got very far with her since.'' He looked at St. James, gave a rueful smile. "I learned that the hard way one holiday here when I was twenty-six and feeling particularly full of myself. Needless to say, Julianna wasn't impressed.''

"Ah. And Mick's father?''

Lynley took up his brandy once again. "Harry's a bit of local colour. Hard drinker, hard smoker, hard gambler. A mouth like a docker. According to Nancy, he had heart surgery last year, however, so perhaps he's had to change his style.''

"Close to Mick?''

"At one time, yes. I couldn't say now. Mick started out working on the *Spokesman* before he went off as a free-lance writer.''

"Did you know Mick, Tommy?''

"Nearly all my life. We were of an age. I spent a great deal of time in Nanrunnel years ago. We saw each other on half-terms and holidays.''

''Friends?''

''More or less. We drank together, sailed together, did some fishing, scouted women in Penzance. As teenagers. I didn't see much of him once I went up to Oxford.''

''What was he like?''

Lynley smiled. ''A man who liked women, controversy, and practical jokes just about equally. At least, he did when he was young. I can't think he changed much.''

''Perhaps we've a motive somewhere in that.''

''Perhaps.'' Lynley explained the allusions to Mick's extramarital affairs which John Penellin had made that afternoon.

''A good explanation for the condition of the body,'' St. James said. ''A husband getting back upon the man who cuckolded him. But that doesn't explain the mess in the sitting room, does it?'' St. James picked up his pen to make a note, but he put it down again without writing. Fatigue was getting the better of him. He could feel it like dust beneath his eyelids and he knew quite well that he wouldn't be good for any useful thinking for very much longer. Still, a half-formed memory plagued him, something said earlier that he knew he ought to recall. He stirred restlessly in his seat, catching sight of the piano in the drawing room and remembering Lady Asherton standing near it earlier in the evening. ''Tommy, didn't your mother say something about a story Mick was working on? Hadn't Nancy told her about it?''

''She told me as well.''

''Then . . .''

''It's a possibility. I got the impression that Mick felt it was a significant piece. Certainly far more significant than the usual feature in the *Spokesman*. In fact, I don't think he intended it for the *Spokesman* at all.''

''Is that something that might have irritated his father?''

''Hardly enough to kill him. And certainly not enough to castrate him, St. James.''

''If,'' St. James pointed out, ''the killing and the castration were done by the same person. We both saw that the castration was done after death, Tommy.''

Lynley shook his head. ''That doesn't work for me. First a killer— later a butcher.''

St. James had to admit that it didn't work for him all that well either. "Why do you suppose Nancy's lying about that phone call?" St. James didn't wait for Lynley's response. He mused aloud. "It doesn't look good for John Penellin that he was seen near the cottage."

"John didn't kill Mick. He's not the type. He couldn't have killed him."

"Not intentionally."

"Not at all."

There was a fair degree of certainty behind Lynley's words. St. James met it by saying, "Good men have been driven to violence before. You know that. Unintentional violence—that sudden blow delivered in rage. How many more deaths is a moment of madness—rather than premeditation—responsible for? And John was there, Tommy. That has to mean something."

Lynley got to his feet. He stretched in an easy, lithe movement. "I'll talk to John in the morning. We'll sort it out."

St. James turned to him but did not rise. "What if the police decide they've found their man? What if the forensic evidence supports an arrest? Penellin's hair on the corpse, his fingerprints in the room, a drop of Mick's blood on the cuff of his trousers or the sleeve of his coat. If he was in the room tonight, there's going to be evidence to support it, far beyond the testimony of neighbours who saw him and other neighbours who heard a row. What will you do then? Does Boscowan know you're CID?"

"It's nothing I broadcast."

"Will he ask the Yard for assistance?"

Lynley answered with obvious reluctance, putting into words St. James' own thoughts. "Not if he thinks he's got his man in John Penellin. Why should he?" He sighed. "It's damned awkward, for all Nancy's request that I help her father. We'll have to be careful, St. James. We can't afford to step on official toes."

"And if we do?"

"There'll be the devil to pay in London." He nodded a good night and left the room.

St. James went back to his notes. From the desk he took out a second sheet of paper and spent several minutes creating columns and categories into which he put what little information they had. John Penellin. Harry Cambrey. Mark Penellin. Unknown Husbands. Newspaper Employees. Potential Motives for the Crime. The Weapon. The Time of Death. He wrote and listed and read and stared. The words began to swim before him. He pressed his fingers to his closed eyes. Somewhere a casement window creaked in the breeze. At the same moment the drawing room door opened and shut. His head jerked up at the sound. Deborah stood in the shadows.

She wore a dressing gown whose ivory colour and insubstantial material made her look like a spectre. Her hair hung loosely round her face and shoulders.

St. James shoved his chair back, pushed himself to his feet. His weight was off balance because of the awkward position of his leg, and he could feel the accompanying stress as it pulled at the muscles of his waist.

Deborah looked down the length of the drawing room and then into the alcove. "Tommy's not with you?"

"He's gone to bed."

She frowned. "I thought I'd heard—"

"He was here earlier."

"Oh," she said. "Right."

St. James waited for her to leave, but instead, she came into the alcove and joined him next to the desk. A lock of her hair caught against his sleeve, and he could smell the fragrance of lilies on her skin. He fixed his eyes on his notes and felt her do likewise. After a moment, she spoke.

"Are you going to get involved in this?"

He bent forward and jotted a few deliberately illegible words in the margin of the paper. A reference to notebooks on the cottage floor. The location of the call box. A question for Mrs. Swann. Anything. It didn't matter.

"I'll help if I can," he answered. "Although this sort of investigating isn't in my line at all, so I don't know how much good I'll do. I was just going through what Tommy and I were talking about. Nancy. Her family. The newspaper. That sort of thing."

"By writing it down. Yes. I remember your lists. You always had dozens of them, didn't you? Everywhere."

"All over the lab."

"Graphs and charts as well, I recall. I never had to feel contrite about the jumble of photographs I shed all over the house while you were in the lab, throwing darts at your own jumble in sheer frustration."

"It was a scalpel, actually," St. James said.

They laughed together, but it was only an instant of shared amusement from which silence grew, first on his part then on hers. In it the sound of a clock's ticking seemed inordinately loud, as did the distant breaking of the sea.

"I'd no idea Helen's been working with you in the lab," Deborah said. "Dad never mentioned it in any of his letters. Isn't that odd? Sidney told me this afternoon. She's so good at everything, isn't she? Even at the cottage. There I was, standing there like an idiot while Nancy fell apart and that poor baby screamed. With Helen all the time knowing just what to do."

"Yes," St. James replied. "She's very helpful."

Deborah said nothing else. He willed her to leave. He added more notations to the paper on the desk. He frowned at it, read it, pretended to study it. And then, when it could no longer be avoided, when to do so would openly declare him the craven he pretended not to be, he finally looked up.

It was the diffusion of light in the alcove that defeated him. In it, her eyes became darker and more luminescent. Her skin looked softer, her lips fuller. She was far too close to him, and he knew in an instant that his choices were plain: He could leave the room or take her into his arms. There was no middle ground. There never would be. And it was sheer delusion to believe a time might come when he would ever be safe from what he felt when he was with her. He gathered up his papers, murmured a conventional good night, and started to leave.

He was halfway across the drawing room when she spoke.

"Simon, I've seen that man."

He turned, perplexed. She went on.

"That man tonight. Mick Cambrey. I've seen him. That's what I'd come to tell Tommy."

He walked back to her, placed his papers on the desk. "Where?"

"I'm not entirely sure if he *is* the same man. There's a wedding picture of him and Nancy in their bedroom. I saw it when I took the baby up, and I'm almost certain he's the same man I saw coming out of the flat next to mine this morning—I suppose yesterday morning now—in London. I didn't want to say anything earlier because of Nancy." Deborah fingered her hair. "Well, I waited to say something because the flat next to mine belongs to a woman. Tina Cogin. And she seems to be . . . of course, I couldn't say for certain, but from the way she talks and dresses and makes allusions to her experiences with men. . . . The impression I got . . . ."

"She's a prostitute?"

Deborah told the story quickly: how Tina Cogin had overheard their row in London; how she had appeared with a drink for Deborah, one that she herself claimed to use after her sexual encounters with men. "But I didn't have a chance to talk to her much because Sidney arrived and Tina left."

"What about Cambrey?"

"It was the glass. I still had Tina's glass and I hadn't thought about returning it till this morning."

She'd seen Cambrey as she approached Tina's door, Deborah explained. He came out of the flat, and realising that she was actually in the presence of one of Tina's "clients," Deborah hesitated, unsure whether to give the glass over to the man and ask him to return it to Tina, whether to walk on by and pretend she didn't notice him, whether to return to her own flat without a word. He had made the decision for her by saying good morning.

"He wasn't embarrassed at all," Deborah said ingenuously.

St. James reflected upon the fact that men are rarely embarrassed about their part in a sexual liaison, but he didn't comment. "Did you talk to him?"

"I just asked him to give the glass to Tina and to tell her I was off to Cornwall. He asked should he fetch her, but I said no. I didn't actually want to see her with him. It did seem so awkward, Simon. I wondered would he put his arm round her or kiss her goodbye? Would they shake hands?" Deborah shot him a fleeting smile. "I don't handle that sort of thing well, do I? Anyway, he went back into the flat."

"Was the door unlocked?"

Deborah glanced away, her expression thoughtful. "No, he had a key."

"Had you seen him before? Or just that once?"

"Just then. And a moment later. He went into the flat and spoke to Tina." She flushed. "I heard him say something about red-headed competition in the hallway. So he must have thought . . . Well, he really couldn't have. He was probably only joking. But she must have led him to believe that I was on the game because when he came out he said that Tina wanted me to know she'd take care of my gentlemen callers while I was gone. And then he laughed. And he looked me over, Simon. At first I thought he'd taken Tina seriously, but he winked and grinned and it just seemed his way." Deborah appeared to go back through what she had said, for her face brightened as she drew a conclusion from the facts. "Then she's probably not a prostitute, is she? If Mick had a key to her flat . . . Prostitutes don't generally give out keys, do they? I mean, s'pose one man stops by while another . . ." She gestured futilely.

"It would create an awkward situation."

"So perhaps she isn't a prostitute. Could he be keeping her, Simon? Or even hiding her? Protecting her from someone?"

"Are you sure it was Mick you saw?"

"I think it was. If I got another look at a photograph, I could be certain. But I remember his hair because it was dark auburn, just exactly the shade I always wished mine might be. I remember thinking how unfair that such a colour should be wasted on a man who probably didn't treasure it nearly as much as I would have done."

St. James tapped his fingers against the desk. He thought aloud. "I'm sure we can manage to get a photograph of Mick. If not the one from the cottage, then surely another. His father would probably have one." He considered the next logical step. "Could you go to London and talk to Tina, Deborah? Good Lord, what am I thinking of? You can't dash off to London in the middle of your weekend here."

"Of course I can. There's a dinner planned here for tomorrow night, but we've nothing after that. Tommy can fly me back Sunday morning. Or I can take the train."

"You need only find out whether she recognises his picture. If she does, don't tell her he's dead. Tommy and I will see to that." St. James folded his papers, slipped them into his jacket pocket, and continued speaking pensively. "If Mick's linked to her sexually, she may be able to tell us something which clarifies his murder, something which Mick might have told her inadvertently. Men relax after intercourse. They feel more important. They let down their guard. They become more honest." He suddenly became aware of the nature of his words and stopped them, shifting in another direction without looking her way. "Helen can go with you. I'll do some questioning here. Tommy'll want to be part of that. Then we'll join you when . . . Damn! The photographs! I left the film from the cottage in your camera. If we can develop it, no doubt we'll . . . I'm afraid I used it all up."

She smiled. He knew why. He was starting to sound exactly like her.

"I'll get it for you, shall I? It's just in my room."

She left him. He walked to the alcove window and looked out over the night-shrouded garden. Shapes alone defined the bushes there. Pathways were muted streaks of grey.

St. James considered the disjointed pieces of Mick Cambrey's life and death that had emerged that night. He wondered how they fit together. Mick had been gone a great deal, Lady Asherton had said. He'd been working on a story in London. A big story. St. James thought about this and the possible connections a story might have to Tina Cogin.

One assumption was that she was Mick's lover, a woman being kept in London for his clandestine pleasure. Yet Deborah, nobody's fool when it came to judgement, had concluded from a first impression, a conversation, and a run-in with Mick that Tina was a prostitute. If this was the case, the resultant tie to a story was both logical and ineluctable. For Mick might be keeping the woman in London not for his pleasure but for her own protection as a source for a story that had the potential to make banner headlines and put Mick's name in the forefront of journalism. It certainly would not be the first time if a prostitute became involved in critically important news, nor would it be the first time if heads were to roll and careers were to fall because of a prostitute. And now with Mick dead and his sitting room ransacked—perhaps in the hope of finding Tina Cogin's address in London—no amalgamation of these details sounded outrageous.

"Simon!" Deborah flew back into the room. He swung round from the window to find her trembling, arms wrapped round herself tightly as if she were cold.

"What is it?"

"Sidney. Someone's with Sidney. I heard a man's voice. I heard her cry. I thought that Justin might be—"

St. James didn't wait for her to finish the sentence. He hurried from the room and rushed down the main corridor towards the northwest wing. With each step his anxiety grew, as did his anger. Every image from the afternoon manifested itself before him once again. Sidney in the water. Sidney on the sand. Brooke straddling her, punching her, tearing at her clothes. But there was no cliff to separate him from Justin Brooke now. He blessed that fact.

Only years of dealing with his sister caused St. James to pause at her door rather than throw himself into her room. Deborah came up next to him as he listened against the wood. He heard Sidney cry out, he heard Brooke's voice, he heard Sidney's moan. Damn and blast, he thought. He took Deborah's arm, guiding her away from the door and down the long corridor that led to her own room in the southern corner of the house.

"Simon!" she whispered.

He didn't reply until they were in her room with the door shut behind them. "It's nothing," he said. "Don't worry."

"But, I heard her."

"Deborah, she's all right. Believe me."

"But . . ." Sudden comprehension swept across Deborah's face. She turned away with a gulp. "I only thought," she said but gave up the effort and concluded with, "Why am I such a fool?"

He wanted to reply, to assuage her embarrassment, but he knew that any comment only held the promise of making things worse. Frustrated, angry at the changes in their lives that seemed to bind him to inaction, he looked aimlessly round her room as if it could formulate an answer for him. He took in the black oak panelling upon the walls, the formal Asherton armorial display in the plaster overmantel of the fireplace, the lofty barrel ceiling that soared into the darkness. An immense four-poster bed dominated the floor space, its headboard carved with grotesques that writhed their way through flowers and fruit. It was a horrible place to be alone. It felt just like a tomb.

"Sidney's always been a bit hard to understand," St. James settled upon saying. "Bear with her, Deborah. You couldn't have known what that was all about. It's all right. Really."

To his surprise, she turned to him hotly. "It isn't all right. It isn't and you know it. How can she make love with him after what he did to her today? I don't understand it. Is she mad? Is he?"

That was the question and the answer all at once. For it was a true madness, white, hot, and indecent, obliterating everything that stood in its way.

"She's in love with him, Deborah," he finally replied. "Aren't people all just a little bit mad when they love?"

Her response was a stare. He could see her swallow.

"The film. Let me get it," she said.

12

The Anchor and Rose benefitted from having the most propitious location in all of Nanrunnel. It not only displayed from its broad bay windows a fine, unobstructed view of the harbour guaranteed to please the most discerning seeker of Cornish atmosphere, but it also sat directly across from Nanrunnel's single bus stop and was, as a result, the first structure a thirsty visitor's eyes fell upon when disembarking from Penzance and regions beyond.

The interior of the pub was engaged in the gentle process of deterioration. Once creamy walls had taken their place on the evolutionary path towards grey, an effect produced by exposure to generations of smoke from fireplace, cigars, pipes, and cigarettes. An elaborate mahogany bar, pitted and stained, curved from the lounge into the public bar, with a brass footrail heavily distressed through years of use. Similarly worn tables and chairs spread across a well-trodden floor, and the ceiling above them was so convex that architectural disaster seemed imminent.

When St. James and Lady Helen entered, shortly after the pub's morning opening, they found themselves alone with a large tabby cat that lounged in the bay window and a woman who stood behind the bar, drying innumerable pint and half-pint glasses. She nodded at them and went on with her work, her eyes following Lady Helen to the window where she stooped to pet the cat.

"Careful with 'um," the woman said. "Watch he doesn't scratch. He's a mean 'un when he wants to be."

As if with the intention of proving her a liar, the cat yawned, stretched, and presented a corpulent stomach for Lady Helen to attend to. Watching, the woman snorted and stacked glasses on a tray.

St. James joined her at the bar, reflecting upon the fact that if this was Mrs. Swann, she was trapped somewhere in the cygnet stage, for there was nothing the least bit swanlike about her. She was stout and solid, with minuscule eyes and a frizz of grey hair, a living contradiction to her name dressed in a dirndl skirt and a peasant blouse.

"What c'n I get you?" she asked and went on with her drying.

"It's a bit early for me," St. James replied. "We've come to talk to you, actually. If you're Mrs. Swann."

"Who wants to know?"

St. James introduced himself and Lady Helen, who had taken a seat next to the cat. "I'm sure you've heard Mick Cambrey's been murdered."

"Whole village knows. About that and the chop-up as well." She smiled. "Looks like Mick got what was coming at last. Separated proper from his favourite toy, wasn't he? No doubt there'll be a regular piss-up here when the local husbands come round to celebrate tonight."

"Mick was involved with some local women?"

Mrs. Swann drove her towel-covered fist into a glass and polished it vigorously. "Mick Cambrey's involved in anyone willing to give him a poke." That said, she turned to the empty shelves behind her and began placing glasses upside down on the mats. The implicit message was unavoidable: She had nothing more to tell them.

Lady Helen spoke. "Actually, Mrs. Swann, Nancy Cambrey's our concern. We've come to see you mostly because of her."

Mrs. Swann's shoulders lost some of their stiffness, although she didn't turn around when she said, "Dim girl, Nance. Married to that sod." Her tight little curls shook with disgust.

"Indeed," Lady Helen went on smoothly. "And she's in the worst sort of situation at the moment, isn't she? Not only to have her husband murdered but then to have her father questioned by the police."

That re-engaged Mrs. Swann's interest quickly enough. She faced them, fists on hips. Her mouth opened and shut. Then opened again. "John Penellin?"

"Quite. Nancy tried to tell the police that she talked to her father on the phone last night so he couldn't have been in Nanrunnel killing Mick. But they—"

"And she did," Mrs. Swann asserted. "That she did. She did. Borrowed ten pence from me to make the call. Not a coin in her bag, thanks to Mick." She began to wax warmly to this secondary topic. "Always took her money, he did. Hers and his father's and anyone else's he could get his hands on. He was always after cash. He wanted to be a swell.''

"Are you sure Nancy spoke to her father?'' St. James asked. "Not to someone else?''

Mrs. Swann took umbrage at St. James' doubt. She pointed her finger for emphasis. "Course it was her father. Didn't I get so tired of waiting for her—she must have been a good ten or fifteen minutes—that I went to the call box and yanked her out?''

"Where is this call box?''

"Outside the school yard. Right on Paul Lane.''

"Did you see her place the call? Could you see the call box itself?''

Mrs. Swann put the questions together and reached a quick conclusion. "You can't be thinking *Nancy* killed Mick? That she slipped off to her cottage, chopped him up, then came back nice as nice to serve up the lager?''

"Mrs. Swann, can you see the call box from the school grounds?''

"No. What of it? I yanked the lass out myself. She was crying. Said her dad was dead angry that she'd borrowed some money and she was trying to set it to rights with him.'' Mrs. Swann pressed her lips together as if she had said all that she would. But then a bubble of anger seemed to grow and burst within her, for she went on, her voice growing fierce. "And I don't blame Nancy's dad for that, do I? Everyone knew where any money would go that Nance gave to Mick. He'd pass it right on to his ladies, wouldn't he? So full of himself, little worm. Got too big in his head when he went to university. Bigger still with his fancy writing. Started thinking he could live by his own rules, didn't he? Right there in the newspaper office. He got what he deserved.''

"In the newspaper office?'' St. James queried. "He met with women in the newspaper office?''

She flipped her head in a vicious nod towards the ceiling. "Right above stairs, it is. Has a nice little room in the back of it. With a cot and everything. Perfect little love nest. And he flaunted his doings. Proud of them all. He even kept trophies.''

"Trophies?''

Mrs. Swann leaned forward, resting her enormous breasts on the bar. She gusted hot breath in St. James' face. "What d'you say to ladies' panties, my lad? Two different pairs right there in his desk. Harry found them. His *dad*. Not six months out of hospital, poor man, and he comes on those. Sitting there real as real in Mick's top drawer and they weren't even clean. Oh, the screaming and shouting that went on then.''

"Nancy found out?"

"Harry was screaming, not Nance. You've a babe on the way, he says. And the paper! Our family! Is it all for nothing so you can please your own fancy? And he hits Mick so hard I thought he was dead from the sound he made when he hit the floor. Sliced his head on the edge of a cabinet as well. But in a minute or two, he comes storming down the stairs with his father just raving behind him."

"When was this?" St. James asked.

Mrs. Swann shrugged. Her outrage seemed spent. "Harry can tell you. He's right above stairs."

John Penellin rolled up the Ordnance Survey map, put an elastic band round it, and placed it with half a dozen others in the old umbrella stand in his office. The late morning sunlight streamed in the windows, heating the room to an uncomfortable degree, and he opened the casement and adjusted the blinds as he spoke.

"So it's been a fairly good year, all way round. And if we let that north acreage lie fallow for another season, the land can only benefit from it. That's my suggestion, at any rate." He resumed his seat behind the desk, and as if he had an inflexible agenda to which he was determined to adhere, he went on immediately with: "May we speak of Wheal Maen?"

It had not been Lynley's intention to go through the account books or to engage in a detailed discussion of Penellin's management of the estate, something he had been doing with great facility and against growing for a quarter of a century. Nonetheless, he cooperated, knowing that patience was more likely to encourage a confidence from Penellin than was a direct enquiry.

The entire appearance of the man suggested that an unburdening of his heart was more than in order. He looked whey-faced. He was still wearing last night's clothes, but they gave no evidence of having been slept in, thus acting as testimony to the fact that Penellin had probably never been to bed. Part of what had kept him from sleep was depicted on his body: His fingers were still lightly stained with ink from having his prints taken by Penzance CID. Evaluating all this, Lynley ignored the real purpose of his visit for a moment and followed Penellin's lead.

"Still a believer, John?" he said. "Mining in Cornwall is well over one hundred years dead. You know that better than I."

"It's not reopening Wheal Maen I want to speak of," Penellin said.

"The mine needs to be sealed. The engine house is a ruin. The main shaft's flooded. It's far too dangerous to be left as it is." He swivelled his chair and nodded towards the large estate map on the office wall. "The mine can be seen from the Sennen road. It's only a quick walk across a bit of moor to get to it. I think it's time we tore the engine house down completely and sealed the shaft over before someone decides to go exploring and gets hurt. Or worse."

"That road isn't heavily trafficked at any time of year."

"It's true that few visitors go down that way," Penellin said. "But local folks use the road all the time. It's the children I worry about. You know how they are with their playing. I don't want any of us having to face the horror of a child falling into Wheal Maen."

Lynley left his seat to study the map. It was true that the mine was less than one hundred yards from the road, separated from it only by a dry stone wall, certainly an insufficient barrier to keep the public off the land in an area where countless footpaths led across private property, through open moors and into combes, joining one village to another.

"Of course you're right," he said and added reflectively, more to himself than to the other man, "How Father would have hated to see a mine sealed."

"Times change," Penellin said. "Your father wasn't a man to hold onto the past." He went to the filing cabinet and removed three more folders which he carried back to his desk. Lynley rejoined him.

"How's Nancy this morning?" he asked.

"Coping."

"What time did the police return you?"

"Half past four. Thereabouts."

"Is that it, then? With the police?"

"For now."

Outside, two of the gardeners were talking to each other as they worked among the plants, the clean sharp snap of their secateurs acting as interjections between their words. Penellin watched them through the blinds for a moment.

Lynley hesitated, caught between his promise to Nancy and his knowledge that Penellin wished to say no more. He was a private man. He did not want help. That much was clear. Yet Lynley felt that beneath Penellin's natural taciturnity an undercurrent of inexplicable anxiety was flowing, and he sought to find the source of the other man's worry in order to alleviate it as best he could. After so many years of relying on Penellin's strength and loyalty, he could not turn away from offering reciprocal strength and loyalty now.

"Nancy told me she spoke to you on the phone last night," Lynley said.

"Yes."

"But someone saw you in the village, according to the police."

Penellin made no response.

"Look, John, if there's some sort of trouble—"

"No trouble, my lord." Penellin pulled the files across the desk and opened the top one. It was a gesture of dismissal, the furthest he would ever go in asking Lynley to leave the office. "It's as Nancy said. We spoke on the phone. If someone thinks I was in the village, it can't be helped, can it? The neighbourhood is dark. It could have been anyone. It's as Nancy said. I was at the lodge."

"Dammit it all, we were standing right there when you walked in after two in the morning! You were in the village, weren't you? You saw Mick. Neither you nor Nancy is telling the truth. John, are you trying to protect her? Or is it Mark? Because he wasn't home either. And you knew that, didn't you? Were you looking for Mark? Was he at odds with Mick?"

Penellin lifted a document from within the file. "I've started the initial paperwork on closing Wheal Maen," he said.

Lynley made a final effort. "You've been here twenty-five years. I should like to think you'd come to me in a time of trouble."

"There's no trouble," Penellin said firmly. He picked up another sheet of paper, and although he did not look at it, the single gesture was eloquent in its plea for solitude.

Lynley terminated the interview and left the office.

With the door closed behind him, he paused in the hall, where the old tile floor made the air quite cool. At the end of the corridor, the southwest door of the house was open, and the sun beat down on the courtyard outside. There was movement on the cobblestones, the pleasant sound of running water. He walked towards it.

Outside, he found Jasper—sometime chauffeur, sometime gardener, sometime stableman, and full-time gossip—washing down the Land Rover they'd driven last night. His trousers were rolled up, his knobby feet bare, his white shirt open on a gaunt chest of grizzled hair. He nodded at Lynley.

"Got it from 'un, did you?" he asked, directing the spray on the Rover's windscreen.

"Got what from whom?" Lynley asked.

Jasper snorted. " 'Ad it all this morning, we did," he said. "Murder 'n police 'n John getting hisself carted off by CID." He spat onto the cobblestones and rubbed a rag against the Rover's bonnet. "With John in Nanrunnel 'n Nance lyin' like a pig in the rain 'bout everthing she can . . . 'oo'd think to see the like?"

"Nancy's lying?" Lynley asked. "You know that, Jasper?"

"Course I know it," he said. "Weren't I down to the lodge at half ten? Din't I go 'bout the mill? Wasn't nobody home? *Course* she be lyin'."

"About the mill? The mill in the woods? Has the mill something to do with Mick Cambrey's death?"

Jasper's face shuttered at this frontal approach. Too late Lynley remembered the old man's fondness for hanging a tale on the thread of innuendo. In reply to the questions, Jasper whimsically chose his own conversational path.

" 'N John never tol' you 'bout them clothes as Nance cut up, did 'e?"

"No. He said nothing about clothes," Lynley replied, and as bait he offered, "They can't have been important, I suppose, or he would have mentioned them."

Jasper shook his head darkly at the folly of dismissing such a piece of information. "Slicin' um to shreds, she were," he said. "Right back of their cottage. Came 'pon her, me and John. Caught her out and she cried like an ol' sick cow when she saw us, she did. Tha's important enough, I say."

"But she didn't talk to you?"

"Said nothin'. All them fancy clothes and Nance cuttin' and slicin'. John went near mad 'en he saw her. Started into the cottage after Mick, 'e did. Nance stopped 'im. 'Ung onto 'is arm till John run outer steam."

"So they were another woman's clothes," Lynley mused. "Jasper, does anyone know who Mick's woman was?"

"Woman?" Jasper scoffed. "More like women. Dozens, from what Harry Cambrey do say. Comes into the Anchor and Rose, does Harry. Sits and asks everbody 'oo'd listen what's to do 'bout Mick's catting round. 'She don' give 'um near enough,' Harry likes to tell it. 'Wha's a man to do when 'is woman's not like to give him enough?' " Jasper laughed derisively, stepped back from the Rover, and sprayed the front tyre. Water splashed on his legs, freckling them with bits of mud. "The way Harry do tell it, Nance been keeping her arms and legs crossed since the babe were born. With Mick just suffering b'yond endurance, swelled up like to burst with nowheres to stick it. 'Wha's a man to do?' Harry do ask. And Mrs. Swann, *she* do tell him, but—" Jasper suddenly seemed to realise with whom he was having this confidential little chat. His humour faded. He straightened his back, pulled off his cap, and ran his hand through his hair. "Anybody'd see the problem easy. Mick din't want the bother o' settling down."

He spat again to punctuate the discussion's end.

St. James and Lady Helen heard Harry Cambrey before they saw him. As they climbed the narrow stairway—ducking their heads to avoid capriciously placed beams in the ceiling—the sound of furniture being shoved on a bare, wooden floor was followed by a drawer being viciously slammed home, and that was followed by a raw curse. When they knocked on the door, a hush fell inside the room. Then footsteps approached. The door jerked open. Cambrey looked them over. They did the same of him.

Seeing him, St. James was reminded of the fact that he'd undergone heart surgery the previous year. He looked all the worse for the experience, thin, with a prominent Adam's apple and a skeletal collar bone meeting in two knobby points beneath it. His yellow skin suggested a dysfunctioning liver, and at the corners of his mouth, red sores cracked his lips and spotted them with dried blood. His face was unshaven, and the fringe of grey hair at the crown of his head crinkled out from his scalp, as if he'd been brought hastily awake and hadn't taken the time to comb it.

When Cambrey stepped back to let them pass into the office, St. James saw that it was one large room with several smaller cubicles opening along one wall and four narrow windows above the street that ran up the hill towards the upper reaches of the village. Aside from Harry Cambrey, no one else was there, an odd circumstance for a place of business, particularly a newspaper. But at least one of the reasons for the absence of employees lay upon work tops, upon desks, upon chairs. Notebooks and files had been taken from storage and strewn here and there. Harry Cambrey was engaged in a search.

He'd obviously been working at it for some hours and with no particular method, considering the state of the room. A series of military green filing cabinets had drawers which gaped open, half-empty; a stack of computer disks sat next to a word processor which was switched on; across a layout table, the current edition of the newspaper had been shoved aside to make way for three stacks of photographs; and the drawers of each one of the five desks in the room had been removed. The air was musty with the smell of old paper, and since the overhead lights had not been switched on, the room possessed a Dickensian gloom.

"What do you want?" Harry Cambrey was smoking a cigarette which he removed from his mouth only to cough or to light another. If he were concerned about the effect of his habit upon his heart, he did not show it.

"No one's here but yourself?" St. James asked as he and Lady Helen picked their way through the debris.

"I gave them the day off." Cambrey eyed Lady Helen from head to toe as he made his reply. "And your business?"

"We've been asked by Nancy to look into what's at the root of Mick's murder."

"You're to *help?* The two of you?" He made no attempt to hide his inspection of them, taking in St. James' leg brace with the same effrontery he used to examine Lady Helen's summer frock.

"The pursuit of news is a dangerous profession, isn't it, Mr. Cambrey?" Lady Helen said from the windows, which was as far as she'd got in her circuit of the room. "If your son's been murdered because of a story, what difference does it make who brings his killer to justice, so long as it's done?"

At this, Cambrey's factitious bravado disappeared. "It's a story," he said. His arms hung limp and lifeless at his sides. "I know it. I feel it. I've been here since I heard, trying to find the lad's notes."

"You've come up with nothing?" St. James asked.

"There's little enough to go on. Just trying to remember what he said and what he did. It's not a Nanrunnel story. It can't be. But that's the limit of what I know."

"You're sure of that?"

"It doesn't fit with how he's been these last months, that he'd be working on a Nanrunnel story. He was off here and there all the time, tracking down a lead, doing research, interviewing this person, locating that one. It wasn't a village story. Couldn't have been." He shook his head. "It would have been the making of this paper once we got it in print. I know it."

"Where did he go?"

"London."

"But with no notes left behind? Isn't that curious?"

"There're notes all right. Here. What you see." Cambrey flung his arm out to encompass the office's disarray. "But nothing I figure would cause the lad's death. Reporters don't lose their lives over interviews with army men, with the local MP, with bedridden invalids, with dairy farmers in the north. Journalists die because they have information worth dying over. Mick's not got that here."

"Nothing unusual among all this material?"

Cambrey dropped his cigarette to the floor and crushed it out. He massaged the muscles of his left arm, and as he did so, his eyes slid towards one of the desks. St. James read his answer in the latter action.

"You've found something."

"I don't know. You may as well have a look. I can make nothing from it." Cambrey went to the desk. From beneath the telephone, he took a piece of paper which he handed to St. James. "Tucked to the back of the drawer," he said.

The paper was grease splodged, originally a wrapper for a sandwich from the Talisman Cafe. The writing was faint. The dull light in the room and the points at which the pen had skipped through grease made it difficult to read, but St. James could see that it consisted mostly of numbers.

> 1 k 9400
> 500 g 55ea
> 27500-M1 Procure/Transport
> 27500-M6 Finance

St. James looked up. "Is this Mick's writing?"

Cambrey nodded. "If there's a story anywhere, that's it. But I don't know what it's about nor what that lot means."

"But there must be notes somewhere that use the same numbers and references," Lady Helen said. "M1 and M6. Surely he means the motorways."

"If there're notes here using the same set of numbers, I've not found them," Cambrey said.

"So they're missing."

"Pinched?" Cambrey lit another cigarette, inhaled, coughed. "I heard the cottage'd been searched."

"Has there been any indication of a break-in here?" St. James asked.

Cambrey looked from them to the room itself. He shook his head. "Boscowan sent a man to tell me about Mick round 4:15 this morning. I went to the cottage, but they'd already taken the body away and they wouldn't let me in. So I came here. I've been here ever since. There'd been no break-in."

"No sign of a search? Perhaps by one of the other employees?"

"Nothing," he said. His nostils pinched. "I want to find the bastard that did this to Mickey. And I won't stop the story. Nothing'll stop it. We have a free press. My boy lived for that, died for that as well. But it won't be in vain.''

"If he died for a story in the first place," St. James said quietly.

Cambrey's face grew dark. "What else is there?"

"Mick's women.''

Cambrey removed the cigarette from his mouth in a movement that was slow, studied, like an actor's. His head gave a tiny nod of approbation. "They're talking like that about Mickey, are they? Well now, why should I doubt it? Men were jealous of his easy way and women were the same if he didn't choose them." The cigarette went back to his mouth. It created a haze through which Cambrey squinted. "He was a man, was Mick. A real man. And a man has his needs. That tight wife of his had ice between her legs. What she denied him, he found somewhere else. If there's fault, it's Nancy's. Turn away from a man and he'll seek another woman. There's no crime in that. He was young. He had needs.''

"Was there anyone special he saw? More than one woman? Had he taken up with anyone new?"

"Couldn't say. It wasn't Mickey's way to boast about it when he did a new woman.''

"Did married women sleep with him?" Lady Helen asked. "Women from the village?''

"Lots of women slept with him." Cambrey pushed aside papers on the desk top, lifted the glass that covered it, and removed a photograph which he passed to her. "See for yourself. Is this the kind of man you'd say no to if he asked you to spread your legs, missy?"

Lady Helen drew in a quick breath to respond, but in an admirable demonstration of self-control, she didn't do so. Nor did she look at the picture which she handed to St. James. In it, a shirtless young man stood on the deck of a sailboat, one hand on a spar as he adjusted the rigging. He was square-jawed and nice looking, but slender like his father, not possessed of the rugged body or features that naturally come to mind when one hears the words *a real man.* St. James turned over the photograph. *Cambrey prepares for America's Cup—the lad's on his way* had been written facetiously across it. It was written in the same hand as was the note from the desk.

"He had a sense of humour," St. James noted.

"He had everything.''

"May I keep the photograph? This note as well?"

"Do what you like. They're nothing to me without Mick." Cambrey examined the office. Defeat was in the set of his shoulders, it lined a weary path across his face. "We were on our way. The *Spokesman* was going to be the biggest paper in South Cornwall. Not just a weekly any longer. I wanted it. Mick wanted it. We were on our way. All of us."

"Mick got on well with the staff? No troubles there?"

"They loved him. He'd made good on his own. Come back to the village. He was a hero to them, what they wanted to be." Cambrey sharpened his voice. "You can't think that someone on the staff would kill him. No one from this office would have laid a hand on my son. They had no reason. He was changing the paper. He was making improvements. He was—"

"Getting ready to give someone the sack?"

"Bloody hell, who?"

St. James looked at the desk closest to the window. A framed photograph of two young children sat on it. "What was his relationship with your copy editor? Is it Julianna Vendale?"

"Julianna?" Cambrey removed his cigarette, licked his lips.

"Was she one of his women? A former lover? Or the female half of an office seduction, about to be given the sack for not cooperating in Mick's quest to have his needs met?"

Cambrey barked a laugh, refusing to react to the manner in which St. James had used his own words about his son to arrive at a more-than-logical and less-than-savoury motive for murder. No noble journalist going to his death over information or the protection of a source, but a squalid little episode of sexual harassment ending in a very sexual crime.

"Mick didn't need Julianna Vendale," Cambrey said. "He didn't have to go begging for what was spread out before him—hot, wet, and willing—everywhere he turned."

On the street once more, they headed in the direction of the harbour car park where Lady Helen had left the Rover. St. James glanced at her as they walked. During the final minutes in the newspaper office, she'd said nothing, although the tension in her body and the fixed expression on her face articulated her reaction to Mick Cambrey's life and his death—not to mention his father—better than any words. The moment they left the building, however, she gave vent to disgust. She marched towards the car park. St. James could barely manage the pace. He only caught snatches of her diatribe.

"Some sort of sexual athlete . . . more like his scorekeeper than his father . . . *time* to put a newspaper out since they were so busy getting their needs met? . . . every woman in Cornwall . . . no wonder to me—absolutely no wonder at all—that someone cut . . . I'd even consider doing it myself . . ." She was quite out of breath when she reached the car. So was he.

They leaned against it, directing their faces into a breeze that was pungent with the odours of kelp and fish. In the harbour just beneath them, hundreds of gulls circled above a small skiff, its morning catch flickering silver in the sun.

"Is that what you thought of me?" Lady Helen asked abruptly.

St. James couldn't have been more surprised by the question. "Helen, for God's sake—"

"Is it?" she demanded. "Tell me. I want to know. Because if it is, you can walk all the way back to Howenstow."

"Then how can I answer? I'll say of course not. You'll say I'm just saying that so I don't have to walk back to Howenstow. It's a no-win situation for me, Helen. I may as well start hobbling on my way right now."

"Oh, get in," she sighed.

He did so before she could change her mind. She joined him but didn't start the car at once. Instead, she gazed through the dirty windscreen to the crusty walls of the harbour quay. A family walked together upon it, mother guiding an infant in a faded blue pushchair, father holding a toddler by the hand. They looked inordinately young to be parents.

"I kept telling myself to consider the source," Lady Helen finally said. "I kept saying, he's mourning, he can't know what he's saying, he can't hear what it sounds like. But I'm afraid I lost myself entirely when he asked me if I'd have spread my legs for Mick. I always wondered what that expression *seeing red* meant. Now I know. I wanted to throw myself at him and tear out his hair."

"He didn't have much."

That broke the tension. She laughed in resignation and started the car. "What do you make of that note?"

St. James removed the paper from his shirt pocket and turned it to the formal printing stamped diagonally across the front. "Talisman Cafe. I wonder where that is."

"Not far from the Anchor and Rose. Just up Paul Lane a bit. Why?"

"Because he couldn't have written this in the newspaper office. It hardly makes sense to use a sandwich wrapper with so much blank paper lying about. So he must have written it somewhere else. In the cafe or elsewhere if he'd taken the sandwich out. Actually, I was hoping the Talisman Cafe was in Paddington.'' He told her about Tina Cogin.

Lady Helen nodded her head at the note. ''Do you think this has to do with her?''

''She's involved somehow, if Deborah's correct in her assumption that it was Mick Cambrey she saw in the hall outside that flat. But if the Talisman Cafe is here in Nanrunnel, Mick must have worked this up locally.''

''With a local source? A local killer as well?''

''Possibly. But not necessarily. He was in and out of London. Everyone agrees to that. I can't think it would be that difficult to trace him back to Cornwall, especially if he did his travelling by train.''

''If he did have a local source of information, whoever it is could be in danger as well.''

''If the story is the motive for his murder.'' St. James returned the paper to his jacket pocket.

''I'd say it's more likely the other, payment for seducing another man's wife.'' Lady Helen pulled out onto the Lamorna Road. It rose in a gentle slope past tourist flats and cottages, veering east to display the bright sea. ''It's more workable as a motive, considering what we know about Mick. Because how would a man feel, coming upon evidence that he cannot deny, evidence that tells him the woman he loves is giving herself to another man.''

St. James turned away. He looked at the water. A fishing boat was chugging towards Nanrunnel, and even at this distance he could see the lobster baskets hanging from its sides. ''He'd feel like killing, I expect,'' he replied. He felt Lady Helen look towards him and knew she realised how he had taken her words. She would want to speak in order to ease the moment. He preferred to let it go and indicated that by saying to her, ''As to the other, Helen. What you asked about us, about how I felt when you and I were lovers . . . Of course not. You know that. I hope you always have.''

''I've not been down here in several years,'' Lynley said as he and St. James went through the gate in the Howenstow wall and began their descent into the woodland. ''Who knows what condition we'll find the place in, if it's not a ruin altogether. You know how it is. A few seasons abandoned and roofs cave in, beams rot, floors disintegrate. I was surprised to hear it was still standing at all.''

He was making conversation and he knew it, in the hope that by doing so he could vanquish the legion of memories that were waiting on the plain of his consciousness, ready to assault him, memories that were intimately associated with the mill and tied to a portion of his life from which he had walked away, making an obstinate vow never to think of it again. Even now, as they approached the building and saw the tile of its roofline emerge through the trees, he could feel the first tentative foray of a recollection: just an image of his mother striding through the woods. But he knew that she was merely an illusion, trying her luck against his protective armour. He fought her off by pausing on the path, taking his time about lighting a cigarette.

"We came this way yesterday," St. James was answering. He walked on ahead for a few paces, stopping when he glanced back and saw that Lynley had fallen behind. "The wheel's overgrown. Did you know?"

"I'm not surprised. That was always a problem, as I recall." Lynley smoked pensively, liking the concrete feel of the cigarette between his fingers. He savoured the sharp taste of the tobacco and the fact that the cigarette in his hand gave him something to which he might attend with more concentration than was necessary.

"And Jasper thinks someone's using the mill? For what? Dossing?"

"He wouldn't say."

St. James nodded, looked thoughtful, walked on. No longer able to avoid it through idle conversation or cigarette smoking or any other form of temporising, Lynley followed.

Oddly enough, he found that the mill wasn't very much changed since he had last been there, as if someone had been caring for it. The exterior needed paint—patches of whitewash had worn completely through to the stone—and much of its woodwork was splintered, but the roof was all of one piece, and aside from a pane of glass that was missing from the single window on the upper floor, the building looked sturdy enough to stand for another hundred years.

The two men climbed the old stone steps, their feet sliding into shallow grooves which spoke of the thousands of entries and exits made during the time that the mill was in operation. Its paint long ago faded and storm-washed to nothing, the door hung partially open. Its wood was swollen from seasons of rain, so the door no longer fit neatly into position. It gave way with a shriek at Lynley's push.

They entered, paused, took stock of what they saw. The bottom floor was nearly empty, illuminated by streaky shafts of sunlight that gained access through gaps in the shuttered windows. Against a far wall, some sacking lay in a disintegrating heap next to a stack of wooden crates. Beneath one of the windows, a stone mortar and pestle were cobwebbed over, while nearby a coil of rope hung from a peg, looking as if it hadn't been touched in half a century. A small stack of old newspapers stood in one corner of the room, and Lynley watched as St. James went to inspect them.

"The *Spokesman,*" he said, picking one up. "With some notations in the text. Corrections. Deletions. A new design for the masthead." He tossed the paper down. "Did Mick Cambrey know about this place, Tommy?"

"We came here as boys. I expect he hadn't forgotten it. But those papers look old. He can't have been here recently."

"Hmm. Yes. They're from a year ago April. But someone's been here more recently than that." St. James indicated several sets of footprints on the dusty floor. They led to a wall ladder that gave access to the mill loft and the gears and shafts which drove its great grindstone. St. James examined the ladder rungs, pulled on three of them to test their safety, and began an awkward ascent.

Lynley watched him make his slow way to the top, knowing quite well that St. James would expect him to follow. He could not avoid doing so. Nor could he any longer avoid the force of reminiscence that the mill—and more so, the loft above him—provoked. For after ages of searching, she'd found him up there, where he had hidden from her and from the knowledge that he had come upon unexpectedly.

Dashing up through the garden from the sea, he'd only had a glimpse of the man passing before a first floor window, a glance that gave him the impression of height and stature, a glance in which he saw only his father's paisley dressing gown, a glance in which he hadn't bothered to think how impossible it was that his father—so ill—would even be out of bed, let alone sauntering round his mother's bedroom. He didn't think of that, only felt instead a sunshot bolt of joy as the words *cured cured cured* sang out in his mind and he ran up the stairs—pounded up the stairs calling to them both—and burst into his mother's room. Or at least tried to. But the door was locked. And as he called out, his father's nurse hurried up the stairs, carrying a tray, admonishing him, telling him he would awaken the invalid. And he got only as far as saying, "But Father's . . ." before he understood.

And then he called out to her in a such savage rage that she opened the door and he saw it all: Trenarrow wearing his father's dressing gown, the covers on her bed in disarray, the clothing discarded hastily on the floor. The air was heavy with the pungent odour of intercourse. And only a dressing room and bath separated them from the room in which his father lay dying.

He'd flung himself mindlessly at Trenarrow. But he was only a slender boy of seventeen, no match for a man of thirty-one. Trenarrow hit him once, a slap on the face with his open palm, the sort of blow one uses to calm an hysterical woman. His mother had cried, "Roddy, no!" and it was over.

She had found him in the mill. From the one small window in the loft, he watched her coming through the woodland, tall and elegant, just forty-one years old. And so very beautiful.

He should have been able to maintain his poise. The oldest son of the earl, after all, he should have possessed the strength of will and the dignity to tell her that he'd have to return to school and prepare for exams. It wouldn't matter whether she believed him. The only object was to be off, at once.

But he watched her approach and thought instead of how his father loved her, how he shouted for her—"Daze! Darling Daze!"—whenever he walked into the house. His life had revolved round making her happy, and now he lay in his bedroom and waited for the cancer to eat away the rest of his body while she and Trenarrow kissed and clung and touched and . . .

He broke. She climbed the ladder, calling his name. He was more than ready for her.

Whore, he screamed. Are you crazy? Or just so itchy that anyone will do? Even someone with nothing more on his mind than sticking you a good one and laughing about it with his mates in the pub when he's done. Are you proud of that, whore? Are you fucking proud?

When she hit him, the blow came completely by surprise because she had stood there, immobile, and accepted his abuse. But with his last question, she struck him so hard with the back of her hand that he staggered against the wall, his lip split open by her diamond ring. Her face never changed. It was blank, carved in stone.

You'll be sorry! he screamed as she climbed down the ladder. I'll make you sorry! I'll make both of you sorry. I will!

And he had done so, over and over again. How he had done so.

"Tommy?"

Lynley looked up to find St. James watching him over the edge of the loft.

"You might want to see what's up here."

"Yes. Of course."

He climbed the ladder.

It had only taken a moment for St. James to evaluate what he found in the loft. The mill shaft, its tremendous gears, and its grindstone took up much of the space, but what was left gave mute evidence of the use to which the mill had been put most recently.

In the centre of the room stood a rusting card table and one folding chair. This latter held a discarded T-shirt, long ago metamorphosed from white to grey, while on the surface of the former an antique postage scale measured the weight of a tarnished spoon and two dirty razor blades. Next to this was an open carton of small plastic bags.

St. James watched as Lynley joined him and inspected these items, his features becoming more settled as he reached his own inescapable conclusion.

"Mick's been here more recently than last April, Tommy," St. James said. "And I dare say his visits had nothing to do with the *Spokesman*." He touched the postage scale lightly, watched the movement of the arrow that indicated weight. "Perhaps we have a better idea why he died."

Lynley shook his head. His voice was dark. "This isn't Mick," he said.

13

At half past seven that evening, St. James knocked on Deborah's bedroom door and entered to find her stepping back from the dressing table, her forehead wrinkled as she studied her appearance.

"Well," she said doubtfully, "I don't know." She touched the necklace at her throat—a double strand of pearls—and her hand fell to the neckline of her dress where she fingered the material experimentally. It appeared to be silk, and its colour was an odd combination of grey and green, like the ocean on an overcast day. Her hair and skin were a contrast to this, and the result was more striking than she appeared to realise.

"A success," St. James said.

She smiled at his reflection in the mirror. "Lord, I'm nervous. I keep telling myself that it's only a small dinner party with Tommy's family and a few of their friends. I keep telling myself that it doesn't matter in the least. But then I have visions of fumbling round with all this silverware. Simon, why on earth does it always come down to silverware?"

"The worst nightmare of a genteel society: Which fork do I use when I eat the shrimp? The rest of life's problems seem inconsequential by comparison."

"What shall I say to these people? Tommy did tell me there'd be a dinner tonight, but at the time I didn't think much about it. If I were only like Helen, I could chat amusingly about a thousand and one different topics. I could talk to anyone. It wouldn't even matter. But I'm not like Helen. Oh, I wish I were. Just for tonight. Perhaps she can pretend to be me and I can fade into the woodwork."

"Hardly a plan to please Tommy."

"I've managed to convince myself that I'll trip on the stairs or spill a glass of wine down the front of my dress or get caught on the tablecloth and pull off half the dishes when I get out of my chair. Last night I had a nightmare that my face had broken out in blisters and hives and people were saying, '*This* is the fiancée?' in funereal tones all round me."

St. James laughed at that and joined her at the dressing table where he peered into the mirror and studied her face. "Not a blister anywhere. Not a hive in sight. As to those freckles, however . . ."

She laughed as well, such a pure sound, such a pleasure. It shot him back through time to memory. He stepped away.

"I've managed . . ." He reached in his jacket pocket for the photograph of Mick Cambrey which he handed to her. "If you'll have a look at him."

She did so, carrying the picture to the light. It was a moment before she answered.

"It's the same man."

"Are you certain?"

"Fairly. May I take this with me and show it to Tina?"

He thought about this. Last night it had seemed an innocent plan to have Deborah verify Mick Cambrey's presence in London through the simple expedient of having Tina Cogin identify his photograph. But after today's conversation with Harry Cambrey, after seeing the cryptographic paper from the Talisman Cafe, after considering the potential motives behind the crime and how Tina Cogin fit into any or all of them, he was not so sure about the role Deborah could play—or any role he wanted her to play—in investigating the crime and contacting those most closely caught up in it. Deborah seemed to sense his hesitation and presented him with a *fait accompli.*

"I've spoken to Tommy about it," she said. "To Helen as well. We thought we'd take the train up in the morning—Helen and I—and go directly to the flat. So we should know something more about Mick Cambrey by the afternoon. Surely that shall be of help."

He couldn't deny this and she seemed to read agreement in his face. She said, "Right. Good," and put the photograph in the drawer of the bedside table with a *that's that* movement. As she did so, the bedroom door opened and Sidney wandered in, reaching with one hand over her shoulder to fiddle with the zip on her dress while with the other she aimlessly attempted to rearrange her tousled hair.

"These blasted Howenstow maids," she was muttering. "They flutter through my room—God knows they mean well—and I can't find a thing.

Simon, will you . . . good Lord, you look wonderful in that suit. Is it new? Here. I can't seem to manage this blasted thing on my own.'' She presented her back to her brother and, as he finished what she had begun with the zip, she looked at Deborah. ''And you look stunning, Deb. Simon, doesn't she look stunning? Oh, never mind. Why on earth would I ask you when the only thing you've found stunning in years is a patch of blood through a microscope. Or perhaps a bit of skin from beneath the fingernail of a corpse.'' She laughed, turned, and patted her brother's cheek before going to the dressing table, where she studied herself in the mirror and picked up a bottle of Deborah's perfume.

''So the maids have straightened everything up''—she continued with her original thought—''and, of course, I can't find a thing. My perfume is utterly gone—may I borrow a splash of yours, Deb?—and just try to find my shoes! Why, I almost had to borrow a pair from Helen until I found them tucked in the very back of my wardrobe as if I'd no intention in the world of ever wearing them again.''

''An odd place for shoes,'' St. James pointed out sardonically. ''In the wardrobe.''

''He's laughing at me, Deborah,'' Sidney said. ''But if he didn't have your father keeping him together, there's no doubt in my mind what the result would be. Chaos. Complete. Utter. Infinite.'' She bent and brought her face closer to the glass. ''The swelling's gone, thank God, although the scratches are stunning. Not to mention the bruise beneath my eye. I look just like a street brawler. D'you think anyone will mention it? Or shall we all just concentrate on keeping our upper lips stiff and our manners impeccable? You know the sort of thing. Eyes forward and no groping at anyone's thighs beneath the tablecloth.''

''Groping at thighs?'' Deborah asked. ''Simon, you never told me. And I've been worrying about the silver!''

''The silver?'' Sidney looked round from the mirror. ''Oh, you mean all the forks and knives? Pooh. Unless people start throwing them, don't give it a thought.'' Unbidden, she fluffed up Deborah's hair, stepped back, frowned, played with it again. ''Where's Justin, d'you know? I've not seen him for ages today. He's probably worried I shall bite him again. I can't think why he reacted the way he did yesterday. I've bitten him before although, now I think, the circumstances *were* a bit different.'' She laughed light-heartedly. ''Well, if the two of us get into another row tonight, let's hope it's at the dinner table. With all those knives and forks, we'll have plenty of weapons.''

*   *   *

Lynley found Peter in the smoking room on the ground floor of the house. Cigarette in hand, he was standing by the fireplace, his attention fixed upon a red fox that was mounted in a glass case above it. A compassionate taxidermist had thoughtfully poised the animal in the act of flight, just inches from a burrow that would have saved him. Other vulpine trophies had not been so fortunately enshrined, however. Their heads hung from plaques fastened intermittently between photographs on the room's panelled walls. Since the only light came from an arabesque brass chandelier, these latter foxes cast long shadows, accusatory wedges of darkness like reverse spotlights that emphasised a devotion to blood sports which no one in the family had actually felt since before the First War.

Seeing his brother's reflection in the glass case, Peter spoke without turning around. "Why do you suppose no one's ever taken this awful thing down from the mantel?"

"I think it was Grandfather's first successful hunt."

"Why blood him when you can give him the poor creature as a prize?"

"That sort of thing."

Lynley noted that his brother had removed the swastika from his ear, replacing it with a single gold stud. He wore grey trousers, a white shirt, a loosely knotted tie—and although the clothes were overly large, at least they were clean. And he had put on shoes if not socks. This seemed cause enough for fleeting gratification, and Lynley briefly considered the value and the wisdom of confronting his brother—as he knew he had to be confronted eventually—at a moment when Peter's appearance suggested concession, compromise, and the promise of change.

Peter tossed his cigarette into the fireplace and opened the liquor cabinet that was a hidden feature of the mantel beneath the fox.

"This was one of my little adolescent secrets," he chuckled as he poured himself a tumbler of whisky. "Jasper showed it to me when I turned seventeen."

"He showed me as well. A rite of passage, I suppose."

"D'you think Mother knew?"

"I imagine so."

"What a disappointment. To think one's clever and to find out just the opposite." He turned from the fireplace for the first time and held his glass up in a rakish salute. "The best, Tommy. Weren't you lucky to have found her."

At that, Lynley noticed his brother's eyes. They were unnaturally bright. He felt a twinge of apprehension. Stifling it, he merely said thank you, and watched as Peter wandered to the desk that abutted the wide bay window. There, he began to play with the items arranged on the leather-edged blotter, spinning the letter opener on its ivory handle, lifting the top of an empty silver inkstand, joggling a rack of cherrywood pipes. Still sipping his whisky, he picked up a photograph of their grandparents and yawned as he idly studied their faces.

Seeing this and knowing it for what it was—an attempt to construct a barrier of indifference—Lynley realised there was no point in temporising. "I'd like to ask you about the mill."

Peter replaced the photograph and picked at a worn spot on the back of the armchair that sat before the desk. "What about the mill?"

"You've been using it, haven't you?"

"I haven't been there in ages. I've been by it, of course, to get down to the cove. But I've not been inside. Why?"

"You know the answer to that."

Peter's face remained blank as Lynley spoke, but a muscle spasm pulled at the corner of his mouth. He made his way to a row of university photographs that decorated one of the walls. He began gliding from one to the next as if he were seeing them for the very first time.

"Every Lynley for one hundred years," he remarked, "crewing at Oxford. What a black sheep I've been." He came to a blank spot on the wall and touched the palm of his hand to the panel. "Even Father had his day, didn't he, Tommy? But of course, we can't have his picture here. It wouldn't do if Father were able to look down from the walls and observe our wicked ways."

Lynley refused to allow the honeyed words to provoke him. "I'd like to talk about the mill."

Peter threw back the rest of his whisky, put his glass on a lowboy, and continued his perusal. He stopped before the most recent photograph and flicked his index finger against his brother's picture. His nail snapped sharply upon the glass like a slap in miniature.

"Even you, Tommy. You've fit the mould. A Lynley to be proud of. You're a regular swell."

Lynley felt his chest tighten. "I've no control over the kind of life you've chosen to lead in London," he said, hoping to sound reasonable and knowing how poor a job he made of it. "You've chucked Oxford? Fine. You've your own digs? Fine. You've taken up with this . . . with Sasha? Fine. But not here, Peter. I won't have this business at Howenstow. Is that clear?"

Peter turned from the wall, cocking his head slightly. "You won't have it? You drop into our lives once or twice a year to announce what you will and won't have, is that it? And this is just one of those momentous occasions.''

"How often I'm here makes no difference to anything. I'm responsible for Howenstow, for every person on the grounds. And I've no intention of putting up with the sort of filth—''

"Oh, I see. Some local drug action's going on at the mill, and you've placed me at the centre in your best DI fashion. Well. Nice job. Have you dusted for prints? Found a lock of my hair? Did I leave behind spittle for you to analyse?'' Peter shook his head in eloquent disgust. "You're a fool. If I want to use, I sure as hell won't go all the way down to the mill. I've nothing to hide. From you or from anyone.''

"There's more than using going on and you know it. You're in over your head.''

"What's that supposed to mean?''

The disingenuous question rubbed Lynley raw. "You're bringing it onto the estate. That's what it means. You're cutting it in the mill. That's what it means. You're taking it to London. To use. To sell. Have I painted the picture well enough for you? God in heaven, Peter, if Mother knew, it would kill her.''

"And wouldn't that be convenient for you? No more worrying about whether she's going to disgrace you by running off with Roderick. No more wondering how much time he's been spending in her bed. If she'd only have the good grace to drop dead because of me, you might even celebrate by bringing Father's photographs back. But that'd be a tough one, wouldn't it, Tommy? Because you'd have to stop acting like such a bleeding little prig and how on earth could you ever manage it?''

"Don't try to avoid the issue by bringing up all that.''

"Oh, no! Avoidance. What a heinous crime! Another sin I've committed. Another black mark on my soul.'' Peter took the university picture from the wall, tossing it in his brother's direction. It landed with a clatter against the legs of a chair. "You're completely unsullied, aren't you, Tommy? Why can't I just follow your faultless example?''

"I don't want a row with you, Peter.''

"It's delicious. Drugs, adultery, and fornication. All in one family. Who knows what else we'd have to work with if only Judy were here as well. But then, she's dabbled a bit in adultery herself, hasn't she, Tommy? Like mother, like daughter. That's what I say. And what about you? Too noble to have it off with some bloke's wife if she strikes your fancy? Too moral? Too ethical? I can't believe that.''

"This is getting us nowhere.''

"What a blight we must be to you. Living hand in glove with the seven deadly sins and enjoying every one of them. Where do we do the worse damage? To your bloody title or your precious career?"

"You'd say anything if you believed it had the power to hurt me, wouldn't you?"

Peter laughed, but he was gripping the back of an armchair tightly. "To hurt *you?* Is that what you actually think? I can't believe it. As far as I know, the world still revolves round the sun, not you. Or hadn't you noticed? There *are* actually people who lead their lives without the slightest worry about how their behaviour affects the Eighth Earl of Asherton, and I'm one of them, Tommy. I don't dance to your tune. I never have. I never will." His features contorted with an angry bitterness. "What I really love about this whole sodding conversation is the implication that you care about anything beyond yourself. About Howenstow. About Mother. About me. What difference would it make to you if this place burned to the ground? What difference would it make if both of us died in the flames? You'd be free of us then. You'd never have to worry about playing the role. Dutiful son. Loving brother. You make me sick." Peter fumbled in his pocket, bringing out a packet of cigarettes. But his hands were shaking so badly that he dropped them to the floor where they spilled out onto the carpet.

"Peter," Lynley said. "Peter, let me help you. You can't go on this way. You know that. You must."

"And if I die, what of it? Then you'll only have Mother and Roderick to contend with. She's invited him tonight, you know. What an insult to the earl! I think she's actually decided to declare independence."

"They don't matter. You know that. Let me help you. Please."

"Help? You?" Peter bent and retrieved his cigarettes. It took him four tries with a match before he was able to light one. "You'd sully your pretty reputation to salvage mine? What a laugh that is! What's it to you what happens to me, as long as your own name stays pure?"

"You're my brother."

Peter drew in on his cigarette deeply before mashing it out in an ashtray. "To hell with your brotherhood." He started for the door.

Lynley grabbed his arm as he passed. "That's easy for you, isn't it? To hell with brotherhood. To hell with everyone. Because a commitment to people takes you away from dope. And you can't bear that."

"You talk to *me* of commitments? You filthy hypocrite. When did you ever commit to anyone besides yourself?"

Lynley refused to be sidetracked. "Seeing the mill was a revelation today. You ought to be proud of what you've become."

"A smuggler! A dealer! An addict! What a nice little footnote in the family history. What a blackguard! What a fiend!" Peter's voice spiralled. He pulled himself from his brother's grasp. "So have me arrested. Or better yet, arrest me yourself. Haul me into the Met. Turning in your own brother should make your career. Here." He extended his hands, wrists together. "Shackle me up. Take me away tonight and have your promotion tomorrow."

Lynley watched the play of emotion on his brother's face. He tried to tell himself that this confrontation had its roots in Peter's addiction. But he knew quite well that his own past behaviour, his obstinate pride, and his need to punish had led inevitably to this ugly outburst. Still, he struggled against the desire to lash out in return.

"Listen to yourself. Look at what it's doing to you. Look at what you've become."

"I've become nothing! It's where I began. It's what I always was."

"In your own eyes, perhaps. But in no one else's."

"In *everyone's* eyes. I've spent a lifetime trying to measure up and I've chucked it. Do your hear? I've chucked it all and I'm bloody well glad of it. So leave me alone, will you? Go back to your nice little townhouse and your nice little life. Make yourself a nice little marriage with a nice little wife. Have some nice little babies to carry on your name and leave me alone! Just leave me alone!" His face was empurpled; his body shook.

"Yes. I can see that's best." Lynley stepped past his brother only to see that their mother, white-faced, had come to the doorway. How long she had been standing there, he couldn't have said.

"My dear, my *dear!* It was simply divine." The Reverend Mrs. Sweeney divided the final word into two, with a dramatic pause between the syllables, as if in the hope of building anticipation in her audience over how her sentence would end, be it with approbation or censure. *Plorable,* her tone implied, was as likely a conclusion as *vine.*

She was seated directly across from St. James, midway down the length of the linen-covered dining table at which were gathered a party of eighteen. They constituted an interesting assortment of Lynley relations, Cornish notables, and community members who had known the family for years. The Reverend Mr. Sweeney and his wife belonged to this latter group.

Mrs. Sweeney leaned forward. Candlelight glimmered across the astounding, wide field of her chest which was amply revealed by a remarkable décolletage. St. James woundered idly what excuse Mrs. Sweeney had concocted for wearing such a gown this evening. Its cut was certainly not what one generally expected from a minister's wife and she wasn't in the role of Beatrice now. Then he noticed the damp, longing, and agitated glances which Mr. Sweeney—three seats away and attempting to converse politely with the wife of the Plymouth MP—was casting in his wife's direction. He put the question to rest.

Fork raised, a bit of salmon pastry caught on its tines, Mrs. Sweeney continued. "My dear, the entire *cast* was simply thrilled with your photographs. Dare we *hope* to make it a yearly event?" She was speaking to Deborah, who sat on Lynley's right at the head of the table. "Just think of it. An annual collection of photographs with our own Lord Asherton. In a different costume every time." She trilled a little laugh. "The actors, I mean. Of course. Not Lord Asherton."

"But why not Tommy in costume as well?" Lady Helen said. "I think it's high time he joined the Nanrunnel Players and stopped hiding his talent under a bushel."

"Oh, we could hardly dare to hope or to think . . ." Mr. Sweeney tore his attention from his wife's cleavage long enough to take up this thought.

"I can just see it," Sidney laughed. "Tommy as Petruchio."

"I've told him time and again it was a mistake to read history at Oxford," Lady Helen said. "He's always had a flair for the stage. Haven't you, Tommy darling?"

"Might we *really* . . ." Mr. Sweeney faltered, caught between the obvious teasing of Lynley's friends and his own unspoken hope that there might be a margin of reality behind Lady Helen's words. He said, as if it were a possible inducement to Lynley's becoming one of the local thespians, "We have so often asked Dr. Trenarrow to join us under the lights."

"A pleasure I must avoid," Trenarrow said.

"And those you don't avoid?"

Peter Lynley asked the question, winking round the table in a manner that suggested skeletons were about to leap out of the cupboards while the dead came springing back to life. He poured more of the white burgundy into his wine glass and did the same for Sasha. Both of them drank. Sasha smiled down at her plate as if enjoying a secret joke. Neither of them had touched their salmon.

A brief hiatus came upon the conversation. Trenarrow broke it. "High blood pressure keeps me from many pleasures, I'm afraid. Such are the failings of middle age."

"You don't have the look of a man who has failings," Justin Brooke said. He and Sidney had twined their hands on the table top. St. James wondered how either of them was managing to eat.

"We all have failings," Trenarrow replied. "Some of us are fortunate in that we manage to keep them better hidden than others. But we all of us have them. It's the way of the world."

Hodge, assisted by two of the dailies who had been induced to stay into the evening, emerged from the warming room as Dr. Trenarrow spoke. The introduction of a second course arrested attention. If Peter Lynley had sought the embarrassment of others with his sly question, food proved to be eminently more interesting to the assembled group.

"You're not sealing Wheal Maen!" The exclamation rose like a wail, emitted from Lady Augusta, Lynley's maiden aunt. His father's sister had always maintained a proprietary interest and watchful eye over Howenstow. As she spoke, she cast a look of outrage upon John Penellin on her right, who remained detached from the conversation.

St. James had been surprised to see Penellin among the guests. Surely a death in the family would have been excuse enough to allow him to beg off a dinner party in which he appeared to have little interest. The estate manager had spoken less than ten words during drinks in the hall, spending most of the time standing at the window and gazing gravely in the direction of the lodge. However, from what he had seen and heard last night, St. James knew Penellin had no love for his son-in-law. So perhaps it was his indifference to Mick Cambrey which prompted him to take part in the gathering. Or perhaps it was an act of loyalty to the Lynleys. Or a behaviour he wished to be seen as such.

Lady Augusta was continuing. She was a woman well-skilled in the art of dinner table dialogue, devoting half her time to the right, the other to the left, and throwing a remark right down the centre whenever she deemed it appropriate. "It's bad enough that Wheal Maen must be closed. But cows were actually grazing in the park when I arrived! Good heavens, I couldn't believe my eyes. My father must be spinning in his grave. I don't understand the reason, Mr. Penellin."

Penellin looked up from his wine glass. "The mine's too close to the road. The main shaft's flooded. It's safer to seal it."

"Piffle!" Lady Augusta proclaimed. "Those mines are individual works of art. You know as well as I that at least two of our mines have beam-engines that are perfectly intact. People want to see that sort of thing, you know. People pay to see it.''

"Guided tours, Aunt?'' Lynley asked.

"Just the thing!''

"With everyone wearing those wonderful cyclops hats with little torches attached to their foreheads,'' Lady Helen said.

"Yes, of course.'' Lady Augusta rapped the table sharply with her fork. "We don't want the Trust here, sniffing round for another Lanhydrock, putting everyone out of house and home, do we? *Do* we?'' She gave a quick nod, accepting no response as agreement. "Quite. We don't. But what other way do we have of avoiding those little beasts than by dealing with the tourist trade ourselves, my dears? We must make repairs, we must open the mines, we must allow tours. Children love tours. They'll be wild to go down. They'll give their parents no peace until they've had a look.''

"It's an interesting idea,'' Lynley said. "But I'll only consider it on one condition.''

"What's that, Tommy dear?''

"That you run the tea shop.''

"That I . . .'' Her mouth closed abruptly.

"In a white cap,'' Lynley went on. "Dressed as a milkmaid.''

Lady Augusta pressed against the back of her chair and laughed with the heartiness of a woman who knew she'd been bested, if only for the moment. "You naughty boy,'' she said and dipped into her soup.

Conversation ebbed and flowed through the remainder of the meal. St. James caught only snatches here and there. Lady Asherton and Cotter talking about a large brass charger, caparisoned and prancing, that hung on the room's east wall; Lady Helen relating to Dr. Trenarrow an amusing tale of mistaken identity at a long ago house party attended by her father; Justin Brooke and Sidney laughing together over a remark Lady Augusta made about Lynley's childhood; the Plymouth MP and the Reverend Mrs. Sweeney wandering in a maze of confusion in which he discussed the need for economic development and she responded with a dreamy reverie about bringing the film industry to Cornwall apparently in order to feature herself in a starring role; Mr. Sweeney—when his eyes were not feasting upon his spouse—murmuring vague responses to the MP's wife, who was speaking about each of her grandchildren in turn. Only Peter and Sasha kept their voices low, their heads together, their attention on each other.

Thus the company moved smoothly towards the end of the meal.

This was heralded by the presentation of the pudding, a flaming concoction that looked as if its intended purpose was to conclude the dinner by means of a conflagration. When it had been duly served and devoured, Lynley got to his feet. He brushed back his hair in a boyish gesture.

"You know this already," he said. "But I'd like to make it official tonight by saying that Deborah and I shall marry in December." He touched her bright hair lightly as a murmur of congratulations rose and fell. "What you don't know, however, because we only decided late this afternoon, is that we'll be coming home permanently to Cornwall then. To make our life here—have our children grow up here—with you."

It was an announcement which, considering the reaction, no one had been prepared to hear. Least of all had St. James expected it. He had an impression only of a general cry of surprise and then a series of images played quickly before him: Lady Asherton saying her son's name and nothing more; Trenarrow turning abruptly to Lynley's mother; Deborah pressing her cheek to Lynley's hand in a movement so quick it might have gone unnoticed; and then Cotter studying St. James with an expression whose meaning was unmistakable. He's expected this all along, St. James thought.

There was no time to dwell upon what it would mean—how it would feel—to have Deborah nearly three hundred miles away from the home she'd known all her life. For champagne glasses had been distributed, and Mr. Sweeney was enthusiastically seizing the moment. He got to his feet, eager to be the first to embrace such welcome news. Only the Second Coming could have given him more pleasure.

"Then I *must* say . . ." Clumsily, he reached for his glass. "Do let me toast you both. To have you with us again, to have you home, to have you . . ." He relinquished the attempt to find an appropriate sentiment and merely raised his glass and burbled, "Simply wonderful," before he sat down.

Other congratulations followed, and with them were voiced the inevitable questions about engagement and wedding and future life. The meal could have disintegrated at that point into one large display of bonhomie, but Peter Lynley put an end to the promise of that happening.

He stood, holding his champagne glass at arm's length towards his brother. He waved it unevenly. Only the shape of the glass prevented the wine from sloshing out. "Then a toast," he said, drawing out the last word. He leaned one hand on Sasha's shoulder for support. She glanced furtively at Lynley and then said something in a low voice which Peter disregarded. "To the perfect brother," he announced. "Who has managed somehow after searching the world over—not to mention doing a fair degree of sampling the goods as he went. Right, Tommy?—to find the perfect woman with whom he can now have the perfect life. What a damned lucky fellow Lord Asherton is." He gulped his drink noisily and fell back into his chair.

That cuts it, St. James thought. He looked to see how Lynley would handle the matter, but his eyes came to rest upon Deborah instead. Face pinched, she ducked her head. No matter that her humiliation was both unwarranted and unnecessary considering its source, the fact of it alone provided a spur. St. James pushed his own chair back and rose awkwardly.

"The issue of perfection is always open to debate," he said. "I'm not eloquent enough to argue it here. I drink instead to Tommy—oldest of my friends—and to Deborah—dearest companion of my exile. My own life has been richer indeed for having had both of you part of it."

A swell of general approbation followed his words, on the heels of which the Plymouth MP lifted his glass and managed to turn his own toast into a speech cataloguing his accomplishments and his steadfast, if highly unlikely, belief in the reincarnation of the Cornish mining industry, a topic upon which Lady Augusta waxed wildly enthusiastic for several more minutes. At the end of this time, it seemed clear that whatever damage Peter Lynley had attempted to do, the company seemed intent upon ignoring him altogether, a determination fortified by Lady Asherton, who announced with a resolute air of good cheer that coffee, port, and all the postprandial etceteras would be in the drawing room.

Unlike the dining room with its silver candelabra and unobtrusive wall sconces, the drawing room was brightly lit by its two chandeliers. Here, a serving table had been laid with a coffee service and another with brandy, balloon glasses, liqueurs. With his own coffee in hand, St. James made his way to a Hepplewhite settee which was centrally located in the room. He sat and placed his coffee on the side table. He didn't really want it, couldn't think why he had taken one in the first place.

"My dear"—Lady Augusta had buttonholed Deborah by the grand piano—"I want to hear about every change you've got planned for Howenstow."

"Change?" Deborah asked her blankly.

"The nurseries need to be updated like mad. You'll know that already."

"Actually, I haven't had a chance to think much about it."

"I know you have this charming little hobby of photography—Daze told me all about it last week—but I'm glad to say you don't look at all the type of a woman who's going to put off having children in favour of a career.'' As if seeking affirmation for her statement, she stepped back and looked Deborah over, like a breeder assessing the potential of a mare.

"I'm a professional photographer," Deborah told her, stressing the adjective politely.

Lady Augusta waved that off like a fly. "You won't let that get in the way of the children."

Dr. Trenarrow, passing by, came to Deborah's rescue. "Times have changed, Augusta. We no longer live in an age where merit is determined by one's ability to reproduce. And thank God for that. Think of the limitless possibilities presented in eschewing procreation. No more thinning of familial gene pools. A future without bleeders. No Saint Vitus' dance."

"Oh, rubbish, you scientists," was Lady Augusta's riposte, but she was abashed enough to seek other conversational prey and headed in the direction of John Penellin, who was standing at the doorway to the Elizabethan gallery, brandy in hand.

St. James watched her close in on the estate manager, her fluttering scarf and ample posterior making her resemble nothing so much as the stern of a ship under sail. He heard her call out, "Those mines, Mr. Penellin," before he turned away to find that Deborah had come to join him.

"Please don't get up." She sat beside him. She was taking neither coffee nor liqueur.

"You've survived." He smiled. "Even with the silver. Not a single mistake, as far as I could tell."

"Everyone's been more than kind," she said. "Well, nearly everyone. Peter was . . ." She looked round the room as if in search of Lynley's brother, and she sighed, perhaps feeling relief that he and Sasha had left the party altogether. "Did I look petrified when I first came downstairs? I must have. Everyone was treating me like porcelain before dinner."

"Not at all." St. James reached for his coffee, but merely turned the cup aimlessly in its saucer. He wondered why Deborah had joined him like this. Her place was with Lynley who, along with Justin Brooke and Sidney, was steeped in conversation with the Plymouth MP. He heard their laughter, heard Brooke say, "Too right," heard one of them comment on the Labour Party. Sidney said something about the Prime Minister's hair. There was another burst of laughter.

Next to him, Deborah stirred, but didn't speak. It was unlikely that she had joined him for the sake of companionship or a quick postmortem of the evening's events. Yet this reticence was out of character as well. He looked up from his contemplation of her engagement ring—a heavy emerald set off with diamonds—and found her studying him with an intensity that brought the heat to his face. This sudden loss of his habitual detachment was as disconcerting as was her unnatural diffidence. We're a fine pair, he thought.

"Why did you call me that, Simon? In the dining room."

So much for diffidence. "It seemed the right thing. After all, it's the truth. You were there through everything, both you and your father."

"I see." Her hand lay next to his. He had noticed this before but had chosen to ignore it, making a deliberate effort not to move away from her like a man afraid of the potential for contact. His fingers were relaxed. He willed them to be so. And although a single movement, wearing the guise of inadvertence, would have been sufficient to cover her hand with his own, he took care to maintain between them an appropriately discreet and utterly hypocritical four inches of beautifully upholstered Hepplewhite.

The gesture, when it came, was hers. She touched his hand lightly, an innocent contact that broke through his barriers. The movement meant nothing, it promised even less. He knew that quite well. But despite this, his fingers caught hers and held.

"I do want to know why you said it," she repeated.

There was no point. It could only lead nowhere. Or worse, it could lead to an unbridled bout of suffering he'd prefer not to face.

"Simon—"

"How can I answer you? What can I possibly say that won't make us both miserable and end up leading to another row? I don't want that. And I can't think you do."

He told himself that he would adhere to every resolution he had made regarding Deborah. She was committed, he thought. Love and honour bound her to another. He would have to take solace in the fact that, in time, they might once again be the friends they had been in the past, taking pleasure in each other's company and wanting nothing more. A dozen different lies rose in his mind about what was right and possible in their situation, about duty, responsibility, commitment, and love, about the anchors of ethics and morals that held each of them fast. And still he wanted to speak, because the reality was that anything—even anger and the risk of estrangement—was better than the void.

A sudden commotion at the drawing room door precluded the possibility of further conversation. Hodge was speaking urgently to Lady Asherton while Nancy Cambrey pulled upon his arm as if she would drag him back into the corridor. Lynley went to join them. St. James did likewise. In the hush that descended upon the company, Nancy's voice rose.

"You can't. Not now."

"What is it?" Lynley asked.

"Inspector Boscowan, my lord," Hodge replied in a low voice. "He's down in the hall. Wanting to speak to John Penellin."

Only part of Hodge's statement proved true, for as he spoke, Boscowan stepped into the drawing room doorway as if he expected some sort of trouble. He looked the group over, his face apologetic, and his eyes came to rest upon John Penellin. It was clear that a duty which gave him no pleasure had brought him to interrupt the party.

The room was absolutely still. John Penellin walked towards them. He handed his brandy to Dr. Trenarrow.

"Edward," he said to Boscowan with a nod. Nancy had faded into the corridor where she slumped against a mule chest and watched the encounter. "Perhaps we can go to the estate office."

"There's no need for that, John," Boscowan said. "I'm sorry."

The implication behind the apology was obvious. Boscowan would never have come to Howenstow in this manner unless he was certain that he had his man.

"Are you arresting me?" Penellin asked the question in a manner that sounded at once both resigned and curiously without panic, as if he'd been preparing himself for this eventuality all along.

Boscowan glanced around. Every eye was fastened on the little group. He said, "Out here please," and walked into the corridor. Penellin, St. James, and Lynley followed. Another plainclothes policeman was waiting at the top of the stairs. He was bulky, with the physique of a boxer, and he watched them warily, arms crossed, hands balled into fists.

Boscowan faced Penellin, his back to the other officer. In speaking next, he crossed the line that divides police and civilian, breaking rules and regulations. But he didn't seem to be fazed by this, his words having their roots in friendship rather than in duty.

"You need a solicitor, John. We've the first of the forensic reports. It doesn't look good." And then again and in a way that left no doubt as to Boscowan's sincerity, "Truly I'm sorry."

"Fingerprints, fibres, hairs? What have you?" Lynley asked.

"The lot."

"Dad's been inside the cottage in the past," Nancy said.

Boscowan shook his head. St. James knew what that sign of negation meant. Penellin's fingerprints in the cottage could indeed be argued away by the fact that he'd been there before. But if Boscowan had fibres and hairs in his possession, the probability was that they'd come from one source: Mick Cambrey's corpse. If that was the case, the reality was that Penellin had indeed lied about his whereabouts the previous night.

"If you'll come now," Boscowan said in a more normal tone of voice. This appeared to be the signal for the other policeman. He walked to Penellin's side and took his arm. In a moment it was over.

As their steps faded down the stairs, Nancy Cambrey fainted. Lynley caught her before she hit the floor.

"Get Helen," he said to St. James and when Lady Helen was with them, they took Nancy down to Lady Asherton's day room in the east wing of the house. It offered the double benefit of being both private and comfortable. A few minutes among its family memorabilia and friendly furniture would no doubt restore Nancy to herself, Lynley decided. And he allowed himself a moment of gratitude that his mother would carry on upstairs without him until such a time as she could deal with John Penellin's arrest privately and face the turmoil that would arrive in its wake.

St. James had possessed the foresight to bring the whisky decanter from the drawing room. He pressed a glass upon Nancy. Lady Helen steadied her hand. She'd only taken a tiny sip when a tentative knock sounded on the door. It was followed, unaccountably, by Justin Brooke's voice.

"May I have a word?" He didn't wait for a response. Rather, he opened the door, popped his head inside, and said nothing until he fixed upon Lynley. "May I have a word with you?"

"A word?" Lynley demanded incredulously, wondering what on earth Brooke could possibly want. "What the devil—"

"It's important," Brooke said. He looked earnestly to the others as if for support and found it in the least likely quarter. Lady Helen spoke.

"I'll take Nancy back to the lodge, Tommy. It doesn't make sense to keep her here. She'll need to see to the baby, I'm sure."

Lynley waited until both women were gone before he spoke to Brooke who took a balloon-backed chair unbidden, straddled it backwards, and folded his arms along its top rail. Lynley leaned against his mother's desk. St. James stood by the fireplace.

"What is it that you wanted?" Lynley said to Brooke. He was

impatient with the interruption and too preoccupied to care much about hiding it.

"It's a private matter, concerning your family." Brooke canted his head towards St. James, an indication of his desire that this conference be held out of the other man's presence. St. James made a move to go.

"No, it's fine," Lynley said to him, finding himself perversely unwilling to allow Brooke the degree of control that would be implied by St. James' departure. There was something about the man that he didn't like: an ease of manner contravened by a flicker of malice in his expression.

Brooke reached for the decanter of whisky and Nancy's glass that were standing on a circular table next to his chair. He poured himself some, saying, "Very well then. I could use a drink. You?" He held the decanter first to Lynley, then to St. James. There were no other glasses in the room, so the invitation was meaningless, as Brooke no doubt knew. He drank appreciatively, said, "Good stuff," and poured himself more. "Word came back to the drawing room fast enough that Penellin's been arrested. But Penellin couldn't have killed this Mick Cambrey."

It was certainly not the sort of pronouncement which Lynley had been expecting. "If you know something about this affair, you need to tell the police. It's only indirectly my concern."

Brooke said, "It's more direct than you think."

"What are you talking about?"

"Your brother."

The clink of decanter upon glass seemed unnaturally grating and loud, as Brooke took more whisky. Lynley refused to think the patently unthinkable, or to draw the conclusion for which those two simple words asked.

"People in the drawing room just now were saying Penellin had an argument with Cambrey before his death. That was the main cause for suspicion, they said. Someone had heard about it in the village today."

"I don't see what this has to do with my brother."

"Everything, I'm afraid. Mick Cambrey didn't have an argument with Penellin. Or if he did, it didn't compare with the row he had with Peter."

Lynley stared at the man. He felt a sudden urge to throw him from the room and recognised how closely the desire was tied to an incipient dread and to the unwanted realisation that somehow this piece of information was not a surprise to him.

"What are you talking about? How do you know?"

"I was with him," Brooke replied. "And it was after Penellin. Cambrey said that much."

Lynley reached for a chair. "The story, please," he said with marked courtesy.

"Right." Brooke nodded his approval. "Sid and I had a bit of a blowup yesterday. She didn't much want to see me last night. So I went into the village. With Peter."

"Why?"

"For something to do, mainly. Peter was low on cash and he wanted to borrow some. He said he knew a bloke who'd be dealing with money that night, so we went to see him. It was Cambrey."

Lynley's eyes narrowed. "What did he need money for?"

Brooke tossed a look in St. James' direction before he replied, as if he expected a reaction from that quarter. "He wanted some coke."

"And he took you with him? Wasn't that rather short-sighted?"

"It was safe enough. Peter knew he could trust me." Brooke seemed to feel a more direct revelation was in order. "Look, I'd a stash with me yesterday, and I'd given him some. It was gone. We wanted more. But I didn't have any more money than he did, so we were on the look for it. We wanted to get high."

"I see. You've managed to get to know my brother with remarkable ease this weekend."

"People get to know others when their interests are the same."

"Quite. Yes." Lynley ignored the need to clench his fist, to strike. "Did Mick lend him money?"

"He wouldn't hear of it. That's what started the row. Peter could see it—I could see it—right there on his desk in six or ten stacks. But he wouldn't part with as much as two quid."

"What happened then?"

Brooke grimaced. "Hell, I didn't even know this bloke. When Mick and Peter started in, I just left the place. I would have liked the dope, yes. But I didn't want to get into a brawl."

"What did you do when you left?"

"Wandered round a bit till I found the pub. Had a drink and hitched a ride back later."

"Hitched a ride? With whom?"

"Farmer and his wife." Brooke grinned and added unnecessarily, "By the smell of them. Dairy, I'd guess."

"And Peter?"

"I left him arguing with Cambrey."

"Where was Sasha all this time?"

"Here. She and Peter'd gone round about a promise he'd made in London to get her some dope on his own. I think she was waiting for him to make good."

"What time did you leave the cottage?" St. James asked. His expression was stony.

Brooke looked at the room's white cornice, fixated upon its egg and dart pattern. Thinking, remembering, or playing at both. "It was ten when I got to the pub. I remember that. I checked the time."

"And did you see Peter again that night?"

"Didn't see him until this evening." Again, Brooke grinned. This time it was a just-between-us-boys sort of look, one that claimed cama-raderie and understanding. "I came back here, made it up with Sid, and spent the night occupied in her room. Fairly well occupied, as a matter of fact. Sid's that way." He pushed himself to his feet and concluded by saying, "I thought it best to tell you about your brother, rather than the police. It seemed to me that you'd know what to do. But if you think I should ring them . . ."

He let the statement slide. All of them knew it was meaningless. Nodding at them both, he left the room.

When the door closed behind him, Lynley felt in his pocket for his cigarette case. Once it was in his grasp, however, he looked at it curi-ously, saw how it winked in the light, and wondered how it had come to find its way into his hand. He didn't want to smoke.

"What shall . . ." The two words emerged hoarsely. He tried again. "What shall I do, St. James?"

"Talk to Boscowan. What else can you do?"

"He's my brother. Would you have me play Cain?"

"Shall I do it for you, then?"

At that, Lynley looked at his friend. He saw how implacable St. James' features had become. He knew that there was no reasonable al-ternative. He saw that even as he searched for one.

"Give me till the morning," he said.

14

Deborah checked the room in a cursory fashion to make sure she hadn't forgotten anything. She locked her suitcase and pulled it from the bed, deciding, as she did so, that it was just as well they were leaving Cornwall. The weather had changed during the night, and yesterday's dazzling cobalt sky was the colour of slate this morning. Sharp gusts of wind coughed intermittently against the windows, and from one which she had left partially open came the unmistakable smell of rain-laden air. However, other than the occasional rattling of windowpanes and the creak of the heavy branches of a beech tree a short distance from the house, the morning brought no additional sounds, for instinctively recognising the approach of a storm, the clamorous gulls and cormorants had vanished, seeking shelter inland.

"Miss?"

At the doorway stood one of the Howenstow maids, a young woman with a cloud of dark hair that quite overwhelmed a triangular face. Her name was Caroline, Deborah recalled, and like the other daily help in the house, she wore no uniform, merely a navy skirt, white blouse, and flat-heeled shoes. She was snug and neat looking, and she carried a tray which she used to gesture as she spoke.

"His lordship thought you'd want something before you leave for the train," Caroline said, taking the food to a small tripod table that stood near the fireplace. "He says you've just thirty minutes."

"Does Lady Helen know that? Is she up?"

"Up, dressing, and having her breakfast as well."

As if in affirmation of this, Lady Helen wandered into the room, simultaneously engaged in all three activities. She was in her stocking feet, she was munching on a wedge of toast, and she was holding up two pairs of shoes at arm's length.

"I can't decide," she said as she scrutinised them critically. "The suede are more comfortable, but the green *are* rather sweet, aren't they? I've had them both on and off a dozen times this morning."

"I should recommend the suede," Caroline said.

"Hmmm." Lady Helen dropped one suede shoe to the floor, stepped into it, dropped one of the other pair, stepped into that. "Look closely, Caroline. Are you really quite sure?"

"Quite," Caroline replied. "The suede. And if you'll give me the other pair, I'll just pop them into your suitcase."

Lady Helen waved her off for a moment. She studied her feet in the mirror that hung on the inside of the wardrobe door. "I can see your point. But look at the green. Surely, there's green in my skirt as well. Or if not, perhaps they'll provide a hint of contrast. Because I've the sweetest handbag that goes with these shoes and I've been dying to put them together somehow. One hates to admit that an impulsive purchase of shoes and bag has been wildly in vain. Deborah, what do you think?"

"The suede," Deborah said. She pushed her suitcase towards the door and went to the dressing table.

Lady Helen sighed. "Outvoted, I suppose." She watched as Caroline left the room. "I wonder if I can steal her from Tommy. Just one look at those shoes and she made up her mind. Heavens, Deborah, she'd save me hours every day. No more standing before the wardrobe, futilely trying to decide what to wear in the morning. I'd be positively liberated."

Deborah made a vague sound of response, and stared, perplexed, at the empty spot next to the dressing table. She went to the wardrobe and peered inside, feeling neither panic nor dismay at first, but merely confusion. Lady Helen chatted on.

"I victimise myself. I hear the word *sale* in reference to Harrod's, and I simply fall apart. Shoes, hats, pullovers, dresses. I even bought a pair of Wellingtons once, simply because they fit. So fetching, I thought, just the thing for mucking round Mother's garden." She inspected Deborah's breakfast tray. "Will you be eating your grapefruit?"

"No. I'm not at all hungry." Deborah went into the bathroom, came out again. She knelt on the floor to look under the bed, trying to recall where she had left the case. Certainly it had been in the room all along. She'd seen it without seeing it last night as well as the night before, hadn't she? She thought about the question, admitted to herself that she couldn't remember. Yet it was inconceivable that she might have misplaced the case, even more inconceivable that it was missing altogether. Because if it was missing and she hadn't misplaced it herself, that could only mean . . .

"Whatever are you doing?" Lady Helen asked, dipping happily into Deborah's grapefruit.

Dread was hitting her as she saw that nothing had been stored beneath the bed or hurriedly shoved there to get it out of the way. Deborah got to her feet. Her face felt cold.

Lady Helen's smile faded. "What is it? What's wrong?"

In a last and utterly useless search, Deborah returned to the wardrobe and tossed the extra pillows and blankets to the floor. "My cameras," she said. "Helen, my cameras. They're gone."

"Cameras?" Lady Helen asked blankly. "Gone? What do you mean?"

"Gone. Just what I said. *Gone.* They were in their case. You've seen it. I brought it with me this weekend. It's gone."

"But they can't be gone. They've just been misplaced. No doubt someone thought—"

"They're gone," Deborah said. "They were in a metal case. Cameras, lenses, filters. Everything."

Lady Helen replaced the bowl of grapefruit on Deborah's tray. She looked round the room. "Are you certain?"

"Of course I'm certain! Don't be so—" Deborah stopped herself and with an effort at calm said, "They were in a case by the dressing table. Look. It's not there."

"Let me ask Caroline," Lady Helen said. "Or Hodge. They may have already been taken down to the car. Or perhaps Tommy came in earlier and got them. Surely that's it. Because I can't think that anyone would actually . . ." Her voice refused to say the word *steal.* Nonetheless, the fact that it was foremost on Lady Helen's mind was obvious in the very omission.

"I haven't left the room since last night. I've only been in the bath. If Tommy came for the cameras, why wouldn't he have told me?"

"Let me ask," Lady Helen said again. She left the room to do so.

Deborah sank onto the stool in front of the dressing table, staring at the floor. The pattern of flowers and leaves in the carpet blurred before her as she considered the loss. Three cameras, six lenses, dozens of filters, all purchased from the proceeds of her first successful show in America, state-of-the-art equipment that served as the hallmark of who she had managed to become at the end of three years on her own. A professional without ties, duties, or obligations. A woman committed to the future.

Every decision she had made during those years in America had taken its legitimacy from the ultimate possession of that equipment. She could look back on every conclusion she had reached, the convictions she had developed, the deeds she had done, and feel neither guilt nor regret because she had emerged with a profession at which she was a bona fide success. That part of a life—which might have been hers to hold and love and nurture—had been mourned in secret made no difference. That she had filled her time with distractions to avoid acknowledging the worst of her loss—indeed, that she had re-evaluated all losses and defined each one as inconsequential—had no impact upon her. Everything was made acceptable and right and completely justifiable because she'd attained her goal. She was a success, possessing all the requisite signs and symbols of that achievement.

Lady Helen came back into the room. "I spoke to both Caroline and Hodge," she said. Regret made the statement hesitant. She had no need to say more. "Deborah, listen. Tommy will—"

"I don't want Tommy to replace the cameras!" Deborah cried fiercely.

A quick flash of surprise passed across Lady Helen's face. It vanished in an instant, leaving in its place an expression of perfectly impartial repose.

"I was going to say that Tommy will want to know at once. I'll fetch him."

She was gone only a few moments, returning with both Lynley and St. James. The former went to Deborah. The latter remained by the door.

"Damn and blast," Lynley muttered. "What next?" He put his arm round Deborah's shoulders and hugged her to him briefly before he knelt next to the stool and gazed into her face.

His own, she could see, was lined by fatigue. He didn't look as if he'd slept at all the previous night. She knew how worried he must be about John Penellin, and she felt a twinge of shame that she should be causing him additional distress.

"Deb darling," he said, "I'm sorry."

So he knew that the cameras had been stolen. Unlike Lady Helen, he didn't even offer the excuse that the equipment had somehow been misplaced.

"When did you last see them, Deborah?" St. James asked.

Lynley touched her hair, smoothed it back from her face. Deborah could smell the clean, fresh scent of his skin. He hadn't smoked yet, and she liked the smell of him when he hadn't yet had his first cigarette. If she could concentrate on Tommy, everything else would go away.

"Did you see them last night when you went to bed?" St. James persisted.

"They were here yesterday morning. I remember that because I replaced the camera I'd used at the play. Everything was here, right by the dressing table."

"And you don't remember seeing them after that? You didn't use them during the day?"

"I didn't use them. I wasn't even in the room until it was time to dress for the party. I might have noticed them then. I ought to have. I was in here, after all. I was right by the dressing table. But I didn't notice them last night at all. Did you, Simon?"

Lynley got to his feet. His glance went from Deborah to St. James in a curious look, perplexed but nothing more.

"I'm sure they were here," St. James said. "It was your old metal case, wasn't it?" When she nodded, he said, "I saw it by the dressing table."

"Saw it by the dressing table." Lynley repeated the comment more to himself than to the others. He looked at the spot on the floor. He looked at St. James. He looked at the bed.

"When, St. James?" He asked the question easily, three simple words. But the fact of his saying them and the deliberation of their tone added a new dimension to the conversation.

Lady Helen said, "Tommy, shouldn't we be off to the train?"

"When did you see the camera case, St. James? Yesterday? The evening? Sometime during the night? When? Were you alone? Or was Deborah—"

"Tommy," Lady Helen said.

"No. Let him answer."

St. James didn't reply. Deborah reached for Lynley's arm. She looked to Lady Helen in eloquent entreaty.

"Tommy," Lady Helen said, "this isn't—"

"I said let him answer."

A moment passed, a small eternity before St. James gave an emotionless recitation of the facts. "Helen and I managed to get a picture of Mick Cambrey yesterday from his father, Tommy. I brought it to Deborah before dinner last night. I saw her camera case then."

Lynley stared at him. A long breath left his body. "Christ," he said. "I'm sorry. That was so bloody stupid. I can't think what made me say it."

St. James could have smiled. He could have brushed off the apology or laughed off the implied insult as an understandable error. He did nothing, said nothing. He looked only at Deborah, and even then it was a glance of a moment before he looked away.

As if seeking to relieve the situation, Lady Helen said, "Were they terribly valuable, Deborah?"

"They're worth hundreds of pounds." Deborah went to the window where the light would be behind her, leaving her face in shadow. She could feel the blood pounding in her chest, on her neck, on her cheeks. She wanted, absurdly, to do nothing more than cry.

"Then someone must hope to sell them. But not in Cornwall, I dare say, at least not locally where they could be tracked down. Perhaps in Bodmin or Exeter or even in London. And if that's the case, they'd have been taken last night, during the party, I should guess. After John Penellin was arrested, things did tend to fall apart, didn't they? People were coming and going from the drawing room all the rest of the evening."

"And not everyone was in the drawing room in the first place," Deborah said. She thought of Peter Lynley and the cruelty of his toast at dinner. What better person to want to hurt her than Peter? What better way to get at Tommy than by hurting her?

St. James looked at his watch. "You ought to get Helen and Deborah to the train," he told Lynley. "There's no real point to their remaining, is there? We can deal with the cameras ourselves."

"That's best," Lady Helen agreed. "I suddenly find myself absolutely longing for the soot and grime of London, my dears." She walked towards the door, briefly grasping St. James' hand as she passed him.

When St. James started to follow her, Lynley spoke. "Simon. Forgive me. I have no excuse."

"Except your brother and John Penellin. Exhaustion and worry. It doesn't matter, Tommy."

"It does. I feel a perfect fool."

St. James shook his head, but his face was drawn. "It's nothing. Please. Forget it." He left the room.

St. James heard, rather than saw, his sister yawning in the dining room doorway. "What an evening," she said as she padded into the room and joined him at the table. She rested her head in one hand, reached for his pot of coffee, and poured herself a cup which she sugared with an air that combined liberality with general indifference. As if she hadn't bothered to look out the window prior to dressing for the day, she wore bright blue shorts, profusely decorated with coruscating silver stars, and a halter top. "Offensive after-dinner toasts, visits from the police, an arrest on the spot. It's a wonder we lived to tell the tale." She eyed the line of covered serving dishes on the sideboard, shrugged them off as possibly too troublesome a venture, and instead took a slice of bacon from her brother's plate. This she placed on a piece of his toast.

"Sid . . ."

"Hmmm?" She pulled part of the newspaper towards her. "What're you reading?"

St. James didn't reply. He'd been going through the *Spokesman,* and he wanted a moment to evaluate what he'd read.

It was a village paper, its contents comprising mostly village news. And no matter the intensity or importance of Mick Cambrey's association with the *Spokesman,* St. James found that he couldn't reasonably attribute the man's murder to what he was reading in this local journal. The news items ran the gamut from a recent wedding held on the quay at Lamorna Cove, to the conviction of a purse snatcher from Penzance, to the innovations developed on a dairy farm not far from St. Buryan. There was coverage of the Nanrunnel production of *Much Ado About Nothing*, including a profile of the girl who played Hero. Sports news consisted of an article on a local tennis match, and whoever covered the crime beat had managed to unearth only a traffic accident involving a right-of-way dispute between a lorry driver and a cow. Just the editorial page held promise, and even here that promise was directed more towards the future of the paper than to a motive for Mick Cambrey's murder.

The page held two opinion columns and seven letters. The first column had been written by Cambrey, an articulate piece on stemming the tide of weapons being run into Northern Ireland. Julianna Vendale had composed the second column on national child care. The letters, which came from both Nanrunnel and Penzance residents, dealt with previous columns on village expansion and on the local secondary school's declining O-level results. All of this reflected Mick Cambrey's efforts to make the newspaper something more than a village gossip sheet. But none of it seemed to have content likely to provoke a murder.

St. James reflected upon the fact that Harry Cambrey believed his son had been working on a story that would have been the making of the *Spokesman.* Ostensibly without confiding his intentions to his father, Mick had planned that this story would reach a wider audience than was available in this remote area of Cornwall. Thus, St. James wondered if

Cambrey could have discovered that his son was spending time, money, and effort away from the *Spokesman,* all for something that wouldn't benefit the newspaper at all. And if Cambrey had discovered that, how would he have reacted to the news? Would he have struck out in anger as he had done once before in the newspaper office?

Every question concerning the murder revolved round a decision between premeditation and passion. The fact that there had been an argument suggested passion, as did the mutilation of the body. But other details—the condition of the sitting room, the missing money—suggested premeditation. And even an autopsy would probably not generate a definitive distinction between the two.

"Where is everyone this morning?" Sidney got up from the table and took her coffee to one of the windows where she curled onto a velvet-covered bench. "What a dreary day. It's going to rain."

"Tommy's taken Deborah and Helen to catch the train for London. I've not seen anyone else."

"Justin and I ought to be off as well, I suppose. He's got work tomorrow. Have you seen him?"

"Not this morning." St. James was no mourner for that fact. He was finding that the less he saw of Brooke, the better he liked it. He could only hope that his sister would come to her senses soon and clear her life of the man.

"Perhaps I'll rout him from his room," Sidney said, but she made no move to do so and she was still sipping coffee and gazing out the window when Lady Asherton joined them. The fact that she had not come in for breakfast was evident in her choice of clothing: She wore blue jeans rolled above her ankles, a man's white cotton shirt, and a baseball cap. She was carrying a pair of heavy gardening gloves which she slapped into her palm emphatically.

"Here you are, Simon. Good," she said. "Will you come with me a moment? It's about Deborah's cameras."

"Have you found them?" St. James asked.

"Found them?" Sidney repeated blankly. "Has Deb lost her cameras on top of everything else?" She shook her head darkly and returned to the table, where she took up the part of her paper which her brother had been reading.

"In the garden," Lady Asherton said and led St. James outside, where a salty wind was fast delivering an angry-looking bank of grey clouds from the sea.

One of the gardeners was waiting for them at the furthest point of the house's south wing. He stood opposite a beech tree, secateurs in his hand and a worn woollen cap pulled low on his brow. He nodded when St. James and Lady Asherton joined him, and he directed St. James' attention to the large yew bush that abutted the house.

"Dead pity, that," the gardener said. "She be right damaged, poor thing."

"Deborah's room is just above," Lady Asherton said.

St. James looked at the plant and saw that the portion of the yew nearest the house had been destroyed, its growth split, broken, and torn off completely by an object which had, most likely, been dropped from above. The damage was recent, all the breakage fresh. The distinct scent of conifer rose from the mangled branches.

St. James stepped back and looked up at the windows. Deborah's room was directly above, with the billiard room beneath it. Both were far removed from the dining and drawing rooms where the party had gathered on the previous evening. And as far as he knew, no one had played billiards, so no one would have been witness to the noise which the camera case must have made as it crashed to the ground.

Lady Asherton spoke quietly as the gardener went back to his work, clipping off the ruined branches and stowing them in a plastic rubbish sack tucked under his arm. "There's a margin of relief in all this, Simon. At least we know no one from the house took the cameras."

"Why do you say that?"

"It hardly makes sense that one of us would take them and drop them outside. Far easier to hide them in one's room and slip off with them later, wouldn't you agree?"

"Easier, yes. But not as wise. Especially if someone inside the house wanted to make it look as if an outsider took the cameras in the first place. But even that's not a wise plan. Because who were the technical outsiders last night? Mr. and Mrs. Sweeney, Dr. Trenarrow, your sister-in-law, the MP from Plymouth."

"John Penellin," she added. "The daily help from the village."

"An unlikely lot to be stealing cameras." From her expression, he could tell that Lady Asherton had already done some considerable thinking about Deborah's cameras, about where they might be, about who had taken them. Her words, however, acted to camouflage this.

"I'm having difficulty understanding why they were stolen in the first place."

"They're valuable. They can be sold by someone who needs money."

Her face crumpled momentarily then regained composure.

St. James showed mercy by saying, "The house was open during the party. Someone could have got in while we were in the dining room.

It would have been no large matter to slip up to Deborah's room and take the cameras then.''

"But why take the cameras at all, Simon, if it's a matter of money? Why not take something else? Something even more valuable?''

"What?'' he asked. "Everything else is too easily associated with Howenstow. The silver's marked. The family crest is on everything. Surely you wouldn't expect someone to cart off one of the paintings and hope it wouldn't be noticed as missing until the next day.''

She turned her head to look out at the park, a movement designed merely to avert her face for a moment. "It can't be a question of money,'' she said, twisting her gardening gloves in her hands. "It can't, Simon. You do know that.''

"Then perhaps Mrs. Sweeney objected to having her photograph taken after all,'' he suggested.

She smiled bleakly at that but went along with his effort to divert her. "Could she have slipped out to the loo sometime after dinner and trundled through the house looking for Deborah's room?''

Her question brought them back to the inescapable reality. Whoever had taken the cameras had also known which room was Deborah's.

"Has Tommy spoken to Peter this morning?'' St. James asked.

"Peter's not up yet.''

"He vanished after dinner, Daze.''

"I know.''

"And do you know where he went? Where Sasha went?''

She shook her head. "A walk on the grounds, down to the cove, for a drive. Perhaps to the lodge to see Mark Penellin.'' She sighed. The effort seemed too much. "I can't believe he's taken Deborah's cameras. He's sold most of his own things. I know that. I pretend not to, but I know it. Still, I don't believe he'd actually steal things and sell them. Not Peter. I won't believe that.''

A shout rose from the park as she finished speaking. Someone was coming towards the house at a hobbling run, a man who alternately clutched his side then his thigh with one hand while with the other he waved a cap in the air. All the time he continued to shout.

"Jasper, m'lady,'' the gardener said, joining them with his rubbish sack trailing behind him.

"Whatever is he up to?'' As he reached the gatehouse, Lady Asherton raised her voice. "Stop shouting like that, Jasper. You're frightening us all to death.''

Jasper dashed to her side, wheezing and gasping. He seemed unable to gather enough breath to put together a coherent sentence.

" 'Tis 'im,'' he panted. "Down the cove.''

Lady Asherton looked at St. James. They shared the same thought. Lady Asherton took a step away as if to distance herself from information she couldn't bear to hear.

"Who?'' St. James asked. "Jasper, who's at the cove?''

Jasper bent double, coughed, " 'N the cove!''

"For heaven's sake—''

Jasper straightened, looked around, and pointed an arthritic finger at the front door where Sidney stood, apparently seeking the source of the disturbance.

" 'Er man,'' he gasped. "He be dead down the cove.''

15

When St. James finally caught up with her, his sister had already reached the cove, far in advance of everyone else. Somewhere in her desperate flight through the park and the woodland, she had fallen, and blood streaked in a furcate pattern down one arm and along one leg. From the cliff top, he saw her fling herself at Brooke's body, snatching him up as if by that action she could infuse him with life. She was speaking in an incoherent fashion—inarticulate words, not sentences—as she held his body to hers. Brooke's head hung in an impossible position, testimony to the manner in which he had died.

Sidney lowered him to the ground. She opened his mouth, covering it with her own in a useless attempt at resuscitation. Even from the cliff top, St. James could hear her small, frantic cries as each breath she gave him produced no response. She pounded on his chest. She pulled open his shirt. She threw herself the length of his body and pressed against him as if to arouse him in death as she had done in life. It was a mindless, grim mimicry of seduction. St. James grew cold as he watched. He said her name, then called to her, to no avail.

Finally, she looked up the face of the cliff and saw him. She stretched out one hand as if in supplication, and at last she began to cry. It was a horrible ululation, part despair and part grief, a weeping the source of which was as primordial as it was timeless. She covered Brooke's bruised face with kisses before she lowered her head and rested it on his chest. And she wept, in sorrow, in anger, in rage. She grabbed the body by the shoulders, lifted and shook it as she shouted Brooke's name. In reply the lifeless head bobbed ghoulishly on its splintered neck in a danse macabre.

St. James stood motionless, forcing himself to keep his eyes on his sister, making himself a witness to the worst part of her grief, accepting the watching as punishment, just and true, for the sin of possessing a body so ruined that it would not allow him to go to her aid. Immobilised and inwardly cursing with a rising ferocity that was fast approaching panic, he listened to Sidney's keening wail. He swung round viciously at the touch of a hand on his arm. Lady Asherton stood there, behind her the gardener and half a dozen others from the house.

"Get her *away* from him." He barely managed the words. But his speaking released the rest of them into action.

With a final, worried look at his face, Lady Asherton began a nimble descent of the cliff. The others followed, carrying blankets, a makeshift stretcher, a thermos, a coil of rope. Although they all climbed down quickly, it seemed to St. James that they moved in slow motion in the manner of mimes.

Three of them reached Sidney simultaneously, and Lady Asherton pulled her away from the body which she continued to shake with a wild futility. As Sidney fought to go back to it, beginning to scream, Lady Asherton shouted something over her shoulder which St. James could not distinguish. In answer, one of the men handed her an open vial. She pulled Sidney to her, grabbed her by the hair, and thrust the vial under her nose. Sidney's head flew back. Her hand went to her mouth. She spoke brokenly to Lady Asherton, who in answer pointed up the cliff.

Sidney began to climb. The gardener helped her. Then the others from the house. All of them saw that she neither stumbled nor fell. And within a few moments, St. James was pulling her fiercely into his arms. He held her, pressing his cheek to the top of her head and fighting back an emotional reaction of his own that promised to overwhelm him if he gave it free rein. When the worst of her weeping had subsided, he began to lead her in the direction of the house, both his arms round her, somehow afraid that if he released her, he would be giving her back to hysteria, back to the body of her lover on the beach.

They passed under the trees of the woodland. St. James was hardly aware of the progress they made. Nor was he aware of the rushing sound of the river, the rich scent of vegetation, the springy feel of the loamy ground beneath their feet. If his clothing was caught or snagged by the bushes that encroached upon the narrow path, he took no notice.

The air had grown quite heavy with an approaching storm by the time they reached the Howenstow wall and went through the gate. The tree leaves susurrated as the swelling wind tossed them, and up the trunk of one ash a grey squirrel scampered, disappearing into its branches for shelter. Sidney raised her head from her brother's chest.

"It'll rain," she said. "Simon, he'll get wet."

St. James tightened his arms. He kissed the top of her head. "No, it's all right." He attempted to sound more like the older brother she knew, the one who had taken care of her nighttime monsters, the one who could make bad dreams go away. *But not this one, Sid.* "They'll take care of him. You'll see."

Large, heavy drops splattered noisily on the leaves. In his arms, Sidney shivered.

"How Mummy shouted at us!" she whispered.

"Shouted? When?"

"You opened all the nursery windows to see how much rain would come into the room. She shouted and shouted. She hit you as well." Her body heaved with a sob. "I never could bear to see Mummy hit you."

"The carpet was ruined. No doubt I deserved it."

"But it was my idea. And I let you take the punishment." She brought her hand to her face. Blood had streaked between her fingers. She began to weep again. "I'm sorry."

He stroked her hair. "It's all right, love. I'd quite forgotten. Believe me."

"How could I do that to you, Simon? You were my favourite brother. I loved you best. Nanny told me how bad it was to love you more than Andrew or David, but I couldn't help it. I loved you best. Then I let you take a beating and it was my fault and I never said a word." Her raised face was wet with tears that, St. James knew, in reality had nothing to do with their childhood disputes.

"Let me tell you something, Sid," he confided, "but you must promise never to say anything to David or Andrew. You were my favourite as well. You still are, in fact."

"Really?"

"Absolutely."

They came to the gatehouse and entered the garden as the wind picked up, tearing at the heads of roses, sending a shower of petals into their path. Although the rain began to beat against them aggressively, they didn't hurry their pace. By the time they reached the doorway, they were both quite wet.

"Mummy will shout at us now," Sidney said as St. James closed the door behind them. "Shall we hide?"

"We'll be safe enough for now."

"I'll not let her beat you."

"I know that, Sid." St. James led his sister towards the stairway, taking her hand when she hesitated and gazed around, clearly confused. "It's just this way," he urged her.

At the top of the stairs, he saw Cotter coming towards him, a small tray in his hands. At the sight of him, St. James gave a moment of thanksgiving over to Cotter's ability to read his mind.

"Saw you comin'," Cotter explained and nodded at the tray. "It's brandy. Is she . . ." He jerked his head towards Sidney, his brow furrowing at the sight of her.

"She'll be all right in a bit. If you'll help me, Cotter. Her room's this way."

Unlike Deborah's room, Sidney's was neither cavelike nor sepulchral. Overlooking a small, walled garden at the rear of the house, it was painted and papered in a combination of yellow and white, with a floral carpet of pastels on the floor. St. James sat his sister on the bed and went to draw the curtains while Cotter poured brandy and held it to her lips. "A bit o' this, Miss Sidney," Cotter said solicitously. "It'll warm you up nice."

She drank cooperatively. "Does Mummy know?" she asked.

Cotter glanced warily at St. James. "Have a bit more," he said.

St. James rooted through a drawer, looking for her nightdress. He found it under a Sidney-like pile of jerseys, jewellery, and stockings.

"You must get out of those wet things," he told her. "Cotter, will you find a towel for her hair? And something for the cuts?"

Cotter nodded, eyeing Sidney cautiously before he left the room. Alone with his sister, St. James undressed her, tossing her wet clothes onto the floor. He drew her nightdress over her head, pulling her arms gently through the thin satin straps. She said nothing and didn't seem to realise he was present at all. When Cotter returned with towel and plaster, St. James rubbed Sidney's hair roughly. He saw to her arms and legs and the muddy splatters on her feet. Swinging her legs up on the bed, he pulled the blankets round her. She submitted to it all like a child, like a doll.

"Sid," he whispered, touching her cheek. He wanted to talk about Justin Brooke. He wanted to know if they had been together in the night. He wanted to know when Brooke had gone to the cliff. Above all, he wanted to know why.

She didn't respond. She stared at the ceiling. Whatever she knew would have to wait.

Lynley parked the Rover at the far end of the courtyard and entered the house through the northwest door between the gun room and the servants' hall. He had seen the line of vehicles on the drive—two police cars, an unmarked saloon, and an ambulance with its windscreen wipers still running—so he was not unprepared to be accosted by Hodge as he quickly passed through the domestic wing of the house. They met outside the pantry.

"What is it?" Lynley asked the old butler. He tried to sound reasonably concerned without revealing his incipient panic. Upon seeing the cars through the wind-driven rain, his first thought had run unveeringly towards Peter.

Hodge gave the information willingly enough and in a fashion designed to reveal nothing of his own feelings in the matter. It was Mr. Brooke, he told Lynley. He'd been taken to the old schoolroom.

If the manner in which Hodge had relayed the information had been fleeting cause for hope—nothing could be terribly amiss if Brooke hadn't been taken directly to hospital—hope dissipated when Lynley entered the schoolroom in the east wing of the house a few minutes later. The body lay shrouded by blankets on a long scarred table at the room's centre, the very same table at which generations of young Lynleys had done their childhood lessons before being packed off to school. A group of men stood in hushed conversation round it, among them Inspector Boscowan and the plainclothes sergeant who had accompanied him to pick up John Penellin on the previous evening. Boscowan was talking to the group in general, issuing some sort of instructions to two crime-scene men whose trouser legs were muddy and whose jacket shoulders bore large wet patches from the rain. The police pathologist was with them, identifiable by the medical bag at her feet. It was unopened, and she didn't look as if she intended to do any preliminary examining of the body. Nor did the crime-scene men seem prepared to do any work at present. Which led Lynley to the only conclusion possible: Wherever Brooke had died, it hadn't been in the schoolroom.

He saw St. James standing in one of the window embrasures, giving his attention to what could be seen of the garden through the rain-streaked glass.

"Jasper found him in the cove." St. James spoke quietly when

Lynley joined him. He did not turn away from the window. His own clothes had had a recent wetting, Lynley saw, and his shirt bore streaks of blood which the rain had elongated like a waterwash of paint. "It looks like an accident. It seems there was slippage at the top of the cliff. He lost his footing." He looked past Lynley's shoulder at the group round the body, then back at Lynley once again. "At least, that's what Boscowan's considering for now."

St. James didn't ask the question that Lynley heard behind the final guarded statement. He was grateful for the respite, however long his friend intended it to be. He said, "Why was the body moved, St. James? Who moved it? Why?"

"Your mother. It had begun to rain. Sid got to him before the rest of us. I'm afraid none of us were thinking too clearly at the moment, least of all myself." A yew branch, struck by a gust of wind, scratched against the window in front of them. Rain created a sharp tattoo. St. James moved farther into the embrasure and lifted his eyes to the upper floor of the wing opposite the schoolroom, to the corner bedroom next to Lynley's own. "Where's Peter?"

The respite had been brief indeed. Lynley felt the sudden need to lie, to protect his brother in some way, but he couldn't do it. Nor could he say what drove him to the truth, whether it was priggish morality or an unspoken plea for the other man's help and understanding. "He's gone."

"Sasha?"

"As well."

"Where?"

"I don't know."

St. James' reaction was a single word, sighed more than spoken. "Great." Then, "How long? Was his bed slept in last night? Was hers?"

"No." Lynley didn't add that he'd seen as much at half past seven this morning when he'd gone to speak to his brother. He didn't tell him that he'd sent Jasper out to search for Peter at a quarter to eight. Nor did he describe the horror he'd felt, seeing the police cars and ambulance lined up in front of Howenstow, thinking Peter had been found dead, and recognising in his reaction to that thought a small measure of relief behind the dread. He saw St. James reflectively considering Brooke's covered body. "Peter had nothing to do with this," he said. "It was an accident. You said that yourself."

"I wonder whether Peter knew that Brooke spoke to us last night," St. James said. "Would Brooke have told him so? And if he did, why?"

Lynley recognised the speculation that drove the questions. It was the very same speculation he was facing himself. "Peter's not a killer. You know that."

"Then you'd better find him. Killer or not, he has a bit of explaining to do, doesn't he?"

"Jasper's been out looking for him since early this morning."

"I did wonder what he'd been doing at the cove. He thought Peter was there?"

"There. At the mill. He's been looking everywhere. Off the estate as well."

"Are Peter's things still here?"

"I . . . no." Lynley knew St. James well enough to see the reasoning that came upon the heels of his answer. If Peter had run from Howenstow with no time to lose, knowing his life was in danger, he'd be likely to leave his belongings behind. If, on the other hand, he had left after committing a murder that he knew wouldn't be discovered for some hours, he'd have plenty of time to pack whatever possessions he'd brought with him to Howenstow. That done, he could steal off into the night, with no one the wiser until Brooke's body was found. If he had killed him. If Brooke had been murdered at all. Lynley forced himself to keep in mind the fact that they were calling it an accident. And surely the crime-scene men knew what they were looking at when they made their observations at the site of an untimely death. Earlier in the morning, the thought of Peter having stolen Deborah's cameras in order to sell them and purchase cocaine had been repellent, a cause for disbelief and denial. Now it was welcome. For how likely was it that his brother had been involved in both the disappearance of the cameras and Justin Brooke's death? And if his mind was focussed on his body's need for cocaine, why pause in his pursuit of the drug to eliminate Brooke?

He knew the answer, of course. But that answer tied Peter to Mick Cambrey's death, a death that no one was calling an accident.

"We'll be taking the body now." The plainclothes sergeant had come to join them. In spite of the rain, he smelled heavily of sweat and his forehead was oily with perspiration. "With your permission."

Lynley nodded sharply in acquiescence and longed for liquor to soothe his nerves. As if in answer, the schoolroom doors opened and his mother entered, pushing a drinks trolley on which she'd assembled two urns, three full decanters of spirits, and several plates of biscuits. Her blue jeans and shoes were stained with mud, her white shirt torn, her hair dishevelled. But as if her appearance were the least of her concerns, when she spoke, she took command of the situation.

"I don't pretend to know your regulations, Inspector," she told Boscowan. "But it does seem reasonable that you might be allowed something to take the edge off the chill. Coffee, tea, brandy, whisky. Whatever you'd like. Please help yourselves."

Boscowan nodded his thanks and, having received this much permission, his officers occupied themselves at the trolley. Boscowan strolled over to Lynley and St. James.

"Was he a drinker, my lord?"

"I didn't know him that well. But he was drinking last night. We all were."

"Drunk?"

"He didn't appear to be. Not when I last saw him."

"And when was that?"

"When the party broke up. Round midnight. Perhaps a bit later."

"Where?"

"In the drawing room."

"Drinking?"

"Yes."

"But not drunk?"

"He could have been. I don't know. He wasn't acting drunk." Lynley recognised the intention behind the questions. If Brooke had been drunk, he fell to his death. If he had been sober, he was pushed. But Lynley felt the need to excuse the death as an accident, whatever Brooke's condition last night. "Drunk or sober, he'd never been here before. He wasn't familiar with the lay of the land."

Boscowan nodded, but nothing in his manner suggested conviction. "No doubt the postmortem will tell the tale."

"It was dark. The cliff's high."

"Dark if the man went out in the night," Boscowan said. "He could have done so this morning."

"How was he dressed?"

Boscowan's shoulders lifted, a partial acknowledgement of the accuracy of Lynley's question. "In his evening clothes. But no one's to say he wasn't up until dawn with one member of the party or another. Until we have a time of death, we can be certain of nothing. Except the fact that he's dead. And we're certain of that." He nodded and joined his men by the trolley.

"A thousand and one questions he's not asking, St. James," Lynley said.

The other man listed them. "Who saw him last? Has anyone else gone missing from the estate? Who was here at the party? Who else was on the grounds? Is there any reason why someone might want to harm him?''

"Why isn't he asking?''

"He's waiting for the postmortem, I should guess. It's to his advantage that this be an accident.''

"Why?''

"Because he's got his man for Cambrey's murder. And John Penellin couldn't have killed Brooke.''

"You're implying there's a connection.''

"There is. There must be.'' A blur of movement on the drive outside caught their attention. "Jasper,'' St. James noted.

The old man was trudging through puddles, heading towards the west wing of the house.

"Let's see what he has to say,'' Lynley said.

They found him just outside the servants' hall where he was shaking the rain off a battered sou'wester. He did the same to an antique mackintosh and hung both on a wall peg before he struggled out of dark green gumboots that were caked with mud. He nodded curtly at Lynley and St. James, and when he was quite ready, followed them back to the smoking room, where he accepted a whisky to ward off the cold.

"Nowheres to be found,'' he told Lynley. "But 'r boat's gone from Lamorna Cove.''

"It's what?'' Lynley said. "Jasper, are you certain?''

"Course I be certain. 'Tain't there.''

Lynley stared at the fox on the overmantel and tried to understand, but all that came to mind were details. They refused to coalesce. The family's thirty-five-foot sloop was docked at Lamorna. Peter had been sailing since he was five years old. The weather had been promising a storm all day. No one with any sense or experience would have taken a boat out. "It must have broken loose of its mooring somehow.''

Jasper made a sound of derision, but his face was blank when Lynley swung towards him again. "Where else did you check?''

"Ever'place. 'Tween Nanrunnel and Treen.''

"Trewoofe? St. Buryan? Did you go inland?''

"Aye. A bit. No need t' go far, m'lord. If the lad be on foot, someone's like to see him. But no one makes the claim.'' Jasper pulled on his jaw, rubbing his fingers through the stubble of his beard. "Way I see, either him and the lady's in hiding round here or they got a ride direct soon's they left Howenstow. Or they took the boat.''

"He wouldn't have done it. He knows better than that. He's not entirely . . .'' Lynley stopped. There was no need for Jasper to hear the worst of his fears. No doubt the man knew every one of them already. "Thank you, Jasper. Make sure you get something to eat."

The old man nodded and headed for the door. He paused at the threshold, however. "John Penellin got took last night, I hear."

"Yes. He did."

Jasper's mouth worked, as if he wished to say more but was hesitant to do so.

"What is it?" Lynley asked.

"He oughtn't take blame for nobody, you ask me," Jasper said and left them.

"What more does Jasper know?" St. James asked when they were alone.

Lynley was staring at the carpet, lost in thought. He roused himself to say, "Nothing, I should guess. It's just what he feels."

"About John?"

"Yes. Peter as well. If there's guilt to be assessed, Jasper knows where it should lie." Lynley had never felt so incapable of either action or decision. It seemed as if his life were spinning out of control and all he could do was watch the various pieces fly haphazardly into space. All he could say was, "He wouldn't take the boat. Not in this weather. Where would he go? And why?"

He heard St. James move and looked up to see the compassion on his face. "Perhaps he's still somewhere on the estate, Tommy. Perhaps he doesn't even know what's happened and his disappearance is altogether unconnected to Justin Brooke."

"And to the cameras?"

"To those as well."

Lynley looked away, to the pictures on the wall, all those generations of Lynleys who fit the mould, did their crewing at Oxford, and took their places at Howenstow without a single howl of protest.

"I don't believe that, St. James. Not for a moment. Do you?"

His friend sighed. "Frankly? No."

16

"Heavens, to what depths have we managed to slither?" Lady Helen said. She dropped her suitcase, sighed, and let her handbag dangle forlornly from her fingertips. "Lunching at Paddington Station. Behaviour so utterly reprehensible that I can hardly believe I allowed myself to engage in it."

"It was *your* suggestion after all, Helen." Deborah set her own luggage on the floor and looked round the bed-sitting room with a smile of contentment. It felt unaccountably good to be home, even if home was only a single room in Paddington. At least it was her own.

"I plead utter guilt. But when one is in the absolute throes of starvation, when demise is the probable consequence of even a moment's epicurean snobbery, what *is* one to do but rush madly towards the first cafeteria that comes into sight?" She shuddered, as if stricken by the recollection of what she'd found heaped upon her luncheon plate. "Can you imagine a more despicable thing to do to a sausage?"

Deborah laughed. "Would you like a restorative? A cup of tea? I've even got a recipe for a health drink you might like. Tina gave it to me. A pick-me-up, she called it."

"No doubt 'picked up' is just what she needed after an encounter with Mick Cambrey, if his father's to be believed," Lady Helen said. "But I'll forego that pleasure for now, if I may. Shall we pop next door with his picture?"

Deborah pulled it from her shoulder bag and led the way. The corridor was narrow, lined with doors on both sides, and the floor gave off the sharp scent of a carpet that was relatively new. It also served to muffle their footsteps, and as if this damper upon their approach encouraged other caution, Deborah rapped upon Tina's door softly.

"Tina's . . . well, she's a night owl, I suppose," she explained to Lady Helen. "So she may not be up yet."

That appeared to be the case, as Deborah's knocking brought no response. She tried a second time, a bit louder. And then a third, calling, "Tina?"

In answer, the door opposite opened and an elderly woman peered out. She wore a large checked handkerchief over her head, tied under her chin like a babushka. It served to cover her hair, which was tightly pinned in what appeared to be an infinite number of grey curls.

"She's not 'ere." The woman clutched to her chest a thin purple dressing gown, printed in a design of hideous orange flowers and palmate green leaves that were enough to make one eschew travelling in the tropics forever. "Been gone two days."

"How distressing," Lady Helen said. "Do you know where she's gone?"

"I'd like to know, wouldn't I?" the woman said. "She's borrowed my iron and I could do with it back."

"No doubt," Lady Helen said with complete sympathy as if the woman's manner of dress in the middle of the afternoon—deshabille with a vengeance—had been provoked solely by the loss of her iron. "Shall I see if I can get it for you?" She turned to Deborah. "Who manages the building?"

"There's a caretaker on the ground floor," Deborah said and added in a low voice, "But, Helen, you can't—"

"Then I'll pop down directly, shall I?" She fluttered her fingers and walked to the lift.

The old woman watched their exchange suspiciously. She eyed Deborah from head to toe. Nervously, Deborah smiled, trying to think of a casual remark about the building, the weather, or anything else that might keep the woman from wondering why Lady Helen was so charmingly intent upon fetching an iron for a complete stranger. She gave up the effort when nothing came to mind, retreating to her own flat where Lady Helen joined her in less than ten minutes, in victorious possession of the key to Tina's door.

Deborah was astonished. "How on earth did you manage it?"

Lady Helen laughed. "Don't you think I look the smallest bit like Tina's only sister, come all the way from Edinburgh to spend a few days catching up on sororal chitchat?"

"You convinced him of that?"

"It was such a performance, I almost convinced myself. Shall we?"

They returned to the flat. Deborah felt a bit weak at the thought of what Lady Helen clearly proposed to do.

"This can't be legal," she said. "Aren't we breaking and entering?"

"Entering perhaps," Lady Helen replied cheerfully as she inserted the key in the lock without the slightest hesitation. "But hardly breaking. After all, we've got the key. Ah. Here we are. And not even a squeak to alert the neighbours."

"I *am* the neighbours."

Lady Helen laughed. "How convenient."

The flat was identical in size and shape to Deborah's, although it contained more furniture, each piece an indication of considerable expense. No chintz-covered three-piece suite for Tina Cogin; no second-hand tables; no cheap prints on the walls. Instead, gleaming hardwoods filled the room—oak and mahogany, rosewood and birch. Beneath them lay a hand-loomed rug while above them a tapestry on the wall had the look of having been crafted by an experienced artisan. Clearly, the room's occupant had a penchant for luxury.

"Well," Lady Helen said as she looked all this over, "there must be something to be said for her line of work. Ah, there's the iron. Let's not forget to take that with us when we leave."

"Helen, aren't we leaving now?"

"In a moment, darling. First, just a peek here and there to get a feeling for the woman."

"But we can't—"

"We'll want something to tell Simon when we phone him, Deborah. As things stand now, if Tina's not back by evening, we'll have nothing to report but a knock gone unanswered at her door. What a waste of everyone's energy that would be."

"What if she walks in on us? Helen! Really."

Every moment anticipating Tina's return and wondering what on earth they would say to her when she walked in the door and found them making fast and loose with her belongings, Deborah followed Lady Helen into the tiny kitchen and watched in an agony of nerves as she blithely opened the cupboards. There were only two, both containing the barest necessities in the smallest sizes available: coffee, salt, sugar, condiments, a package of savoury biscuits, a tin of soup, another of grapefruit segments, another of cereal. On one shelf sat two plates, two bowls, two cups, and four glasses. On the work top beneath was a bottle of wine, previously opened and two-thirds full. Beyond a small tin coffee pot, a dented pan, and an enamel kettle, the kitchen contained nothing else. And even what there was provided little enough information about Tina Cogin herself. Lady Helen summed it up.

"She doesn't seem to cook her meals here, does she? Of course, there are dozens of take-aways on Praed Street, so I suppose she could be bringing food in."

"But if she entertains men?"

"That's the question, isn't it? Well, there's the bottle of wine. Perhaps that's all the entertainment she provides before she and her caller get down to business. Let's see what else we have."

Lady Helen crossed to the wardrobe and pulled it open to reveal a row of evening and cocktail dresses, half a dozen wraps—one of which was fur—with an array of high-heeled pumps lined beneath them. A top shelf held a collection of hat boxes; a middle shelf contained a stack of folded negligees. The bottom shelf was empty, but it had collected no dust, giving the impression that something had been kept there regularly.

Lady Helen tapped her cheek and gave a quick inspection to the chest of drawers. "Just her underclothes," she told Deborah after a cursory glance inside. "They appear to be silk, but I shall draw the line at fingering my way through them." She pushed the drawers closed and leaned against the chest, arms crossed in front of her, frowning at the wardrobe. "Deborah, there's something . . . just a moment. Let me see." She went into the bathroom and called out behind her, "Why don't you have a go with the desk?"

The medicine cabinet opened, a drawer scraped against wood, a catch clicked, paper rustled. Lady Helen murmured to herself.

Deborah looked at her watch. Less than five minutes had passed since they'd entered the flat. It felt like an hour.

She went to the desk. Nothing was on its top save a telephone, an answering machine, and a pad of paper which Deborah, feeling ridiculously like a celluloid detective yet all the time lacking any better idea of what to do with herself, held up to the light to check for the indentations that previous writing might have made. Seeing nothing save the single pressure point of a full stop or a dot of an *i*, she went on to the drawers but found two of them empty. The third held a savings passbook, a manila folder, and a solitary index card. Deborah picked this up.

"Odd," Lady Helen said from the bathroom doorway. "She's been gone two days, according to your neighbour, but she's left all her make-up behind. She's taken none of her evening clothes, but every ordinary garment she owns is missing. And there's a set of those dreadful fingernail tips in the bathroom. The kind one glues on. Why on earth would she take her fingernails off? They're such hell to put on in the first place.''

"Perhaps they're spares," Deborah said. "Perhaps she's gone to the country. She might be somewhere she won't need fancy clothes, where artificial fingernails would get in the way. The Lake District. Fishing in Scotland. To see relatives on a farm." Deborah saw where her trail of ideas was leading. Lady Helen completed it.

"To Cornwall," she said and nodded at the index card. "What have you there?"

Deborah examined it. "Two telephone numbers. Perhaps one is Mick Cambrey's. Shall I copy them?"

"Do." Lady Helen came to look over her shoulder. "I'm beginning to admire her. Here I am, so attached to my appearance that I wouldn't even consider venturing anywhere without at least one vanity case crammed to the brim with cosmetics. And there she is. The all-or-nothing woman. Either casual to a fault or dressed to . . ." Lady Helen faltered.

Deborah looked up. Her mouth felt dry. "Helen, she couldn't have killed him." Yet even as she said it, her discomfort grew. What, after all, did she know about Tina? Nothing really, beyond a single conversation which had revealed little more than a weakness for men, an affinity for nightlife, and a concern about ageing. Still one could certainly *sense* evil in people, no matter their attempts to disguise it. One could certainly sense the potential for rage. And none of that had been present in Tina. Yet as she considered Mick Cambrey's death and the very fact of his presence in Tina Cogin's life, Deborah had to admit that she wasn't so sure.

She reached blindly for the folder as if it contained a verification of Tina's lack of guile. *Prospects* was printed across the tab. Inside, a clip held together a sheaf of papers.

"What is it?" Lady Helen asked.

"Names and addresses. Telephone numbers."

"Her client list?"

"I shouldn't think so. Look. There are at least a hundred names. Women as well as men."

"A mailing list?"

"I suppose it might be. There's a savings book as well." Deborah slid this out of its plastic folder.

"Tell all," Lady Helen said. "Is her lifestyle profitable? Shall I change my line of work?"

Deborah read the list of deposits, flipped back to the name. She felt a rush of surprise. "This isn't hers," she said. "It belongs to Mick Cambrey. And whatever he was doing, it was wildly profitable."

"Mr. Allcourt-St. James? This *is* a pleasure." Dr. Alice Waters rose from her chair and shooed off the lab assistant who had shown St. James to her office. "I thought I recognised you at Howenstow this morning. Hardly the time for introductions, however. What brings you to my den?"

It was an apt choice of words, for the office of Penzance CID's forensic pathologist was little more than a windowless cubicle on the verge of being overcome by bookshelves, an ancient roll-top desk, a medical school skeleton wearing a World War II gas mask, and stacks of scientific journals. All that remained of the floor space was a trail that led from the doorway to the desk. A chair sat next to this—curiously out of place and intricately carved in a design of flowers and birds that was more suggestive of a country house dining room than a department of forensic pathology—and after offering St. James her hand in a cool, firm shake, she waved him into it.

"Take the throne," she said. "Circa 1675. It was a good period for chairs if one doesn't mind a bit of excessive ornamentation."

"You're a collector?"

"Takes one's mind off the job." She sank into her own chair—a piece of wounded leather whose surface was cracked and wrinkled—and rooted through the papers on her desk until she found a small carton of chocolates which she presented to him. When he had made his selection, a process she watched with a good deal of interest, she took a chocolate herself, biting into it with the satisfaction of a discerning gourmet. "Just read your piece on A-B-O secretors last week," she said. "I hardly thought I'd be having the pleasure of meeting you as well. Have you come about this Howenstow business?"

"The Cambrey death, actually."

Behind her large-framed spectacles, Dr. Waters' eyebrows rose. She finished her chocolate, wiped her fingers on the lapel of her lab coat, and took a folder from beneath an African violet that looked as if it hadn't been watered in months.

"Not the smallest indication of activity for weeks, and suddenly I've two corpses on my hands in less than forty-eight hours." She flipped the folder open, read for a moment, then snapped it shut. She reached for a skull which grinned at them from one of the bookshelves and dislodged a paperclip from its eye socket. It had obviously been a demonstration piece in many previous explanations, for pen marks dotted it liberally and a large red X had at one time been drawn directly upon the squamosal suture. "Two blows to the head. He took the more severe of the two here on the parietal region. A fracture resulted."

"Have you an idea of the weapon?"

"I wouldn't say weapon so much as source. He fell against something."

"He couldn't have been struck?"

She took another chocolate, shaking her head and pointing to the skull. "Look at where the fracture would be, my good man. He wasn't overly tall—between five-eight and five-nine—but he'd have to be sitting for anyone to hit him there with enough force to kill him."

"Someone creeping up on him?"

"Couldn't have happened. The blow didn't come from above. Even if it had, to have placed a blow there, the killer would have had to stand in such a way that Cambrey would have seen him in his peripheral vision. He would have made an attempt to block the blow in some way and we'd have evidence on the body. Bruising or abrasions. But we've neither."

"The killer may have been too fast for him."

She turned the skull. "Possibly. But that wouldn't explain the second blow. Another fracture, less severe, in the right frontal region. For your scenario, the killer would have hit him in the back of the head, asked him to kindly turn round, then hit him in the front."

"Are we talking about an accident, then? Cambrey stumbling on his own, falling, and then later someone coming to the cottage, finding the body, and mutilating it for the sheer enjoyment of castration?"

"Hardly." She replaced the skull and learned back in her chair. The light from the ceiling winked against her spectacles and shone in her hair, which was short, straight, and artificially blue-black. "Here's the scenario as I've worked it out. Cambrey's standing, having a conversation with the killer. It grows into an argument. He takes a tremendous blow on the jaw—there was heavy bruising of the submaxilla and that was the only significant bruising on the body—which sends him falling back against an object perhaps four and a half feet from the floor."

St. James thought about the sitting room in Gull Cottage. He knew Dr. Waters had been there herself. She would have done a preliminary examination of the body there on Friday night. And no matter one's determination to wait for autopsy results before formulating an opinion, she would have begun developing ideas the moment she saw the corpse. "The mantel?"

She cocked an affirmative finger at him. "Cambrey's weight increases the velocity of his fall. The result is our first fracture. From the mantel, then, he falls again, but slightly to the side this time. And he hits the right frontal region of his skull on another object."

"The hearth?"

"Most likely. This second fracture is less severe. But it makes no difference. He died within moments because of the first. Intracranial haemorrhage. He couldn't have been saved."

"The mutilation was done after death, of course," St. James said reflectively. "There was virtually no blood."

"A mess none the less," Dr. Waters commented poetically.

St. James tried to picture the events as Dr. Waters had laid them out. The conversation, the escalation into argument, the evolution of anger to rage, the blow itself. "How long would you estimate the mutilation took? If someone were in a frenzy, running to the kitchen, finding a knife, perhaps with a knife already—"

"There was no frenzy involved. Depend upon that. At least not when the mutilation occurred." He saw that she recognised his confusion. She answered as if in anticipation of his questions. "People in frenzies tend to hack and stab, over and over. You know the sort of thing. Sixty-five wounds. We see that all the time. But in this case, it was just a couple of quick cuts. As if the killer had nothing more in mind than making a statement on Cambrey's body."

"With what sort of weapon?"

She lingered over her box of chocolates again. Her hand hesitated before pushing them aside with a look that combined both regret and determination. "Anything sharp. From a butcher knife to a pair of good scissors."

"But you've found no weapon yet?"

"Forensic are still working through the cottage. Imaginative lot, they are. Testing everything from kitchen knives to the safety pins used on the baby's nappies. They're tearing apart the village as well, looking in dustbins and flower gardens, busy earning their salaries. It's a waste of time."

"Why?"

She flipped a thumb back and forth over her shoulder as she answered his question, quite as if they were standing in the village and not several miles away in Penzance. "We have the hills behind us. We have the sea in front of us. We have a coastline honeycombed with thousands of caves. We have disused mines. We have a harbour filled with fishing boats. We have, in short, an infinite number of places in which one could deposit a knife with no one's being the wiser for decades as to how it got here. Just think of the fishermen's fillet knives. How many of those must be lying about?''

"So the killer might even have gone prepared to do this bit of work."

"Might. Might not. We've no way of telling."

"And Cambrey hadn't been tied up?"

"According to Forensic, nothing indicates that. No fragments of hemp, nylon, or anything else. He was very fit, actually. As to the other—the Howenstow business this morning—that's appearing to be quite another matter.''

"Drugs?" St. James asked.

She looked immediately interested. "I couldn't say. We've only done the preliminaries. Is there something—"

"Cocaine."

She made a note to herself on a pad of paper. "Not surprising, that. What people put into their bodies in the name of excitement . . . silly fools.'' She gave a moment over to what was apparently a dark consideration of drug use in the country. Rousing herself, she went on. "We've done a blood-alcohol on him. He was drunk."

"Capable of functioning?"

"Impaired, but capable. Enough to get out there and take a tumble. Four vertebrae were broken. Spinal cord was severed.'' She removed her spectacles and rubbed the bridge of her nose where they rested upon skin that was red and raw. Without them she looked curiously defenceless and somehow unmasked. "Had he lived, he'd have been a quadriplegic. So I wonder if we say he was lucky to have died.'' Her glance dropped unconsciously to St. James' bad leg. She pulled back fractionally into her chair. "I'm terribly sorry. Too many hours on the job.''

Less-than-perfect life versus no life at all. It was always the question, certainly one that St. James had asked himself many times in the years since his accident. He brushed off her apology by ignoring it altogether.

"Did he fall? Or was he pushed?"

"Forensic are combing both the body and the clothing to see if he may have grappled with someone. But as far as I can tell at the moment, it's a straightforward fall. He was drunk. He was at the top of a dangerous cliff. Time of death seems to be round one in the morning. So it was dark. And there was a heavy cloud cover last night as well. I'd say an accidental fall is a safe conclusion.''

How relieved Lynley would be to hear that, St. James thought. Yet even as Dr. Waters gave her opinion, he felt tugged by a reluctance to accept it. Appearances suggested an accident, to be sure. But no matter the appearance of the death, Brooke's presence at the cliff top in the middle of the night suggested a clandestine meeting that led to murder.

Outside the dining room, what had that morning been a summer storm was growing into a tempest, with gale-force winds howling round the house and rain striking the windows in angry flurries. The curtains were drawn, so the noise was somewhat muted, but an occasional blast shook the windows with enough force that they rattled ominously, impossible to ignore. When this happened, St. James found his thoughts torn from the deaths of Mick Cambrey and Justin Brooke and refastened upon the disappearance of the *Daze*. He knew that Lynley had spent the remainder of the day in a futile search for his brother. But the coastline was rugged and difficult to reach by land. If Peter had put the boat into a natural harbour somewhere to escape the worst of the storm, Lynley had not found him.

"I didn't think to alter the menu," Lady Asherton was saying in reference to the elaborate array of food with which they had been presented. "So much has been happening, I've forgotten how to think straight. There were supposed to be at least nine of us here. Ten, if Augusta had stayed. It's a blessing she went home last night. Had she been here this morning when Jasper found the body . . ." She toyed with a spear of broccoli, as if suddenly aware how disjointed her comments actually sounded. Candlelight and shadows played against the turquoise dress she wore and softened the lines of worry that, with the advancing day, had grown more prominent between her eyebrows and from her nose to her chin. She hadn't mentioned Peter since first being told he was gone.

"People 'ave to eat, Daze, and that's all there is to it," Cotter said, although he'd touched no more of his food than had the others.

"But we've not much heart for it, have we?" Lady Asherton smiled at Cotter, but her anxiety was palpable. It showed itself in her quick movements, in the fleeting glimpses she took of her older son who sat nearby. Lynley had been home only ten minutes prior to dinner. He had spent that time in the estate office making phone calls. St. James knew he had not spoken to his mother about Peter, and he did not have the look of a man who intended to speak about Peter now. As if she realised this, Lady Asherton said to St. James, "How's Sidney?"

"Sleeping now. She wants to go back to London in the morning."

"Is that wise, St. James?" Lynley asked.

"She doesn't appear to be willing to have it any other way."

"Will you go with her?"

He shook his head, fingered the stem of his wineglass, and thought about his brief conversation with his sister just an hour ago. Mostly he thought about her refusal to speak of Justin Brooke. *Don't ask me, don't make me,* she'd said, all the time looking ill, with her hair in soaked ringlets from a feverish dream. *I can't, I can't. Don't make me, Simon. Please.*

"She says she'll do well enough taking the train up alone," he said.

"Perhaps she wants to speak to his family. Have the police contacted them?"

"I don't know that he has any family. I don't know much about him at all." Beyond the fact, he added silently, that I'm glad he's dead.

His conscience had demanded the admission all day, ever since the moment when he'd held his sister in his arms on the top of the cliff, gazed down on Brooke's body, and known a moment of exultation that had its roots in his need for revenge. Here was justice, he'd thought. Here was retribution. Perhaps the hand of reprisal had been momentarily stayed after Brooke had attacked his sister on the beach. But the savagery of his assault upon her had called for an accounting. It had been made in full. He was glad of it. He was relieved that Sidney was free of Brooke at last. And the strength of his relief—so utterly foreign to what he had always believed was a civilised response to the death of another human being—disquieted him. He knew without a doubt that, given the opportunity, he himself could easily have done away with Justin Brooke.

"At any rate," he said, "I think it's probably wise that she get away. No one's asked her to stay. Officially, that is." He saw that the others understood his meaning. The police had not asked to speak with Sidney. As far as they were concerned, Brooke's death was due to an accidental fall.

The others mulled over this piece of information as the dining room door opened and Hodge came into the room. "A telephone call for Mr. St. James, my lady." Hodge had a way of making announcements with an intonation that suggested nothing less than impending doom: a phone call from fate, Hecate on the line. "It's in the estate office. Lady Helen Clyde."

St. James rose at once, grateful for an excuse to be gone. The atmosphere in the dining room was overhung with too many unspoken questions, and scores of issues asking to be discussed. But everyone seemed determined to avoid discussion, preferring the growing tension to the risk of facing a potentially painful truth.

He followed the butler to the west wing of the house, down the long corridor that led to the estate office. A single light burned upon the desk, creating a bright oval of illumination in the centre of which lay the telephone receiver. He picked it up.

"She's disappeared," Lady Helen said when she heard his voice. "It looks as if she's taken herself off on a casual holiday because her ordinary clothes are gone—but none of her dressy clothes—and there's no suitcase in the flat."

"You got inside?"

"Sheer audacious fast talking and the key was mine."

"You've missed your calling, Helen."

"Darling, I know. Con man extraordinaire. It comes from spending my youth in finishing schools instead of university. Modern languages, decorative arts, dissembling, and prevaricating. I was certain it would all be useful someday."

"No idea where's she gone?"

"She's left behind her makeup and her fingernails, so—"

"Her fingernails? Helen, what sort of business is this?"

She laughed and explained the artificial nails to him. "They're not what one would wear to do a bit of hiking, you see. Or mucking about. Or rock climbing, sailing, fishing. That sort of thing. So we think she's off in the country somewhere."

"Here in Cornwall?"

"That was our first thought as well, and we've come up with fairly solid evidence, we think. She has Mick Cambrey's savings book—with some rather hefty deposits made to his account, by the way—and we've found two telephone numbers. One's for a London exchange. We phoned it and got a recording for a place called Islington, Ltd., giving their business hours. I'll check into that in the morning."

"And the other number?"

"It's Cornwall, Simon. We've tried it twice and got no answer. We thought it might be Mick Cambrey's."

St. James pulled an envelope from the side drawer of the desk. "Did you try directory enquiries?"

"To compare it to Cambrey's number? He's ex-directory, I'm afraid. Let me give you the number. Perhaps you can do something more with it."

He jotted it down on the envelope, shoved it into his pocket. "Sid's coming back to London tomorrow." He told Lady Helen about Justin Brooke. She listened in silence, asking no questions and making no comment until he had completed the tale. He left nothing out, concluding with, "And now Peter's gone missing as well."

"Oh, no," she said. Dimly in the background, St. James could hear music playing softly. A flute concerto. It made him wish he were sitting in her drawing room in Onslow Square, talking idly about nothing, with nothing more on his mind than blood or fibre or hair analyses associated with people he did not know and would never meet. She said, "Poor Tommy. Poor Daze. How are they holding up?"

"They're coping."

"And Sid?"

"She's taken it badly. Will you see to her, Helen? Tomorrow night? When she's back?"

"Of course. Don't worry. Don't give it a thought." She hesitated momentarily. Again, the music came over the line, delicate and elusive, like a fragrance in the air. Then she said, "Simon, wishing didn't make it happen, you know."

How well she knew him. "When I saw him on the beach, when I knew that he was dead—"

"Don't be so hard on yourself."

"I could have killed him, Helen. God knows I wanted to."

"Which of us can say we've never felt the same? Towards someone at some time. It means nothing, my dear. You need some rest. We all do. It's been a dreadful time."

He smiled at her tone. Mother, sister, loving friend. He accepted the ephemeral absolution which she offered. "You're right, of course."

"So go to bed. Surely we can depend upon nothing else happening before morning."

"Let's hope so." He replaced the receiver and stood for a moment watching the storm. Rain lashed the windows. Wind tore at the trees. Somewhere a door banged open and shut. He left the office.

He considered climbing the southwest stairway to spend the rest of the evening in his room. He felt drained of energy, incapable of thought, and unwilling to face the task of making polite conversation that deliberately avoided the topics foremost on everyone's mind. Peter Lynley. Sasha Nifford. Where they were. What they had done. Still, he knew that Lynley would be waiting to hear about Lady Helen's call. So he headed back towards the dining room.

Voices drifting down the northwest corridor arrested his attention as he approached the kitchen. Near the servants' hall, Jasper stood conversing with a rugged-looking man who dripped water from a brimming sou' wester onto the floor. Seeing St. James, Jasper motioned him over.

"Bob's found 'r boat," he said. "Broke up on Cribba Head."

"It's the *Daze,* all right," the other man put in. "No mistakin' 'er."

"Is anyone—"

"There don't appear to be anyone with 'er. Don't see how 'tis possible. Not in the shape she be in."

17

St. James and Lynley followed the fisherman's rusty Austin in the estate Land Rover. Their headlamps illuminated the havoc created by the continuing storm. Newly dismembered rhododendrons lined the drive, round them a thick carpet of purple flowers which the vehicles crushed beneath their tyres. A large sycamore branch, sheared from a tree, nearly bisected the road. Leaves and twigs hurtled in every direction while tremendous gusts of wind lashed pebbles from the drive and fired them like bullets against the cars. At the lodge, shutters banged angrily against the stone walls. Water streamed down eaves and gushed from rainpipes. Climbing roses, ripped from their trellis, lay in sodden heaps on the flagstones and the ground.

Lynley braked the Rover, and Mark Penellin dashed out to join them. Framed in the doorway, Nancy Cambrey watched, a shawl clutched to her throat and the wind whipping her dress round her legs. She shouted something that was lost in the gale. Lynley lowered his window a few inches as Mark climbed into the car's rear seat.

"Any word of Peter?" Nancy caught the front door as the wind drove it against the wall. Over the sound of her voice came the baby's thin, faint wail. "Shall I do something?"

"Stay by the phone," he shouted back. "I may need you to go on to the house. To Mother."

She nodded, gave a wave, and slammed the door home. Lynley shifted gears. They lurched onto the drive, through a pool of water and a bank of mud.

"She's at Cribba Head?" Mark Penellin asked. His hair was slicked back, drenched from the rain.

"According to what we know right now," Lynley replied. "What's happened to you?"

Mark tentatively touched his fingers to a fresh plaster above his right eyebrow. Abrasions covered his knuckles and the back of his hand. He shook his head self-effacingly. "I was trying to fix the shutters so the baby'd stop crying. Nearly knocked myself out in the process." He turned up the collar of his oilskin and buttoned it at the throat. "You're sure it's the *Daze*?"

"It seems to be."

"And no word of Peter?"

"None."

"Bloody fool." Mark took out a pack of cigarettes, offering it to both Lynley and St. James. When they refused, he lit one for himself but only smoked for a minute before crushing it out.

"You've not seen Peter?" Lynley asked.

"Not since Friday afternoon. At the cove."

St. James glanced at the boy over his shoulder. "Peter said he didn't see you then."

Mark raised a brow, winced, touched the plaster there. "He saw me," he replied, and with a cautious look at Lynley added, "Maybe he forgot."

Following the Austin, the Rover crawled along the narrow lane. Aside from their vehicles' lights and the occasional glimmer from a cottage or a farmhouse window, the darkness was complete, and the gloom, in conjunction with the storm made the going slow. Water filmed the road. Hedgerows bent perilously towards the car. Their headlamps glared upon the torrential rain. Stopping twice to clear the road of debris, they took fifty minutes to make what should have been a quarter of an hour's drive.

Outside of Treen, they jolted over the uneven track to Cribba Head, pulling the cars to a halt some twenty yards from the path that led down to Penberth Cove. From the rear seat, Mark Penellin handed Lynley a fisherman's oilskin which he pulled on over his worn, grey guernsey.

"You'd best wait here, St. James." Even in the closed confines of the car, Lynley had to raise his voice to be heard over the wind and the roar of surf which pounded the shore below them. The Rover rocked ominously like a lightweight toy. "It's a rough walk."

"I'll come as far as I can."

Lynley nodded, shoving open his door. The three of them climbed out into the storm. St. James found that he had to use the entire weight of his body to shut his own door once Mark Penellin hopped out.

"Jesus!" The boy shouted. "Some blow, this." He joined Lynley in pulling ropes, life jackets, and life rings out of the car's boot.

Ahead of them, the fisherman had left his headlamps burning, and they illuminated the distance to the cliff. Sheets of rain drove through the arc of light, angled by the bellowing wind. The fisherman began to trudge through weeds which clung to his trousers. He carried a coil of rope.

"She be down in the cove," he shouted over his shoulder as they approached. "Some fifty yard from shore. Bow to stern, northeast on the rocks. Most o' the mast and yards 's gone, I fear."

Bent into the wind which was not only fierce but icy cold, as if it took its inspiration from an Arctic storm, they struggled towards the cliff's edge. There, made slick and dangerous by water, a narrow path led steeply down to Penberth Cove where lights glimmered from small granite cottages at the water's edge. Torches bobbed and glittered near the surf where locals brave enough to contend with the storm were watching the broken sloop disintegrate. There was no way they could get to the boat. Even if a small skiff could have managed the surf, the reef that was destroying the *Daze* would have done as much for any other vessel. Beyond that, storm-driven waves impeded them, crashing upon a natural spur of granite, sending plumes of spray towering into the air.

"I can't manage it, Tommy," St. James shouted when he saw the path. "I'll have to wait here."

Lynley lifted a hand, nodded, and began the descent. The others followed, picking their way among the boulders, finding handholds and footholds in outcroppings of rock. St. James watched them disappear into a patch of heavy shadow before he turned, fighting the wind and the rain to get back to the car. He felt weighted down by the mud on his shoes and the snarl of weeds that tangled in the heel piece of his brace. When he reached the Rover, he was out of breath. He pulled open the door and threw himself inside.

Out of the storm, he stripped off his ill-fitting oilskin and sodden guernsey. He shook the rain out of his hair. He shivered in the cold, wished for dry clothes, and thought about what the fisherman had said. At first it seemed to St. James that he hadn't heard him correctly. Northeast bow to stern on the rocks. There had to be a mistake. Except that a Cornish fisherman would know his directions, and the brief glimpse St. James had had of the sloop acted as confirmation of the fact. So there was no mistake. That being the case, either the boat wasn't the *Daze* at all, or they needed to take a new look at their theories.

It was nearly thirty minutes before Lynley returned with Mark at his heels, the fisherman a short distance behind them. Hunched against the rain, they stood at the Austin talking for a moment, the fisherman gesturing with hands and arms. Lynley nodded once, squinted towards the southwest, and with a final shouted comment, he tramped through the mud and weeds to the Rover. Mark Penellin followed. They stowed their gear in the boot once again and fell rather than climbed inside the car. They were soaking.

"She's destroyed." Lynley was gasping like a runner. "Another hour and there'll be nothing left."

"It's the *Daze*?"

"Without a doubt."

Ahead of them, the Austin roared. It reversed, made the turn, and left them on the clifftop. Lynley stared into the darkness which the Austin left behind. Rain pelted the windscreen.

"Could they tell you anything?"

"Little enough. They saw the boat coming in towards dusk. Apparently the fool was attempting to run through the rocks into the cove to be winched out of high water, as the other boats are."

"Someone saw it hit?"

"Five men were working round the capstan winch on the slip. When they saw what was happening, they gathered a crew and went to see what could be done. They're fishing people, after all. They'd be unlikely to let anyone run aground without trying to help in some way. But when they finally got a clear sight of the boat, no one was on deck."

"How is that possible?" St. James regretted the impulsive question the moment he asked it. There were two explanations, and he saw them himself before Lynley and Mark put them into words.

"People get swept overboard in this kind of weather," Mark said. "If you're not careful, if you don't wear a safety line, if you don't know what you're doing—"

"Peter knows what he's doing," Lynley interrupted.

"People panic, Tommy," St. James said.

Lynley didn't respond at once, as if he were evaluating this idea. He looked across St. James to the passenger's window in the direction of the sodden path that led to the cove. Water from his hair trickled crookedly down his brow. He wiped it away. "He could have gone below. He could still be below. They both could be there."

This wasn't an immediately untenable assumption, St. James thought, and it fitted rather nicely with the position in which the *Daze* had gone aground. If Peter had been using when he'd made the decision to take the boat out in the first place—as was clearly indicated by the fact that he had done so in the face of a coming storm—his reasoning would have been clouded by the drug. Indeed, the effects of cocaine would probably have prompted him to see himself as invincible, superior to the elements, in full command. The storm itself would have been not so much a clear and present danger as a source of excitement, the ultimate high.

On the other hand, taking the boat might have been a final act of desperation. If Peter needed to run away in order to avoid answering questions about Mick Cambrey and Justin Brooke, he may have decided the sea was his best means of escape. On land, he would have been noticed by someone. He had no transportation. He would need to thumb a ride. And with Sasha with him, whoever picked them up would be quite likely to remember them both when, and if, the police came calling. Peter was wise enough to know that.

Yet everything about the position and the destruction of the boat suggested something other than flight.

Lynley switched on the ignition. The car rumbled to life.

"I'll get up a party tomorrow," he said. "We're going to have to look for any signs of them."

His mother met them in the northwest corridor where they were hanging their dripping oilskins and guernseys on the wall pegs. She didn't speak at first. Rather, she held one hand, palm outward, between her breasts, as if in some way this would allow her to ward off a coming blow. With the other hand, she clasped a wrap she'd thrown on, a paisley stole of red and black that did battle with her colouring and the shade of her dress. She appeared to be using it more for security than for warmth, for the material was thin and perhaps with the cold or with trepidation, her body quivered beneath it. She was very pale, and Lynley thought that for the first time in his recollection, his mother looked every one of her fifty-six years.

"I've coffee for you in the day room," she said.

Lynley saw St. James look from him to his mother. He knew his friend well enough to recognise his decision. It was time he told his mother the worst about Peter. He had to prepare her for whatever she would have to face in the coming days. And he couldn't do that with St. James present, no matter how he longed to have his friend at his side.

"I'd like to check on Sidney," St. James said. "I'll be down later."

The northwest staircase was nearby, round the corner from the gun room, and St. James disappeared in that direction. Alone with his mother, Lynley didn't know what to say. Like a cooperative guest, he settled on a polite: "I could do with a coffee. Thank you."

His mother led the way. He noticed how she walked, her head upright, her shoulders back. He read the underlying meaning beneath her posture. Should someone see her—Hodge, the cook, or one of the dailies—she would give them no sign of any personal turmoil. Her estate manager had been arrested for murder; one of her houseguests had died in the night; her youngest child was missing, and her middle child was a man with whom she hadn't spoken intimately in more than fifteen years. But if any of this bothered her, no one would see it. If gossip flourished behind the green baize door, its subject would not be the myriad ways in which God's punishment had fallen upon the dowager Countess of Asherton at last.

They walked along the corridor that ran the length of the body of the house. At its eastern end, the day room door was closed, and when Lady Asherton opened it, the room's sole occupant got to his feet, crushing out his cigarette in an ashtray.

"Have you found anything?" Roderick Trenarrow asked.

Lynley hesitated in the doorway. He was all at once aware of the fact that his clothes were wet. Great oblongs of damp caused the wool of his trousers to adhere scratchily to his legs. His shirt clung to both his chest and his shoulders, and its collar pressed damply to the back of his neck. Even his socks were soaked, for although he'd worn gumboots down to Penberth Cove, he'd removed them in the car and he'd stepped directly into a substantial puddle of rainwater when he'd parked in the courtyard upon their return.

So he wanted to leave. He wanted to change his clothes. But instead, he forced himself forward and went to the bentwood cart next to his mother's desk. A coffee pot sat on it.

"Tommy?" his mother said. She had sat upon the least comfortable chair in the room.

Lynley took his cup of coffee to the sofa. Trenarrow remained where he was by the fireplace. A coal fire burned there, but its warmth did not cut through the clammy weight of Lynley's clothes. He glanced at Trenarrow, nodding in acknowledgement of the question he'd asked, but saying nothing. He wanted the other man to depart. He couldn't imagine having a conversation about Peter in front of him. Yet he knew that any request on his part for some privacy with his mother would be misinterpreted by both of them. Clearly, as on the previous evening, Trenarrow was there at her behest. This was no social call which he had designed to lead to seduction, and the concern on Trenarrow's face, when he looked at Lady Asherton, gave evidence of that.

It appeared he would have no choice in the matter. He rubbed his forehead, brushed back his damp hair. "No one was with the boat," he said. "At least we couldn't see anyone. They might have been below."

"Has anyone been called?"

"The lifeboat, you mean?" He shook his head. "She's breaking up too fast. By the time they got there, she'd be gone."

"Do you think he was swept overboard?"

They were speaking of her child, but they might have been discussing the replanting of the garden that would have to be done after the storm. He marvelled at her calm. She maintained it only until he replied, however.

"There's no way of knowing. Whether he was below with Sasha. Whether they were both swept overboard. We won't know anything until we find the bodies. And even then, if they've sustained enough damage, we might only be left with inferences and not a lot more."

At that, she lowered her head and covered her eyes. Lynley waited for Trenarrow to cross the room to her. He could feel the other man's need to do so. It was like a current that snapped in the air. But he made no move.

"Don't torture yourself," Trenarrow said. "We don't know a thing. We don't even know yet if it was Peter who took the boat. Dorothy, please. Listen to me."

Lynley remembered with a pain that rushed and receded. Trenarrow had always been the only person who used his mother's real name.

"You know he took the boat," she said. "We all know why. But I've ignored every sign, haven't I? He's been in clinics having treatment. Four clinics now and I wanted to believe that he was over it. But he's not. I knew that the moment I saw him Friday morning. But I couldn't bear to face another round of addiction, so I simply ignored it. I've actually begun praying that he'll find his way on his own because I don't know how to help him any longer. I've never known. Oh, Roddy . . ."

If she hadn't said his name, Trenarrow probably would have maintained his distance. But as it was, he went to her, touched her face, her hair, said her name again. Her arms went round him.

Lynley looked away. His muscles ached. His bones felt leaden.

"I don't understand it," Lady Asherton was saying. "No matter what he intended by taking the boat, he would have seen what the weather was like. He would have known the danger. He can't have been as desperate as that.'' And then gently pushing herself away from Trenarrow, ''Tommy?''

''I don't know,'' Lynley said. He kept his tone guarded.

His mother got to her feet, came to the sofa. ''There's something else, isn't there? Something you've not told me. No, Roddy''—this as Trenarrow made a move towards her—''I'm all right. Tell me what it is, Tommy. Tell me what you've not wanted me to know. You argued with him last night. I heard you. You know that. But there's more, isn't there? Tell me.''

Lynley looked up at her. Her face had become remarkably calm again, as if she had managed to find and draw upon a new source of strength. He dropped his eyes to the coffee cup that warmed the palm of his hand.

''Peter was at Mick Cambrey's cottage after John Penellin's visit on Friday night. Later, Mick died. Justin told me about that after John's arrest last night. And then''—he looked back at her—''Justin died.''

Her lips parted as he spoke, but otherwise her expression remained impassive. ''You can't think your own brother—''

''I don't know what to think.'' His throat felt raw. ''For God's sake, tell me what to think, if you will. Mick's dead. Justin's dead. Peter's disappeared. So what would you have me think of it all?''

Trenarrow took a step as if with the intention of deflecting the strength of Lynley's words. But as he moved, Lady Asherton did likewise. She joined her son on the sofa, put her arm round his shoulders. She pressed her cheek against his and brushed her lips against his damp hair.

''Dearest Tommy,'' she murmured. ''My dear, my dear. Why on earth do you believe you must bear it all?''

It was the first time she had touched him in more than a decade.

18

The morning sky, a cerulean arc under which a froth of cumulus clouds drifted inland, acted as a contradiction to the previous day's storm. As did the seabirds, who once again filled the air with their raw, importunate cries. The ground below them, however, was a testament to foul weather, and from his bedroom window, a cup of tea in his hand, St. James surveyed the consequences of those hours of rain and bluster.

Slate tiles from the roof lay shattered on the drive which entered the south courtyard over which his room looked. A twisted weathervane had fallen among them, no doubt blown there from the roof of one of the outbuildings that formed part of the courtyard wall. Crushed flowers created occasional mats of bright colour: purple canterbury bells, pink begonias, entire spikes of larkspur, and everywhere the petals of ruined roses. Bits of broken glass made a jewellike glitter on the cobblestones, and one small, curiously unbroken windowpane covered a puddle of water like newly formed ice. Already the gardeners and groundsmen were taking steps to repair the damage, and St. James could hear their voices from the park, drowned out by the intermittent roar of a power saw.

A sharp double rap on the door brought Cotter into the room. "Got what you need," he said. "Bit of a surprise, that, as well." He crossed the room and handed St. James the envelope which he'd removed from the estate office desk during his telephone conversation with Lady Helen Clyde. "It's Dr. Trenarrow's number."

"Is it?" St. James placed his tea cup on the cheveret. He took the envelope and thoughtfully turned it in his hands.

"Didn't even need to ring it, Mr. St. James," Cotter said. "Hodge knew whose it was the moment I showed it to him. Seems 'e's rung it enough times over the years.''

"Did you phone the number anyway, to be certain?"

"I did. It's Dr. Trenarrow's, all right. And 'e knows we're coming."

"Any word from Tommy?"

"Daze said 'e phoned from Pendeen." Cotter shook his head. "He's got nothing."

St. James frowned, wondering about the efficacy of Lynley's plan, one which stubbornly avoided the participation of either coastguard or police. He had headed out before dawn with six men from the surrounding farms to check the coastline from St. Ives to Penzance. They were operating two launches, one setting sail from Penzance harbour and the other across the peninsula at St. Ives Bay. The boats were small enough to give them fairly good visual access to the shore and fast enough to complete at least a cursory search in relatively few hours. But if that gleaned them nothing, a second search would have to be conducted by land. That would take days. And, whether Lynley liked it or not, it could not be orchestrated without the inclusion of the local police.

"I feel done in by this whole flipping weekend," Cotter commented as he replaced St. James' teacup on the tray that sat on the table next to the bed. "I'm that glad Deb's gone back to London. Get 'er out o' this mess is what I say."

He sounded as if he hoped St. James would make a response that would encourage further conversation along these lines. St. James had no intention of doing so.

Cotter shook out St. James' dressing gown and hung it in the wardrobe. He spent a moment straightening the neat row of his shoes. He banged a set of wooden coat hangers together and snapped the locks on the suitcase which sat on the top shelf. Then he burst out with, "What's to become of the girl? There's no closeness 'mong them. Not a bit an' you know it. It's not like with you, is it? It's not like your family. Oh, they're rich, bloody rich, but Deb's not drawn to money. You know that well as I do. You know what draws the girl."

Beauty, contemplation, the colours of the sky, a sudden new idea, the sight of a swan. He knew, had always known. And he needed to forget. His bedroom door opened, promising escape. Sidney entered, but with the wardrobe door obstructing his vision, Cotter didn't seem to notice that he and St. James were no longer alone.

"You can't say you feel nothing," Cotter asserted vigorously. "I c'n see it all over you. I have done for ages, no matter what you say."

"Am I interrupting something?" Sidney asked.

Cotter swung the wardrobe door home. He looked from St. James to his sister, then back to St. James.

"I'll see to the car," he said abruptly, excused himself, and left them alone.

"What was that about?" Sidney asked.

"Nothing."

"It didn't sound like nothing."

"It was."

"I see."

She remained by the door, the knob beneath her hand. St. James felt a stirring of concern at the sight of her. She looked caught somewhere between numb and ill, with blue-black crescents beneath her eyes providing the only colour on her face and her eyes themselves holding no expression, reflecting rather than absorbing the light. She wore a faded denim skirt and an oversized pullover. Her hair looked uncombed.

"I'm off," she said. "Daze's taking me to the station."

What had seemed reasonable only last night seemed out of the question when he saw his sister in the light of day. "Why don't you stay, Sid? I can take you home myself later on."

"This is best. I really want to go. It's better this way."

"But the station will be—"

"I'll take a cab home. I'll be all right." She turned the knob of the door, as if experimentally. "I understand Peter's missing," she said.

"Yes." St. James told her what had happened since he'd taken her to her room the previous morning. She listened without looking at him. As he spoke, he could sense her increasing tension, and he knew that it took its definition from an anger growing out of her comment about Peter Lynley. After the docility which shock had produced in her yesterday, he wasn't prepared for the change even though he knew that her anger was natural, a need to strike out and wound so that someone, somehow, would feel some of her pain. The worst part of a death was always that moment of knowing beyond a doubt that no matter how many people share it—be they family, friends, or even an entire nation—no two people can ever feel it the same way. So it always seems as if one experiences it alone. How much worse for Sidney, who *was* experiencing it alone, who was the sole mourner of Justin Brooke.

"How convenient," she said when he'd completed his story.

"What do you mean?"

"I mean he told me."

"Told you?"

"Justin told me, Simon. Everything. About Peter's being at Mick Cambrey's cottage. About the row Mick and Peter had. He told me. He *told* me. All right? Am I being clear?" She didn't move beyond the door. Had she done so, had she flung herself into the room, had she begun to tear at curtains and bedclothes, had she dashed the single vase of flowers to the floor, St. James would have felt less disturbed. All of those behaviours were decidedly Sidney. This was not. Only her voice gave testimony to the state of her spirit, and even it was only a fraction away from being perfectly controlled. "I told him that he had to tell you or Tommy," she went on. "Once John Penellin was arrested, I told him he had to say something. He couldn't keep quiet. It was his duty, I said. He had to tell the truth. But he didn't want to get involved. He knew he'd be making things bad for Peter. But I insisted. I said, 'If someone saw John Penellin at Gull Cottage, then someone probably saw you and Peter as well.' Better come forward with the story, I told him, rather than let the police drag it out of some neighbour."

"Sid—"

"But he was worried because he'd left Peter with Mick. He was worried because Peter was getting wild about the cocaine. He was worried because he didn't know what had happened after he left them. But I convinced him that he had to speak to Tommy. So he did. Now he's dead. And how perfectly convenient that Peter's disappeared just at a moment when we all have so many questions we'd like to put to him."

St. James crossed the room to her and shut the door. "CID think Justin's death was an accident, Sid. They've nothing at all to suggest it was murder."

"I don't believe that."

"Why not?"

"I just don't."

"Was he with you Saturday night?"

"Of course he was with me." She flung her head back and stated it like a fine point of honour. "We made love. He wanted to. He came to me. I didn't ask him. He came to me."

"What excuse did he give for leaving you afterwards?"

Her nostrils flared. "He loved me, Simon. He wanted me. We were good together. But you can't accept that, can you?"

"Sid, I don't want to argue about—"

"Can you? *Can you?*"

Somewhere in the corridor two women were talking, having a mild argument over who would vacuum and who would clean the baths. Their voices grew louder for a moment, then faded away as they descended the stairs.

"What time did he leave you?"

"I don't know. I didn't notice."

"Did he say anything?"

"He was restless. He said he couldn't sleep. He's like that sometimes. He's been like that before. We make love and he gets all wound up. Sometimes he wants to do it again right away."

"But not Saturday night?"

"He said he thought he could sleep better in his own room."

"Did he dress?"

"Did he . . . yes, he dressed." She drew the conclusion herself. "So he *was* meeting Peter. Because why would he have dressed when his own room was right across the hall? And he did dress, Simon. His shoes and socks, his trousers and shirt. Everything but his tie." She clenched at the material of her skirt. "Peter's bed wasn't slept in. I heard that this morning. Justin didn't fall. You know he didn't fall."

St. James didn't argue with her. He reflected upon the possibilities suggested by the simple act of donning clothes. If Peter Lynley had wanted to have an innocent conversation with Brooke, it would have been more sensible for them to have had it somewhere in the house. If, on the other hand, he had wanted to be rid of Brooke, far wiser to do it in a location where it would look like an accident. But if that were the case, why on earth would Justin agree to meet Peter anywhere alone?

"Sid, it doesn't make sense. Justin wasn't a fool. Why would he agree to meet Peter at the cliff? And in the middle of the night? After his conversation with Tommy, for all he knew, Peter was out for his blood." Then he thought about Friday afternoon's scene on the beach. "Unless, of course, Peter got him down there on false pretences. With some sort of bait."

"What?"

"Sasha?"

"That's absurd."

"Then cocaine. They'd gone to Nanrunnel looking for it. Perhaps that was the carrot Peter used."

"It wouldn't have worked. Justin wasn't going to use any longer. Not after what happened between us on the beach. He apologised for that. He said he was off it. He wouldn't use again."

St. James could not keep the scepticism from his face. He saw the hard edge of his sister's features begin to disintegrate as she read his reaction.

"He promised, Simon. You didn't know him as I did. You wouldn't understand. But if he promised when we were making love . . . especially when . . . There were certain things he liked me to do."

"My God, Sidney."

She began to cry. "Of course. My God, Sidney. What else can you say? Why should you of all people even begin to understand? You've never been close to feeling anything for anyone. Why on earth should you? After all, you've got science. You don't have to feel passion. You can feel busy instead. With projects and conferences and lectures and the guidance of all those future pathologists who come to worship at your knee."

Here was the need to wound that he'd recognised before. Still, it came out of nowhere. He hadn't expected it. And whether the attack was accurate or not, he found that he could not summon a response.

Sidney drew a hand across her eyes. "I'm leaving. Just tell little Peter when you find him that I have lots to discuss with him. Believe me, I can hardly wait for the opportunity."

Trenarrow's house was easy enough to find, for it sat just off the upper reaches of Paul Lane on the outskirts of the village, the largest structure within view. By the standards of Howenstow, it was a humble enough dwelling. But in comparison to the cottages that stacked one upon the other on the hillside beneath it, the villa was very grand, with broad bay windows overlooking the harbour and a stand of poplar trees acting like a backdrop against which the house's ashlar walls and white woodwork were displayed to some considerable effect.

With Cotter at the wheel of the Rover, St. James saw the villa at once as they came over the last rise of the coastal road and began their descent into Nanrunnel. They wound past the harbour, the village shops, the tourist flats. At the Anchor and Rose, they made the turn onto Paul Lane. Here debris from yesterday's storm littered the pitted asphalt: rubbish from cottage dustbins, assorted food wrappers and tins, a wrecked sign that once had advertised cream teas. The road twisted on itself and climbed above the village, where it was strewn with broken foliage from hedges and shrubs. Pools of rainwater reflected the sky.

A narrow drive branching north off Paul Lane was discreetly marked *The Villa*. Fuchsias lined it, drooping heavily over a dry-stone wall.

Behind this, a terraced garden covered much of the hillside where a carefully plotted, meandering path led upward to the house, through beds of phlox and nemesia, bellflowers and cyclamen.

The drive ended in a curve round a hawthorn tree, and Cotter parked beneath it, a few yards from the front door. A doric-columned portico sheltered this, with two urns of vermilion pelargoniums standing on either side.

St. James studied the front of the house. "Does he live here alone?" he asked.

"Far's I know," Cotter replied. "But a woman answered the phone when I rang."

"A woman?" St. James thought of Tina Cogin and Trenarrow's telephone number in her flat. "Let's see what the doctor can tell us."

Their knock was not answered by Trenarrow. Rather, a young West Indian woman opened the door, and from the expression on Cotter's face when she first spoke, St. James knew he could dismiss Tina Cogin as the woman who had answered the phone. The mystery of her whereabouts, it seemed, would not be solved through the expediency of her clandestine presence at Trenarrow's house.

"Doctor see nobodies here," the woman said, looking from Cotter to St. James. The words sounded rehearsed, perhaps frequently and not always patiently said.

"Dr. Trenarrow knows we're coming to see him," St. James said. "It's not a medical call."

"Ah." She smiled, showing large teeth which protruded like ivory against her coffee skin. She held wide the door. "Then in with you, man. He's looking at his flowers. Every morning in the garden before he goes off to work. Same thing. I'll fetch him for you."

She showed them to the study where, with a meaningful look at St. James, Cotter said, "I could do with a walk round the garden myself," and followed the woman from the room. Cotter would, St. James knew, find out what he could about who she was and why she was there.

Alone, he turned to look at the room. It was the sort of study he particularly liked, with air faintly scented by the smell of the old leather chairs, bookcases filled to absolute capacity, a fireplace with coals newly laid and ready to be lit. A desk sat in the large bay window overlooking the harbour, but as if the view would be a distraction from work, it faced into the room, rather than outward. An open magazine lay upon it with a pen left in the center crease as if the reader had been interrupted in the middle of an article. Curious, St. James went to examine it, flipping it closed for a moment.

Cancer Research, an American journal, with a photograph of a white-coated scientist on its cover. She leaned against a working area on which sat an immense electron microscope. *Scripps Clinic, La Jolla* was printed beneath the photograph, along with the phrase *Testing the Limits of Bio-Research.*

St. James went back to the article, a technical treatise on an extra-cellular matrix protein called proteoglycans. Despite his own extensive background in science, it made little sense to him.

"Not quite what one would call light reading, is it?"

St. James looked up. Dr. Trenarrow stood in the doorway. He was wearing a well-tailored three-piece suit. He'd pinned a small rosebud to its lapel.

"It's certainly beyond me," St. James replied.

"Any word of Peter?"

"Nothing yet, I'm afraid."

Trenarrow shut the door and gestured St. James into one of the room's wingback chairs.

"Coffee?" he asked. "I've been discovering it's one of Dora's few specialities."

"Thank you, no. She's your housekeeper?"

"Using the term in the loosest possible fashion." He smiled briefly, without humour. The remark seemed largely an effort to be light-hearted, an effort he dismissed with his very next words. "Tommy told us last night. About Peter seeing Mick Cambrey the night he died. About Brooke as well. I don't know where you stand in all this, but I've known that boy since he was six years old, and he's not a killer. He's incapable of violence, most especially the sort that was done to Mick Cambrey."

"Did you know Mick well?"

"Not as well as others in the village. Just as his landlord. I let him Gull Cottage."

"How long ago was that?"

Trenarrow began an automatic answer, but then his brow furrowed, as if he'd suddenly wondered about the nature of the question. "About nine months."

"Who lived there before him?"

"I did." Trenarrow made a quick movement in his chair, an adjustment in position that betrayed irritation. "You can't have come here on a social call at this time of morning, Mr. St. James. Did Tommy send you?"

"Tommy?"

"No doubt you know the facts. We've years of bad blood between us. You're asking about Cambrey. You're asking about the cottage. Are these questions his idea or yours?''

"Mine. But he knows I've come to see you.''

"About Mick?''

"Actually, no. Tina Cogin's disappeared. We think she may have come to Cornwall.''

"Who?''

"Tina Cogin. Shrewsbury Court Apartments. In Paddington. Your telephone number was among her things.''

"I haven't the slightest . . . Tina Cogin, you say?''

"She's not a patient of yours? Or a former patient?''

"I don't see patients. Oh, perhaps the occasional terminal case who volunteers for an experimental drug. But if Tina Cogin was one of them and she's disappeared . . . Excuse me for the levity, but there's only one place she'd be disappearing to and it wouldn't be Cornwall.''

"Then you may well have seen her in a different light.''

Trenarrow looked perplexed. "Sorry?''

"She may be a prostitute.''

The doctor's gold-rimmed spectacles slid fractionally down his nose. He knuckled them back into place and said, "And she had my name?''

"No. Just your number.''

"My address?''

"Not even that.''

Trenarrow pushed himself out of his chair. He walked over to the window behind the desk. He spent a long moment studying the view before he turned back to St. James. "I've not set foot in London in a year. Perhaps more. But I suppose that makes little enough difference if she's come to Cornwall. Perhaps she's making house calls.'' He smiled wryly. "You don't really know me, Mr. St. James, so you have no way of knowing if I'm telling you the truth. But let me say that it's not been my habit to pay a woman for sex. Some men do it without flinching, I realise. But I've always preferred lovemaking to grow out of a passion other than avarice. This other—the negotiating first, the exchange of cash later—that's not my style.''

"Was it Mick's?''

"Mick's?''

"He was seen leaving her flat Friday morning in London. He may well have given her your number, in fact. Perhaps for some sort of consultation.''

Trenarrow's fingers went to the rosebud on his lapel, touching its tightly furled petals. "That's a possibility,'' he said thoughtfully. "Although referrals generally come from physicians, it *is* a possibility if she's seriously ill. Mick knew cancer research is my line of work. He'd done an interview with me shortly after he took over the *Spokesman*. It's not inconceivable that he might have given her my name. But Cambrey and a prostitute? That's going to put a wrench in his reputation. His father's been fanning the fires of Mick's sexual profligacy for the last year at least. And believe me, nothing he's said has ever alluded to Mick having to pay for a woman's favours. According to Harry, so many women were throwing themselves at the poor lad that he barely had time to pull his trousers up before someone was moaning to have them back down. If involvement with a prostitute led to Mick's murder, it'll be sad times for Harry. He seems to be hoping it was from a row with a dozen or two jealous husbands.''

"Or one jealous wife?''

"Nancy?'' Trenarrow said incredulously. "I can't see her hurting anyone, can you? And even if she had somehow been driven beyond endurance—it was no secret, after all, that Mick saw other women—when could she have done it? She couldn't have been in two places at once.''

"She was gone from the refreshment booth for a good ten minutes or more.''

"Time to run home, murder her husband, and reappear as if everything were well? The thought's a bit absurd, considering the girl. Someone else might have managed it with aplomb, but Nancy's no actress. If she'd killed her husband during the evening, I doubt she could have hidden it from a soul.''

There was certainly a weight of evidence to support Trenarrow's declaration. From start to finish, Nancy's reactions had borne the unmistakable stamp of authenticity. Her shock, her numb grief, her rising anxiety. None of them had seemed in the least bit factitious. It hardly seemed likely that she'd run home, killed her husband, and feigned horror later. That being the case, St. James considered the problem of suspects. John Penellin had been in the area that night, as had Peter Lynley and Justin Brooke. Perhaps Harry Cambrey had paid a visit to the cottage as well. And Mark Penellin's whereabouts were still unaccounted for. Yet a motive for the crime was not clearly emerging. Each one they considered was nebulous at best. And more than anything, a motive needed clear definition if anyone was to understand the full circumstances of Mick Cambrey's death.

*   *   *

St. James noticed Harry Cambrey almost immediately as Cotter pulled the car back onto Paul Lane. He was climbing towards them. He waved energetically as they approached. The cigarette between his fingers left a tiny plume of smoke in the air.

"Who's this?" Cotter slowed the car.

"Mick Cambrey's father. Let's see what he wants."

Cotter pulled to the side of the road, and Harry Cambrey came to St. James' window. He leaned into the car, bringing with him the mixed odours of tobacco smoke and beer. His appearance had undergone some improvement since St. James and Lady Helen had seen him on Saturday morning. His clothes were fresh, his hair was combed, and although a few overlooked whiskers sprouted here and there like grey bristles on his cheeks, his face was largely shaven as well.

He was panting, and he winced as if the words hurt him when he spoke. "Howenstow folks said you'd be here. Come down to the office. Something to show you."

"You've found notes?" St. James asked.

Cambrey shook his head. "Worked it all out, though." When St. James opened the car door, Cambrey clambered inside. He nodded at the introduction to Cotter. "It's those numbers I found. The ones from his desk. I've been playing with them since Saturday. I know what they mean."

Cotter remained in the pub with Mrs. Swann, chatting amiably over a pint of ale. He was saying, "I wouldn't say no to one o' them Scotch eggs," as St. James followed Harry Cambrey up to the newspaper office.

Unlike his former visit to the *Spokesman,* on this morning the staff was at work. All the lights were on—creating an entirely different atmosphere from the previous gloom—and in three of the four cubicles newspaper employees either pecked at typewriters or talked on the phones. A long-haired boy examined a set of photographs on a display board while next to him a compositor engaged in the process of laying out another edition of the newspaper on an angled green table. He held an unlit pipe between his teeth and tapped a pencil in staccato against a plastic holder of paperclips. At the word processor on the table next to Mick Cambrey's desk, a woman sat typing. She had soft, dark hair drawn back from her face and—when she looked up—intelligent eyes. She was very attractive. Julianna Vendale, St. James decided. He wondered how and if her responsibilities at the newspaper had altered with Mick Cambrey's death.

Harry Cambrey led the way to one of the cubicles. It was sparsely furnished, hung with wall decorations which suggested that not only was the office his own, but nothing had been done to change it during his convalescence after heart surgery. Everything spoke of the fact that, no matter Harry Cambrey's desire, his son had not intended to assume either his office or his job. Framed newpaper clippings, gone yellow with age, appeared to represent the older man's proudest stories: a piece on a disastrous sea-rescue attempt in which twenty of the would-be rescuers had drowned; an accident which dismembered a local fisherman; the rescue of a child from a mine shaft; a brawl during a fete in Penzance. These were accompanied by newspaper photographs as well, the originals of those which had been printed with the stories.

On the top of an ancient desk, the most recent edition of the *Spokesman* lay open to the editorial page. Mick's contribution had been heavily circled in red. On the wall opposite, a map of Great Britain hung. Cambrey directed St. James to this.

"I kept thinking about those numbers," he said. "Mick was systematic about things like that. He wouldn't have kept that paper if it wasn't important." He felt in the breast pocket of his shirt for a packet of cigarettes. He shook one out and lit it before going on. "I'm still working on part of it, but I'm on my way."

St. James saw that next to the map Cambrey had taped a small piece of paper. On it he had printed part of the cryptic message which he'd found beneath his son's desk. *27500-M1 Procure/Transport* and, beneath that, *27500-M6 Finance*. On the map itself, two motorways had been traced in red marking pen, the M1 heading north from London and the M6 heading northwest below Leicester towards the Irish Sea.

"Look at it," Cambrey said. "M1 and M6 run together south of Leicester. The M1 only goes as far as Leeds, but the M6 continues. It ends in Carlisle. At Solway Firth."

St. James considered this. He made no reply. Cambrey sounded agitated when he continued.

"Look at the map, man. Just look at it square. M6 gives access to Liverpool, doesn't it? It takes you to Preston, to Morecambe Bay. And they every bloody one of them—"

"—give access to Ireland," St. James concluded, thinking of the editorial he'd read only the morning before.

Cambrey went for the paper. He folded it back. His cigarette bobbed between his lips as he talked. "He knew someone was running guns for the IRA."

"How could he have stumbled onto a story like that?"

"Stumbled?" Cambrey removed his cigarette, picked tobacco from his tongue and shook the newspaper to make his point. "My lad didn't stumble. He was a journalist, not a fool. He listened. He talked. He learned to follow leads." Cambrey returned to the map and used the folded newspaper as a pointer. "Guns must be coming into Cornwall in the first place, or if not into Cornwall, then through a south harbour. Shipped from sympathisers, maybe in North Africa or Spain or even France. They come in anywhere along the south coast—Plymouth, Bournemouth, Southampton, Portsmouth. They're shipped disassembled. Trucked to London and put together. Then from there, up the M1 to the M6, and then to Liverpool or Preston or Morecambe Bay."

"Why not ship them directly to Ireland in the first place?" St. James asked, but he knew the answer even as he asked it. A foreign ship docking at Belfast would be more likely to rouse suspicion than would an English ship. It would undergo a thorough customs check. But an English ship would be largely accepted. For why would the English be sending arms to assist an uprising against themselves?

"There was more on the paper than M1 and M6," St. James pointed out. "Those additional numbers have to mean something."

Cambrey nodded. "Likely to be some sort of registration numbers, I think. References to the ship they'd be using. Numbers on the type of weapons they'd be supplying. It's some sort of code. But make no mistake about it. Mick was on his way to breaking it."

"Yet you've found no other notes?"

"What I've found's enough. I know my lad. I know what he was about."

St. James reflected upon the map. He thought about the numbers Mick had jotted on the paper. He noted the fact that the editorial about Northern Ireland had appeared on Sunday, more than thirty hours after Mick's death. If the two were connected somehow, then the killer had known about the editorial in advance of the paper's appearance on Sunday morning. He wondered how likely a possibility that was.

"Do you keep your back issues of the newspaper here?" he asked.

"This isn't a back issue problem," Cambrey said.

"Nonetheless, do you have them?"

"Some. Out here."

Cambrey led him from his office to a storage cabinet that sat to the left of the casement windows. He pulled open the doors to reveal stacks of newspapers upon the shelves. St. James glanced at them, pulled the first set off the shelf, and looked at Cambrey.

"Can you get me Mick's keys?" he asked.

Cambrey looked puzzled. "I've a spare cottage key here."

"No. I mean all his keys. He has a set, doesn't he? Car, cottage, office? Can you get them? I expect Boscowan has them now, so you'll need to come up with an excuse. And I'll want them for a few days."

"Why?"

"Does the name Tina Cogin mean anything to you?" St. James asked in answer.

"Cogin?"

"Yes. A woman from London. Mick knew her apparently. I think he may have had the key to her flat."

"Mick had the key to half a dozen flats, if I know him." Cambrey pulled out a cigarette and left him to his papers.

An hour's search through the past six months gleaned him nothing save hands that were stained with newsprint. As far as he could tell, Harry Cambrey's conjecture about gunrunning was as likely a motive for his son's death as was anything else the paper had to offer. He shut the cupboard doors. When he turned, it was to find Julianna Vendale watching him, a coffee cup raised to her lips. She'd left the word processor, coming to stand near a coffee maker that was bubbling noisily in the corner of the room.

"Nothing?" She put her cup down on the table and pushed a lock of long hair back from her shoulder.

"Everyone seems to think he was working on a story," St. James said.

"Mick was always working on something."

"Did most of his projects get into print?"

She drew her eyebrows together. A faint crease appeared between them. Otherwise, her face was completely unlined. St. James knew from his previous conversation with Lynley that Julianna Vendale was in her middle thirties, perhaps a bit older. But her face denied her age.

"I don't know," she answered. "I wasn't always aware of what his projects were. But it wouldn't surprise me to find out he'd begun something and then let it die. He'd shoot out of here often enough, convinced he was hot on the trail of a feature he could sell in London. Then he'd never complete it."

St. James had seen that himself in his perusal of the newspapers. Dr. Trenarrow had said Mick interviewed him for a story. But nowhere in the back issues of the paper was there a feature that in any way related to a conversation the two of them might have had. St. James related this to Julianna Vendale.

She poured herself another cup of coffee and spoke over her shoulder. "That doesn't surprise me. Mick probably thought he was going to get a Mother Teresa piece out of it—Cornish Scientist Dedicates his Life to Saving Others—only to discover that Dr. Trenarrow's no more on the path to heaven than the rest of us are."

Or, St. James thought, the potential story was a ploy to get an interview with Trenarrow in the first place in order to gather information, and to pass it along with Trenarrow's phone number to a needy friend.

Julianna was continuing. "That was largely his way, ever since he came back to the *Spokesman*. I think he was looking for a story as a means of escape."

"He didn't want to be here?"

"It was a step backwards for him. He'd been a free-lance journalist. He'd been doing quite well. Then his father fell ill and he had to chuck it all and come back to hold the family business together."

"You couldn't have done that?"

"I could have done, of course. But Harry wanted Mick to take over the paper. More than that, I should guess, he wanted him back in Nanrunnel permanently."

St. James thought he saw the direction Harry Cambrey had intended things to move once Mick returned to Nanrunnel. Nonetheless, he asked, "How did you fit into the plans?"

"Harry made certain we worked together as much as possible. Then, I suppose, he just hoped for the best. He had great faith in Mick's charm."

"And you?"

She was holding her coffee cup between her hands, as if to keep them warm. Her fingers were long, she wore no rings. "He didn't appeal to me. When Harry saw that, he started having Nancy Penellin come to do the books during our regular office hours instead of on weekends."

"And as to developing the newspaper's stature?"

She indicated the word processor. "Mick made the attempt at first. He started with new equipment. He wanted to update. But then he seemed to lose interest."

"When?"

"Just about the time he made Nancy pregnant." She lifted her shoulders in a graceful shrug. "After they married, he was gone a great deal."

"Pursuing a story?"

She smiled. "Pursuing."

*   *   *

They strolled across the narrow street to the harbour. The tide was out. Five sunbathers lay on the narrow strand. Near them, a group of small children dabbled their hands and feet in the water, shrieking with excitement as it lapped at their legs.

"Get what you need?" Cotter asked.

"Pieces, that's all. Nothing seems to fit together. I can't make a connection between Mick and Tina Cogin, between Tina Cogin and Trenarrow. It's nothing more than conjecture."

"P'raps Deb was wrong. P'raps she didn't see Mick in London."

"No. She saw him. Everything indicates that. He knew Tina Cogin. But as to how and why, I don't know."

"Seems 'ow and why's the easiest part, 'cording to Missus Swann."

"She's not an admirer of Mick's, is she?"

"She hated 'im, and there's the truth." Cotter watched the children playing for a moment. He smiled as one of them—a little girl of three or four—fell onto her bottom, splashing water on the others. "But if there's truth to her talk about Mick Cambrey and women, then far's I can see, looks to me that John Penellin did it."

"Why?"

"It's 'is daughter involved, Mr. St. James. A man's not likely to let another man hurt 'is daughter. Not if it can be stopped in some way. A man does what 'e can."

St. James recognised the bait and acknowledged the fact that their morning's discussion was not yet concluded in Cotter's eyes. But he had no need to ask the question which Cotter's comment called for: *And what would you do?* He knew the answer. Instead he said, "Did you learn anything from the housekeeper?"

"Dora? A bit." Cotter leaned against the harbour railing, resting his elbows on the top metal bar. "Great admirer of the doctor, is Dora. Works 'is fingers to the bone. Gives 'is life to research. And when 'e's not doing that, 'e's visiting folks at a convalescent 'ome outside St. Just."

"That's the extent of it?"

"Seems to be."

St. James sighed. Not for the first time did he admit to the fact that his field was science, crime scene investigation, the analysis of evidence, the interpretation of data, the preparation of reports. He had no expertise in an arena that demanded insightful communication and intuitive deduction. More, he didn't have the taste or the talent for either. And the further he waded into the growing mire of conjecture, the more frustrated he felt.

From his jacket pocket, he pulled out the piece of paper which Harry Cambrey had given him Saturday morning. It seemed as reasonable a direction to head in as any. *When you're lost,* he thought mordantly, *you may as well head somewhere.*

Cotter joined him in studying it. "MP," he said. Then, "Member of Parliament?"

St. James looked up. "What did you say?"

"Them letters. MP."

"MP? No——" As he spoke, St. James held the paper to the sunlight. And he saw what the gloom of the newspaper office and his own preconceived notions had prevented him from realising before. The pen, which had skipped in the grease on other spots on the paper, had done as much again next to the words *procure* and *transport.* The result was an imperfectly formed loop for the letter *P,* not the number *1* at all. And the *6,* if the thought followed logically, had to be instead a hastily scrawled *C.*

"Good God." He frowned, examining the accompanying numbers. Dismissing gunrunning and Ireland and every other side issue from his mind, it wasn't long before he saw the obvious. *500. 55. 27500.* The last was the multiple of the previous two.

And then he recognised the first connection of the circumstances surrounding Mick Cambrey's death. The position of the *Daze* had told him, bow to stern northeast on the rocks. He should have clung to that thought. It had been pointing to the truth.

He thought about the coastline of Cornwall. He knew without a doubt that Lynley's party of men could scour every cove from St. Ives to Penzance, but it would be as limitedly useful an activity for them as it had been for the excise officers who had patrolled the same area for two hundred years. The coast was honeycombed with caves. It was scalloped by coves. St. James knew that. He did not need to clamber among the rocks and slither down the faces of cliffs to see what he knew quite well was already there, a haven for smugglers. If they knew how to pilot a boat among the reefs.

It could have come from anywhere, he thought. From Portgwarra to Sennen Cove. Even from the Scillys. But there was only one way to know for sure.

"What next?" Cotter asked.

St. James folded the paper. "We need to find Tommy."

"Why?"

"To call off the search."

19

After nearly two hours, they found him on the quay at Lamorna Cove. He was squatting on the edge, talking to a fisherman who had just docked his boat and was trudging up the harbour steps, three coils of greasy-looking rope dangling from his shoulder. He paused halfway, listening to Lynley above him. He shook his head, covered his eyes to examine the other boats in the harbour, and with a wave towards the scattering of buildings set back from the quay, he continued his climb.

Up above, on the road that dipped into the cove, St. James got out of the car. "Go back to Howenstow," he told Cotter. "I'll ride in with Tommy."

"Any message for Daze?"

St. James considered the question. Any message for Lynley's mother seemed a toss-up between relieving her mind about one set of circumstances only to fire her worries about another. "Nothing yet."

He waited as Cotter turned the car around and headed back the way they had come. Then he began the descent into Lamorna, with the wind whipping round him and the sun warming his face. Below him, the crystalline water reflected the colour of the sky, and the small beach glistened with newly washed sand. The houses on the hillside, built by Cornish craftsmen who had been testing the strength of the southwestern weather for generations, had sustained no damage from the storm. Here, that which had been the ruin of the *Daze* might not even have occurred.

St. James watched as Lynley walked along the quay, his head bent forward, his hands deep in trouser pockets. The posture said everything about the condition of his spirit, and the fact that he was alone suggested either that he had disbanded the search altogether or that the others had gone on without him. Because they'd been at it for hours already, St. James guessed the former. He called Lynley's name.

His friend looked up, raised a hand in greeting, but said nothing until he and St. James met at the land end of the quay. His expression was bleak.

"Nothing." He lifted his head and the wind tossed his hair. "We've completed the circuit. I've been talking to everyone here as a last-ditch effort. I thought someone might have seen them getting the boat ready to sail, or walking on the quay, or stocking supplies. But no one in any of the houses saw a blasted thing. Only the woman who runs the cafe even noticed the *Daze* yesterday."

"When was that?"

"Just after six in the morning. She was getting ready to open the cafe—adjusting the front blinds—so she can't have been mistaken. She saw them sailing out of the harbour."

"And it *was* yesterday? Not the day before."

"She remembers it was yesterday because she couldn't understand why someone was taking the boat out when rain had been forecast."

"But it was in the morning that she saw them?"

Lynley glanced his way, flashed a tired but grateful smile. "I know what you're thinking. Peter left Howenstow the night before, and because of that, it's less likely he's the one who took the boat. That's good of you, St. James. Don't think I haven't considered it myself. But the reality is that he and Sasha could have come to Lamorna during the night, slept on the boat, then taken her out at dawn."

"Did this woman see anyone on deck?"

"Just a figure at the helm."

"Only one?"

"I can't think Sasha knows how to sail, St. James. She was probably below. She was probably still asleep." Lynley looked back at the cove. "We've done the whole coastline. But so far, nothing. Not a sighting, not a garment, not a sign of them." He took out his cigarette case and flipped it open. "I'm going to have to come up with something to tell Mother. But God only knows what it'll be."

St. James had been placing most of the facts together as Lynley spoke. His thoughts elsewhere, he'd heard not so much the words as the desolation behind them. He sought to bring that to an immediate end.

"Peter didn't take the *Daze*," he said. "I'm sure of it."

Lynley's head turned to him slowly. It looked like the sort of movement one makes in a dream. "What are you saying?"

"We need to go to Penzance."

Detective Inspector Boscowan took them to the officers' mess. "The yellow submarine," he'd called it, and the name was very apt: yellow walls, yellow linoleum, yellow formica-topped tables, yellow plastic chairs. Only the crockery was a different colour, but as this colour was carmine, the overall effect was one which did not encourage the thought of lingering over a meal with one's mates. Nor did it suggest the possibility of consuming one's food without developing a ferocious headache in the process. They took a pot of tea to a table overlooking a small courtyard in which a dispirited ash tree attempted to flourish in a circle of dirt the colour of granite.

"Designed and decorated by madmen," was Boscowan's only comment as he hooked his foot round the leg of an extra chair and dragged it to their table. "Supposed to take one's mind off one's work."

"It does that," St. James remarked.

Boscowan poured the tea while Lynley ripped open three packages of digestive biscuits and shook them onto an extra plate. They fell upon it with a sound like small artillery fire.

"Baked fresh daily." Boscowan smiled sardonically, took a biscuit, dunked it into his tea and held it there. "John's spoken to a solicitor this morning. I had a devil of a time getting him to do it. I've always known the man's stubborn, but he's never been like this."

"Are you going to charge him?" Lynley asked.

Boscowan examined his biscuit, dunked it again. "I've no choice in the matter. He was there. He admits it. The evidence supports it. Witnesses saw him. Witnesses heard the row." Boscowan took a bite of his biscuit after which he appreciatively held it up at eye level and nodded his head. He wiped his fingers on a paper napkin and urged the plate upon the other two men. "Not half bad. Just put your faith in the tea." He waited until they had each taken one before he went on. "Had John only *been* there it would be a different matter. Had there not also been that flaming row which half the neighbourhood appear to have heard . . ."

St. James looked at Lynley. He was adding a second cube of sugar to his tea. His index finger played along the handle of the cup. But he said nothing.

St. James said, "As to Penellin's motive?"

"An argument over Nancy, I dare say. Cambrey was trapped into the marriage, and he made no bones about hating every minute of it. There's not one person I've talked to who hasn't said that."

"Then why marry her in the first place? Why not simply refuse? Why not insist on an abortion?"

"According to John, the girl wouldn't hear of abortion. And Harry Cambrey wouldn't hear of Mick's refusing to marry her."

"But Mick was a grown man after all."

"With a dad sick and likely to die after his surgery." Boscowan drained his cup of tea. "Harry Cambrey recognised a string when he saw one. Don't think he didn't pull it to keep Mick in Nanrunnel. So the lad got trapped here. He started stepping out on his wife. Everyone knows it, including John Penellin."

Lynley said, "But you can't truly believe that John—"

Boscowan raised a hand quickly. "I know the facts. They're all we have to work with. Nothing else can matter, and you damn well know it. What difference does it make that John Penellin's my friend? His son-in-law's dead and that has to be seen to, whether it's convenient in my life or not." Having said this, Boscowan looked abashed, as if his brief outburst had come as a surprise to him. He went on more quietly. "I've offered to let him go home pending arraignment, but he's refused. It's as if he wants to be here, as if he wants to be tried." He reached for another biscuit but rather than eat it, he broke it in his hands. "It's as if he did it."

"May we see him?" Lynley asked.

Boscowan hesitated. He looked from Lynley to St. James, then out the window. "It's irregular. You know that."

Lynley pulled out his warrant card. Boscowan waved it off. "I know you're Scotland Yard. But this isn't a Yard case, and I've my own Chief Constable's sensibilities to consider. No visitors save family and solicitor when it's a homicide. That's standard procedure in Penzance, regardless of what you allow at the Met."

"A woman friend of Mick Cambrey's has gone missing from London," Lynley said. "Perhaps John Penellin can help us with that."

"A case you're working on?"

Lynley didn't reply. At the next table a girl in a stained white uniform began stacking plates onto a metal tray. Crockery crashed and scraped. A mound of mashed potatoes fell to the floor. Boscowan watched her work. He tapped a hard biscuit on the table top.

"Oh hell," he murmured. "Come on with you both. I'll arrange it somehow."

He left them in an interrogation room in another wing of the building. A single table and five chairs were the only furnishings besides a mirror on one wall and a ceiling light fixture from which a spider was industriously constructing a web.

"Do you think he'll admit to it?" Lynley asked as they waited.

"He doesn't really have a choice."

"And you're sure, St. James?"

"It's the only reasonable explanation."

A uniformed constable escorted John Penellin into the room. When he saw who his visitors were, he took a single step backwards as if he would leave. The door was already closed behind him, however. It had a small window set at eye level, and although Penellin glanced at this as if considering whether to signal the constable to take him back to his cell, he made no move to do so. Instead, he joined them. The table wobbled on uneven legs as he leaned against it when he sat.

"What's happened?" he asked warily.

"Justin Brooke took a fall at Howenstow early Sunday morning," Lynley said. "The police think it was an accident. It may well have been. But if it wasn't, there's either a second killer on the loose locally or you yourself are innocent and there's only one killer. Which do you think is more likely, John?"

Penellin twisted a button on the cuff of his shirt. His expression did not change although a muscle contracted as quickly as a reflex beneath his right eye.

St. James spoke. "The *Daze* was taken from Lamorna early yesterday morning. She was wrecked at Penberth Cove last night."

The button Penellin was twisting fell onto the table. He picked it up, used his thumb to flip it onto its other side. St. James went on.

"I think it's a three-tiered operation, with a main supplier and perhaps half a dozen dealers. They seem to be running the cocaine in two possible ways: Either the dealers pick it up from the supplier—perhaps on the Scillys—and then sail back to the mainland, or the supplier arranges to meet the dealers in any number of coves along the coast. Porthgawarra comes to mind at once. The shore's accessible, the village is too far off for anyone to notice clandestine comings and goings in the cove. The cliff is riddled with caves and caches in which an exchange could take place if it seems too risky to try it on the open sea. But no matter how he gets it from his supplier, once the dealer has it—either from the Scillys or from one of the coves—he sails back to Lamorna in the *Daze* and then takes the cocaine to the mill at Howenstow where he packages it. With no one the wiser.''

Penellin said only, "You know, then.''

"Who is it that you've been trying to protect?'' St. James asked. "Mark or the Lynleys?''

Penellin reached in his pocket and brought out a packet of Dunhills. Lynley leaned across the table with the lighter. Penellin looked at him over the flame.

"It's a bit of both, I should guess,'' Lynley said. "The longer you keep silent, the longer you protect Mark from arrest. But keeping him from arrest makes him available to Peter unless you do what you can to keep them apart.''

"Mark's dragging Peter down,'' Penellin said. "He'll kill him eventually if I don't stop him.''

"Justin Brooke told us that Peter intended to make a buy here in Cornwall,'' St. James said. "Mark was his source, wasn't he? That was why you were trying to keep them from seeing each other on Friday at Howenstow.''

"I thought Mark might try to sell to Peter and the girl. I've suspected him of dealing in drugs for some time, and I thought if I could just find where he was bringing the stuff in, where he was packaging it . . .'' Penellin rolled his cigarette restlessly between his fingers. There was no ashtray on the table, so he knocked the growing cylinder of ash onto the floor and smashed it with his foot. "I thought I could stop him. I've been watching him for weeks, following him when I could. I'd no idea he was doing it right on the estate.''

"It was a solid plan,'' St. James said, "both parts of it. Using the *Daze* as a means of getting the cocaine. Using the mill to cut and package it. Everything was associated with Howenstow in some way. And since Peter was—and is—the known Howenstow user, he stood to take the fall if things didn't work out. He'd protest his innocence wildly, of course. He'd blame Mark when it came down to it. But who'd believe him? Even yesterday, we immediately assumed he'd taken the boat. No one gave a thought to Mark. It was clever of them.''

Penellin's head lifted slowly at St. James' final word. "You know that part as well.''

"Mark didn't have the capital to orchestrate this alone,'' St. James said. "He needed an investor, and I should guess it was Mick. Nancy knew that, didn't she? You both knew it.''

"Suspected. Suspected is all.''

"Is that why you went to see him on Friday night?"

Penellin gave his attention back to his cigarette. "I was looking for answers."

"And Nancy must have known you'd be going there. So when Mick was killed, she feared the worst."

"Cambrey'd taken out a bank loan to update the newspaper," Penellin said, "but little enough got spent on that. Then he started going all the time to London. And he started talking money to Nance. How there wasn't enough. How they were close to bankrupt. Rent money. Baby money. They were going to sink, according to Mick. But none of it made sense. He had money. He'd managed to get the loan."

"Which he was investing rather copiously in cocaine."

"She didn't want to believe he was involved. She said he didn't take drugs, and she wouldn't see that one doesn't have to take them in order to sell them. She wanted proof."

"That's what you were after Friday night when you went to the cottage."

"I'd forgotten that it was one of the Fridays when he did the pay envelopes. I'd thought he'd not be home and I'd be able to have a thorough search. But he was there. We had a row."

St. James took the Talisman sandwich wrapper from his pocket. "I think this is what you wanted," he said and handed it to Penellin. "It was in the newspaper office. Harry found it in Mick's desk."

Penellin looked the paper over, handed it back. "I don't know what I wanted," he said and gave a low, self-derisive laugh. "I think I was looking for a typed confession."

"This is more design than confession," St. James admitted.

"What does it mean?"

"Only Mark could verify it, but I think it represents the original deal the two of them struck together. *1 K 9400* would signify the cost of the original purchase of cocaine. A kilo for £9400. They'd split that between them to sell, which is what the second line tells us. 500 grams for each of them at £55 per gram. Their profit: £27,500 each. And next to their profit, the particular talent each of them would bring to the plan. MP—Mark—would provide the transportation in order to procure the drug. He'd take the *Daze* and meet the dealer. MC—Mick—would provide the initial financing from the bank loan he'd secured in order to purchase new equipment for the newspaper. And Mick covered himself by beginning those initial equipment purchases so no one's suspicions would be aroused."

"Then it fell apart," Penellin said.

"Perhaps. It could be that the cocaine didn't sell as well as they thought it would and he lost money on the deal. Perhaps things didn't work out between the partners. Or there may have been a double cross somewhere along the line."

"Or the other," Penellin said. "Go ahead with the other."

"That's why you're in here, John, isn't it?" Lynley asked. "That's why you're saying nothing. That's why you're taking the blame."

"He must have discovered how easy it was," Penellin said. "He didn't need Mick once he'd made the initial purchase, did he? Why bother with an added person who'd expect part of the profits?"

"John, you can't take the blame for Cambrey's death."

"Mark's only twenty-two."

"That doesn't matter. You didn't—"

Penellin cut Lynley short by speaking to St. James. "How did you know it was Mark?"

"The *Daze*. We thought Peter had taken her to get away from Howenstow. But the boat was northeast on the rocks at Penberth Cove. So she had to be returning to Howenstow, not leaving. And she'd been there for several hours when we arrived, so there was plenty of time for Mark to abandon her, to make his way back to Howenstow, and be ready—somewhat banged up, admittedly—to help us search for Peter."

"He'd have needed to abandon her," Penellin said numbly.

"The cocaine gave him good enough reason to do so. If anyone at Penberth phoned the coastguard, he'd be in serious trouble. Better risk his life by jumping ship near the shore than risk a jail sentence by getting caught with a kilogram of cocaine on the boat."

"John," Lynley said insistently, "you've got to tell Boscowan the truth. About all of this. About Friday night."

Levelly, Penellin looked at him. "And what of Mark?" he asked. Lynley didn't reply. Penellin's features became a wash of anguish. "I can't do what you ask of me. He's my son."

Nancy was working in front of the lodge while Molly cooed in a pram nearby, gurgling over a string of bright plastic ducks which her mother had suspended above her. When Lynley pulled the car to a halt on the drive, Nancy looked up. She was raking up the foliage, flowers, loose pebbles, and debris that the wind had blown up against the house.

"No word of Peter?" she asked, walking towards them as they got out of the car.

"Is Mark here, Nancy?"

She faltered. The fact that Lynley had not aswered her question seemed to disconcert her at the same time as it acted as presage of an unpleasantness to come. She drew the rake to her side, holding it upright.

"Did Mark fix the shutters for you last night?" Lynley asked.

"The shutters?"

Her two simple words were verification enough. "Is he in the house?" St. James asked.

"I think he's just gone out. He said he was planning to—"

A sudden blast of rock and roll music negated her words. She brought a fist to her lips.

"We've spoken to your father," Lynley told her. "You've no need to protect Mark any longer. It's time he told the truth."

Leaving her in the garden, they went into the house, following the sound of drums and guitars in the direction of the kitchen where Mark sat at the table, making adjustments to his portable stereo. As he had done in the early hours of Saturday morning following Mick Cambrey's death, St. James noted the details about the boy. Then, they had suggested the possibility of his taking money from Gull Cottage upon discovering his brother-in-law's death. Now they acted in concert to corroborate his part in the cocaine partnership: a heavy gold chain round his right wrist, a new watch round his left, designer blue jeans and shirt, snakeskin boots, the stereo itself. Not one of them was the sort of possession one would purchase on the salary his father paid him to work round the estate.

On the table sat a half-eaten ham sandwich, a bottle of beer, a bag of vinegar crisps. This latter provided the air with a pungent smell. Mark dipped into it for a handful, looked up, and saw the other two men in the doorway. He turned down the volume on the stereo and got to his feet, dropping the crisps onto his plate.

"What's wrong?" he asked. "Is it Peter? Is he all right?" He ran the heel of his hand against his temple as if to straighten his hair. It was neatly combed as usual.

"We've not come about my brother," Lynley said.

Mark frowned. "I haven't heard a thing. Nance phoned your mother. She said there was no word. Have you . . . is there something . . ." He held out a hand, a gesture of camaraderie.

St. James wondered how Lynley would get past the boy's posturing. He had his answer when his friend swept the stereo from the table so forcefully that it crashed against the kitchen cupboards and gouged the wood.

"*Hey!*"

As Mark began to move, Lynley came round the table. He pushed the boy into his chair. Mark's head snapped back against the wall.

"What the hell—"

"You can talk to me or Penzance CID. Make up your mind."

Quick comprehension darted across the boy's face. He rubbed his collar bone. Nevertheless, he merely said, "You're daft."

Lynley tossed the Talisman sandwich wrapper onto the table. "What's it to be? Make up your mind."

Mark's expression was unchanging as he glanced at the paper, at the numbers, the notations, at his own initials. He snorted a laugh. "You're in heavy shit over Brooke's death, aren't you? You'd do anything to keep the police from looking into that. You're trying to keep the coppers off Peter."

"We're not here about Peter."

"No. I dare say. Let's not talk about Peter or you might hear the truth. Well, you can't have me arrested for anything. You don't have a shred of evidence."

"You took the *Daze* from Lamorna. You abandoned her off Penberth. My guess is that the reason why is sitting right here in this house. Or perhaps in the mill. How does felony theft sound? What about smuggling? Possession of narcotics? We can start with any one of them. I'll put my money on Boscowan's willingness to listen to just about anything to get your father out of the nick. I rather doubt he's as sentimental about you. So shall I give him a ring? Or shall we talk?"

Mark looked away. On the floor his stereo was giving off bursts of static.

"What do you want to know?" The question was sullen.

"Who's dealing the cocaine?"

"Me. Mick."

"You've been using the mill?"

"It was Mick's idea. He'd spent most of last spring boffing Nancy in the loft. He knew no one ever went there."

"And the *Daze*?"

"Free transportation. No overhead. Nothing to cut into the profits."

"What profits? Nancy claims they have no money."

"We turned the take around from the first go last March and reinvested in another buy. A bigger one this time." A smile pulled at his mouth. He didn't bother to conceal it. "Thank God the stuff was wrapped in oilskins. Otherwise, it'd be sitting in Penberth Cove at the moment, making the fish as happy as hell to be there. As it is"—he dumped more crisps on his plate—"Mick'll miss out on the profits."

"Convenient for you that he's dead."

Mark was unimpressed. "Am I supposed to blanch with fear at the implication? Oops, the poor berk's just given himself a motive for murder?" He took a bite from his sandwich, chewed it deliberately, and washed it down with a swallow of beer. "Let's avoid the drama. I was in St. Ives Friday night."

"No doubt with someone who'd be only too happy to step forward and confirm that fact?"

Mark maintained his bravado. "Sure. No problem."

"Honour among drug dealers?"

"A man needs to know his friends."

"Peter was one once."

Mark studied his fingernails. The stereo squawked. St. James switched it off.

"Did you sell to my brother?"

"When he had the money."

"When did you last see him?"

"I've told you before. There's no change in the story. Friday afternoon at the cove. He phoned the lodge earlier and said he wanted to see me. I had to hunt the bloody ass down as it was. Jesus, I don't even know why I bothered."

"What did he want?"

"What he always wanted. Dope on credit."

"Did he know how you were using the mill?" Lynley asked.

Mark gave a sardonic laugh in response. "D'you think I'd tell him that and have him slobbering down my neck for free samples every time I was working there? We may be old mates, but I like to think I know where to draw the line."

"Where is he?" Lynley asked.

Mark was silent.

Lynley crashed his fist onto the table top. "Where is he? Where's my brother?"

Mark pushed his arm away. "I don't know, all right? I bloody don't know. Dead with a needle in his arm, most likely."

"Tommy."

St. James' admonition came too late. Lynley dragged the boy to his feet. He threw him against the wall, pressed his arm against his larynx, and held him there.

"You piece of filth," he said. "God damn you, I'll be back." He dropped him abruptly and left the room.

Mark stood for a moment, rubbing his throat. He brushed at the collar of his shirt as if to remove any trace of Lynley's quick assault. Stooping, he picked up his stereo, put it back on the table, and began to play with its knobs. St. James left him.

He found Lynley in the car, his hands gripping the wheel. Nancy and her baby were gone.

"We're their victims." Lynley stared at the drive that wound towards the great house. Shadows dappled it. A breeze danced sycamore leaves across the lane. "We're all of us their victims. I as much as anyone, St. James. No. *More* than anyone, because I'm supposed to be a professional."

St. James saw the conflicts that confronted his friend. The ties of blood, the call of duty. Responsibility to family, betrayal of self. He waited for Lynley, always at heart an honest man, to put his struggle into words.

"I should have told Boscowan that Peter was at Gull Cottage on Friday night. I should have told him that Mick was alive after John left him. I should have told him about the row. About Brooke. About everything. But God help me, I couldn't, St. James. What's happening to me?"

"You're trying to deal with Peter, with Nancy, with John, with Mark. With everyone, Tommy."

"The walls are crashing in."

"We'll sort it out."

Lynley looked at him then. His dark eyes seemed filmed over by a mist. "Do you believe that?" he asked.

"I've got to believe something."

"Actually, Islington-London is its formal name," Lady Helen said. "Islington-London, Ltd. It's a pharmaceutical company."

St. James' attention was on the section of the garden that he could still see in the growing darkness. He stood in the small alcove off the drawing room while behind him Lady Asherton, Lynley, and Cotter drank their evening coffee.

"Deborah and I went there this morning," Lady Helen continued. In the background, St. James heard Deborah's voice, followed by her laughter, light and engaging. "Yes, all right, darling," Lady Helen said to her. And then to St. James, "Deborah's most unforgiving about the fact that I wore my fox fur. Well, perhaps I *was* just a bit overdressed for the occasion, but the ensemble did make a statement, I think. And besides, as far as I'm concerned, if one's going to do anything incognita, one ought to do it well. Don't you agree?''

''Decidedly.''

''And it was a success. The receptionist even asked me if I'd come about a job. Senior Director of Project Testing. Sounds absolutely divine. Have I a future in it?''

St. James smiled into the telephone. ''I suppose it depends upon what project's being tested. What about Tina? What's the connection?''

''There doesn't seem to be one at all. We described her to the receptionist—and what a blessing to have Deborah there because her eye for detail, not to mention her memory, is quite remarkable. But the girl hadn't a clue. She didn't recognise the description at all.'' Lady Helen paused as Deborah interjected a comment in the background. She went on to say, ''Considering what Tina apparently looks like, it's hard to believe anyone would forget her. Although the girl did ask if she might be a biochemist.''

''That seems a bit far-fetched.''

''Hmm. It does. Except that Deborah did tell me about a drink she's developed. A health drink. Perhaps Tina hoped to sell it to the pharmaceutical company?''

''Unlikely, Helen.''

''I suppose so. She'd go to a beverage company with it, wouldn't she?''

''That's more probable. Has anyone heard from her? Has she returned?''

''Not yet. I spent part of the afternoon going to each flat in the building to see if anyone knew anything about where she might be.''

''No luck, I take it.''

''None at all. No one seems to know her very well. In fact, Deborah appears to be the only person who's had any close contact with her, aside from a peculiar woman across the hall who loaned her an iron. Several people have seen her about, of course—she's lived here since September—but no one's spent any time talking to her. Besides Deborah.''

St. James jotted the word *September* into his notes. He underlined it, drew a circle round it. He topped the circle with a cross. The symbol of woman. He scribbled over it all.

''What next?'' Lady Helen was asking.

"See if the building manager has a Cornish address for her," St. James said. "You might try to find out what she pays for the flat."

"Quite. I should have thought to ask that earlier. Although heaven knows why. Are we getting anywhere?"

St. James sighed. "I don't know. Have you spoken to Sidney?"

"That's a problem, Simon. I've been phoning her flat, but there's no answer. I tried her agency, but they've not heard from her either. Did she talk about going to see friends?"

"No. She talked about going home."

"I'll keep trying, then. Don't worry. She may have gone to Cheyne Row."

St. James thought this unlikely. He felt the first bite of concern. "We need to find her, Helen."

"I'll pop round to her flat. She may not be answering the phone."

Having secured this assurance, St. James rang off. He remained in the alcove, staring down at the scribbled mess he'd made of the word *September*. He wanted it to mean something. He knew that it probably did. But what that something was he could not have said.

He turned as Lynley came into the alcove. "Anything?"

St. James related the bits of information which Lady Helen had managed to gather that day. He saw the change in Lynley's expression after he'd heard the very first fact.

"Islington-London?" he asked. "Are you sure of that, St. James?"

"Helen went there. Why? Does it mean something to you?"

Warily, Lynley glanced back into the drawing room. His mother and Cotter were chatting together quietly as they looked through a family album which lay between them.

"Tommy? What is it?"

"Roderick Trenarrow. He works for Islington-Penzance."

Part V

IDENTITIES

20

"Then Mick must have left both of those telephone numbers in Tina Cogin's flat," St. James said. "Trenarrow's as well as Islington's. That explains why Trenarrow didn't know who Tina was."

Lynley didn't reply until he'd made the turn onto Beaufort Street, to head in the general direction of Paddington. They had just dropped Cotter at St. James' Cheyne Row house where he'd greeted the sight of that brick building like a prodigal son, scurrying inside with a suitcase in each hand and undisguised, wholehearted relief buoying his footsteps. It was ten past one in the afternoon. Their drive into the city from the airfield in Surrey had been plagued by a snarl of slow-moving traffic, the product of a summer fete near Buckland which apparently was drawing record crowds.

"Do you think Roderick's involved in this business?"

St. James took note not only of the dispassionate tone of Lynley's question but also of the fact that he'd deliberately phrased it to leave out the word *murder*. At the same time, he saw the manner in which his friend attended to the driving as he spoke, both hands high on the steering wheel, eyes fixed straight ahead. He knew only the barest details of Lynley's past relationship with Trenarrow, all of them circling round a general antipathy that had its roots in Lady Asherton's enduring relationship with the man. Lynley would need something to compensate for that dislike if Trenarrow was even tangentially involved in the deaths in Cornwall, and it seemed that he'd chosen scrupulous impartiality as a means of counterbalancing the animosity that coloured his long association with the man.

"I suppose he could be, even if only unconsciously." St. James told him about his meeting with Trenarrow, about the interview Mick Cambrey had done with him. "But if Mick was working on a story that led to his death, Trenarrow may have merely given him a lead, perhaps the name of someone at Islington-London with information Mick needed."

"But if, as you say, there were no notes in the newspaper office from any story connected to Roderick . . ." Lynley braked at a traffic signal. It would have been natural to look at St. James. He did not do so. "What does that suggest to you?"

"I didn't say there were no notes about him, Tommy. I said there was no story about him. Or about anything relating to cancer research. That's a different matter than an absence of notes. There may be hundreds of notes for all we know. Harry Cambrey was the one who looked through Mick's files. I had no chance to do so."

"So the information may still be there, with Harry unable to recognise its importance."

"Quite. But the story itself—whatever it was, if it's even connected to Mick's death—may have nothing to do with Trenarrow directly. He may just be a source."

Lynley looked at him then. "You didn't want to phone him, St. James. Why?"

St. James watched a woman push a pram across the street. A small child clung to the hem of her dress. The traffic signal changed. Cars and lorries began to move.

"Mick may have been on the trail of a story that caused his death. You know as well as I that it makes no sense to alert anyone to the fact that we may be on the trail as well."

"So you do think Roderick's involved."

"Not necessarily. Probably not at all. But he could inadvertently give the word to someone who is. Why phone him and allow for that chance?"

Lynley spoke as if he hadn't heard St. James' words. "If he is, St. James, if he is . . ." He turned the Bentley right, onto the Fulham Road. They passed the dress shops and antique dealers, the bistros and restaurants of trendy London where the streets were peopled by fashionably dressed shoppers and trim-looking matrons on their way to rendezvous.

"We don't have all the facts yet, Tommy. There's no sense in tormenting yourself about it now."

Again, St. James' words seemed to make no difference. "It would destroy my mother," Lynley said.

They drove on to Paddington. Deborah met them in the small lobby of the Shrewsbury Court Apartments where she had apparently been waiting for them, pacing back and forth across the black and white tiles. She pulled the door open before they'd had a chance to ring the bell.

"Dad phoned to tell me you were on your way. Tommy, are you all right? Dad said there's still been no sign of Peter."

Lynley's response was to say her name like a sigh. He drew her to him. "What a mess this weekend's been for you. I'm sorry, Deb."

"It's all right. It's nothing."

St. James looked past them. The sign *concierge* on a nearby door was done in calligraphy, he noted. But the hand was inexpert and the dot above the *i* had blurred and become a part of the second *c*. He examined this, considered this—each letter, each detail—keeping his eyes fastened to the sign until Deborah spoke.

"Helen's waiting up above." She moved with Lynley towards the lift.

They found Lady Helen on the telephone in Deborah's flat. She was saying nothing, merely listening, and from her look in his direction and the expression on her face when she replaced the receiver, St. James realised whom she had been trying to reach.

"Sidney?" he asked her.

"I can't find her, Simon. Her agency gave me a list of names, friends of hers. But no one's heard a word. I just tried her flat again. Nothing. I've phoned your mother as well, but there's no answer there. Shall I keep trying her?"

Cold prickling ran its way down St. James' spine. "No. She'll only worry."

Lady Helen spoke again. "I've begun to think about Justin Brooke's death."

She didn't need to say more. St. James' own thoughts had made that same leap forward the moment she had told him that his sister had still not turned up. Again, he cursed himself for allowing Sidney to leave Cornwall alone. If she had walked into danger, if she was hurt in any way . . . He felt the fingers of his right hand dig into his palm. He forced them to relax.

"Has Tina Cogin returned?"

"Not yet."

"Then perhaps we ought to make certain about the key." He looked at Lynley. "Have you brought them?"

"Brought them?" Lady Helen asked blankly.

"Harry Cambrey's managed to get us Mick's set of keys from Boscowan," Lynley explained. "We wanted to see if one of them might unlock Tina's door."

He kept them in suspense only as long as it took to get to the next flat, to insert and turn the proper key in the lock. He swung the door open. They walked inside.

"All right. He had his own key," Lady Helen said. "But, really, Tommy, where does that get us? It can't be a surprise. We already knew he'd been here. Deborah told us that. So all we know beyond that fact is that he was special enough to Tina Cogin to merit a key to her door."

"It changes the nature of their relationship, Helen. This obviously isn't a call girl and her client. Prostitutes don't generally give out their keys."

From his position near the tiny kitchen, St. James was scrutinising the room. Its furnishings were expensive, but they told little about the inhabitant. And there were no personal objects on display: no photographs, no mementoes, no collection of any kind. Indeed, the entire bed-sitting-room had the look of having been put together by a decorator for a hotel. He walked to the desk.

The red light of the answering machine was blinking, indicating a message. He pushed the button. A man's voice said, "Colin Sage. I'm phoning about the advert," and he gave a number for a return call. A second message was much the same. St. James wrote down the numbers and gave them to Lady Helen.

"An advertisement?" she asked. "That can't be how she makes her arrangements."

"You said there was a savings book?" St. James replied.

Deborah came to his side. "Here," she said. "There's this as well."

From a drawer she took both the savings book and a manila folder. He looked at the latter first, frowning down at the neatly typed list of names and addresses. Mostly London. The furthest was Brighton. Behind him, he heard Lynley going through the chest of drawers.

"What is this?" Meditatively, St. James asked the question of himself, but Deborah replied.

"We thought of clients at first. But of course, that can't be. There are women on the list. And even if there weren't any women at all, it's hard to imagine anyone managing to . . ." She hesitated. St. James looked up. Her cheeks had coloured.

"Service this many men?" he asked.

"Well, of course, she's indicated on the tab that they're just prospects, hasn't she? So at first we thought that she was using the list to

. . . before we actually opened up the file and saw . . . I mean, how exactly *would* a prostitute build up a clientele? Through word of mouth?'' Her colour deepened. ''Lord. Is that a dreadful sort of pun?''

He chuckled at the question. ''What did you imagine she was doing with this list, sending out brochures?''

Deborah gave a rueful laugh. ''I'm so hopeless at this sort of thing, aren't I? A hundred clues shrieking to be noticed and I can't make sense of a single one.''

''I thought you'd decided she wasn't a prostitute. I thought we'd all decided that.''

''It's just something about the way she talked and her appearance.''

''Perhaps we can let go of whatever her appearance might have suggested,'' Lynley said.

Across the room, he stood at the wardrobe with Lady Helen at his side. He had taken down the four hatboxes from the top shelf, had opened and placed them on the floor in a line. He was bending over one of these, separating the folds of white tissue paper. From the centre of the nest which the paper created, he withdrew a wig. Long black hair, wispy fringe. He balanced it on his fist.

Deborah gaped at it. Lady Helen sighed.

''Wonderful,'' she said. ''The woman actually wears a *wig?* So what little we know of her—not to mention Deborah's description—must be virtually meaningless. She's a chimera, isn't she? False fingernails. False hair.'' She glanced at the chest of drawers. Something seemed to occur to her, for she went to them, pulled one open, and fingered through the undergarments. She held up a black brassiere. ''False everything else.''

St. James joined them. He took the wig from Lynley and carried it to the window where he opened the curtains and held it under the natural light. The texture told him that the hair was real.

''Did you know she wore a wig, Deb?'' Lynley asked.

''No, of course not. How could I have known?''

''It's a high quality piece,'' St. James said. ''You'd have no cause to think it a wig.'' He examined it closely, running his fingers across the inner webbing. As he did so, a hair came loose, not one of those which comprised the wig, but another shorter hair that had detached itself from the wearer, becoming caught up in the webbing. St. James plucked it completely free, held it up to the light, and handed the wig back to Lynley.

''What is it, Simon?'' Lady Helen asked.

He didn't reply at once. Instead, he stared at the single hair between his fingers, realising what it had to imply and coming to terms with what that implication had to mean. There was only one explanation that made any sense, only one explanation that accounted for Tina Cogin's disappearance. Still, he took a moment to test his theory.

"Have you worn this, Deborah?"

"I? No. What makes you think that?"

At the desk, he took a piece of white paper from the top drawer. He placed the hair on this and carried both back to the light.

"The hair," he said. "It's red."

He looked up at Deborah and saw her expression change from wonder to realisation.

"Is it possible?" he asked her, for since she was the only one who had seen them both, she was also the only one who could possibly confirm it.

"Oh, Simon. I'm no good at this. I don't know. I don't *know*."

"But you saw her. You were with her. She gave you a drink."

"The drink," Deborah said. She dashed from the room. In a moment, the others heard her door crash back against the wall of her flat.

Lady Helen spoke. "What is it? You can't possibly be thinking Deborah has anything to do with all this. The woman's incognita. That's all it is, plain and simple. She's been in disguise."

St. James placed the piece of paper on the desk. He placed the hair on top of it. He heard over and over that single word. *Incognita, incognita*. What a monumental joke.

"My God," he said. "She was telling everyone she met. Tina Cogin. *Tina Cogin*. The name's a bloody anagram."

Deborah flew into the room, in one hand the photograph she had brought with her from Cornwall, in the other hand a small card. She handed both to St. James.

"Turn them over," she said.

He didn't have to do so. He knew already that the handwriting would be identical on each.

"It's the card she gave me, Simon. The recipe for her drink. And on the back of Mick's picture . . ."

Lynley joined them, taking the card and the photograph from St. James. "God almighty," he murmured.

"What on earth is it?" Lady Helen asked.

"The reason Harry Cambrey's been building Mick's reputation as a real man's man, I should guess," St. James said.

*   *   *

Deborah poured boiling water into the teapot and carried it to the small oak table which they had moved into the sitting area of her flat. They took places round it, Deborah and Lynley sitting on the day bed, Lady Helen and St. James on ladder-back chairs. St. James picked up the savings book which lay among the other items attached to Mick Cambrey's life and his death: the manila folder entitled *prospects,* the card upon which he'd written the phone number of Islington-London, the Talisman sandwich wrapper, his photograph, the recipe for the drink which he'd given to Deborah on the day that he'd appeared—as Tina Cogin—at her door.

"These ten withdrawals from the account," Lady Helen said, pointing to them. "They match what Tina—what Mick Cambrey paid in rent. And the time works right with the facts, Simon. September through June."

"Long before he and Mark began dealing in cocaine," Lynley said.

"So that's not how he got the money for the flat?" Deborah asked.

"Not according to Mark."

Lady Helen ran her finger down the page which listed the deposits. She said, "But he's put money in every two weeks for a year. Where on earth did it come from?"

St. James flipped to the front of the book, scanning the entries. "Obviously, he had another source of income."

The amount of money comprising each deposit, St. James saw, was not consistent. Sometimes it was significant, other times barely so. Thus, he discounted the second possibility that had risen in his mind upon noting the regularity of the payments into Mick's account. They couldn't be the result of blackmail. Blackmailers generally increase the cost of suppressing a damaging piece of information. Greed feeds on itself; easy money begs for more.

"Beyond that," Lynley said, "Mark told us that they'd reinvested their profits in a second, larger buy. His taking the *Daze* on Sunday confirms that story."

Deborah poured the tea. St. James scooped up his customary four spoonfuls of sugar before Lady Helen shuddered and handed the bowl to Deborah. She picked up the manila folder.

"Mick must have been selling his share of the cocaine in London. Surely if he'd been doing so in Nanrunnel, someone would have discovered it eventually. Mrs. Swann, for instance. I can hardly think she would have let something like that go unnoticed."

"That makes sense," Lynley agreed. "He had a reputation as a journalist in Cornwall. He'd hardly have jeopardized it by selling cocaine there when he could just as easily have done so here."

"But I've got the impression he had a reputation here in London as well," St. James said. "He'd worked here, hadn't he, before returning to Cornwall?"

"But not as Tina Cogin," Deborah pointed out. "Surely he must have sold the drugs as a woman."

"He became Tina in September," Lady Helen said. "He took this flat in September. He began selling the following March. Plenty of time to amass a list of buyers." She tapped her fingers against the folder. "We were wondering what was meant by *prospects*, weren't we? Perhaps now we know. Shall we see what sort of prospects these really are?"

"If they're prospective cocaine buyers," Lynley said, "they're hardly going to admit the fact."

Lady Helen smiled serenely. "Not to the police, Tommy darling. Of course."

St. James knew what that angelic smile meant. If anyone could wrangle information from a total stranger, it would be Lady Helen. Lighthearted chitchat leading down the primrose path to disclosure and cooperation was her special talent. She had already proved that with the caretaker of Shrewsbury Court Apartments. Obtaining the key to Mick's flat had been child's play for her. This list of prospects was merely one step advanced, a moderate challenge. She would become Sister Helen from the Salvation Army, or Helen the Saved from a drug rehabilitation programme, or Helen the Desperate looking for a score. But ultimately, in some way, she would ferret out the truth.

"If Mick was selling in London, a buyer may have followed him to Cornwall," St. James said.

"But if he was selling as Tina, how would someone know who he really was?" Deborah asked.

"Perhaps he was recognised. Perhaps a buyer, who knew him as Mick, saw him when he was posing as Tina."

"And followed him to Cornwall? Why? Blackmail?"

"What better way to get cocaine? If the buyer was having a hard time coming up with the money, why not blackmail Cambrey for a payment in drugs?" St. James picked up items one by one. He studied them, fingered them, dropped them back on the table. "But Cambrey wouldn't want to risk his reputation in Cornwall by giving in to the blackmail. So he and the buyer argued. He was hit. He struck his head and died. The buyer took the money that was in the cottage sitting room. Anyone who's desperate for drugs—and who's just killed a man—is hardly going to draw the line at taking money lying right in the open."

Lynley got up abruptly. He walked to the open window and leaned on the sill, looking down at the street. Too late, St. James recognised whose portrait he had been painting with his series of conjectures.

"Could he have known about Mick?" Lynley asked. No one answered at first. Instead, they listened to the rising sound of traffic in Sussex Gardens as afternoon commuters began to make their way towards the Edgware Road. An engine revved. Brakes screeched in reply. Lynley repeated the question. He did not turn from the window. "Could my brother have known?"

"Possibly, Tommy," St. James said. When Lynley swung to face him, he went on reluctantly. "He was part of the drug network in London. Sidney saw him not that long ago in Soho. At night. In an alley." He paused thoughtfully, remembering the information his sister had given him, remembering her fanciful description of the woman Peter had been assaulting. *Dressed all in black with flowing black hair.*

He had the impression that Lady Helen was recalling this information even as he did, for she spoke with what seemed a determination to relieve Lynley's anxiety by looking for another focus for the crime. "Mick's death might revolve round something entirely different. We've thought that from the first and I don't think we ought to dismiss it now. He was a journalist, after all. He might have been writing a story. He could even have been working on something about transvestites."

St. James shook his head. "He wasn't writing about transvestites. He *was* a transvestite. The expense of the flat tells us that. The furniture. The woman's wardrobe. He wouldn't need all that just to gather information for a story. And there's the newspaper office to consider as well, with Harry Cambrey finding the underwear in Mick's desk. Not to mention the row the two of them had."

"Harry knew?"

"He seems to have figured it out."

Lady Helen fingered the Talisman wrapper, as if with the resolution of making yet another effort to put Lynley's mind at rest. "Yet Harry was sure it was a story."

"It might have been a story. We've still got the connection to Islington-London."

"Perhaps Mick was investigating a drug of some kind," Deborah offered, "A drug that wasn't ready to be marketed yet."

Lady Helen took up her thought. "One with side effects. One that's already available to doctors. With the company pooh-poohing the possibility of problems."

Lynley came back to the table. They looked at one another, struck

by the plausibility of this bit of idle conjecture. Thalidomide. Thorough
testing, regulations, and restrictions had so far precluded the possibility
of another teratogenic nightmare. But men were greedy when it came to
fast profits. Men had always been so.

"What if, in researching an entirely different subject, Mick got wind
of something suspicious," St. James proposed. "He pursued it here. He
interviewed people here at Islington-London. And that was the cause of
his death."

In spite of their efforts, Lynley did not join them. "But the castration?" He sank down onto the day bed, rubbing his forehead. "We can't
seem to turn in any direction that explains it all."

As if to underscore the futility behind his words, the telephone began to ring. Deborah went to answer it. Lynley was back on his feet an
instant after she spoke.

"Peter! Where on earth are you? . . . What is it? . . . I can't
understand . . . Peter, please . . . You've called where? . . . Wait,
he's right here."

Lynley lunged for the phone. "Damn you, where have you been!
Don't you know that Brooke . . . Shut up and listen to me for once,
Peter. Brooke's dead as well as Mick. . . . I don't care what you want
any longer . . . What?" Lynley stopped, frozen. His body was rigid.
His voice all at once was perfectly calm. "Are you certain? . . . Listen
to me, Peter, you must pull yourself together . . . I understand, but you
mustn't touch anything. Do you understand me, Peter? Don't touch anything. Leave her alone. . . . Now, give me your address . . . All right.
Yes, I've got it. I'll be there at once."

He replaced the phone. It seemed that entire minutes passed before
he turned back to the others.

"Something's happened to Sasha."

"I think he's on something," Lynley said.

Which would explain, St. James thought, why Lynley had insisted
that Deborah and Helen remain behind. He wouldn't want either of them
to see his brother in that condition, especially Deborah. "What happened?"

Lynley pulled the car into Sussex Gardens, cursing when a taxi cut
him off. He headed towards the Bayswater Road, veering through Rad-
nor Place and half a dozen side streets to avoid the worst of the afternoon
crush.

"I don't know. He kept screaming that she was on the bed, that she wasn't moving, that he thought she was dead."

"You didn't want him to phone the emergency number?"

"Christ, he could be hallucinating, St. James. He sounded like someone going through the D.T.'s. Damn and blast this bloody traffic!"

"Where is he, Tommy?"

"Whitechapel."

It took them nearly an hour to get there, battling their way through a virtual gridlock of cars, lorries, buses, and taxis. Lynley knew the city well enough to run through countless side streets and alleys, but every time they emerged onto a main artery, their progress was frustrated again. Midway down New Oxford Street, he spoke.

"I'm at fault here. I've done everything but buy the drugs for him."

"Don't be absurd."

"I wanted him to have the best of everything. I never asked him to stand on his own. What he's become is the result. I'm at fault here, St. James. The real sickness is mine."

St. James gazed out the window and sought a reply. He thought about the energy people expend in seeking to avoid what they most need to face. They fill their lives with distraction and denial, only to find at an unexpected eleventh hour that there is in reality no absolute escape. How long had Lynley been engaged in avoidance? How long had he himself done the same thing? It had become a habit with both of them. In scrupulously avoiding what they needed to say to each other, they had learned to adopt evasion in every significant area of their lives.

He said, "Not everything in life is your responsibility, Tommy."

"My mother said practically the same thing the other night."

"She was right. You punish yourself at times when others bear equal responsibility. Don't do that now."

Lynley shot him a quick look. "The accident. There's that as well, isn't there? You've tried to take the burden from my shoulders all these years, but you never will, not completely. I drove the car, St. James. No matter what other facts exist to attenuate my guilt, the primary fact remains. I drove the car that night. And when it was over, I walked away. You didn't."

"I've not blamed you."

"You don't need to do so. I blame myself." He turned off New Oxford Street and they began another series of side street and back alley runs, edging them closer to the City and to Whitechapel which lay just beyond it. "But at least I must let go of blaming myself for Peter if I'm not to go mad. The best step I can take in that direction at the moment is to swear to you that no matter what we find when we get to him, it shall be Peter's responsibility, not mine.''

They found the building on a narrow street directly off Brick Lane, where a shouting group of Pakistani children were playing football with a caved-in ball. They were using four plastic rubbish sacks for goal posts, but one sack had split open and its contents lay about, smashed and trodden under the children's feet.

The sight of the Bentley called an abrupt halt to the game, and St. James and Lynley climbed out of the car into a curious circle of faces. The air was heavy, not only with the apprehension that accompanies the appearance of strangers in a closely-knit neighbourhood but also with the smell of old coffee grounds, rotting vegetables, and fruit gone bad. The shoes of the football players contributed largely to this pungent odour. They appeared to be caked with organic refuse.

"Wha's up?" one of the children murmured.

"Dunno," another replied. "Some motor, that, i'n it?"

A third, more enterprising than the others, stepped forward with an offer to "watch the motor f'r you, mister. Keep this lot off it." He nodded his head towards the rest of the crew. Lynley raised his hand slightly, a response which the boy seemed to take as affirmation, for he posted himself with one hand on the bonnet, the other on his hip, and one grubby foot on the bumper.

They had parked directly in front of Peter's building, a narrow structure five floors high. Originally, its bricks had been painted white, but time, soot, and lack of interest had dirtied them to a repellent grey. The woodwork of windows and front door appeared to have been untouched for decades. Where handsome blue paint had once made a pleasing contrast to the white of the bricks, mere flecks remained, azure spots like freckles on a skin being eaten by age. The fact that someone on the third floor had tried to ease the aspect of the building by planting freesias in a splintered window box did nothing to combat the general feeling of poverty and decay.

They climbed the four front steps to the door. It stood open. Above it, the words *last few days* had been sprayed onto the bricks with red paint. They seemed a suitable epigraph.

"He said he's on the first floor," Lynley said and headed for the stairs.

Once covered with a cheap linoleum, they were worn through in the centre to their black backing, and the edges that remained were crusted with a combination of old wax and new dirt. Large, greasy discolourations splodged the stairway walls which were pockmarked with bolt holes where once a handrail had been mounted. Handprints covered them, as well as an enormous gravylike stain which oozed down from an upper floor.

On the landing, a dusty pram tilted on three wheels, surrounded by several sacks of rubbish, two tin pails, a broom, and a blackened mop. A gaunt cat, ribs showing and an ulcerated sore in the middle of its forehead, slunk by them as they climbed upward, assailed by the odour of garlic and urine.

In the uncarpeted first floor corridor, the building came to life. Televisions, music, voices raised in an argument, a baby's sudden wail—the discordant sounds of people going about the daily business of living. This was not the case in Peter's flat, however, which they found at the far end of the corridor where a grimy window admitted a weak shaft of light from the street. The door was shut, but neither closed nor latched, so when Lynley knocked, it swung inward to reveal a single room whose windows—closed and covered by bedsheets—seemed to entrap the odours of the entire building, mingling them with the stronger stench of unwashed bodies and dirty clothes.

Although the room was not altogether much smaller than the bedsit they had just left in Paddington, the contrast was unnerving. There was virtually no furniture. Instead, three large, stained pillows lay on the floor among discarded newspapers and open magazines. In lieu of either wardrobe or chest of drawers, a single chair held a pile of unfolded clothing which spilled down to four cardboard cartons in which more clothing lay. Upended fruit packing crates served as tables, and a shadeless floor lamp provided the room with light.

Lynley said nothing at all as they entered. For a moment, he didn't move from the threshold, as if he were summoning the strength of purpose to shut the door behind them and face the truth.

He pushed the door closed so that nothing further obstructed their line of vision. Against the near wall, a threadbare sofa had been folded out into a bed. On this, a partially shrouded figure lay motionless. On the floor, just beyond the sofa, Peter Lynley was curled into a foetal position, his hands curved round his head.

"Peter!" Lynley went to him, knelt, cried his name again.

As if roused by the sound, Peter gasped and made a convulsive movement. His eyes focused, found his brother.

"She won't move." He stuffed part of his T-shirt into his mouth for a moment as if in an attempt to prevent himself from crying. "I came home and she was there and she won't move."

"What's happened?" Lynley asked.

"She won't move, Tommy. I came home and she was there and she won't move."

St. James went to the sofa. He removed the sheet which covered most of the figure. Beneath it, Sasha lay naked on her side on the filthy linen with one arm stretched out and one hand dangling from the edge of the bed. Her thin hair fell forward to cover her face, and where her neck was exposed, its flesh looked grey with dirt. He put his fingers to the wrist of her outstretched arm although even as he did so, he knew the exercise was mere rote formality. He'd once been a member of the Met's crime-scene team. This wasn't the first time he'd looked upon a dead body.

He straightened and shook his head at Lynley. The other man came to join him.

St. James pushed the fallen hair to one side and moved the arm gently to check for rigor. He took a step back, however, when he saw the hypodermic needle embedded in her flesh.

"Overdose," Lynley said. "What's she taken, Peter?"

He went back to his brother. St. James remained with the body. The hypodermic, he noticed, was empty, the plunger down, as if she'd mainlined a substance that had killed her in an instant. It was hard to believe. He looked for some indication of what she had taken to bring about such a death. There was nothing on the packing crate next to the bed, save an empty glass with a tarnished spoon inside it and a residue of white powder on its rim. The bed itself held nothing other than the corpse. He stepped back, looking on the floor between the bed and the crate. And then, with a rush of horror, he saw it.

A silver bottle lay on its side, almost out of sight. It spilled forth a white powder, undoubtedly the same substance which clung to the rim of the glass, the same substance which ended Sasha Nifford's life. Unprepared for the sight, St. James felt his heart begin to pound. He felt burned all at once by a sudden heat. He refused to believe it.

The bottle was Sidney's.

21

"Get control of yourself, Peter," Lynley was saying to his brother. He took Peter's arm, pulling him to his feet. Peter clung to him, weeping. "What's she taken?"

St. James stared at the bottle. He could hear Sidney's voice with utter clarity. She might have been standing right there in the room. *"We drove him home,"* she had said. *"Squalid little flat in Whitechapel."* And then later, more damning and completely undeniable, *"Just tell little Peter when you find him that I have lots to discuss with him. Believe me, I can hardly wait for the opportunity."*

In the light from the lamp the bottle glinted, winking at him and demanding recognition. He gave it, admitted it without hesitation. For from where he stood, St. James could see part of the engraving that comprised her initials, and he'd insisted upon the delicacy of that engraving himself because he'd given the bottle to his sister four years ago on her twenty-first birthday.

"You were my favourite brother. I loved you best."

There was no time. He did not have the luxury in which to consider his various options and weigh the relative morality of each. He could only act or let her face the police. He chose to act, bending, reaching out his hand.

"Good. You've found it," Lynley said, coming to his side. "It looks like—" He suddenly seemed to recognise the significance of St. James' posture, of his outstretched hand. Certainly, St. James thought, from the chill that had rapidly followed the heat in his body, Lynley must have seen something in the pallor of his face. For directly after his words faded away, Lynley drew St. James back from the bed. "Don't protect him for my sake," he said quietly. "That's finished, St. James. I meant what I said in the car. If it's heroin, I can only help Peter by allowing him to face the consequences. I'm going to telephone the Met." He walked from the room.

Heat returned, a wave of it. St. James felt it on his face and in his joints. Oblivious of Peter, who leaned against the wall, weeping into his hands, he moved woodenly to the window. He fumbled behind the bed-sheet curtain to open it, only to find that sometime in the past it had been painted shut. The room was stifling.

Less than twenty-four hours, he thought. The bottle was marked with the silversmith's identification, a small, fanciful escutcheon worked into its base. It wouldn't take long for the police to trace the piece back to Jermyn Street where he'd bought it. Then, it would be a simple matter. They would go through the files and look at orders. These they would compare to the bottle itself. After making some telephone calls to patrons, they would follow up with discreet enquiries at those patrons' homes. The most he could hope for was twenty-four hours.

Dimly, he heard Lynley's voice, speaking into the telephone in the hallway, and nearer, the sound of Peter's weeping. Above that, the harsh grating of stertorous breathing rose and fell. He recognised it as his own.

"They're on their way." Lynley closed the door behind him. He crossed the room. "Are you all right, St. James?"

"Yes. Quite." To prove this beyond doubt, he moved—it took an effort of will—away from the window. Lynley had dumped the clothes from the room's only chair and placed it at the foot of the bed, its back towards the body.

"The police are on their way," he repeated. Firmly, he led his brother to the chair and sat him down. "There's a bottle of something over by the sofa that's likely to get you arrested, Peter. We've only a few minutes to talk."

"I didn't see a bottle. It isn't mine." Peter wiped his nose on his arm.

"Tell me what happened. Where have you been since Saturday night?"

Peter squinted as if the light hurt his eyes. "I've been nowhere."

"Don't play games with me."

"Games? I'm telling—"

"You're on your own in this. Are you capable of understanding that? You're entirely on your own. So you can tell me the truth or talk to the police. Frankly, I don't care one way or the other.''

"I'm *telling* you the truth. We've been nowhere but here.''

"How long have you been back?''

"Since Saturday. Sunday. I don't know. I don't remember.''

"What time did you arrive?''

"After dawn.''

"What *time*?''

"I don't know the time! What difference does it make?''

"The difference it makes is that Justin Brooke's dead. But you're lucky for the moment because the police seem to believe it was an accident.''

Peter's mouth twisted. "And you think *I* killed him? What about Mick? Are you setting me up for that as well, Tommy?'' His voice broke when he said his brother's name. He began to cry again, thin body wracked by the force of dry sobs. He covered his face with his hands. His fingernails were bitten, crusted with dirt. "You always think the worst of me, don't you?''

St. James saw that Lynley was preparing for verbal battle. He spoke to intervene. "You're going to be asked a great many questions, Peter. In the long run, it might be easier to answer them with Tommy so that he can help you, rather than with someone you don't even know.''

"I can't talk to him,'' Peter sobbed. "He won't listen to me. I'm nothing to him.''

"How can you say that?'' Lynley demanded hotly.

"Because it's true, and you know it. You just buy me off. It's what you've always done. You were there with the chequebook all right because that was easy for you. You didn't have to be involved. But you were *never* there—never once in my life—for anything else.'' He leaned forward in the chair, his arms cradling his stomach, his head on his knees. "I was six years old when he got sick, Tommy. I was seven when you left. I was twelve when he died. Do you know what that was like? Can you even imagine it? And all I had—all I *had,* damn you— was poor old Roderick. Doing what he could to be a father to me. Whenever he thought he could get away with it. But always in secret because you might find out.''

Lynley pushed him upright. "So you turned to drugs and it's all my fault? Don't put that on me. Don't you dare.''

"I put nothing on you,'' his brother spat back. "I despise you.''

"You think I don't know it? Every second you breathe is a second you live to hurt me. You even took Deborah's cameras to get back at me, didn't you?''

"That's really rich, Tommy. Get out of here, will you? Leave me to the police."

St. James forced himself to intercede, desperate to get the information he needed. "What did she take, Peter?" he asked. "Where did she get it?"

Peter scrubbed his face on his tattered T-shirt. It was ancient, faded, bearing the figure of a skeleton, a cluster of roses, and the words *Grateful Dead*. "I don't know. I was out."

"Where?" Lynley demanded.

Peter shot him a contemptuous look. "Buying bread and eggs." He flung his hand towards the string bag that lay on the floor by the wall, the two items within it. He directed the rest of his answer to St. James. "When I came back, she was like that. I thought she was asleep at first. But then I could tell . . . I could see." He faltered, lips trembling. "I rang Tommy's office, but they said he wasn't there. I rang his house, but Denton said he was still in Cornwall. I rang Cornwall, but Hodge said he was in London. I—"

"Why were you looking for me?" Lynley asked.

Peter dropped his hands. He stared at the floor. "You're my brother," he said hollowly.

Lynley looked as if his heart were being torn from his chest. "Why do you do these things, Peter? Why? God, *why?*"

"What does it matter?"

St. James heard the sirens. They had made good time. But then, they would have had the advantage of being able to clear away traffic with those shrieking alarms and flashing lights. He spoke quickly, determined to know the worst. "There's a silver container by the bed. Could it be Sasha's?"

Peter gave a short laugh. "Hardly. If she owned a piece of silver, we would have sold it long ago."

"She never showed it to you? You never saw it among her things? She never said where she got it?"

"Never."

There was time for nothing more. The noise of the arriving police swelled to a crescendo, then ceased abruptly. St. James went to the window and pushed back the curtain to see two panda cars, two unmarked police cars, and one van pulling up behind the Bentley. They took up most of the street. The children had scattered, leaving the garbage-sack goal posts behind.

While a uniformed constable remained at the front of the building, tying the police line from the handrail on the front steps to a nearby lamp post, the rest of the group entered. From his own years at the Yard, St. James recognised most of them, either by name or by function: two CID detectives, the scenes-of-crime team, a photographer, the forensic pathologist. It was unusual for all of them to effect an arrival at the same time, so there was no doubt that they knew it was a colleague who had placed the call. That would be why Lynley had telephoned the Met in the first place and not the local station—Bishopsgate—in whose jurisdiction Whitechapel lay. While he intended Peter to face whatever consequences grew from Sasha Nifford's death, he did not intend that his brother should face them without his own indirect participation. It was one thing to swear off assisting Peter if drugs were involved. It was quite another to leave him to his fate in a situation that could possibly turn into an investigation of an entirely different nature. For if Peter had known about the drugs, if he had passed them on to Sasha, if he had even helped her to take them, intending to shoot up himself upon his return from the market . . . These were all possibilities of which St. James knew that Lynley was well aware. And they could all be moulded into various degrees of homicide. Lynley would want the entire investigation handled by a team he could trust, so he'd called the Met. St. James wondered which officer on Victoria Street was phoning the Bishopsgate Station right now with the explanation of why Scotland Yard were invading a foreign patch.

The officers pounded up the stairs. Lynley met them at the door.

"Angus," he said to the man at the head of the group.

He was Detective Inspector Angus MacPherson, a hefty Scot who habitually wore old worsted suits that looked as if they doubled at night as his pyjamas. He nodded at Lynley and walked to the bed. The other officer followed him, removing a small notebook from her shoulder bag and a ballpoint pen from the breast pocket of her rumpled puce blouse. Detective Sergeant Barbara Havers, MacPherson's partner. St. James knew them both.

"What hae we here?" MacPherson murmured. He fingered the bedsheet and looked over his shoulder as the rest of the team crowded into the room. "Ye havena moved anything, Tommy?"

"Just the sheet. She was covered when we got here."

"I covered her," Peter said. "I thought she was asleep."

Sergeant Havers raised an expressive, disbelieving eyebrow. She wrote in her notebook. She looked from Lynley, to his brother, to the corpse on the bed.

"I went to buy eggs. And bread," Peter said. "When I got back—"

Lynley stepped behind his brother, dropping his hand to Peter's shoulder. It was enough to still him. Havers glanced their way again.

"When you got back?" She spoke entirely without inflection.

Peter looked at his brother as if for guidance. First his tongue then his teeth sought his upper lip. "She was like that," Peter said.

Lynley's fingers whitened on his brother's shoulder. It was obvious that Sergeant Havers saw this, for she exhaled in a brief, knowing snort, a woman who possessed no affinity for Thomas Lynley and no fellow-feeling for his situation. She turned back to the bed. MacPherson began speaking to her in a low, quick voice. She jotted down notes.

When MacPherson had completed his preliminary inspection, he joined Peter and Lynley. He drew them to the far corner of the room as the forensic pathologist took over, pulling on surgical gloves. The pathologist probed, touched, poked, and examined. In a few minutes, it was over. He murmured something to Havers and made way for the scenes-of-crime officers.

St. James watched them begin to gather the evidence, his every sense alive to the presence of Sidney's silver bottle on the floor. The water glass on the packing crate was placed into a sack and marked. The tarnished spoon likewise. A fine residue of powder, which St. James himself had not seen in his first inspection of the fruit packing crate, was carefully brushed from its surface into a container. Then the crate was inched to one side, and the bottle itself was plucked from the floor. When it, too, had been dropped into a sack, the twenty-four hours had begun.

St. James signaled to Lynley that he was going to leave. The other man joined him.

"They'll be taking Peter in," Lynley said. "I'll go with him." And then, as if he believed that his intention to accompany his brother in some way negated his prior determination to let Peter stand on his own, he went on to say, "I must do that much, St. James."

"That's understandable."

"Will you tell Deborah for me? I've no idea how long I'll be."

"Of course." St. James thought how to phrase his next question, knowing that Lynley, upon hearing it, would leap to a conclusion which might make him refuse. Still, he had to have the details, and he had to have them without Lynley's knowing why. He led into it cautiously. "Will you get me some information from the Yard? As soon as they have it?"

"What sort of information?"

"The postmortem. As much as you can. As soon as you can."

"You don't think that Peter—"

"They're going to rush things through for you, Tommy. It's the most they can do, all things considered, and they'll do it. So will you get the information?"

Lynley glanced at his brother. Peter had begun to shake. Mac-Pherson rooted through the pile of clothing on the floor until he found a striped sweatshirt which he handed over to Havers who inspected it with deliberate slowness before passing it on to Peter.

Lynley sighed. He rubbed the back of his neck. "All right. I'll get it."

In the back of the taxi spinning towards St. Pancras, St. James tried to remove every thought of his sister from his mind, replacing her image with an unsuccessful attempt to formulate some sort of plan of action. But he could come up with nothing other than a host of memories, each one more importunate than the last, making its own demand that he save her.

He had stopped briefly in Paddington to deliver Lynley's message to Deborah. There, he had used her telephone, ringing his sister's flat, her modelling agency, his own home, knowing all along that he was duplicating Lady Helen's earlier efforts, knowing and not caring, not even thinking, doing nothing but trying to find her, seeing nothing but the silver bottle on the floor and the intricate scrollwork of initials that identified it as Sidney's.

He was aware of Deborah standing nearby, watching and listening. She was alone in the flat—Helen having gone her way to do what she could with the messages on Mick's answering machine and the file marked *prospects*—and he could read her concern in the fine tracery of lines that appeared on her brow as he continued to dial, continued to ask for his sister, continued to meet with no success. He found that, more than anything, he wanted to keep from Deborah the true nature of his fear. She knew Sasha was dead, so she assumed his concern revolved only round Sidney's immediate safety. He was determined to keep it that way.

"No luck?" Deborah asked, when he finally turned from the telephone.

He shook his head and went to the table upon which they had left the material they'd gathered from Mick Cambrey's flat. He sorted it, stacked it, tapped it into a neat pile which he folded and put into his jacket pocket.

"Can I do anything?" she asked. "Anything at all? Please. I feel so useless." She looked stricken and afraid. "I can't believe someone would actually want to hurt Sidney. She's just gone off somewhere, Simon. Hasn't she? She's in agony over Justin. She needs to be alone."

He heard the penultimate statement and knew it for the truth. He had seen his sister's grief in Cornwall and had felt the inchoate fury which that grief provoked. Still, she had gone and he had allowed her to do so. Whatever fell upon Sidney now was in large part his responsibility.

"There's nothing you can do," he said. He started for the door. His face was impassive. He could feel each feature settle until he wore a perfectly insensate mask. He knew that Deborah wouldn't understand such a reaction to her offer. She would read it as rejection, seeing it, perhaps, as an adolescent retaliation for everything that had passed between them since her return. But that couldn't be helped.

"Simon. Please."

"There's nothing more to be done."

"I can help. You know I can."

"There's no need, Deborah."

"Let me help you find her."

"Just wait here for Tommy."

"I don't *want*—" She stopped. He could see a pulse beating in her throat. He waited for more. There was nothing. Deborah took in a slow breath, but she didn't look away. "I'll go to Cheyne Row."

"There's no point to that. Sidney won't be there."

"I don't care. I'm going."

He had neither the time nor the wish to argue with her. So he left, forcing himself back to his original purpose in returning to London. He hoped that a visit to Islington-London might somehow reveal the truth behind Mick Cambrey's death and that this additional death in White-chapel were somehow tied to the previous two. For tying them together would serve as a means of exonerating Sidney. And tying them together meant a pursuit of the ghost of Mick Cambrey. He was determined to incarnate this spectre from Cornwall. Islington-London seemed to offer the final opportunity of doing so.

But in the back of the taxi, he felt his weary mind lose the battle against images that attacked his calm, forcing him back to a time and a place he thought he had left behind forever. There, he saw them as they had appeared at the hospital, distorted faces emerging out of the fugue created by alternating states of consciousness and by the drug that deadened his most immediate suffering. David and Andrew in hushed consultation with the doctors; his mother and Helen, riven by sorrow; Tommy, driven by guilt. And Sidney. Just seventeen years old, with a butchered-up haircut and earrings that looked like communication satellites. Outrageous Sidney, reading to him from the most ridiculous of the London dailies, laughing uproariously at the worst of their gruesome and titillating stories. She was always there, never missing a day, refusing to allow him to sink into despair.

And then later in Switzerland. He remembered the bitterness with which he had looked at the Alps from his hospital window, loathing his body, despising its weakness, confronting for the very first time the inescapable reality of never being able to walk with ease in those mountains—or any others—again. But Sidney was with him, bullying, shouting, harassing him back to health, stubbornly insisting he would live to an old age even when he prayed each night that he might die.

Remembering all this, he fought against the facts that nagged at his consciousness: Sidney's presence in Soho, the nature of her relationship with Justin Brooke, her easy access to drugs from the life she led, the people she knew, and the work she did. And while he tried to convince himself that she did not know—could not possibly have known—Mick Cambrey and thus could not be involved in his death in any way, he could not dismiss the fact that Deborah had told him Sidney had seen Tina Cogin that day in her flat. Sidney herself had talked about seeing Peter assaulting a woman in Soho, a woman whose description was identical to Tina's. Even though it was tenuous enough to be disregarded as meaningless, the connection was there. He could not overlook it. So he wondered where she was and what she had done, while twenty-five years of mutual history cried out that he find her before the police.

Islington-London was an unprepossessing building not far from Gray's Inn Road. A small, gated courtyard set the structure back from the street, and it was crammed with half a dozen small cars and a minivan with the letters ISLINGTON spread across a map of Great Britain and white stars scattered here and there in all three countries, obviously indicating the location of branch offices. There were ten in all, as far north as Inverness, as far south as Penzance. It appeared to be quite an operation.

Inside the lobby, the sound from the street was muted by thick walls, thick carpet, and a Muzak track currently playing an all-strings rendition of "Lucy in the Sky with Diamonds." Handsome sofas lined the walls beneath large, modern canvases in the style of David Hockney. Across from these a receptionist, who couldn't have been more than an erstwhile fifth form student who'd decided not to continue in school, tapped away at a word processor with impossibly long magenta-coloured fingernails. Her hair was dyed to match.

Out of the corner of her eye, she appeared to see St. James approach, for she did not turn from her word processing screen. Rather she wiggled her fingers vaguely in the direction of a stack of papers on her desk and popped her chewing gum before saying, "Take an application form."

"I've not come about a job."

When the girl didn't respond, St. James noticed that she was wearing the small kind of headset earphones that are usually attached to a tape recorder either giving dictation or blaring out rock and roll music that, mercifully, no one else has to hear. He repeated his statement, louder this time. She looked up, removing the headset hastily.

"Sorry. One gets used to the automatic response." She pulled a ledger towards her. "Have an appointment?"

"Do people generally have appointments when they come here?"

She chewed her gum more thoughtfully for a moment and looked him over as if searching for hidden meanings. "Generally," she said. "Right."

"So no one would come to make a purchase?"

The gum snapped in her mouth. "The sales force goes out. No one comes here. There's the odd telephone order, isn't there, but it's not like a chemist's shop." She watched as St. James took the folded materials from his jacket pocket and produced the photograph of Mick Cambrey. He gave it to her, his hand making contact with her talon nails which, glistening wetly, grazed his skin. She wore a tiny gold musical note glued onto the nail of her ring finger, like a piece of odd jewelery.

"Has this man had an appointment to see anyone?" he asked.

She smiled when her eyes dropped to the picture. "He's been here all right."

"Lately?"

She tapped her nails on the desktop as she thought. "Hmm. That's a bit difficult, isn't it? A few weeks past, I think."

"Do you know who he saw?"

"His name?"

"Mick—Michael—Cambrey."

"Let me check." She opened the ledger on her desk and scanned several pages, an activity which seemed to allow her the opportunity of showing off her fingernails to their best advantage, since every time she turned a page, she used a new nail to guide her eyes down the column of times and names.

"A visitor's log?" St. James asked.

"Everybody signs in and out. Security, you know."

"Security?"

"Drug research. You can't be too careful. Something new comes out and everyone in the West End's hot to try it with drinks that night. Ah. Here it is. He's signed into Project Testing, Department Twenty-Five." She flipped back through several more pages. "Here he is again. Same department, same time. Just before lunch." She slipped back several months. "Quite a regular, he was."

"Always the same department?"

"Looks that way."

"May I speak to the department head?"

She closed the ledger and looked regretful. "That's a bit rough. No appointment, you see. And poor Mr. Malverd's balancing two departments at once. Why don't you leave your name?" She shrugged noncommitally.

St. James wasn't about to be put off. "This man, Mick Cambrey, was murdered Friday night."

The receptionist's face sharpened with immediate interest. "You're police?" she asked. And then sounding hopeful, "Scotland Yard?"

St. James gave a moment's thought to how easily it could all have been managed had Lynley only come with him. As it was, he removed his own card and handed it over. "This is a private endeavour," he told her.

She glanced at the card, moved her lips as she read it, and then turned it over as if more information might be printed on the back. "A murder," she breathed. "Just let me see if I can reach Mr. Malverd for you." She punched three buttons on the switchboard and pocketed his card. "Just in case I need you myself," she said with a wink.

Ten minutes later, a man came into the reception area, swinging shut a heavy, panelled door behind him. He introduced himself as Stephen Malverd, offered his hand in an abbreviated greeting, and pulled on his earlobe. He was wearing a white lab coat which hung below his knees, directing attention to what he wore upon his feet. Sandals, rather than shoes, and heavy argyle socks. He was very busy, he said, he could spare only a few minutes, if Mr. St. James would come this way . . .

He strode briskly back into the heart of the building. As he walked, his hair—which sprang up round his head wild and unruly like a pad of steel wool—fluttered and bounced, and his lab coat blew open like a cape. He slowed his pace only when he noticed St. James' gait, but even then he looked at the offending leg accusingly, as if it too robbed him of precious moments away from his job.

They rang for the lift at the end of a corridor given over to administrative offices. Malverd said nothing until they were on their way to the building's third floor. "It's been chaos round here for the last few days," he said. "But I'm glad you've come. I thought there was more involved than I heard at first."

"Then you remember Michael Cambrey?"

Malverd's face was a sudden blank. "Michael Cambrey? But she told me—" He gestured aimlessly in an indication of the reception area and frowned. "What's this about?"

"A man named Michael Cambrey visited Project Testing, Department Twenty-Five, several times over the past few months. He was murdered last Friday."

"I'm not sure how I can help you." Malverd sounded perplexed. "Twenty-Five isn't my regular patch. I've only stepped in briefly. What is it that you want?"

"Anything you—or anyone else—can tell me about why Cambrey was here."

The lift doors opened. Malverd didn't exit at once. He appeared to be trying to decide whether he wanted to talk to St. James or merely to dismiss him and get back to his own work.

"This death has something to do with Islington? With an Islington product?"

That certainly was a possibility, St. James realised, although not in the manner that Malverd obviously thought. "I'm not sure," St. James said. "That's why I've come."

"Police?"

He took out another card. "Forensic science."

Malverd looked moderately interested at this piece of information. At least, his expression indicated, he was talking to a fellow. "Let's see what we can do," he said. "It's just this way."

He led St. James down a linoleum-tiled corridor, a far cry from the reception and administration offices below. Laboratories opened to either side, peopled by technicians who sat on tall stools at work areas that time, the movement of heavy equipment, and the exposure to chemicals had bleached from black-topped to grey.

Malverd nodded at colleagues as they walked, but he said nothing. Once he removed a schedule from his pocket, studied it, glanced at his watch, and cursed. He picked up speed, dodged past a tea cart round which a group of technicians gathered for an afternoon break, and in a second corridor, he opened a door.

"This is Twenty-Five," he said.

The room they entered was a large, rectangular laboratory, brightly illuminated by long ceiling tubes of fluorescent lights. At least six incubators sat at intervals on a work top that ran along one wall. Interspersed among them, centrifuges squatted, some open, some closed, some humming at work. Dozens of pH metres lay among microscopes, and everywhere glass-fronted cabinets held chemicals, beakers, flasks, test tubes, pipettes. Among all these accoutrements of science, two technicians copied the orange digital numbers which flickered on one of the incubators. Another worked at a hood, from which a glass cover had been pulled down to protect cultures from contamination. Four others peered into microscopes while another prepared a set of specimens on slides.

Several of them looked up as Malverd led St. James towards a closed door at the far end of the lab, but none of them spoke. When Malverd rapped once sharply upon that door and entered without waiting for a reply, the few who had given him their attention lost interest.

A secretary, who appeared as harried as Malverd, turned from a filing cabinet as they entered. A desk, a chair, a computer, and a laser printer hemmed her in on all sides.

"For you, Mr. Malverd." She reached for a pile of telephone messages which were joined together by a paper clip. "I don't know what to tell people."

Malverd picked them up, flipped through them, dropped them onto her desk. "Put them off," he said. "Put everyone off. I've no time to answer phone calls."

"But—"

"Do you people keep engagement diaries up here, Mrs. Courtney? Have you evolved that far, or would that be too much to expect?"

Her lips whitened, even as she smiled and made a polite effort to take his questions as a joke, something which Malverd's tone made difficult. She pushed her way past him and went behind her desk where she took out a leather volume and handed it over. "We always keep records, Mr. Malverd. I think you'll find everything in perfect order."

"I hope so," he said. "It'll be the first thing that is. I could do with some tea. You?" This to St. James, who demurred. "See about it, will you?" was Malverd's final comment to Mrs. Courtney, who fired a look of nuclear quality in his direction before she went to do his bidding.

Malverd opened a second door which led to a second room, this one larger than the first but hardly less crowded. It was obviously the office of the project director and it looked the part. Old metal bookshelves held volumes dedicated to biomedicinal chemistry, to pharmacokinetics, to pharmacology, to genetics. Bound collections of scientific journals vied with these for space, as did a pressure reader, an antique microscope, and a set of scales. At least thirty leather notebooks occupied the shelves nearest the reach of the desk, and these, St. James assumed, would contain the reported results of experiments which the technicians in the outer lab carried out. On the wall above the desk, a long graph charted the progress of something, using green and red lines. Below this in four framed cases hung a collection of scorpions, splayed out as if in demonstration of man's dominion over lesser creatures.

Malverd frowned at these latter objects as he took a seat behind the desk. He gave another, meaningful glance at his watch. "How can I help you?"

St. James removed a stack of typescript from the only other chair in the room. He sat down, gave a cursory look at the graph, and said, "Mick Cambrey evidently came to this department a number of times in the last few months. He was a journalist."

"He was murdered, you said? And you think there's some connection between his death and Islington?"

"Several people feel he might have been working on a story. There could be a connection between that and his death. We don't know yet."

"But you've indicated you're not from the police."

"That's right."

St. James waited for Malverd to use this as an excuse to end their conversation. He had every right to do so. But it seemed that their previously acknowledged mutual interest in science would be enough to carry the interview forward for the moment, since Malverd nodded thoughtfully and flipped open the engagement diary in what appeared to be an arbitrary selection of date. He said, "Well. Cambrey. Let's see." He began to read, running his finger down one page and then another much as had the receptionist a few minutes before. "Smythe-Thomas, Hallington, Schweinbeck, Barry—what did he see *him* for?—Taversly, Powers . . . Ah, here it is: Cambrey; half past eleven"—he squinted at the date—"two weeks ago Friday."

"The receptionist indicated he'd been here before. Is his name in the diary other than that Friday?"

Cooperatively, Malverd flipped through the book. He reached for a scrap of paper and made note of the dates which he handed to St. James when he had completed his survey of the diary. "Quite a regular visitor," he said. "Every other Friday."

"How far back does the book go?"

"Just to January."

"Is last year's diary available?"

"Let me check that."

When Malverd had left the office to do so, St. James took a closer look at the graph above the desk. The ordinate, he saw, was labelled *tumour growth,* while the abcissa was called *time-post injection.* Two lines marked the progress of two substances: one falling rapidly and bearing the identification *drug* and the other, marked *saline,* rising steadily.

Malverd returned, cup of tea in one hand and engagement diary in the other. He tapped the door shut with his foot.

"He was here last year as well," Malverd said. Again, he copied the dates as he found them, pausing occasionally to slurp a bit of tea. Both the lab and the office were almost inhumanly quiet. The only sound was the scratching of Malverd's pencil on paper. At last he looked up. "Nothing before last June," he said. "June second."

"More than a year," St. James noted. "But nothing to tell us why he was here?"

"Nothing. I've no idea at all." Malverd tapped the tips of his fingers together and frowned at the graph. "Unless . . . it may have been oncozyme."

"Oncozyme?"

"It's a drug Department Twenty-Five's been testing for perhaps eighteen months or more."

"What sort of drug?"

"Cancer."

Cambrey's interview with Dr. Trenarrow rose instantly in St. James's mind. The connection between that meeting and Cambrey's trips to London was finally neither conjectural nor tenuous.

"A form of chemotherapy? What exactly does it do?"

"Inhibits protein synthesis in cancer cells," Malverd said. "Our hope is that it'll prevent replication of oncogenes, the genes that cause cancer in the first place." He nodded at the graph and pointed to the red line that descended it steeply, a sharp diagonal that indicated the percentage of inhibited tumour growth versus the time after the drug had been administered. "As you can see, it looks like a promising treatment. The results in mice have been quite extraordinary."

"So it's not been used on human subjects?"

"We're years away from that. The toxicology studies have only just begun. You know the sort of thing. What amount constitutes a safe dosage? What are its biological effects?"

"Side effects?"

"Certainly. We'd be looking closely for those."

"If there are no side effects, if there's nothing to prove oncozyme a danger, what happens then?"

"Then we market the drug."

"At some considerable profit, I should guess," St. James noted.

"For a fortune," Malverd replied. "It's a breakthrough drug. No doubt about it. In fact, I should guess that oncozyme's the story this Cambrey was writing. But as to its being a potential cause for his murder"—he paused meaningfully—"I don't see how."

St. James thought he did. It would have taken the form of a random piece of knowledge, a source of concern, or an idea passed on by someone with access to inside information. He asked, "What's the relationship between Islington-London and Islington-Penzance?"

"Penzance is one of our research facilities. We have them scattered round the country."

"Their purpose? More testing?"

Malverd shook his head. "The drugs are created at the research labs in the first place." He leaned back in his chair. "Each lab generally works in a separate area of disease control. We've one on Parkinson's, another on Huntington's chorea, a new one dealing with AIDS. We've even a lab working on the common cold, believe it or not." He smiled.

"And Penzance?"

"One of our three cancer locations."

"Did Penzance produce oncozyme, by any chance?"

Malverd looked meditatively at the graph again. "No. Our Bury lab in Suffolk was responsible for oncozyme."

"And you've said they don't test the drugs at these facilities?"

"Not the sort of extensive testing we do here. The initial testing, of course. They do that. Otherwise, they'd hardly know what they've developed, would they?"

"Would it be safe to assume that someone at one of these associate labs would have access to results? Not only that local lab's results but London's results as well."

"Of course."

"And he or she might recognise an inconsistency? Perhaps some detail glossed over in the rush to market a new product?"

Malverd's benign expression altered. He thrust out his chin and pulled it back as if adjusting his spinal cord. "That's hardly likely, Mr. St. James. This is a place of medicine, not a science fiction novel." He got to his feet. "I must get back to my own lab, now. Until we've a new man to take over Twenty-Five, I'm in a bit of a frazzle. I'm sure you understand."

St. James followed him out of the office. Malverd handed the secretary both of the engagement diaries and said, "They were in order, Mrs. Courtney. I do congratulate you on that."

She responded coldly as she took the diaries from him. "Mr. Brooke kept everything in order, Mr. Malverd."

St. James heard the name with a rush of surprise. "Mr. Brooke?" he asked. It couldn't be possible.

Malverd proved that it was. He led him back into the lab. "Justin Brooke," he said. "Senior biochemist in charge of this lot. Bloody fool was killed last weekend in an accident in Cornwall. I thought at first that's why you'd come."

22

Before he nodded at the constable to unlock the interrogation room's door, Lynley looked through the small, thick-glassed window, a plastic tray of tea and sandwiches in his hand. Head bowed, his brother was sitting at the table. He still wore the striped sweatshirt that MacPherson had given him in Whitechapel, but whatever protection it had afforded him earlier was no longer adequate. Peter shook—arms, legs, head, and shoulders. Lynley had no doubt that every internal muscle was quivering as well.

When they had left him in the room thirty minutes before—alone save for a guard outside to make sure he did nothing to harm himself—Peter had asked no questions; he had made neither statement nor request. He merely stood, hands on the back of one of the chairs, glancing over the impersonal room. One table, four chairs, a dull beige linoleum floor, two ceiling lights only one of which worked, a red, dented tin ashtray on the table. All he had done before taking a seat was to look at Lynley and open his mouth as if to speak. His face limned entreaty upon every feature. But he said nothing. It was as if Peter were finally seeing how irreparable was the damage he had done to his relationship with his brother. If he believed that blood tied them inextricably to each other, that he could call upon that blood to save himself in some way, he apparently did not intend to mention the fact now.

Lynley nodded at the constable, who unlocked the door and re-locked it once Lynley had entered. Always a sound of grim finality, Lynley found that the key grating upon metal was even more so now that it was being turned against the freedom of his own brother. He hadn't expected to feel this way. He hadn't expected to feel the desire to rescue or the exigent need to protect. For some delusional reason, he had actually believed that he would feel a closure had been reached once Peter finally faced the criminal implications of the lifestyle he'd chosen these past few years. But now that the justice system had caught Peter up, Lynley found himself feeling not at all righteously vindicated at having been the brother who had chosen the clean, the moral, the ethical life, the life guaranteed to make him society's darling. Rather, he felt himself the hypocrite and knew beyond a doubt that if punishment were to be meted out to the greater sinner—the man who had been given the most and had therefore thrown the most away—he would be its rightful recipient.

Peter looked up, saw him, looked away. The expression on his face was not sullen, however. It was dazed by both confusion and fear.

"We both need something to eat," Lynley said. He sat opposite his brother and placed the tray on the table between them. When Peter made no move towards it, Lynley unwrapped a sandwich, fumbling with the seal. The crinkling of the paper made that curious sound like fire eating wood. It was unusually loud. "The Yard food's unspeakable. Either sawdust or institutional mush. I had these brought in from a restaurant down the street. Try the pastrami. It's my favourite." Peter didn't move. Lynley reached for the tea. "I can't recall how much sugar you use. I've brought a few packets. There's a carton of milk as well." He stirred his own tea, unwrapped his sandwich, and tried to avoid considering the inherent idiocy of his behaviour. He knew he was acting like a hovering mother, as if he believed that food was going to take the illness away.

Peter raised his head. "Not hungry." His lips, Lynley saw, were cracked, raw from having been bitten during the half hour in which he'd been left alone. In one spot they had begun to bleed although already the blood was drying in a ragged, dark blot. Other blood—in the form of small, crusty scabs—ringed the inside of his nose, while dry skin caked his eyelids, embedding itself between his lashes.

"The appetite goes first," Peter said. "Then everything else. You don't realise what's happening. You think you're fine, the best you've ever been. But you don't eat. You don't sleep. You work less and less and finally not at all. You don't do anything but coke. Sex. Sometimes you do sex. But in the end, you don't even do that. Coke's so much better."

Lynley carefully placed his sandwich, untouched, onto the paper in which it had been wrapped. He was suddenly unhungry. And wanting to

be nothing more than unfeeling as well. He reached for his tea and circled his hands around it. A dull but comforting warmth emanated from
the cup.

"Will you let me help you?"

Peter's right hand gripped his left. He made no reply.

"I can't change the kind of brother I was when you needed me,"
Lynley said. "I can only offer you what I am right now, however little
that may be."

Peter seemed to withdraw at this. Or perhaps it was that the cold—
within and without—was causing him to diminish in size, conserving
energy, garnering whatever small resources he had left. When he finally
answered, his lips scarcely moved. Lynley had to strain to hear him.

"I wanted to be like you."

"Like me? Why?"

"You were perfect. You were my standard. I wanted to be like you.
When I found I couldn't, I just gave it up. If I couldn't be you, I didn't
want to be anything."

Peter's words sounded the sure ring of finality. They sounded not
only like the end of an interview that had barely begun, but also like the
end of any possibility to put things right between them. Lynley sought
something—words, images, a common experience—that would allow him
to reach back through those fifteen years and touch the little boy he had
abandoned at Howenstow. But he could find nothing. There was no way
to go back and no way to make amends.

He felt leaden. He reached in his jacket pocket, brought out his
cigarette case and lighter, and laid them on the table. The case had been
his father's, and the elaborately engraved *A* on the cover had worn through
time. Portions of it had disappeared altogether, but the case was familiar
to him, dear to him, nicked and dented with age though it was. He
wouldn't have considered replacing it with another. Staring at it—small
rectangular symbol of everything he had run from, all the areas of his
life he had chosen to deny, the welter of emotions he had refused to
face—he found the words.

"It was knowing that she was sleeping with Roderick while Father
was alive. I couldn't stand that, Peter. It didn't matter to me that they'd
fallen in love, that they hadn't set out to but that it just happened between them. It didn't matter that Roderick had every intention of mar-
rying her when she was free. It didn't matter that she still loved Father
—and I knew she loved him, because I saw how she acted with him
even after she'd begun the affair with Roderick. Still, I didn't understand, and I couldn't abide my own blind ignorance. How could she love

them both? How could she be devoted to one—take care of him, bathe him, read to him, see to him hour after hour and day after day, feed him, sit with him . . . all of that—and still sleep with the other? And how could Roderick go into Father's bedroom—talk to him about his condition—and all the time know that he would be having Mother directly afterwards? I couldn't understand it. I didn't see how it was possible. I wanted life simple and it wasn't. They're savages, I thought. They have no sense of propriety. They don't know how to behave. They have to be taught. I'll teach them. I'll show them. I'll punish them."

Lynley took a cigarette and slid the case across the table to his brother. "My leaving Howenstow, my coming back so seldom, had nothing to do with you, Peter. You just turned out to be the victim of my need to avenge something which Father probably never even knew was happening. For what it's worth—God knows it's little enough—I'm sorry."

Peter took a cigarette. But he held it in his fingers, unlit, as if to light it would be taking a step further than he wished to go.

"I wanted you to be there, but you weren't," he said. "No one would tell me when you'd be home again. I thought it was a secret for some reason. Then I finally realised that no one would tell me because no one knew. So I stopped asking. Then after a while, I stopped caring. When you did come home, it was easier to hate you so that when you left again—as you always did—it wouldn't really matter."

"You didn't know about Mother and Trenarrow?"

"Not for a long time."

"How did you find out?"

Peter lit his cigarette. "Parents' Day at school. Both of them came. Some blokes told me then. 'That chap Trenarrow's been boffing your mum, Pete. You too daft to know it?'" He shrugged. "I pretended to be cool. I pretended I knew. I kept thinking they'd get married. But they never did."

"I made certain of that. I wanted them to suffer."

"You didn't have that sort of control over them."

"I did. I do. I knew where Mother's loyalties lay. I used them to hurt her."

Peter asked for no further explanation. He put his cigarette into the ashtray and watched its fragile plume of smoke rise. Lynley chose his next words carefully, feeling his way in a land that should have been old and familiar but was instead quite foreign.

"Perhaps we can make our way through this together. Not try to go back, of course. That's impossible. But try to go on."

"As restitution on your part?" Peter shook his head. "You don't have to make anything up to me, Tommy. Oh, I know you think you do. But I chose my own path. I'm not your responsibility.'' And then, as if he thought his final statement sounded petulant, he finished with, ''Really.''

''None of this has anything to do with responsibility. I want to help. You're my brother. I love you.''

Uttered so simply as a declaration of fact, the statement might have been a blow to his brother. Peter recoiled. His raw lips trembled. He covered his eyes. ''I'm sorry,'' he finally said. And then only, ''Tommy.''

Lynley said nothing more until his brother lowered his hand. He was alone in the interrogation room with Peter solely because of Inspector MacPherson's compassion. MacPherson's partner, Sergeant Havers, had protested vociferously enough when Lynley had asked for these few minutes. She had cited regulations, procedures, Judge's Rules, and civil law until MacPherson had silenced her with a simple ''I dae know the law, lass. Gie me credit for that, if ye will,'' and sent her to sit by a phone and await the results of the toxicological analysis of the powder they had found in Peter's Whitechapel room. After which, MacPherson himself had lumbered off, leaving Lynley at the interrogation room's door, and saying, ''Twenty minutes, Tommy'' over his shoulder. So in spite of what needed to be said about the years of suffering he and Peter had caused each other, there was little enough time for gathering information and none at all for restoring the relationship they had destroyed. That would have to wait.

''I need to ask you about Mick Cambrey,'' Lynley said. ''About Justin Brooke as well.''

''You think I killed them.''

''It doesn't matter what I think. The only thing that matters is what Penzance CID think. Peter, you must know I can't let John Penellin take the blame for Mick's death.''

Peter's eyebrows drew together. ''John's been arrested?''

''Saturday night. You'd already left Howenstow when they came for him, then?''

''We left directly after dinner. I didn't know.'' He touched a finger to the sandwich in front of him and pushed it aside with a grimace of distaste.

''I need the truth,'' Lynley said. ''It's the only thing that's going to help anyone. And the only way to get John released—since he doesn't intend to do anything to help himself—is to tell the police what really happened on Friday night. Peter, did you see Mick Cambrey after John went to Gull Cottage?''

"They'll arrest me," he mumbled. "They'll put me on trial."

"You've nothing to fear if you're innocent. If you come forward. If you tell the truth. Peter, were you there? Or did Brooke lie about that?"

Escape was well within Peter's reach. A simple denial would do it. An accusation that Brooke had lied. Even a manufactured reason why Brooke might have done so since the man himself was dead and couldn't refute it. Those were the possibilities of response. As was a decision to help a man who had been part of their extended family for Peter's entire life.

Peter licked his dry lips. "I was there."

Lynley didn't know whether to feel relief or despair. He said, "What happened?"

"I think Justin didn't trust me to see to things on my own. Or else he couldn't wait."

"For the coke?"

"He'd had a stash with him at Howenstow." Briefly, Peter related the scene that had occurred between Sidney and Justin Brooke on the beach. "She threw it in the water," he concluded. "So that was that. I'd already phoned Mark about getting some more, but I didn't have enough money and he wouldn't trust me for it, not even for a few days."

"So instead you went to Mick?" A positive answer would be the first fissure in the tale Brooke had told. But it was not forthcoming.

"Not for coke," Peter said, unconsciously corroborating the first part of Brooke's story. "For cash. I remembered he did the pay envelopes for the newspaper on alternate Fridays."

"Did you know Mick was a cross-dresser as well?"

Peter smiled wearily. There was an element of grudging admiration in it, a ghost of the little boy he had been. "I always thought you'd make a decent detective."

Lynley didn't tell him how little of his own talent for inference and deduction had gone into the discovery of Mick Cambrey's second life in London. He merely said, "How long have you known?"

"About a month. I bought from him occasionally in London when my other sources were dry. We'd meet in Soho. There's an alley near the square where deals go down. We'd meet in a club there. I'd buy a gram, half a gram, less. Whatever I could afford."

"That seems damn risky. Why not meet at your flat? At his?"

Peter shot him a look. "I didn't even know he had a flat. And I sure as hell didn't want him to see mine."

"How would you get in touch? How would you make the arrangements?"

"Like I said. Sometimes my other sources went dry. So I'd phone him in Cornwall. If he was due to come to London, we'd set up a buy."

"Always in Soho?"

"Always the same place. At this club. That's where I found out about the cross-dressing."

"How?"

Peter's face coloured as he related the story of how he had waited an hour for Mick Cambrey to appear at Kat's Kradle; how a woman approached him when he went to the bar for matches; how they had three drinks together; how they finally went outside. "There's a bit of an alcove there," Peter said. "It's private, more or less. I was drunk as hell by then. I didn't know what I was doing, much less care, so when she started rubbing against me, really feeling me up, I was willing all right. Then when things had gone as far as she wanted them to go, she started laughing. Laughing and laughing like a crazy woman. I saw it was Mick."

"You couldn't tell before that?"

Peter gave a rueful shake of his head. "Mick looked good, Tommy. I don't even know how he did it. But he looked damn good. Sexy. He probably could have fooled his own father. He sure as hell fooled me."

"And when you saw the woman was Mick?"

"I wanted to beat the shit out of him. But I was too drunk. I took a swing. We both fell. At least, I know we ended up on the ground somehow. And then, of all people, Sidney St. James showed up out of nowhere—Christ, it was like a nightmare. She was with Brooke. He pulled me off Mick and Mick took off. I didn't see him again until Friday night in Nanrunnel."

"How did you find out Mick dealt cocaine in the first place?"

"Mark told me."

"But you didn't try to get cocaine from him in Nanrunnel?"

"He wouldn't sell there. Only in London."

"He wasn't in London all that often, was he? Who were his buyers?"

"There's a whole network, Tommy. Dealers know the buyers. Buyers know the dealers. Everyone knows everyone. You get a number. You ring it. You make arrangements."

"And if your caller turns out to be from the Met's drug squad?"

"Then you're busted. But not if you're smart. And not if you know how to set up your network. Mick knew how to do that. He was a journalist. He knew how to establish good sources. He just looked for a different kind of source once he started dealing. He had hundreds of connections.''

That was true, Lynley thought. It would have been simple for a man in Mick Cambrey's position. ''What happened between you on Friday night? The neighbours heard a row.''

''I was getting desperate. Mark picked up on that in the afternoon and obliged me by raising his price. I didn't have the cash, so I went to see Mick to borrow some. He said absolutely not. I promised I'd be good for it. I swore that I'd have it back in a week.''

''How?''

Peter stared at his bitten fingernails. Lynley saw that he was struggling with his conscience, choosing how far to go, and costing out the consequences. ''Things from Howenstow,'' he finally said. ''The silver. I thought I could sell a few pieces in London and no one would be the wiser. At least not for a while.''

''Is that why you went to Cornwall in the first place?'' Lynley waited for the answer and tried to remain indifferent to the idea of his brother's selling what had been part of their family for generations merely to feed his drug addiction.

''I don't know why I went to Cornwall. I wasn't thinking straight. One minute I was going there to make a buy from Mark. The next it was to pinch a bit of silver to take back to London. The next it was to get some money from Mick. That's what it's like. You don't even know what you're doing after a while. It's like being dizzy.''

''And when Mick refused to lend you the money?''

''It was stupid. I threatened to let it out in the village what he was up to in London. The cross-dressing. The drug dealing as well.''

''I take it that didn't convince him to hand over a few pounds?''

''Not at all. He just laughed. He said if I wanted money I should threaten him with death, not blackmail. People pay a hell of a lot more to stay alive than to have a secret kept, he said. That's where the real money is. And all the time he kept laughing. Like he was egging me on.''

''What was Brooke doing?''

''Trying to get us both to shut up. He could tell I was crazy. I think he was scared that something weird would go down.''

''But you didn't shut up?''

''Mick kept after me. He said that if I wanted to put his dirty linen on the table, that he'd be willing to spread mine out as well. He said you and Mother might find my return to drug use of interest. But as to that, I didn't even care.'' Peter bit at his thumbnail, anxious little nibbling bites. "It didn't matter to me if he told you since you'd guessed I was using again anyway. As for Mother . . . nothing mattered to me except getting high. You don't know what it feels like to be willing to do anything just to get your hands on some coke."

It was a damning admission. Lynley only thanked the luck of the moment that neither MacPherson nor Havers was there to hear it. The former, he knew, might well take it as a meaningless slip of the tongue. The latter, however, would pounce upon it like a starving mongrel.

"I just exploded at that point," Peter said. "It was that or start to beg."

"Is that when Brooke left?"

"He tried to get me to go as well, but I said no. I said I wanted to finish what I'd started with the little pouffe."

Again, the damning choice of words. Lynley felt himself wince inwardly. "What happened then?"

"I called Mick every foul name I could think of. I raved. Screamed. I was strung out and mad and I *needed* . . ." He picked up his cup of tea, swallowed a large mouthful. A trickle of the liquid dripped down his chin. "I ended up begging and snivelling for just fifty quid. He threw me out."

Peter's cigarette had gone untouched in the ashtray. It had burnt to nothing, creating a perfect cylinder of grey ash. He tapped it with the broken nail of his index finger. It dissolved into a wispy pile. He said:

"The money was still there when I left him, Tommy. You've no cause to believe that. But the money was there. And Mick was alive."

"I believe you." Lynley tried to make his words ring with the assurance that his personal belief was all that would be necessary to restore Peter to the safety of his family. But that was nothing more than irresponsible fantasy. For as things stood now, once Peter's story was relayed to the Penzance police, he would surely stand trial. And once his extensive drug use was revealed to a jury, his position would be perilous at best, no matter Lynley's earlier avowals of the inherent value of telling the truth.

Peter seemed to take comfort from his brother's words. He seemed to feel an encouragement to continue, a fragile bond between them that allowed for revelation. "I didn't take them, Tommy. I wouldn't have done that." Lynley looked at him blankly. Peter went on. "Her cameras. I didn't take them. I didn't. I swear it."

The fact that Peter had been willing to sell off the family silver made it hard to believe he'd suddenly developed a conscience when it came to Deborah. Lynley avoided a direct reply. "What time did you leave Mick on Friday?"

Peter considered the question. "I went to the Anchor and Rose and had a pint," he said. "It must have been about a quarter to ten."

"Not ten o'clock? Not later?"

"Not when I arrived."

"Were you still there at ten?" When Peter nodded, Lynley asked, "Then why did Justin hitchhike back to Howenstow alone?"

"Justin?"

"Wasn't he there in the pub?"

Peter looked at him in some confusion. "No."

Lynley felt a measure of relief at this. It was the first exonerating piece of information that his brother had offered. And the fact that he had offered it, so completely unconscious of its importance, told Lynley that in this instance his brother was telling the truth. It was a detail to be checked upon, a blemish on Brooke's story, the vague promise that the case against Peter could indeed be broken by a barrister in court.

"What I don't understand," Lynley said, "is why you left Howenstow so suddenly. Was it the row we had in the smoking room?"

Peter smiled briefly. "Considering how many other rows we'd had, one more would hardly have made me turn tail, would it?" He looked away. At first Lynley thought he was fabricating a story, but he saw the spots of colour on his brother's face and realised he was embarrassed. "It was Sasha," he said. "She wouldn't let up on me. She kept insisting we come back to London. I'd taken a matchbox from the smoking room—the silver piece that usually sits on the desk—and once she knew I couldn't get any money from Mick or some dope from Mark, she wanted to bring the box back to London and sell it here. She was in a rush. She wanted the coke bad. She used a lot, Tommy. All the time. More than me."

"Did you make the buy? Is that where you got whatever she took this afternoon?"

"I couldn't find a buyer. Everyone knows the box's hot. I'm surprised I wasn't arrested."

Before now remained unspoken. But there was no doubt that the two words were foremost on both of their minds. The key turned in the door. Someone knocked upon it sharply. MacPherson swung it open. He'd loosened his tie and removed his jacket. His heavy-rimmed spectacles rode high on his forehead, shoved there out of his way. Behind him, Sergeant Havers stood. She made no effort to hide the smile of gratification on her face.

Lynley got to his feet but motioned his brother to stay where he was. MacPherson thumbed towards the hallway where Lynley followed him, shutting the door on his brother.

"Has he a solicitor?" MacPherson asked.

"Of course. We've not phoned, but . . ." Lynley looked at the Scot. His face, in contrast to Havers', was grave. "He's said he doesn't recognise that container, Angus. And surely we'll find any number of witnesses who can verify his story of going out to buy bread and eggs when she took the drug." He tried to keep his voice calm and reasonable so they would not wander beyond the death of Sasha Nifford. The idea that MacPherson and Havers had somehow connected Peter to the Cornwall deaths was unthinkable. But the mention of a solicitor suggested nothing else. "I spoke to the print men just before coming to see him. Evidently, only Sasha's are on the needle. And none of Peter's are on that bottle. For an overdose of this kind—"

MacPherson's face had creased with growing worry. He lifted a hand to stop Lynley's words, dropped it heavily when he said, "Aye, for an overdose. Aye, laddie. Aye. But we do hae more of a problem than an overdose."

"What do you mean?"

"Sergeant Havers'll gie ye the facts."

It took an effort for Lynley to move his eyes from MacPherson to the snubby-faced sergeant. She held a paper in her hand.

"Havers?" he said.

Again, that slight smile. Condescending, knowing, and more than that, enjoying. "The toxicology report indicates it's a mixture of quinine and a drug called ergotamine," she said. "Mixed together appropriately, Inspector, they not only resemble but also taste exactly like heroin. That's what the girl must have thought it was when she injected it."

"What are you saying?" Lynley asked.

MacPherson shuffled his feet. " 'Ye know as well as I. It's a murder."

23

Deborah had been as good as her word. When St. James returned home, Cotter told him that she had arrived herself only an hour before. With an overnight case, he added significantly. "She talked of 'aving a load o' work ahead, printing up some fresh snaps, but I think the girl means to stay till there's word of Miss Sidney." As if in the expectation that St. James would interfere with her plans upon his own arrival, Deborah had gone directly up to her darkroom where the red light glowing above the door told him she was not to be disturbed. When he knocked and said her name, she shouted cheerfully, "Out in a bit" and banged about with what sounded like unnecessary vigour. He descended to his study and placed a call to Cornwall.

He found Dr. Trenarrow at home. He did nothing more than identify himself before Trenarrow asked about Peter Lynley, with a forced calm that said he expected the worst but was keeping up the pretence of all being well at the heart of the matter. St. James guessed Lady Asherton was with him. Bearing that in mind he gave Trenarrow only the barest information.

"We found him in Whitechapel. Tommy's with him at the moment."

Trenarrow said, "He's all right?"

St. James affirmed this in as indirect a fashion as he could, leaving out most of the details, knowing that their recitation to Trenarrow or to anyone else was something that belonged by rights to Lynley. He went on to explain Tina Cogin's true identity. At first Trenarrow sounded relieved to hear that his telephone number had been in the possession of Mick Cambrey all along, and not in the possession of an unknown London prostitute. But that relief was fleeting, and it faded to what seemed to be discomfort and then finally comprehension as the full implications of Mick Cambrey's double life dawned on the man.

"Of *course* I didn't know about it," he responded to St. James' question. "He'd have had to keep something like that completely to himself. Sharing that sort of secret in a village like Nanrunnel would have been the death—" He stopped abruptly. St. James could imagine the process of Trenarrow's thoughts. They certainly weren't out of the realm of possibility.

"We've traced Mick's activities to Islington-London," St. James said. "Did you know Justin Brooke worked there?"

"For Islington? No."

"I wondered if Mick's trip there somehow grew out of the interview you and he had all those months ago."

Over the line, he heard the distinct sound of china upon china, something being poured into a cup. It was a moment before Trenarrow answered. "It may well have. He was doing a feature on cancer research. I spoke of my work. I no doubt mentioned how the Islington company operates, so the London facility would have come into it."

"Would oncozyme have come into it as well?"

"Oncozyme? You know . . ." A shuffling of papers. The sound of a watch alarm going off. It was quickly silenced. "Damn, just a moment." A swallow of tea. "It must have come up. As I recall, we were discussing an entire range of new treatments, everything from monoclonal antibodies to advances in chemotherapy. Oncozyme fits into the latter category. I doubt that I would have passed it by."

"So you knew about oncozyme yourself when Mick interviewed you?"

"Everyone at Islington knew about oncozyme. Bury's Baby we called it. The branch lab at Bury St. Edmunds developed it."

"How much can you tell me about it?"

"It's an anti-oncogene. It prohibits DNA replication. You know what cancer is all about, cells reproducing, killing one off with a large dose of the body's own functions gone completely haywire. An anti-oncogene puts an end to that."

"And the side effects of an anti-oncogene?"

"That's the problem, isn't it? There always are side effects to chemotherapy. Hair loss, nausea, weight loss, vomiting, fever."

"All of those are standard, though, aren't they?"

"Standard but nonetheless inconvenient. Often dangerous. Believe me, Mr. St. James, if someone could develop a drug without side effects, the scientific world would be dazzled indeed.''

"What if a drug was found to be an effective anti-oncogene but, unfortunately, it was also the cause of more serious side effects?''

"What sort do you have in mind? Renal dysfunction? Organ failure? Something like that?''

"Perhaps something worse. A teratogen, for example.''

"Every form of chemotherapy is a teratogen. Under normal circumstances, it would never be used on a pregnant woman.''

"Something else, then?'' St. James considered the possibilities. "Something that might damage progenitor cells?''

There was an extremely long pause which Dr. Trenarrow finally ended by clearing his throat. "You're suggesting a drug causing long-range genetic defects in both men and women. I don't see how that's possible. Drugs are too well tested. It would have come out somewhere. In someone's research. It couldn't have been hidden.''

"Suppose it was,'' St. James said. "Would Mick have been able to stumble upon it?''

"Perhaps. It would have shown up as an irregularity in the test results. But where would he have got test results? Even if he went to the London office, who would have given them to him? And why?''

St. James thought he knew the answer to both those questions.

Deborah was eating an apple when she entered the study ten minutes later. She had cut the piece of fruit into eighths which she'd then arranged on a plate with half a dozen unevenly sliced pieces of cheddar cheese. Because food was involved in her current activity, Peach and Alaska—the household dog and cat—attended closely at her heels. Peach kept a vigilant eye hovering between Deborah's face and the plate while Alaska, who found overt begging beneath his feline dignity, leapt onto St. James' desk and strolled through the pens, pencils, books, magazines, and correspondence. He settled comfortably next to the telephone as if expecting a call.

"Finished with your pictures?'' St. James asked. He was sitting in his leather armchair where he had spent the time following his conversation with Trenarrow by brooding into the unlit fireplace.

Deborah sat opposite him, cross-legged on the sofa. She balanced the plate of cheese and apple on her knees. A large chemical stain ran from calf to ankle on her blue jeans, and in several places her white shirt bore spots of damp from her work in the darkroom. "For the moment. I'm taking a break."

"Came up rather suddenly, your need to print pictures. Wouldn't you say?"

"Yes," she said placidly. "Indeed, I would."

"Using them for a show?"

"Possibly. Probably."

"Deborah."

"What?" She looked up from her plate, brushed hair from her forehead. She held a wedge of cheese in her hand.

"Nothing."

"Ah." She pinched off a bit of the cheese, offered it with a portion of apple to the dog. Peach gobbled down both, wagged her tail, barked for more.

"After you left, I broke her of begging like that," St. James said. "It took me at least two months."

In answer, Deborah gave Peach another bit of cheese. She patted the dog's head, tugged her silky ears, and then looked up at him. Her expression was guileless. "She's just asking for what she wants. There's nothing wrong with that, is there?"

He could feel the provocation behind the words. He pushed himself out of his chair. There were phone calls to make about Brooke, about oncozyme; there was checking to do into his sister's whereabouts; there were at least half a dozen studies unrelated to the Cambrey-Brooke-Nifford deaths awaiting his attention in the lab and half a dozen other reasons for leaving the room. But instead of doing so, he stayed.

"Would you get that blasted cat off my desk?" He walked to the window.

Deborah went to the desk, scooped up the cat, deposited him onto St. James' chair. "Anything else?" she asked as Alaska began enthusiastically kneading the worn leather.

St. James watched the cat curling up for a lengthy stay. He saw Deborah's mouth twitch with a smile. "Minx," he said.

"Brat," she responded.

A car door slammed in the street. He turned to the window. "Tommy's here," he said, and Deborah went to open the front door.

St. James could see that Lynley bore no good news. His gait was slow, without its natural grace. Deborah joined him outside, and they spoke for a moment. She touched his arm. He shook his head, reached for her hand.

St. James left the window. He went to a bookshelf. He chose a volume at random, pulling it down and opening it at random as well. *"I wish you to know that you have been the last dream of my soul,"* he read. *"In my degradation I have not been so degraded but that the sight of you with your father, and of this home made such a home by you, has stirred old shadows . . ."* Good God. He snapped the book shut. *A Tale of Two Cities.* Great, he thought wryly.

He shoved the book back among the others and considered making another selection. *Far from the Madding Crowd* looked promising, a good bout of psychic suffering with Gabriel Oak.

". . . spoke to Mother afterwards," Lynley was saying as he and Deborah came into the study. "She didn't take it well."

St. James greeted his friend with a small whisky which Lynley accepted gratefully. He sank into the sofa. Deborah perched next to him on the sofa's arm, her fingertips brushing his shoulder.

"Brooke appears to have been telling the truth," Lynley began. "Peter was in Gull Cottage after John Penellin left. He and Mick had a row." He shared the information which he'd gathered from his interview with Peter. He added the Soho story as well.

"I did think that might have been Cambrey with Peter in the alley," St. James said when Lynley had finished. "Sidney told me about seeing them. The description seemed to fit," he added, answering the unasked question that immediately appeared on Lynley's face. "So if Peter recognised Cambrey, there's a good chance Justin Brooke did as well."

"Brooke?" Lynley queried. "How? He was there with Sidney in the alley, I know, but what difference does that make?"

"They knew each other, Tommy. Brooke worked for Islington." St. James related his own information about Brooke's position at Islington-London, about Cambrey's visits to Department Twenty-Five, about oncozyme and the potential for a story.

"How does Roderick Trenarrow fit into all this, St. James?"

"He's the prime mover. He gave Mick Cambrey some key information. Cambrey used it to pursue a story. That appears to be the extent of his involvement. He knew about oncozyme. He mentioned it to Mick."

"And then Mick died. Trenarrow was in the vicinity that night."

"He has no motive, Tommy. Justin Brooke did." St. James explained. His theory—the product of those minutes brooding alone in the study—was simple enough. It involved the promise of cocaine in exchange for key background information from an unnamed source that would evolve into an important story about a potentially dangerous drug.

A deal between Cambrey and Brooke that had somehow gone bad, coming to a head on the night Brooke had gone with Peter to Gull Cottage.

"But that doesn't account for Brooke's death."

"Which the police have said from the first was an accident."

Lynley took his cigarette case from his jacket pocket, staring down at it thoughtfully before he spoke. He flipped open his lighter but did not use it at once. "The pub," he said. "Peter said Brooke wasn't in the Anchor and Rose on Friday night, St. James."

"After he left Gull Cottage?"

"Yes. Peter went to the pub. He was there at a quarter to ten and beyond. Brooke never showed up."

"So it fits, doesn't it?"

Deborah spoke. "Did Justin Brooke know Peter was taking him to see Mick Cambrey? Did Peter name Mick before they left for the village? Or did he just say it was someone in Nanrunnel?"

"He must not have known in advance," St. James said. "He'd hardly have gone had he known Mick Cambrey was the man with the money Peter intended to borrow. He wouldn't have wanted to run the risk of exposure."

"It seems that Mick was in more danger of exposure than Justin Brooke," Deborah said. "The cocaine, the cross-dressing, his second life in London. God knows what else you've yet to tumble up."

Lynley lit his cigarette, spoke with a sigh that expelled a gust of smoke. "Beyond that, there's Sasha Nifford. If Brooke killed Cambrey and then fell to his death, what happened to Sasha?"

St. James attempted to look noncommittal. He made himself ask, "What did the Met have to say about Sasha?"

"It was ergotamine and quinine." Lynley took a white envelope from his inner breast pocket. He handed it to St. James. "She seems to have thought it was heroin."

He read the brief report, finding it all at once difficult to assimilate technical information that should have been like a natural second language. Lynley was continuing to speak, giving facts which St. James had himself possessed for years.

"A massive dose constricts all the arteries. Blood vessels rupture in the brain. Death is immediate. But we saw that, didn't we? She still had the needle in her arm."

"The police aren't calling it an accident."

"Quite. They were still questioning Peter when I left."

"But if it wasn't an accident," Deborah said, "doesn't that mean . . ."

"There's a second killer," Lynley concluded.

St. James went to his bookshelves once again. He was sure his movements, jerky and awkward, gave him away.

"Ergotamine," he said. "I'm not entirely sure . . ." He let his voice drift off, hoping for a display of natural curiosity, the reaction typical to a man of science. But all the time, dread and knowledge were seeping through his skin. He pulled down a medical volume.

"It's a prescription drug," Lynley was saying.

St. James flipped through the pages. His hands were clumsy. He was at *G* and then *H* before he knew it. He aimlessly read without seeing a word.

"What's it for?" Deborah asked.

"Migraine headaches mostly."

"Really? Migraine headaches?" St. James felt Deborah turn towards him, willed her not to ask. Innocently, she did so. "Simon, do you take it for your migraines?"

Of course, of course. She had known he took it. Everyone knew. He never counted the tablets. And the bottle was large. So she had gone to his room. She'd taken what she needed. She'd crushed them. She'd mixed them. She'd created the poison. And she'd handed it over, intending it for Peter, but killing Sasha instead.

He had to say something to direct them back to Cambrey and Brooke. He read for another moment, nodded as if caught in heavy contemplation, then shut the book.

"We need to go back to Cornwall," he said decisively. "The newspaper office should give us the definite connection between Brooke and Cambrey. Harry was looking for a story right after Mick's death. But he was looking for something sensational: gunrunning into Northern Ireland, call girls visiting Cabinet ministers. That sort of thing. Something tells me he would have overlooked oncozyme." He didn't add the fact that leaving London by tomorrow would buy him time, making him unavailable to the police when they came calling to question him about a silver bottle from Jermyn Street.

"I can manage that," Lynley said. "Webberly's been good enough to extend my time off. And it'll clear Peter's name. Will you come as well, Deb?"

St. James saw that she was watching him closely. "Yes," she said slowly. Then, "Simon, is there—"

He couldn't allow the question. "If you'll both excuse me, I've a number of reports to see to in the lab," he said. "I've got to make at least some sort of start on them before tomorrow."

He hadn't come down for dinner. Deborah and her father had finally taken their meal alone after nine o'clock in the dining room. Dover sole, asparagus, new potatoes, green salad. A glass of wine with the food. A cup of coffee afterwards. They didn't speak. But every few minutes, Deborah caught her father glancing her way.

A division had come into their relationship since her return from America. Where once they had spoken freely to each other, with great affection and trust, now they were wary. Entire subjects were taboo. She wanted it that way. She had been in such a rush to move from the Chelsea house in the first place to avoid a sharing of confidences with her father. For in the long run, he knew her better than anyone. And he was the most likely person to push back through the present to examine the past. He had, after all, the most at stake. He loved them both.

She pushed back her chair and began gathering their plates. Cotter stood as well. "Glad to have you here tonight, Deb," he said. "Old times, seems like. The three of us."

"The two of us." She smiled in what she hoped would be affectionate and dismissive at once. "Simon didn't come to dinner."

"Three of us in the house, I meant," Cotter said. He handed her the tray from the sideboard. She stacked the plates on it. "Works too much, does Mr. St. James. I worry the man'll wear 'imself down to nothing."

Cleverly, he'd moved to stand near the door. She couldn't escape without making obvious her desire to do so. And surely, her father would pounce upon that. So she cooperated by saying, "He *is* thinner, Dad, isn't he? I can see that."

"That 'e is." And then adroitly he took the opening. "These last three years didn't go easy on Mr. St. James, Deb. You think they did, don't you? But you've got it wrong."

"Well, of course, there were changes in all of our lives, weren't there? I expect he hadn't thought much about my running round the house until I wasn't here to do it any longer. But he got used to it in time. Anyone can see—"

"You know, luv," her father interrupted, "you've never in your life been one to talk false to yourself. I'm sorry to see you start doing it now."

"Talk false? Don't be ridiculous. Why would I do that?"

"You know the answer. Way I see it, Deb, you and Mr. St. James both know the answer more'n quite well. All it takes is one o' you to be brave enough to say it and the other brave enough to stop living a lie."

He put their wine glasses on the tray and took it from her hands. She had inherited her mother's height, Deborah knew, but she'd forgotten how that only made it easier for her father to look directly into her eyes. He did so now. The effect was disconcerting. It drew a confidence from her when she wanted to avoid giving it.

"I know how you want it to be," she said. "But it can't be that way, Dad. You need to accept it. People change. They grow up. They grow apart. Distance does things to them. Time makes their importance to each other fade away."

"Sometimes," he said.

"*This* time." She saw him blink rapidly at the firmness of her voice. She tried to soften the blow. "I was just a little girl. He was like my brother."

"He was that." Cotter moved to one side to let her pass.

She felt bereft by his reaction. She wanted nothing so much as his understanding but didn't know how to explain the situation in any way that would not destroy the dearest of his dreams. "Dad, you must see that it's different with Tommy. I'm not a little girl to him. I never was. But to Simon, I've always been . . . I'll always be . . ."

Cotter's smile was gentle. "You've no need to convince me, Deb. No need." He straightened his shoulders. His tone became brisk. "At least we need to get some food in the man. Will you take a tray up? He's still in the lab."

It was the least she could do. She followed him down the stairs to the kitchen and watched him put together a tray of cheese, cold meats, fresh bread, and fruit, which she carried up to the lab where St. James was sitting at one of the worktables, gazing at a set of photographed bullets. He held a pencil, but it lay unused between his fingers.

He'd turned on several lights, high intensity lamps scattered here and there throughout the sprawling room. They created small pools of illumination within great caverns of shadow. In one of these, his face was largely screened by the darkness.

"Dad wants you to eat something," Deborah said from the doorway. She entered the room and set the tray on the table. "Still working?"

He wasn't. She doubted that he'd got a single thing done in all these past hours he'd spent in the lab. There was a report of some sort lying next to one of the photographs, but its front page didn't bear even a crease from having been folded back. And although a pad of paper lay beneath the pencil he held, he'd written nothing upon it. So all of this was rote behaviour on his part, a falling back on his work as an act of avoidance.

It all involved Sidney. Deborah had seen that much in his face when Lady Helen told him she hadn't been able to find his sister. She had seen it again when he had returned to her flat and placed call after call, trying to locate Sidney himself. Everything he had done from that moment— his journey to Islington-London, his discussion with Tommy about Mick Cambrey's death, his creation of a scenario to fit the facts of the crime, his need to get back to work in the lab—all of this was diversion and distraction to escape the trouble that had Sidney at its core. Deborah wondered what St. James would do, what he would allow himself to feel, if someone had hurt his sister. Once again, she found herself wanting to help him in some way, giving him a peace of mind that appeared to elude him.

"It's just a bit of meat and cheese," she said. "Some fruit. Bread." All of which was obvious. The tray was lying in his line of vision.

"Tommy's gone?" he asked.

"Ages ago. He went back to Peter." She drew one of the lab stools to the other side of the table and sat facing him. "I've forgotten to bring you something to drink," she said. "What would you like? Wine? Mineral water? Dad and I had coffee. Would you like a coffee, Simon?"

"Thank you, no. This is fine." But he made no move to eat. He straightened on the stool, rubbed the muscles of his back.

The darkness did much to alter his face. Harsh angles were softened. Lines disappeared. The years drained away, taking with them the evidence of their companion pain. He was left looking younger and far more vulnerable. He seemed all at once so much easier to reach, the man to whom Deborah had once said anything at all, without fear of either derision or rejection, secure in the knowledge that he would always understand.

"Simon," she said and waited until he had looked up from the plate of food which she knew he would not touch. "Tommy told me what you tried to do for Peter today. That was so kind of you."

His expression clouded. "What I tried—"

She reached across the table, grasping his hand lightly. "He said that you were going to take the container so that it wouldn't be there when the police arrived. Tommy was so moved by that act of friendship.

He would have said something this afternoon in the study, but you left before he had the chance.''

She saw that his eyes were on her ring. The emerald shimmered like a translucent liquid in the light. His hand beneath hers was very cool. But as she waited for him to respond, it balled into a fist and then jerked away. She pulled her own hand back, feeling momentarily struck, feeling that any foolhardy lowering of her defences, any attempt to reach him in simple friendship, condemned her to failure again and again. Across from her, he swung to one side. The shadows deepened on the planes of his face.

"God," he whispered.

At the word, at his expression, she saw that his pulling away had nothing to do with her. "What is it?" she asked.

He leaned into the light. Every line reappeared with every angle newly honed. Dominant bones seemed to draw the skin against his skull. "Deborah . . . how can I tell you? I'm not the hero that you think I am. I did nothing for Tommy. I didn't think of Tommy. I didn't care about Peter. I *don't* care about Peter."

"But—"

"The container belongs to Sidney."

Deborah felt herself drawing back at this statement. Her lips parted, but for a moment she did nothing but stare incredulously at his face. Finally, she managed, "What are you saying?"

"She thinks Peter killed Justin Brooke. She wanted to even the score. But somehow, instead of Peter—"

"Ergotamine," Deborah whispered. "You do take it, don't you?"

He shoved the tray to one side. But that was the only reaction he appeared to be willing to allow himself. His words—if not their connotation—were perfectly cool. "I feel like an idiot. I can't even think what to do to help my own sister. I can't even find her. It's pathetic. Obscene. I'm perfectly useless and this entire day has been nothing more than an illustration of that fact."

"I don't believe it," Deborah said slowly. "Sidney wouldn't . . . she didn't . . . Simon, I can't think you believe it yourself."

"Helen's looked everywhere, phoned everywhere. So have I. Nothing's any good. And they'll trace that container within twenty-four hours."

"How could they? Even if her fingerprints are on it—"

"It has nothing to do with fingerprints. She's used her perfume bottle. It's from Jermyn Street. That's not going to give the police any difficulty. They'll be here by four o'clock tomorrow afternoon. You can bet on that.''

"Her perfume . . . Simon, it's not Sidney!" Quickly, Deborah pushed off the lab stool, going round to join him. "It's not Sidney. It can't be. Don't you remember? She came to my room the night of the dinner. She used my perfume. Hers was missing, she said. Someone had straightened her room. She couldn't find anything. Don't you remember?''

For an instant, he looked momentarily stunned. His vision was fixed upon her although he didn't appear to be seeing her at all. "What?" he whispered and then went on in a voice that was stronger. "That was Saturday evening. That was before Brooke died. Someone was planning to kill Peter even then.''

"Or Sasha," Deborah said.

"Someone's trying to frame Sidney." He pushed himself off the lab stool, walked to the end of the worktable, swung round, walked back. He did it a second time, more quickly and with growing agitation. "Someone got into her room. It could have been anyone. Peter—if Sasha was the intended victim—or Trenarrow or any one of the Penellins. Good God, even Daze.''

The truth was all of a piece in a moment. "No," Deborah said. "It was Justin.''

"Justin?''

"It never made sense to me that he went to her bedroom Friday night. Not after what happened between them on the beach that afternoon. He had a grievance against Sidney. The cocaine, their fight, Peter and Sasha laughing at them both. Laughing at *him*.''

"So he went to her room," St. James said slowly, "made love to her, and took the bottle then. He *must* have done. Damn him to hell.''

"And Saturday when Sid couldn't find him for most of the day—remember, she told us that?—he must have got the ergotamine and quinine then. He made the mixture and passed it on to Sasha.''

"A chemist," St. James said thoughtfully. "A biochemist. Who would know drugs better?''

"So who was he after? Peter or Sasha?''

"It was always Peter.''

"Because of the visit to Mick Cambrey?''

"The room had been searched. The computer was on. There were notebooks and photographs all over the floor. Peter must have seen something when he was there with Brooke, something Brooke knew he might remember once Cambrey was dead.''

"Then why give the drugs to Sasha? When Peter died, she would have told the police at once where she'd gotten them.''

"Not at all. She'd have been dead as well. Brooke was betting on that. He knew she was a user. So he gave her the drugs, hoping she and Peter would use them together and die at Howenstow, I imagine. When it became apparent that the plan wasn't working, he tried to be rid of Peter in a different way: by telling us about their visit to Cambrey so that Peter would be arrested and out of the way. What he couldn't have known is that Sasha and Peter would leave before Peter could be arrested in Cornwall and that Sasha's addiction was worse than Peter's. He especially had no way of knowing that she would hoard the drugs and use them alone. Nor did he know that Peter would go to the Anchor and Rose and get himself seen by a dozen or more people who could provide him with an alibi for the time of Cambrey's death.''

"So it was Justin," Deborah said. "Everything was Justin.''

"I've been blinded by the fact that he died *before* Sasha. I never considered that he might have given her the drugs first.''

"But his own death, Simon?''

"An accident all along.''

"Why? How? What was he doing on the cliff in the middle of the night?''

St. James glanced over her shoulder. She'd left the warning light on above the darkroom door. It cast an eery glow of blood red on the ceiling. It also gave him the answer. "Your cameras,'' he said. "That's where he got rid of them.''

"Why?''

"He was wiping out every trace of his connection to Cambrey. First Cambrey himself. Then Peter. Then—''

"My film,'' she said. "The pictures you took in the cottage. Whatever Peter saw, you must have photographed as well.''

"Which means the state of the sitting room was merely a blind. He hadn't searched for anything. He hadn't taken anything. Whatever he wanted was too big to be removed.''

"The computer?'' Deborah asked. "Even so, how could he have known you even took any pictures in the first place?''

"He knew we had your camera with us Friday night. Mrs. Sweeney made certain of that at dinner on Saturday. He knew my line of work. Sidney would have told him. He had to have known Tommy is with

Scotland Yard. He might have risked our coming upon a murder scene and doing nothing save calling the police. But why take the risk if there was something in that room—something on the film—that could tie him to Cambrey?''

"But the police would have found it eventually, wouldn't they?''

"They'd made their arrest. Penellin was as good as confessing to the crime. The only thing Justin had to fear was that someone other than the local police wouldn't accept the idea of Penellin as a killer. Which is exactly what happened less than twenty-four hours after Cambrey's death. We were nosing about. We were asking questions. He had to take steps to protect himself.''

She asked a final question. "But why all my equipment? Why not just the film?''

"He didn't have time. It was easier to take the entire case, drop it from your window, and then trot down to see Tommy and me in the day room where he told us all about Peter. Then later on he took the cameras to the cove. He went out on the rocks and disposed of them in the water. He climbed back up the cliff. And that's when he fell.''

She smiled, feeling the release that comes with relief. He looked as if he'd shaken off a terrible burden. "I wonder if we can prove any of it.''

"Indeed we can. In Cornwall. First at the cove to find the cameras, then at the newspaper office to find whatever Mick Cambrey was writing about oncozyme. Tomorrow.''

"And the film? The pictures?''

"Icing on the cake.''

"Shall I develop them for you?''

"Would you?''

"Of course.''

"Then let's be about it at once, little bird. It's time to put Justin Brooke in his place.''

24

Deborah worked with a lightness of both heart and spirit that she would have thought impossible a mere two hours before. She found herself humming, occasionally singing a line or two from old songs that popped into her head out of nowhere: the Beatles, Buddy Holly, an ancient Cliff Richard she didn't even know she knew. In the darkroom, she clipped the leader from the roll of exposed film, spooling it into the developing tank in an automatic process that was second nature to her. She didn't pause to reflect upon the work itself or upon the carefree manner in which she did it. Nor did she pause to think about how and why time and circumstances had somehow reversed themselves, allowing her former childhood affection for St. James to blossom, renewed, while they talked together in the lab. She was merely grateful that it had somehow happened, she was merely grateful for the promise it held that rancour could at last be put to rest between them.

How right she had been to follow her instincts and come to Chelsea to be with Simon tonight. How happy she had felt to see his face alter the moment he realised that no blame could be laid at his sister's feet. How comfortable she had been to follow him to his bedroom, to stand chatting and laughing while he rooted out the roll of film. They were comrades again, sharing their thoughts, listening to each other, debating, and reflecting.

Joy in communicating had been the hallmark of their relationship prior to her three-year stay in America. And those minutes in the lab, in his bedroom afterwards, had brought back to her the vivid memory of that joy, if not the full intensity of the joy itself. She saw what he had once been to her as a series of images, playing in the field of her mind.

These whirled her back through childhood and adolescence, vast periods of time that she shared with him.

He was her history in a thousand different ways: listening to her woes, softening the blow of disappointments, reading to her, talking to her, watching her grow. He had seen the very worst that she was—her temper tantrums, her stubborn pride, her inability to accept defeat, the demands for perfection which she placed upon herself, the difficulty she faced in forgiving weakness in others. He had seen this and more, and never had he been anything less than completely accepting. He might advise or instruct, he might warn or admonish. But he always accepted. And she had known he always would from the moment when, as an eighteen-year-old boy, he had squatted before her at the side of her mother's grave where she was trying to be brave, striving for indifference, making a show of the fact that at seven years old she could stand the terror of a devastating loss that she barely understood. He had drawn her into his arms with five simple words which effectively freed her to be who and what she really was for the rest of her life: "It's all right to cry."

He had helped her grow up, encouraged her in every way, and let her go when it was time for her to leave. But it was that final action— his obvious willingness to release her into her own adulthood without a word or action to stop her from leaving him—which had undermined their relationship, creating a rankling that had gnawed within her. And because the very worst she could be was the part of her that rose to the surface when she was first confronted with his intention to subject them both to three years of separation heightened by silence, she had let joy wither, she had let warmth die, she had given herself over to a need to hurt him. And she had done so, achieving a revenge that was at once initially satisfying, pure and simple. But now she saw that the attainment of such a goal was at best a Pyrrhic victory, and any vengeance she had wrought upon Simon had merely ricocheted, wounding herself.

Only in speaking the truth did there exist any hope to rebuild a friendship with him. Only in confession, expiation, and forgiveness did there lie the possibility of retrieving joy. And she wanted joy. Nothing meant more than being comfortable with him again, talking to him as she had in her childhood, as his little sister, his comrade, and his friend. She wanted nothing more. For what had long been at the festering core of her painful separation from Simon was the thwarted desire to be taken to his bed so that she might know that he truly wanted her, so that she might finally be assured that she hadn't just imagined those long ago moments when he had allowed her to see what she had convinced herself was honest desire.

But the need for that satisfaction and knowledge had long since been consumed by the flames of her love for Tommy. And it was Tommy now who would give her the courage to speak the truth. For as she held the film's negatives to the light, searching for the pictures of the Cambrey cottage, she saw the pictures of Lynley as well, cooperatively posing with the Nanrunnel players. She felt a rush of gratitude and devotion just studying him—the way he threw back his head in a burst of laughter, the way his hair shone, the shape of his mouth. She knew that Tommy was where the loyalty of her adulthood lay. He was the future towards which she was moving. But she couldn't reach him with an unfettered heart without laying rest to the past.

She worked through the process of enlarging the photographs which St. James had taken in the Cambrey cottage. From enlarger, to developer, to stop bath, to fixer. All the time her mind was taken up with what she would say to him, how she would say it, and whether her explanation and apology could possibly suffice to end their estrangement.

It was nearly midnight when she'd completed her work in the darkroom: the developing, the washing, the drying, the cleaning up. She switched off the lights, gathered up the photographs, and went in search of St. James.

He heard her movement on the stairs before he saw her. Across his bed he'd spread out every document that pertained to the case, and he was studying them all, deciding which of them could be used to exonerate not only his sister but Peter Lynley and John Penellin as well. A flash at his doorway stirred him from his contemplation of these items. It was Deborah's white shirt against the shadows in the hall. She was holding the photographs.

He smiled. "Have them finished?"

"Yes. It took a bit longer than I thought. I wasn't used to the enlarger. Because it's new and . . . well, you know that, don't you? How silly."

He thought she might give the photographs to him, but she didn't do so. Instead, she came to stand at the foot of his bed. One hand held the photographs pressed against her side, the other curved round the bed's tall, fluted poster.

"I need to talk to you, Simon."

Something in her face reminded him instantly of a bottle of ink spilled on a dining room chair and a scuffy-shoed ten-year-old's quavering confession. Something in her voice, however, told him that, for Deborah, a moment of accounting had arrived, and as a result he felt that sudden draining of strength that comes with an onslaught of dread.

"What is it? What's wrong?"

"The photograph. I knew that you'd see it one day or another, and I wanted you to see it. It was my dearest wish. I wanted you to know that I sleep with Tommy. I wanted you to know because then I might hurt you. And I wanted to hurt you, Simon. I was desperate to punish you. I wanted you to think of us making love together. I wanted you to be jealous. I wanted you to care. And I . . . Simon, I despise myself for having done that to you."

Her words were so unexpected that the very surprise of them buffeted him into a form of shock. For one ridiculous moment, he talked himself into misunderstanding the direction she was heading in, allowing himself to assume that she was speaking of the Cambrey pictures and making references to them that he simply couldn't comprehend. In that instantaneous way that minds have of working, he made a quick decision to direct the conversation along those lines. *What are you talking about? Jealous of Tommy? What photograph, Deborah? I don't understand.* Or better yet, laughing it off, indifferent. *Just a practical joke that didn't work out.* But even as he gathered the resources to respond, she continued, making her meaning quite clear.

"I wanted you so much when I left for America. I loved you so much, and I was sure you loved me. Not as a brother or an uncle or a sort of second father. But as a man, an equal. You know what I mean." Her words were so gentle, her voice so quiet. He felt compelled to keep watching her face. He stood immobilised, unable to go to her even as every sinew in his body insisted he do so. "I don't know if I can even explain what it was like for me, Simon. So confident when I left, so sure of what you and I had together. And then waiting for you to answer my letters. At first not understanding, even believing something had happened to the post. Phoning you after two months and hearing how distant you were. Your career was making such demands on you, you said. Responsibilities were piling up. Conferences and seminars and papers to write. You'd answer my letters when you could. And how is school, Deborah? Are you getting on? Are you making friends? I'm sure you'll do well. You've the talent. You've the gift. You've nothing but a brilliant future ahead of you."

He said the only thing he could manage. "I remember."

"I judged myself." Her fleeting smile was a fragile thing. "Not pretty enough for you, not clever enough, not amusing, not compassionate, not loving, not desirable . . . not enough."

"That wasn't the truth. That isn't the truth."

"Most mornings I woke and despaired of the fact that I was still alive. And that became part of my loathing as well. I wasn't even enough of a person to take my own life. Worthless, I thought. Totally without value. Stupid and ugly and utterly useless."

Each word was more difficult to bear than the last.

"I wanted to die. I prayed to die. But I didn't. I just went on. Which is what most people do."

"They do go on. They heal. They forget. I understand." He hoped those four statements would be enough to stop her. But he saw that she was determined to carry their conversation through to an end of her own devising.

"Tommy was my forgetting at first. When he came to visit, we laughed. We talked. The first time he made an excuse why he'd come. But not after that. And he never pushed me, Simon. He never once made demands. I didn't talk about you, but I think somehow he knew and was determined to wait until I was ready to open my heart to him. So he wrote, he phoned, he laid a real foundation. And when he took me to bed, I wanted to be there. I'd finally let you go."

"Deborah, please. It's all right. I understand." He stopped looking at her. Turning his head was the only movement he seemed capable of making. He stared at the items he'd placed on the bed.

"You'd rejected me. I was angry. I was hurt. I got over you in the end, but for some reason I still believed that I had to show you how things were now. I had to make you see that if you didn't want me, someone else did. So I put that photograph on the wall in my flat. Tommy didn't want me to. He asked me not to. But I pointed out the composition, the colour, the texture of the curtains and the blankets, the shapes of clouds in the sky. It's just a photograph, I said, are you embarrassed about what it implies about us?"

For a moment, she said nothing more. St. James thought she was finished, and he looked up to see that her hand was at her throat, her fingers pressing along her collarbone. "What a terrible lie to tell Tommy. I just wanted to hurt you. As deeply as I could."

"God knows I deserved it. I hurt you as well."

"No. There's no excusing a need for retaliation like that. It's adolescent. Disgusting. It says things about me that make me ill. I'm so sorry. Truly."

It's nothing. Really. Do forget it, little bird. He couldn't bring himself to say it. He couldn't say anything. He couldn't bear the thought that, through his own cowardice, he had driven her to Lynley. It was more than he could suffer. He despised himself. As he watched, seeking words that he didn't know, feeling wrenched by emotions he couldn't bear to possess, she placed the photographs on the edge of the bed, pressing their corners down to keep them from curling.

"Do you love him?" The question sounded as if he had flung it.

She had gone to the door, but she turned to answer. "He's everything to me," she said. "Loyalty, devotion, affection, warmth. He's given me things—"

"Do you love him?" The question was shaken this time. "At least can you say that you love him, Deborah?"

For a moment he thought she might leave without answering. But he saw Lynley's power sweep right through her body. Her chin raised, her shoulders straightened, her eyes shone with tears. He heard the answer before she gave it. "I love him. Yes. I love him. I do." And then she was gone.

He lay in bed and stared at the shifting patterns of black shadow and dim light on the ceiling. The night was warm, so his bedroom window was open, the curtains were undrawn, and he could hear, occasionally, cars rumbling along Cheyne Walk just a block away, the noise of their engines amplified by the open expanse of the river. His body should have been tired—demanding sleep—but instead it ached, muscles excruciatingly tense in his neck and shoulders, hands and arms feeling strung with external nerves, chest sore and constricted as if pressed by a weight. His mind was a maelstrom in which were swirling fragments of former conversations, half-formed hazy fantasies, things needing to be said.

He tried to think of anything other than Deborah. A fibre analysis he needed to complete, a deposition he was due to give in two weeks, a conference at which he was to present a paper, a seminar in Glasgow he had been asked to teach. He tried to be what he had been during her absence, the cool scientist meeting commitments and facing responsibilities, but instead he saw the man he really was, the coward who filled his life with denial and distraction to avoid running the risk of vulnerability.

His entire life was a lie, founded on noble aphorisms in which he knew he did not believe. Let her go. Let her find her own way. Let her have a world of expanding horizons filled with people who could give her riches far beyond the paucity of what he had to offer. Let her find a kindred soul with whom she could share herself, one unburdened by the weaknesses that plagued his own life. But even this listing of the specious regulations that had governed his behaviour still left him safe from having to confront the final truth.

Fear dominated him. It left him useless. Any action he chose could be the source of rejection. So he chose by not choosing, by letting time pass, by believing that conflicts, difficulties, and turmoil would sort themselves out on their own in the long run. And indeed they had done so. Loss was the result.

Too late he saw what he should have seen all along, that his life with Deborah had been a long-forming tapestry in which she had held the thread, had created the design, and had ultimately become the fabric itself. That she should leave him now was a form of dying, leaving him not death's peace of the void but an infinite hellfire of recrimination, all of it the product of his contemptible fear. That the years had passed and he had not told her how he loved her. His heart soared in her presence but he would not say the words. Now, he could only thank God that she and Lynley planned to take up a new life in Cornwall after their marriage. If she was gone from his presence, what remained of life here would at least be bearable.

He turned his head on the pillow and looked at the glowing red numbers of the digital clock. It was ten past three. The effort to sleep was useless. He could at least admit that. He switched on the light.

The stack of photographs still lay on the table next to the bed where he had placed them over two hours ago. In what he knew quite well was an act of deliberate avoidance—more cowardice for which he would despise himself with the dawn—he picked them up. As if this action could eradicate Deborah's words, as if the knowledge of how she had once wanted him were not tearing at his soul, he began to examine them, a study in detachment with his world in ruins.

Without emotion, he looked at the corpse, its mutilation, its position near the sofa. He observed the debris that lay in the room: the letters and envelopes; the pens and pencils; the notebooks and folders; the scraps of paper covered with writing; the poker and fire irons tumbled to the floor; the computer—switched on—with black floppy disks spread out on the desk. And then closer to the corpse, the glint of silver—perhaps a coin—half-hidden under his thigh; the five-pound note, a small wedge torn from it, lying disregarded near his hand on the floor; above him the mantel on which he had struck his head; to the right the hearth to which he had fallen. St. James flipped through the photographs again and again, looking for something he could not have identified even if he saw it. The computer, the disks, the folders, the notebooks, the money, the mantel. He thought only of Deborah.

Giving up the game, he admitted that there would be neither sleep, nor peace, nor even the possibility of a moment's distraction. He could only make the hours till dawn slightly more liveable. He reached for his crutches and swung out of bed. Throwing on his dressing gown, belting it clumsily, he headed for the door. There was brandy in the study. It would not be the first time he had sought its oblivion. He made his way down the stairs.

The study door was partially closed, and it swung inward noiselessly upon his touch. A soft glow—dancing between gold and dusky rose—came from two candles that should have stood on the overmantel but had been placed side by side and lit upon the hearth. Hands clasped round her knees, Deborah sat on the ottoman and watched the candles' flames. Seeing her, St. James wanted to retreat. He thought about doing so. He didn't move.

She looked towards the door, looked away again quickly when she saw it was he. "Couldn't sleep," she said unnecessarily as if she thought she needed to explain her presence in his study—wearing dressing gown and slippers—after three in the morning. "I can't think why. I ought to be exhausted. I *feel* exhausted. But I couldn't sleep. Too much excitement these past few days."

Her words were casual enough, well-chosen and indifferent. But there was something hesitant in her voice. It tried but failed to ring true. Hearing this, he made his way across the room and lowered himself onto the ottoman next to her. It was the sort of gesture he'd never made before. In the past, her place had been on the ottoman, while he sat above her, in the chair or on the sofa.

"I couldn't sleep either," he said, laying his crutches on the floor. "I thought I'd have a brandy."

"I'll get it for you." She began to rise.

He caught her hand, stopped her. "No. It's all right." And when she kept her face averted, "Deborah."

"Yes?"

The single word was calm. Her curly mass of hair hid her face from view. She made a quick movement, like a lifting of her body, and he thought it was prelude to rising and leaving. But instead of doing so, he heard her take a choked breath and realised with a swift dawning of surprise that she was struggling not to cry.

He touched her hair, so tentatively that he knew she couldn't possibly feel that he had done so. "What is it?"

"Nothing."

"Deborah—"

"We were friends," she whispered. "You and I. We were mates. I wanted that back. I thought if I talked to you tonight . . . but I just couldn't find it. It's gone. And I . . . it hurts so much to know that. If I talk to you, if I see you, I still feel torn. I don't want that feeling. I can't face it again."

Her voice broke. Without a thought, he encircled her shoulders with his arm. It didn't matter what he said. Truth or lie made no difference. He had to say something to alleviate her pain.

"We'll survive all this, Deborah. We'll find our way back. We'll be what we were. Don't cry." Roughly, he kissed the side of her head. She turned into his arms. He held her, stroked her hair, rocked her, said her name. And all at once felt flooded by peace. "It doesn't matter," he whispered. "We'll always be mates. We'll never lose that. I promise."

At his words, he felt her arms slip round him. He felt the soft pressure of her breasts against his chest. He felt her heart beating, felt his own heart pounding, and accepted the fact that he had lied to her again. They would never be friends. Friendship was absolutely impossible between them when with so simple a movement—her arms slipping round him—every part of his body lit on fire for her.

Half a dozen admonitions rang out in his head. She was Lynley's. He had hurt her quite enough already. He was betraying the oldest friendship in his life. There were boundaries between them that couldn't be crossed. His resolve was acceptance. We aren't meant to be happy. Life isn't always fair. He heard each one of them, vowed to leave the room, told himself to release her, and stayed where he was. Just to hold her, just to have her like this for one moment, just to feel her near him, just to catch the scent of her skin. It was enough. He would do nothing else . . . save touch her hair again, save brush it back from her face.

She lifted her head to look at him. Admonitions, intentions, boundaries, and resolves were shot to oblivion. Their cost was too high. They didn't matter. Nothing mattered. Just the moment, now, with her.

He touched her cheek, her brow, traced the outline of her lips. She whispered his name, a single word that finally obliterated fear. He wondered how he had ever been afraid to lose himself in the love of this woman. She was himself. He saw that now. He accepted that truth. It was a form of fulfillment. He brought his mouth to hers.

*   *   *

Nothing existed save being in his arms. Nothing mattered save the warmth of his mouth and the taste of his tongue. It was as if only this single moment counted, allowing her life to be defined by his kiss.

He murmured her name, and a sure current passed between them, gathering force from the wellspring of desire. It swept away the past and took in its flow every belief, every intention, every aspect of her life but the knowledge that she wanted him. More than loyalty, more than love, more than the promise of the future, she wanted him. She told herself that this had nothing to do with the Deborah who was Tommy's, who slept in Tommy's bed, who would be Tommy's wife. This had to do only with a settling of accounts, one hour in which she would measure her worth.

"My love," he whispered. "Without you—"

She drew his mouth back to hers. She bit his lips gently and felt them curve in a smile. She wanted no words. In their place, she wanted only sensation. His mouth on her neck, describing a curve to the hollow of her throat; his hands on her breasts, teasing and caressing, dropping to her waist to the belt of her dressing gown, loosening it, pushing the gown from her shoulders, slipping the thin straps of her nightdress down the length of her arms. She stood. The nightdress slid to the floor. She felt his hand on her thigh.

"Deborah."

She didn't want words. She bent to him, kissed him, felt him drawing her down to him, heard her own sigh of pleasure as his mouth found her breast.

She began to touch him. She began to undress him.

"I want you," he whispered. "Deborah. Look at me."

She couldn't. She saw the candles' glow, the stone surround of the fireplace, the bookshelves, the glint of a single brass lamp on his desk. But not his eyes or his face or the shape of his mouth. She accepted his kiss. She returned his caress. But she did not look at him.

"I love you," he whispered.

Three years. She waited for the rush of triumph, but it didn't come. Instead, one of the candles began to gutter, spilling wax in a messy flow onto the hearth. With a hiss, the flame died. The burnt wick sent up a wisp of smoke whose smell was sharp and disturbing. St. James turned to the source.

Deborah watched him do so. The single small flame of the remaining candle flickered like wings against his skin. His profile, his hair, the sharp edge of his jaw, the curve of his shoulder, the sure quick movement of his lovely hands . . . She got to her feet. Her fingers trembled as she put on her dressing gown and fumbled uselessly with its slippery satin belt. She felt shaken to her core. No words, she thought. Anything else, but no words.

"Deborah . . . ."

She couldn't.

"For God's sake, Deborah, what is it? What's wrong?"

She made herself look at him. His features were washed by a storm of emotion. He looked young and so vulnerable. He looked ready to be struck.

"I can't," she said. "Simon, I just can't."

She turned away from him and left the room. She ran up the stairs. Tommy, she thought.

As if his name were a prayer, an invocation that could keep her from feeling both unclean and afraid.

Part VI

EXPIATION

25

The day's fair weather had begun to change by the time Lynley touched the plane down onto the tarmac at Land's End. Heavy grey clouds were scuttling in from the southwest and what had been a mild breeze back in London was here gathering force as a rain-laden wind. This transformation in the weather was, Lynley thought bleakly, a particularly apt metaphor for the alteration that his mood and his circumstances had undergone. For he had begun the morning with a spirit uplifted by hope, but within mere hours of his having decided that the future held the promise of peace in every corner of his life, that hope had been swiftly overshadowed by a sick apprehension which he believed he had put behind him.

Unlike the anxiety of the past few days, this current uneasiness had nothing to do with his brother. Instead, from his meetings with Peter throughout the night had grown a sense of both renewal and rebirth. And although, during his lengthy visit to New Scotland Yard, the family's solicitor had depicted Peter's danger with transparent simplicity unless the death of Mick Cambrey could be unassailably pinned upon Justin Brooke, Lynley and his brother had moved from a discussion of the legal ramifications of his position to a fragile communion in which each of them took the first tentative steps towards understanding the other's past behaviour, a necessary prelude to forgiving past sins. From the hours Lynley had spent talking to his brother had come the realisation that understanding and forgiveness go hand-in-hand. To call upon one is to experience the other. And if understanding and forgiveness were to be seen as virtues—strengths of character, not illustrations of personal weakness—surely it was time he accepted the fact that they could bring harmony to the single relationship in his life where harmony was most needed. He wasn't certain what he would say to her, but he knew he was ready to speak to his mother.

This intention—a resolution which lightened his steps and lifted his shoulders—began to disintegrate upon his arrival in Chelsea. Lynley dashed up the front steps, rapped on the door, and came face to face with his most irrational fear.

St. James answered the door. He was pleasant enough with his offer of a coffee before they left, and confident enough with his presentation of his theory about Justin Brooke's culpability in Sasha Nifford's death. Under any other circumstances the information about Brooke would have filled Lynley with the surge of excitement that always came with the knowledge that he was heading towards the conclusion of a case. Under these circumstances, however, he barely heard St. James' words, let alone understood how far they went to explain everything that had happened in Cornwall and London over the past five days. Instead, he noted that his friend's face was etiolated as if from an illness; he saw the deepening of the lines on his brow; he heard the tension beneath St. James' exposition of motive, means, and opportunity; and he felt a chill through his skin and settle in every vital organ of his body. His confidence and his will—both flagships of the day—lost a quick battle with his growing dismay.

He knew there could be only one source of the change that had come over St. James, and she walked down the stairs not three minutes after his arrival, adjusting the leather strap of a shoulder bag. When she reached the hallway and Lynley saw her face, he read the truth and was sick at heart. He wanted to give sway to the anger and jealousy that he felt in that instant. But instead, generations of good breeding rose to commandeer his behaviour. The demand for an explanation became meaningless social chitchat designed to get them through the moment without so much as a hair of feeling out of place.

"Working hard on your photos, darling?" he asked her and added, because even good breeding had its limits, "You look as if you haven't had a moment's rest. Were you up all night? Are you finished with them?"

Deborah didn't look at St. James, who went into the study where he began rooting in his desk. "Nearly." She came to Lynley's side, slipped her arms round him, lifted her mouth to kiss him, and said in a whisper against his lips, "Good morning, darling Tommy. I missed you last night."

He kissed her, feeling the immediacy of her response to him and wondering if everything else he had seen was merely the product of pathetic insecurity. He told himself that this was the case. Nonetheless he still said, "If you've more work to do, you don't need to go with us."

"I want to go. The photographs can wait." And, with a smile, she kissed him again.

All the time with Deborah in his arms, Lynley was acutely aware of St. James. During the journey to Cornwall, he was aware of them both. He studied every nuance in their behavior towards him, in their behavior towards each other. He examined each word, each gesture, and remark under the unforgiving microscope of his own suspicion. If Deborah said St. James' name, it became in his mind a veiled avowal of her love. If St. James looked in Deborah's direction, it was an open declaration of commitment and desire. By the time Lynley taxied the plane to a halt on the Land's End airstrip, he felt tension coiling like a spring in the back of his neck. The resulting pain was only a secondary consideration, however. It was nothing compared to his self-disgust.

His roiling emotions had prevented him from engaging in anything other than the most superficial of conversations during the drive to Surrey and the flight that followed it. And since not one of them was gifted with Lady Helen's capacity for smoothing over difficult moments with amusing chatter, their talk had ground itself down to nothing in very short order so that when they finally arrived in Cornwall, the atmosphere among them was thick with unspoken words. Lynley knew he was not the only one to sigh with relief when they stepped out of the plane and saw Jasper waiting with the car next to the tarmac.

The silence during their ride to Howenstow was broken only by Jasper telling him that Lady Asherton had arranged to have two of the farm lads waiting at the cove "at half-one like you said 'at you wanted." John Penellin was still being held in Penzance, he confided, but the happy word had gone out to everyone that "Mister Peter be found."

"Her ladyship's looking tenyers younger this morning for knowing the lad's safe," Jasper concluded. "She was wacking her tennis balls at five past eight."

They said nothing more. St. James riffled through the papers in his briefcase, Deborah watched the scenery, Lynley tried to clear his mind. They met neither vehicle nor animal on the narrow lanes, and it wasn't until they made the turn onto the estate drive that they saw anyone at all. Nancy Cambrey was sitting on the front steps of the lodge. In her arms, Molly sucked eagerly at her bottle.

"Stop the car," Lynley said to Jasper, and then to the others, "Nancy knew about Mick's newspaper story from the first. Perhaps she can fill in the details if we tell her what we know."

St. James looked doubtful. A glance at his watch told Lynley that he was concerned about getting to the cove and from there to the newspaper office before much more time elapsed. But he didn't protest. Nor did Deborah. They got out of the car.

Nancy stood when she saw who it was. She led them into the house and faced them in the entry hall. Above her right shoulder, an old, faded sampler hung on the wall, a needlepoint scene of a family picnic, with two children, their parents, a dog, and an empty swing hanging from a tree. The wording was nearly obscure, but it probably had spoken, with well-meaning inaccuracy, of the constant rewards of family life.

"Mark's not here?" Lynley asked.

"He's gone to St. Ives."

"So your father's still said nothing to Inspector Boscowan about him? About Mick? About the cocaine?"

Nancy didn't pretend to misunderstand. She merely said, "I don't know. I've heard nothing," and walked into the sitting room where she placed Molly's bottle on top of the television and the baby herself into her pram. "There's a good girl," she said and patted her back. "There's a good little Molly. You sleep for a bit."

They joined her. It would have been natural to sit, but none of them did so at first. Instead, they took positions like uneasy actors who do not yet know how their play will be blocked: Nancy with one hand curled round the push bar of the pram; St. James with his back to the bay window; Deborah near the piano; Lynley opposite her by the sitting room door.

Nancy looked as if she anticipated the worst from this unexpected visit. Her glance went among them skittishly.

"You've news of Mick," she said.

Together, Lynley and St. James laid out both facts and conjectures. She listened to them without question or comment. Occasionally, she seemed struck by fleeting sorrow, but for the most part she seemed deadened to everything. It was as if, far in advance of their arrival, she had anaesthetised herself against the possibility of feeling anything more, not only about her husband's death but also about some of the less-than-creditable aspects of his life.

"So he never mentioned Islington to you?" Lynley asked when they had concluded their story. "Or oncozyme? Or a biochemist, Justin Brooke?"

"Never. Not once."

"Was that typical of him to be so secretive about a story?"

"Before we married, no. He talked of everything then. When we were lovers. Before the baby."

"And after the baby?"

"He went away more and more. Always about some story."

"To London?"

"Yes."

"Did you know he kept a flat there?" St. James asked.

When she shook her head, Lynley said, "But when your father spoke about Mick keeping other women, did you never think he might be keeping one in London? That would be a reasonable enough assumption, wouldn't it, considering how often he was travelling up there?"

"No. There were . . ." The decision she faced evidenced itself in her hesitation. It was a choice between loyalty or truth. And a question of whether truth in this case really constituted a betrayal. She appeared resolved. She lifted her head. "There were no other women. Dad only thought that. I let him believe Mickey was having other women. It was easier that way."

"Easier than letting your father discover that his son-in-law liked to wear women's clothes?"

Lynley's question appeared to release the young woman from months of secrecy. If anything, she looked monumentally relieved. "No one knew," Nancy murmured. "For ever so long, no one knew but me." She sank into the armchair next to the pram. "Mickey," she said. "Oh God, poor Mickey."

"How did you find out?"

She pulled a crumpled tissue from the pocket of her housedress. "Right before Molly was born. There were things in his chest of drawers. I thought he was having an affair at first and I didn't say anything because I was eight months gone and Mick and me couldn't . . . so I thought . . ."

How reasonable it all was as she haltingly explained it. Pregnant, she couldn't accommodate her husband so if he sought another woman she would have to accept it. She had, after all, entrapped him into marriage. She had only herself to blame if he hurt her as a result. So she wouldn't confront him with the evidence of betrayal. She would put up with it and hope to win him back in the end.

"Then I came home one night, not long after I'd started serving behind bar at the Anchor and Rose. I found him. He was all dressed in my clothes. He'd put on makeup. He'd even got himself a wig. I thought it was my fault. See, I liked to buy things, new clothes. I wanted to be trendy. I wanted to look nice for him. I thought it would get him back. I thought at first he was making a scene to punish me for spending money. But I saw soon enough that . . . he got really . . . it made him excited.''

"What did you do after you found him?''

"Threw away my makeup. Every bit of it. Shredded my clothes. Went after them with a butcher knife in the back garden.''

Lynley remembered Jasper's account of the scene. "Your father saw you doing it, didn't he?''

"He thought I'd found things that someone left behind. So he believed Mick was having other women on the side. I let him believe it. How could I tell him the truth? Besides, Mick promised me that he'd never do it again. And I thought he could do it. I'd got rid of all my good clothes so he wouldn't be tempted. And he tried to be good. He did try. But he couldn't stop. He started bringing things home. I'd find them. I'd try to talk. We'd try to talk together. But nothing worked. He got worse. It was like he needed the dressing more and more. He even did it once at night in the newspaper office and his father caught him. Harry went mad.''

"So his father knew?''

"He beat him silly. Mick came home. He was bleeding and cursing. Crying as well. I thought then he'd stop.''

"But instead he took up a second life in London.''

"I thought he was better.'' She wiped her eyes and blew her nose. "I thought he was cured. I thought we had a chance to be happy. Like when we were lovers. We were happy then.''

"And no one else knew about Mick's cross-dressing? Not Mark? Not someone from the village? Or from the newspaper office?''

"Just me and Harry. That's all,'' she said. "Jesus God, wasn't that enough?''

"What do you think? Was it enough, St. James?''

Jasper had gone on ahead. They were on the drive, walking the final distance to the house. Above them, the sky had given up its last vestiges of blue, turning to the colour of ageing pewter. Deborah walked between them, her hand through Lynley's arm. He looked over the top of her head to St. James.

"The killing itself has looked like a crime of passion all along,'' St. James said. "A blow to his jaw that sent him crashing against the overmantel. No one premeditates a death like that. We've always agreed that some sort of argument took place.''

''But we've been trying to tie it into Mick's profession. And who sent us in that direction in the first place?''

St. James nodded in rueful acceptance. ''Harry Cambrey.''

''He had opportunity. He had motive.''

''Rage over his son's cross-dressing?''

''They'd come to violence over it before.''

''And Harry Cambrey had other grievances,'' Deborah said. ''Wasn't Mick supposed to be making improvements on the newspaper? Hadn't he taken out a bank loan? Perhaps Harry wanted a full accounting of how the money was being spent. And when he found out it was being spent on what he hated most—Mick's cross-dressing—he went over the edge.''

''Then how do you explain the condition of the sitting room?''

''A blind,'' Lynley said. ''Something he could use to support his contention that Mick was murdered because of a story.''

''But that leaves the other two deaths unaccounted for,'' St. James said. ''It also puts Peter into jeopardy again. If Brooke didn't fall to his death, someone pushed him, Tommy.''

''It always comes back to Brooke.''

''Which should tell us how likely it is that he's responsible, no matter what other wrinkles we find in Mick's relationships with anyone else.''

''The cove and the newspaper office, then.''

''I expect that's where we'll dig up the truth.''

They walked through the Tudor gatehouse and crossed the drive. In the garden they paused to greet Lady Asherton's retriever who came running to meet them, a tennis ball between his jaws. Lynley wrested it from him, hurled it in the direction of the west courtyard, and watched as the dog went yelping joyfully on his way. As if in response to her retriever's barking, the front door was pulled open, and Lady Asherton came out of the house.

''I've lunch waiting,'' she said by way of greeting and continued to speak, this time only to Lynley. ''Peter phoned. The Yard's released him for now, but they want him to stay in London. He asked to go to Eaton Terrace. Was it all right to say that would be fine with you, Tommy? I wasn't quite sure if you'd want him at your house.''

''It's fine.''

''He sounded quite different from the way he's talked in the past. I wondered if this time he's prepared for a change. For good.''

"He is. Yes, I think so. And I am as well." Lynley felt a moment's trepidation. He looked at St. James and Deborah. "If you'll give us a few minutes," he said and was grateful for their immediate understanding. They went into the house.

"What is it, Tommy?" Lady Asherton asked. "Is there something you've not told me? Is there more about Peter?"

"I'm going to tell Penzance CID about him today," Lynley said. His mother's face blanched. "He didn't kill Mick. You and I know that. But he was in the cottage after John's visit there on Friday. And Mick was still alive. That's the truth of the matter. The police need to know it."

"Does Peter know . . ." She didn't appear to be willing to complete the thought. He did it for her.

"That I intend to tell the police? Yes, he knows. But St. James and I think we'll be able to clear his name today. He trusts us to do that."

Lady Asherton forced a smile. "Then I shall trust you to do that as well." She turned and began to go into the house.

"Mother." Even now he didn't know how much it might cost him to speak. Nearly sixteen years of his bitterness had created a minefield between them. To attempt to cross it called upon resources of character he wasn't sure he possessed.

She had hesitated, her hand flat on the door to push it open. She was waiting for him to speak.

"I've made a mess out of Peter. Out of everything else as well."

Her head cocked. A quizzical smile touched her lips. "You've made a mess of him?" she said. "Peter's my son, Tommy. He's my responsibility. Don't take the blame when there isn't any need."

"He didn't have a father. I could have been more to him. I chose not to be. I would have had to come home to spend time with Peter, but I couldn't bear that, so I left him to himself."

He saw that she understood the intention behind his words. She dropped her hand from the door and came back to the drive where he was standing. He looked above her to the Asherton coat of arms that was mounted high on the front wall of the house. He had never considered the heraldic device anything more than an amusing anachronism, but now he saw it as a declaration of strength. The hound and the lion facing off in combat, the hound overpowered but showing no fear.

"I knew you loved Roderick," he said. "I saw that you loved him. I wanted to punish you."

"But I loved you as well. What I felt for Roddy had nothing to do with you."

"It wasn't a question of thinking you didn't love me. It was more an unwillingness to see you and forgive you for being what you were."

"For wanting someone besides your father?"

"For giving in to the wanting while Father was alive. I couldn't deal with that. I couldn't stand what it meant."

She looked beyond him, towards the Tudor gatehouse. "I gave in," she said. "Yes. I did that. I wish I'd had the nobility or the courage or whatever it would have taken to send Roddy away when I first realised how much I did love him. But I didn't possess whatever strength it would have taken to do that, Tommy. Other women probably do. But I was weak. I was needy. I asked myself how evil it could be if Roddy and I truly loved each other. How great a wrong were we committing if we turned a blind eye to social condemnation and acted on that love? I wanted him. To have him and still live with myself, I made neat compartments out of my life—children in one, your father in another, Roddy in a third—and I was a different person for each part. What I didn't expect was that you would burst out of the section I'd reserved for you and see the person who wanted Roddy. I didn't think you'd ever see me for what I was."

"What were you really, Mother? Nothing more or less than a human being. I couldn't accept that."

"It's all right. I understand."

"I had to make you suffer. I knew Roderick wanted to marry you. I swore it would never happen. Your primary loyalty was to the family and to Howenstow. I knew he wouldn't marry you unless you'd promise to leave the estate. So I kept you here like a prisoner, all these years."

"You don't have that power. I chose to stay."

He shook his head. "You would have left Howenstow the moment I married." He saw in her face that this was the truth. She dropped her eyes. "I knew that, Mother. I used that knowledge as a weapon. If I married, you were free. So I didn't marry."

"You never met the right woman."

"Why on earth won't you let me take the blame I deserve?"

She looked up at that. "I don't want you in pain, darling. I didn't want it then. I don't want it now."

Nothing could have stirred him to greater remorse. No rebuke, no recrimination. He felt like a swine.

"You seem to think the burden is all on your shoulders," his mother said. "Don't you know a hundred thousand times I've wished that you hadn't found us together, that I hadn't struck out at you, that I had done something—said something, anything—to help you with your grief. Because it *was* grief you were feeling, Tommy. Your father was dying right here in the house, and I'd just destroyed your mother as well. But I was too proud to reach out to you. What a supercilious little monster, I thought. How dare he try to condemn me for something he can't even understand. Let him simmer in his anger. Let him weep. Let him rage. What a prig he is. He'll come round in the end. But you never did." She touched his cheek lightly with the back of her hand, a tentative pressure that he barely felt. "There was no greater punishment than the distance between us. Marriage to Roddy would have done nothing to change that."

"It would have given you something."

"Yes. It still can."

A lightening of her voice—an underlying gentleness—told him what she had not yet said. "He's asked you again? Good. I'm glad of it. It's more forgiveness than I deserve."

She took his arm. "That time is finished, Tommy." Which was so much her way at the heart of the matter, offering a forgiveness that swept away the anger of half a lifetime.

"That simply?" he asked.

"Darling Tommy, that simply."

St. James walked some paces behind Lynley and Deborah. He watched their progress, making a study of their proximity to each other. He memorised the details of Lynley's arm round Deborah's shoulders, hers round his waist, the angle of their heads as they talked, the contrast in the colour of their hair. He saw how they walked in perfect rhythm, their strides the same length, fluid and smooth. He watched them and tried not to think about the previous night, about his realisation that he could no longer run from her and continue to live with himself, about the moment when his stunned awareness had finally absorbed the fact that he would have to do so.

Any man who had known her less well would have labelled her actions on the previous night as a clever manipulation whose end-product gleaned her the witnessing of a measure of suffering to pay for the suffering he'd inflicted upon her. A confession of her adolescent love for him; an admission of that love's attendant desire; an encounter that blended the strongest elements of emotion and arousal; an abrupt conclusion when she was certain that he intended no further flight. But even if he wanted to evaluate her behaviour as a manipulative woman's act of spite, he could not do it. For she had not known he would leave his bedroom and join her in the study, nor could she have anticipated that after years of separation and rejection he would finally let go of the worst of his fears. She had not asked him to join her, she had not asked him to drop onto the ottoman next to her, she had not asked him to take her into his arms. He had only himself to blame for having crossed the boundary into betrayal and for having assumed in the white heat of the moment that she would be willing to cross it as well.

He had forced her hand, he had called for a decision. She had made it. If he was to survive from this time on, he knew he would have to do it alone. Unbearable now, he tried to believe that the thought would become more endurable in time.

Propitiable gods held back the rain although the sky was growing rapidly more tenebrous when they reached the cove. Far out to sea, the sun burst through a ragged tear in the clouds, casting beams like a golden spotlight on the water below. But it was only a momentary break in the weather. No sailor or fisherman would have been deceived by its transitory beauty.

Below them on the beach, two teenaged boys were idly smoking near the rocks. One was tall and big boned with a shock of bright orange hair, the other small and whip-thin with great knobs on his knees. Despite the weather, they were dressed for swimming. On the ground at their feet lay a stack of towels, two face masks, two snorkels. Looking up, the orange-haired boy saw Lynley and waved. The other glanced over his shoulder and tossed his cigarette aside.

"Where do you suppose Brooke threw the cameras in?" Lynley asked St. James.

"He was on the rocks Friday afternoon. My guess is that he'd have edged out as far as he could go and heaved the case into the water. What's the bottom like?"

"Mostly granite."

"And the water's clear. If the camera case is there, they'll be able to see it."

Lynley nodded and made the descent, leaving St. James with Deborah on the cliff. They watched as he crossed the narrow strand and shook both boys' hands. They grinned, the one driving his fingers into his hair and scratching his scalp, the other shifting from foot to foot. They both looked cold.

"Not exactly the best weather for a swim," Deborah remarked.

St. James said nothing.

The boys pulled on face masks, adjusted their snorkels and headed for the water, one on either side of the rocks. Alongside them, Lynley climbed the granite outcropping and picked his way out to its furthest point.

The surface of the water was extraordinarily calm since a natural reef protected the cove. Even from the cliff, St. James could see the anemones that grew on the outcropping beneath the water, their stamen swaying in the gentle current. Above and around them, broad-leafed kelp undulated. Beneath them, crabs hid. The cove was a combination of reef and tide pools, sea life and sand. It was not the best location for a swim, but it had no match as a site for the disposing of an object one wished to go unrecovered for years. Within weeks, the camera case would be shrouded by barnacles, sea urchins, and anemones. Within months, it would lose both shape and definition, ultimately coming to resemble the rocks themselves.

If the case was there, however, the two boys were having difficulty finding it. Again and again, they bobbed to the surface on either side of Lynley. Each time, they carried nothing with them. Each time, they shook their heads.

"Tell them to go farther out," St. James shouted when the boys made their sixth return empty-handed.

Lynley looked up, nodded, and waved. He squatted on the rocks and talked to the boys. They dove under the water again. Both were good swimmers. They clearly understood what they were looking for. But neither found a thing.

"It looks hopeless." Deborah seemed to be speaking more to herself than to St. James. Nonetheless, he replied.

"You're right. I'm sorry, Deborah. I thought to have recovered at least something for you." He glanced her way, saw by her expression of misery that she'd read the meaning behind his words.

"Oh, Simon, please. I couldn't. When it came down to it, I couldn't do it to him. Can you try to understand?"

"The saltwater would have ruined them anyway. But at least you'd have had something to remind you of your success in America. Besides Tommy, of course." She stiffened. He knew he had hurt her and felt a whisper of triumph at his power to do so. It was replaced almost immediately by a roar of shame. "That was unforgivable. I'm sorry," he said.

"I deserve it."

"No. You don't deserve it." He walked away from her, giving his attention back to the cove. "Tell them to finish, Tommy," he shouted. "The cameras aren't there."

Below, the two boys were surfacing once more. This time, however, one of them clutched an object in his hand. Long and narrow, it glinted in the dull light as he handed it to Lynley. Wooden handle, metal blade. Both bearing no sign of having been in the water more than a few days.

"What's he got?" Deborah asked.

Lynley held it up so that they both could see it from the top of the cliff. St. James felt a quick rush of excitement.

"A kitchen knife," he said.

26

A lazy rain had begun to fall by the time they reached the harbour car park in Nanrunnel. It was no precursor of a Cornish southwester, but rather the herald of a brief summer shower. Thousands of gulls accompanied it, screaming in from the sea to seek havens on chimney tops, along the quay, and upon the decks of boats secured to the harbour walls.

On the path that skirted the circumference of the harbour, they passed overturned skiffs, lopsided piles of fishing nets redolent with the odours of the sea, and waterside buildings whose windows reflected the unchanging grey mask of the weather. Not until they reached the point at which the path inclined between two buildings as it led into the village proper did any of them speak. It was then that Lynley noticed that the cobbled pavement was already slick with rain. He glanced uneasily at St. James.

The other man answered his look. "I can manage it, Tommy."

They'd talked little about the knife. Just that it was obviously a kitchen utensil, so if it had been used on Mick Cambrey and if Nancy could identify it as having come from the cottage, it served as further evidence that the crime against her husband had not been planned. Its presence in the cove did nothing to absolve Justin Brooke from blame. Rather, the knife merely changed his reason for having gone there in the first place. Not to rid himself of Deborah's cameras but to rid himself of something far more damning.

Thus the cameras remained a piece still not tucked into position in the jigsaw of the crime. They all agreed that it was reasonable to continue to conclude Brooke had taken them from Deborah's room. But where he had disposed of them was once again as elusive a location as it had been two days ago.

Rounding the corner of an antique silver shop on the Lamorna Road, they found the streets of the village deserted. This was an unsurprising summertime phenomenon in an area where the vicissitudes of the weather often forced holiday makers to be flexible in matters concerning how they spent their time. Where sun would see them strolling the village streets, exploring the harbour, and taking pictures on the quay, rain usually provoked a sudden need to try their luck in a game of chance, a sudden hunger for tucking into a fresh crab salad, a sudden thirst for real ale. An inclement afternoon was a welcome boon to the proprietors of bingo parlours, restaurants, and pubs.

This proved to be the case at the Anchor and Rose. The pub teemed with fishermen forced to shore by the weather as well as day visitors seeking shelter from the rain. Most of them were packed into the public bar. The formal lounge beyond it was largely empty.

In any other circumstances, two such diverse groups, inhabiting the same watering hole, would hardly be likely to blend into a cohesive unit. But the presence of a teenaged mandolin player, a fisherman conversant with the Irish whistle, and a pale-legged man wearing running shorts and playing the spoons had broken the barrier of class and experience, melding what should have been motley into montage.

In the wide bay window overlooking the harbour, a leather-skinned fisherman—backlit by the dull light outside—engaged a fashionably clad tot in a game of cat's cradle. His weathered hands held out the string to the child; his broken teeth flashed in a grin.

"Go on, Dickie. Take it. You know how to play," Mummy coaxed the little boy.

Dickie cooperated. Approving laughter ensued. The fisherman rested his hand on the child's head.

"It's a photograph, isn't it?" Lynley said to Deborah in the doorway where they stood watching.

She smiled. "What a wonderful face he has, Tommy. And look how the light just barely strikes the side of it."

St. James was on the stairs, climbing up to the newspaper office. Deborah followed, Lynley behind her.

"You know," she went on, pausing briefly on the landing, "I was worried for a time about the scope for my photographs in Cornwall. Don't ask me why. I'm a creature of habit, I suppose, and my habit has been to do most of my work in London. But I love it here, Tommy. There's a photograph everywhere. It's grand. Truly. I've thought that from the first."

At her words, Lynley felt shamed by his earlier doubts. He paused on the steps. "I love you, Deb."

Her expression softened. "And I you, Tommy."

St. James had already opened the door of the newspaper office. Inside, two telephones were ringing, Julianna Vendale was typing at a word processor, a young photographer was cleaning half a dozen camera lenses lined up on a desk, and in one of the cubicles three men and a woman leaned into a circle of conversation. Harry Cambrey was among them. *Advertising and Circulation* was painted in faded black letters on the upper half of the wood and glass door.

Harry Cambrey saw them and left his meeting. He was wearing suit trousers, a white shirt, a black tie. As if in the need to explain this, he said, "Buried him this morning. Half past eight."

Odd, Lynley thought, that Nancy hadn't mentioned it. But it explained the acceptance with which she had greeted their presence. There was a degree of finality to burial. It didn't end sorrow, but it did make easier the acknowledgement of loss.

"Half a dozen coppers hanging about in the graveyard," Cambrey continued. "First thing they've done besides trying to stick the killing on John Penellin. And isn't that a thought? John killing Mick."

"Perhaps he had a motive after all," St. James said. He handed Mick Cambrey's set of keys to his father. "Mick's dressing. Would a man be driven to kill another man over that?"

Cambrey's fist closed over the keys. He turned his back on his employees and lowered his voice. "So. Who knows about it?"

"You covered up well. Nearly everyone sees Mick exactly as you painted him. A real man's man, an insatiable womaniser."

"What the hell else could I do?" Cambrey asked. "God damn, he was my son. He was a *man*."

"Whose main source of arousal was dressing like a woman."

"I never could break him. I did try."

"So this wasn't something recent?"

Shoving the keys into his pocket, Cambrey shook his head. "He'd been doing it all his life, off and on. I'd catch him at it. Whip his arse. Push him buck naked into the street. Tie him to a chair and paint his face and make like I'd plan to cut off his cock. But nothing made a difference."

"Save his death," Lynley said.

Cambrey didn't seem to care about the implication behind Lynley's words. He merely said, "I protected the lad as best I could. I didn't kill him."

"The protection worked," St. James said. "People saw him as you wished him to be seen. But in the end, he didn't need your protection because of the cross-dressing, but because of a story, just as you thought."

"It was the guns, wasn't it?" Cambrey asked. "Like I said."

St. James looked at Lynley as if wanting direction or perhaps permission to add to the man's mourning. An explanation of the "notes" Cambrey had found in Mick's desk would do it. Through their real meaning, nearly everything could be revealed. Not only cross-dressing, but dealing drugs as well. Not only spending money frivolously instead of using it to upgrade the newspaper, but filtering much of it off in order to support a double life.

Every delusion, Lynley thought, deserved destruction. Building anything on the foundation of a lie—be it a single relationship or an entire way of life—was to rely upon sand to remain unshifting. While the illusion of solidity might exist for a while, whatever was built would ultimately crumble. The only question seemed to be at what point Harry Cambrey's inaccurate vision of his son ought to be laid to rest.

Lynley looked at the old man, studying the face that was creased with age and failure, jaundiced by ill health. He saw the stark bones of his chest pressing against his shirt, the ugly nicotine stains on his fingers, the arthritic curl of those fingers as he reached for a bottle of beer on a desk. Let someone else do the telling, he decided.

"We know he was working on a story about a drug called oncozyme," Lynley said.

St. James followed his lead. "He was spending time in London visiting a company called Islington and a biochemist there called Justin Brooke. Did Mick ever speak of Brooke? Of Islington?"

Cambrey shook his head. "A drug, you say?" He still seemed to be adjusting to the fact that his previous idea about gunrunning had led nowhere.

"We need access to his files—here and in the cottage—if we're to prove anything," St. James said. "The man who killed Mick is dead himself. Only Mick's notes can give us his motive and some sort of foundation to build a case against him."

"And if the killer found the notes and destroyed them? If they were in the cottage and he pinched them that night?"

"Too many other things have occurred that needn't have happened had the killer found the notes." Lynley thought about St. James' explanation once more: how Brooke tried to eliminate Peter because of something Peter must have seen or heard that evening in Gull Cottage; how he'd taken Deborah's cameras to get at the film. This second circumstance alone spoke more loudly than anything else in support of the existence of a piece of hard evidence. It had to be somewhere, however disguised. Brooke had known that.

Cambrey spoke. "He kept files in those cabinets"—he nodded in their direction—"and more at the cottage. The police're done with it and I've the key when you're ready to go there. Let's get to work."

There were three cabinets of four drawers apiece. While the business of putting out a newspaper went on round them, Lynley, St. James, Deborah, and Cambrey began going through the drawers one by one. Look for anything, St. James told them, that bore any resemblance to a report on oncozyme. The name of the drug itself, a mention of cancer, a study of treatments, interviews with doctors, researchers, or patients.

The search began through folders, notebooks, and simple scraps of paper. They saw immediately that it would be no easy task. There was no logical manner in which Mick Cambrey had done his filing. It bore signs of neither organisation nor unity. It would take hours, perhaps days, to go through it all, for each piece had to be read separately for the slightest allusion to oncozyme, to cancer, to biochemical research.

They had been at it for over an hour when Julianna Vendale said, "If you're looking for notes, don't forget his computer," and opened a drawer in his desk to reveal at least two dozen floppy disks.

No one groaned, although Deborah looked dismayed and Harry Cambrey cursed. They continued to wade through the detritus of the dead man's career, interrupted by the telephone just after four o'clock. Someone answered it in one of the cubicles, then stuck his head out the door and said, "Is Mr. St. James here?"

"Salvation," Deborah sighed, rubbing the back of her neck. "Perhaps someone's phoning to confess."

Lynley stood to stretch. He walked to the window. Outside, a gentle rain was continuing to fall. It was hours before dark, but in two of the buildings across Paul Lane lamps had been lit. In one of the cottages, a family sat round a table drinking afternoon tea and eating biscuits from a tin. In another, a young woman cut a man's hair. She was concentrating on the sides, standing in front of him to examine her work. He sat patiently for a moment, then pulled her between his legs and kissed her soundly. She cuffed his ears, laughed, gave herself to his embrace. Lynley smiled, turning back to the office.

He saw St. James watching him from the cubicle in which he spoke on the phone. His face looked troubled. Contemplatively, he was pulling at his lip. Whomever he was speaking to was doing much of the talking. Only at long intervals did St. James say a few words. When at last he hung up, he spent what seemed like two or three minutes looking down at the phone. He picked it up once as if to make a call, but then replaced the receiver without having done so. At last he came out to rejoin the others.

"Deborah, can you manage for a bit on your own? Tommy and I need to see to something."

She looked from him to Lynley. "Of course. Shall we go on to the cottage when we've finished here?"

"If you will."

Without another word, he headed for the door. Lynley followed. He said nothing on the way down the stairs. Near the bottom, they skirted two children who were running a collection of small metal lorries along the banister. They stepped past the crowded doorway of the Anchor and Rose, stepped into the street. They turned up the collars of their coats against the rain.

"What is it?" Lynley asked. "Who was on the phone?"

"Helen."

"*Helen?* Why on earth—"

"She's found out about the list of Cambrey's prospects, Tommy, and about the telephone messages on the machine in his flat."

"And?"

"It seems they all have one thing in common."

"From the expression on your face, it's not cocaine, I take it."

"Not cocaine. Cancer." St. James walked towards Paul Lane, his head bent into the rain.

Lynley's eyes went to the harbour, to the huddled seabirds in a mass on the quay, protected from harm by their very numbers. He turned from them and looked at the rain-misted hills above the village. "Where are we going?" he called to his friend.

St. James paused, saying over his shoulder, "We need to talk to Dr. Trenarrow."

It hadn't been easy for Lady Helen to uncover the truth that lay behind the list of prospects, St. James explained. The first dozen names she tried gave her nothing to go on, and more importantly no piece of leading information upon which she could hang any enquiry at all. The recipient of each one of her phone calls was tight-lipped to begin with, becoming even more so the moment she mentioned the name Michael Cambrey. Considering their reactions, that they had heard of Mick in some fashion or another was a fact beyond doubt. As was their determination to reveal nothing substantial about what their connection to Cambrey was. Had he interviewed them for a story? she would ask. Had he been seeking testimony of some sort? Had he visited their homes? Had he written them letters? No matter which tack she tried, the persona she adopted to try it, the subject matter she attempted to pursue, they were always one step ahead of her, as if the first person on the list had telephoned the rest and warned them of an impending call. Not even the mention of Cambrey's murder was enough to jar an admission from anyone. Indeed, the few times she tried that as an opening gambit—posing as a reporter seeking information for a feature story on another journalist's death—the result had been an even stonier reticence than her previous fabrications had inspired.

It was not until she reached the fifteenth name, that the direction of these fruitless conversations changed. For the fifteenth name belonged to Richard Graham. And he was dead. As was the sixteenth name, Catherine Henderford. And the seventeenth, Donald Highcroft. As well as the eighteenth, the nineteenth, and the twentieth. All of them dead of cancer. Lung, ovarian, liver, intestinal. And all of them dead within the last two months.

"I went directly back to the first name on the list," Lady Helen had said. "Of course, I couldn't phone him myself, so I went to Chelsea and had Cotter do it for me. We invented the name of an organisation. Cancer Cooperative, something like that. Checking in to see how the patient was doing, Cotter said. Right down the list. They'd all had cancer. And those that were alive were all in remission, Simon."

The two callers who had left their messages on the answering machine in Mick Cambrey's flat had placed their calls about cancer as well. The exception being that they were willing, even eager, to talk to Lady Helen. They had phoned Mick's number in answer to an advertisement that had run for months in the Sunday *Times*—"You CAN beat cancer!"—followed by a telephone number.

"It's my wife," one of the callers had said when Lady Helen phoned him. "One gets so desperate. We've tried diets, meditation, prayer, group therapy. Mind over matter. Every kind of drug. When I saw the advert, I thought what the hell. But no one returned my call."

Because Mick never received it. Because Mick was dead.

"What was Mick doing, Simon?" Lady Helen had asked at the end of her story.

The answer was simple. He'd changed from journalist to merchant of dreams. He was selling hope. He was selling the possibility of life. He was selling oncozyme.

"He'd learned about oncozyme in his interview with Trenarrow," St. James said to Lynley as they passed the Methodist church on their way up Paul Lane. The wind had picked up. The rain was beading his hair. "He followed the story to Islington-London where Brooke gave him more details. I should imagine the two of them hatched the scheme between them. It was simple enough, noble if one disregards the fact that they were probably making a fortune from the effort. They were providing cancer patients with a miracle drug, years before the drug would be legally approved and available for use. Look at the countless terminally ill people with nothing more to hang onto but the hope that something might work. Think of what people get involved with in an attempt to put themselves into remission: macrobiotic diets, laetrile, psychic healers. Mick was taking no risk that there'd be a lack of interest. Nor did he have to worry that people might not be willing to pay whatever price he was asking for the chance of a cure. He had only two problems. The first would be getting his hands on a steady supply of the drug."

"Justin Brooke," Lynley said.

St. James nodded. "For payments in cash initially. In cocaine later on, I expect. But once Mick had the oncozyme, he had to find someone who would administer it. Monitor the dosage. Assess the results. For part of the profits, of course. No one would take such a risk without some sort of payoff."

"Good God. Roderick."

"Trenarrow's housekeeper told Cotter that he spends a great deal of time visiting at a convalescent home in St. Just. I didn't think much of it at the time except Trenarrow himself told me that experimental drugs are often used on terminal patients. Look at how those two pieces of information fit together to explain what's been going on. A small clinic in St. Just where Trenarrow sees a select group of patients, filtered his way by Mick Cambrey. An illegal clinic—posing as a very private convalescent home—where people pay a hefty fee to be injected with oncozyme. And then the profits get divided three ways: Cambrey, Brooke, and Trenarrow."

"Mick's bankbook in London?"

"His share of the pickings."

"Then who killed him? Why?"

"Brooke. Something must have gone wrong with the deal. Perhaps Mick got greedy. Or perhaps he made a slip of the tongue in Peter's presence that put them all in jeopardy. Perhaps that's the reason Brooke was after Peter."

Lynley paused momentarily, gripped St. James' arm. "Peter told me that Mick made a remark. Blast, I can't remember it exactly. Peter threatened to blackmail him about his cross-dressing and about cocaine. But Mick didn't care. He advised Peter to look for another source. He said something about people being willing to pay a hell of a lot more to stay alive than to have a secret kept."

"And Justin heard that, didn't he? He must have known that Mick was inches away from telling the tale to Peter."

"He wanted to leave the cottage. He wanted Peter to leave."

"You can see why. Brooke stood to lose everything if Mick started playing fast and loose with their secret. His career, his reputation as a scientist, his job at Islington. He stood to go to jail if it all came out. He must have returned to the cottage after Peter left. He and Mick must have got into it. Things escalated between them—God knows they were both breaking enough laws to be as tightly strung as the devil—and Justin took a swing at him. That did it."

"And Trenarrow?" Lynley paused once again opposite the primary school grounds.

St. James looked past him. The stage of the open air theatre was still set up. Performances of one sort or another would continue through the summer. Now, however, the grounds were sodden by rain. "Trenarrow knows about everything. I'd wager he'd known the moment he was introduced to Brooke at Howenstow on Saturday night. I should guess he'd never actually seen Brooke before then. Why should he have when Mick was playing the middleman? But the moment he was introduced, he must have put together the rest. Mick's death, everything."

"But why hold his tongue?"

St. James looked not at Lynley but at the school grounds as he replied. "You know the answer to that."

Lynley gazed up the hill. From where they stood, just the roof of the villa and part of its white cornice showed against the grey sky. "He faced jail as well. The clinic, the drug, the payments people made. His career. His research."

"And most importantly?"

"He stood to lose my mother."

"I expect the payments people made for oncozyme allowed him to buy the villa in the first place."

"A home he could be proud to offer to her."

"So he said nothing."

They continued their climb. "What do you suppose he intends now, with Brooke and Cambrey dead?"

"With Brooke dead, the source of oncozyme is dried up. He'll have to close the clinic in St. Just and make do with what he's managed to save from the profits."

"And our part in all of this, St. James? Do we turn him over to the police? Do we phone his superiors? Do we take the opportunity to ruin him?"

St. James examined his friend. Broad shoulders wet, hair beginning to drip, mouth set in a line. "That's the hell of this, isn't it, Tommy? That's the irony: to have the foulest wish you've ever possessed granted in spades. Just at the moment when, I expect, you no longer wish it."

"Are you leaving it up to me?"

"We've got Brooke and Cambrey tied together well enough. We've got Mick's visits to Islington, we've got Peter and Justin together at Gull Cottage, we've got Justin's lie about being in the Anchor and Rose afterwards, we've got Justin's use of cocaine. As far as the police need to know, Mick was his supplier, a deal went bad, and Justin killed him. Sasha as well. So, yes. The rest is yours. You're the policeman."

"Even if it means letting part of the truth go, letting Roderick go?"

"I'll not stand in judgement. At the bottom of it Trenarrow was trying to help people. The fact that they paid him for the help makes it ugly, but at least he was trying to do something good."

They made the rest of the climb in silence. As they turned up the drive to the villa, lights went on in the ground floor as if they were expected visitors. Below them, village lights began to shine through the gloom as well, making an occasional nimbus glitter behind glass.

Dora answered the door. She was dressed for cooking, wrapped round by an enormous red apron that bore smudges of flour on both breasts and along the thighs. More flour powdered the creases of her blue turban, and an additional dusting had greyed one eyebrow.

"Doctor's in his study," she said when they asked for him. "Come in with you. Rain don't do a bit o' good for bodies out in it." She led them to the study, rapped on the door, and opened it when Trenarrow answered. "I bring tea for these good mans," she said, nodded sharply, and left them.

Dr. Trenarrow got to his feet. He'd been seated behind his desk, in the act of polishing his spectacles. He put them back on his nose. "Everything's all right?" he asked Lynley.

"Peter's at the house in London."

"Thank God. Your mother?"

"I think she'd probably like to see you tonight."

Behind his spectacles, Trenarrow blinked once. He obviously didn't know what to make of Lynley's remark. He said, "You're both soaked." He went to the fireplace and lit the fire, doing it the old-fashioned way by placing a stubby candle beneath the coals.

St. James waited for Lynley to speak. He wondered if this final interview between them would better be held without his presence. Although he'd given lip service to Lynley's opportunity to make a free decision, he really had no doubt what that decision would be. Still, he knew it would not be easy for his friend to turn a blind eye to Trenarrow's part in the illegal sale of oncozyme, no matter how noble the doctor's motives had been. It would be easier for Lynley to do it alone, but St. James' own need to put every detail to rest kept him where he was, listening and noting and prepared to say nothing.

The burning coal hissed. Dr. Trenarrow returned to his desk. St. James and Lynley sat in the wingchairs in front of it. Rain made a sound like delicate waves against the windows.

Dora returned with the tea which she poured, leaving with a gentle admonition to "mind that you take your med'cine when the time come," which Trenarrow accepted with a dutiful nod.

When they were alone once again with the fire, the tea, and the rain, Lynley spoke. "We know about oncozyme, Roderick, and the clinic in St. Just. About the newspaper advertisement that brought you the patients. About Mick and Justin and the parts they played, Mick filtering the applicants to get those best able to pay for the treatment, Justin supplying the drug from London."

Trenarrow pushed fractionally back from the desk. "Is this an official visit, Tommy?"

"No."

"Then what—"

"Had you met Brooke before Saturday night at Howenstow?"

"I'd only spoken to him on the phone. But he came here Friday night."

"When?"

"He was here when I got back from Gull Cottage."

"Why?"

"The obvious reasons. He wanted to talk about Mick."

"But you didn't report him to the police?"

Trenarrow's brow furrowed. He answered simply, "No."

"Yet you knew he'd killed him. Did he tell you why?"

Trenarrow's eyes moved between the other two men. He licked his lips, gripped the handle of his teacup, and studied its contents. "Mick wanted to raise the cost of treatment. I'd already opposed him. Evidently that evening, Justin had as well. They argued about it. Justin lost his temper."

"And when you joined us at the cottage, did you know Justin Brooke had killed Mick?"

"I'd not seen Brooke yet. I'd no more idea than you who had done it."

"What about the condition of the room and the missing money?"

"I didn't put it together until I saw Brooke. He was looking for anything that could connect him to Cambrey."

"And the money?"

"I don't know. He may have taken it, but he didn't admit to it."

"To the killing, however?"

"Yes. To that."

"And the mutilation?"

"To misdirect the police."

"His cocaine use. Did you know about that?"

"No."

"And that Mick dealt cocaine on the side?"

"Good God, no."

St. James listened, feeling the vague discomfort of uncertainty. A tantalising fact danced on the edge of his consciousness, something not quite right that was asking to be noticed.

The other two men continued talking. Their voices were low, barely much more than a murmur with nothing more at stake than an exchange of information, a straightening out of details, and a plan for going on. Into the conversation, a sudden noise was interjected, a dim bleeping that came from Trenarrow's wrist. He pressed a tiny button on the side of his watch.

"Medicine," he said. "Blood pressure."

He reached into his jacket pocket, brought out a flat silver case, and opened it. It contained a neatly arranged layer of white pills. "Dora would never forgive me if she came in one morning and found me dead of a stroke." He popped a pill into his mouth and downed it with tea.

St. James watched him do so, feeling fixed to his chair as every piece of the jigsaw finally fell into place. How it had been done, who had done it, and most of all why. Some in remission, Lady Helen had said, but the rest of them dead.

Dr. Trenarrow lowered his cup, replaced it in the saucer. As he did so, St. James cursed himself inwardly. He cursed every sign he had overlooked, those details he had missed, and each piece of information he had disregarded because it could not be assigned a convenient place in the puzzle of the crime. Once again, he cursed the fact that his field was science, not interview and investigation. He cursed the fact that his interest lay in objects and what they could reveal about the nature of a crime. Had his interest lain in people, surely he would have seen the truth from the first.

27

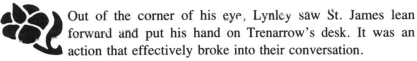Out of the corner of his eye, Lynley saw St. James lean forward and put his hand on Trenarrow's desk. It was an action that effectively broke into their conversation.

"The money," he said.

"I beg your pardon?"

"Tommy, who did you tell about the money?"

Lynley tried to catch his drift. "What money?"

"Nancy said Mick was doing the pay envelopes. She said there was money in the sitting room that evening. You and I discussed it later that night, after she told us about it at the lodge. Who else did you tell? Who else knew about the money?"

"Deborah and Helen. They were there when Nancy told us. John Penellin as well."

"Did you tell your mother?"

"Of course not. Why on earth would I?"

"Then how did Dr. Trenarrow know?"

Lynley realized at once what the question meant. He saw the answer on Trenarrow's face. He fought a battle for professional indifference. He lost it, saying only, "Jesus God."

Trenarrow said nothing. Lynley couldn't think beyond a simple *no*, recognising that what his friend had said earlier was coming to pass. His every foul wish of the last fifteen years was about to be granted in absolute spades.

"What are you saying, St. James?" he managed to ask, although he knew the answer without having to hear it.

"That Dr. Trenarrow killed Mick Cambrey. He didn't intend to.

They argued. He hit him. Mick fell. He began to haemorrhage. He was dead within minutes."

"Roderick." Lynley felt desperate for the man to exonerate himself in some way, knowing only that Trenarrow's exoneration was tied intimately into Lynley's own future life. But St. James went on, utterly calm. Only the facts counted. He wove them together.

"When he saw Cambrey was dead, he acted quickly. It wasn't a search. Even if Mick had been stupid enough to keep records of the oncozyme transactions in the cottage, there was no time to look for them then. There was only time to make it look like a search, or a possible robbery, or a sexual crime. But it was none of those things. It was a fight about oncozyme."

Dr. Trenarrow's face looked implacable. When he spoke, his lips moved, but the rest of him was immobile. And his words seemed nothing more than a futile, if expected, effort at denial. They carried no conviction. "I was at the play Friday night. You know that very well."

"An open air play in a school yard," St. James said. "Hardly a difficult feat to slip out for a while, especially since you'd placed yourself in the back. I expect you went to him after the interval, during the second act. It's not a long walk—three minutes, no more. You went to see him then. You intended only to talk to him about oncozyme, but instead you killed him and came back to the play."

"And the weapon?" Trenarrow's bravado was weak. "Was I supposed to be carrying it round Nanrunnel in my jacket?"

"For the fracture of the skull, there was no weapon. The castration was another matter. You took the knife from the cottage."

"To the play?" Scorn this time, yet no more successful than the bravado had been.

"I should think you hid it somewhere en route. On Virgin Place. Perhaps on Ivy Street. In a garden or a dustbin. You returned for it later that night and got rid of it Saturday at Howenstow. Which is where, I dare say, you got rid of Brooke as well. Because once Brooke knew that Cambrey had been killed, he knew who must have done it. But he couldn't afford to turn you in to the police without damaging himself. The oncozyme scheme bound the two of you together."

"This is all conjecture," Trenarrow said. "According to what you've said so far, I had more reason to keep Mick alive than to kill him. If he was supplying me with patients, what purpose would his death serve?"

"You didn't intend to kill him. You struck out in anger. Your interest was in saving people's lives, but Mick's was in collecting their money. That attitude pushed you right over the edge."

"There's no evidence. You know that. Not for a murder."

"You've forgotten the cameras," St. James said.

Trenarrow looked at him steadily, his expression unchanging.

"You saw the camera at the cottage. You assumed I'd taken pictures of the body. During the chaos Saturday when John Penellin was arrested, you dropped the cameras from Deborah's room."

"But if that's so," Lynley said, feeling himself Trenarrow's advocate for the moment, "why didn't he take the cameras to the cove? If he disposed of the knife there, why not the cameras as well?"

"And risk being seen hiking across the grounds with the case in his possession? I don't know why I didn't realise the stupidity of that idea before. He could conceal the knife on his person, Tommy. If someone saw him on the grounds, he could have claimed to be taking a walk to clear his head of drink. It would have been a believable story. People were used to seeing him at Howenstow. But the cameras, no. I imagine he took them somewhere else—in his car, perhaps—later that night. To a place where he could be relatively certain they'd never be found."

Lynley listened, coming to terms with the truth. They'd all been at the dinner to hear the conversation. They'd all laughed at the absurdity of tourists in the mines. He said the name, two words that acted as final acceptance of what his heart told him was an incontrovertible fact. "Wheal Maen." St. James looked at him. "At dinner Saturday night. Aunt Augusta was up in arms about sealing Wheal Maen."

"This is supposition," Trenarrow broke in sharply. "Supposition and madness. Beyond our oncozyme connection, you've nothing else to go on besides what you're inventing right here in this room. And once our mutual history is out in public, Tommy, who's going to believe this story? If, indeed, you actually want our mutual history to be known."

"It comes down to that in the long run, doesn't it?" Lynley asked. "It always begins and ends with my mother."

For an instant, he allowed himself to see past the call for justice to its attendant scandal. He could have ignored Trenarrow's use of oncozyme, his illegal clinic, and the exorbitant price that patients no doubt paid for treatment there. He could have overlooked all this and allowed his mother to remain in ignorance for the rest of her life. But murder was different. It demanded retribution. He could not ignore that.

Lynley saw how the next few months would play out. A court of law, his accusations, Trenarrow's denial, the sort of case the defence would build with his mother caught in the middle and ultimately named as the reason behind Lynley's public denunciation of her long-time lover.

"He's right, St. James," Lynley said hollowly. "This is conjecture. Even if we got the cameras from the mine, the main shaft's been flooded for years. The film's ruined by now, no matter what was on it.''

St. James shook his head. ''That's the only thing Dr. Trenarrow didn't know. The film's not in the camera. Deborah gave it to me.''

Lynley heard the swift breath hiss between Trenarrow's teeth. St. James went on.

''And the evidence is there, isn't it?'' St. James asked. ''Your silver pillbox under Mick Cambrey's thigh. You may be able to explain away everything else, you may be able to accuse Tommy of attempting to fabricate evidence in order to separate you from his mother. But you'll never be able to deal with the fact that in the photograph of the body, the pillbox is there. The very same one you took from your pocket only minutes ago.''

Trenarrow looked at the misty view of the harbour. ''It proves nothing.''

''When it's in our photographs but missing from the police photographs? That's hardly the case and you know it.''

Rain pattered on windows. Wind sounded in the chimney. A distant foghorn moaned. Trenarrow moved in his chair, turning back towards the room. He grasped its arms and said nothing.

''What happened?'' Lynley asked him. ''Roderick, for the love of God, what happened?''

For a long time, Trenarrow didn't answer. His dull eyes were fixed upon the space between Lynley and St. James. He reached for the pull of the top drawer of the desk and aimlessly played it between his fingers.

''Oncozyme,'' he said. ''Brooke couldn't get enough of it. He was juggling the London inventory books as it was. But we needed more. If you could only know how many people phoned—still phone—how frantic they are for help. We couldn't get enough. But Mick kept funnelling patients my way.''

''Brooke eventually substituted something for the oncozyme, didn't he?'' St. James said. ''Your first patients went into remission just as Islington's research indicated they would. But after a while, things started to go wrong.''

''He'd been sending the drug down from London with Mick. When it became impossible to get and they saw the clinic would have to close, they made a substitution. People who should have gone into remission began to die. Not all at once, of course. But a pattern emerged. I became suspicious. I tested the drug. It was a saline solution.''

''And that was the fight.''

"I went to see him Friday night. I wanted to close the clinic." He stared across the room at the fire. Its glow was reflected in his spectacles like two points of heat. "Mick wasn't at all concerned. These weren't people to him. They were a source of income. Look, just keep the clinic running until we get more of the stuff, he said. So we lose a few? So what? Others'll come. People pay anything for the chance of a cure. What are you so hot about? You're bringing the money in hand over fist and don't pretend you aren't happy as hell about it." Trenarrow looked at Lynley. "I tried to talk to him, Tommy. I couldn't make him see. I couldn't get him to understand. I kept talking. He kept brushing it off. I finally . . . I just snapped."

"When you saw he was dead, you decided to paint it as a sexual crime," St. James said.

"I thought he was after the village women. I thought it would look like someone's husband finally got to him."

"And the money in the cottage?"

"I took it as well. And then made it look like the room had been searched. I took my handkerchief from my pocket so I wouldn't leave prints. I must have lost the pill case then. I saw it the moment I knelt by his body later."

Lynley leaned forward. "As black as it is, Mick's death started out as an accident, Roderick. An assault, an accident. But what about Brooke? You were tied together. What did you have to fear from him? Even if he assumed you'd killed Mick, he'd have kept quiet about it. Bringing you down would only have brought himself down as well."

"I had nothing to fear from Brooke," Trenarrow said.

"Then why—"

"I knew he wanted Peter."

"Wanted—"

"To be rid of him. He was here Friday night when I got home from the play. We'd never actually met, of course, but he had no trouble finding the villa. He said Mick had been talking in front of Peter. He was worried. He wanted me to do something to tighten Mick's tongue."

"Which you'd already done," St. James noted.

Trenarrow accepted the grim statement without reaction. "When he heard about the killing the next morning, he panicked. He came to see me. He thought it was only a matter of time before Peter put together some remarks Mick had made and either went to the police or started sniffing round for someone to blackmail. Peter had a habit to support, he didn't have money, he'd already threatened Mick. Brooke wanted him dead. I wasn't about to let that happen."

"God. Oh, God." Lynley felt the sharp blade of regret pierce through him.

"He said there was no risk involved, that he could make it look like an overdose of some sort. I didn't know what he intended, but I thought I could stall him. I told him I had a better plan and asked him to meet me on the cliff after the party Saturday night."

"And then you killed him?"

"I'd taken the knife, but he was drunk. It was easy enough to shove him over the edge and hope it would look like an accident." For a moment Trenarrow fell silent. He studied a few folders, a magazine, three photographs, a pen that were arranged on his desk. "I didn't regret that. Not for a moment. I still don't."

"But he'd already passed the drug on to Sasha. It was ergotamine and quinine. He told her to give it to Peter."

"I've been too late every way I've turned. What a mess. What a blasted horror." Trenarrow began uselessly to gather a few papers, arranging them in a pile, tapping them together. He fondly looked round the room. He said, "I wanted this for her. I couldn't offer her Gull Cottage. What a ludicrous thought. But she would have come here. And oncozyme made it possible, so it seemed a double good. Can you understand that? People, who otherwise faced death, would live and be cured, while your mother and I would finally be together. I wanted this for her." He held the papers in one hand and with the other slid open the middle drawer of his desk. "Had oncozyme existed then, I would have saved him, Tommy. Without hesitation. Without a second thought. No matter what I felt for your mother. I hope you believe me." He placed the papers in the drawer, rested his hand on top of them. "Does she know about this?"

Lynley thought of his father, wasting away. He thought of his mother, trying to make the best of her life. He thought of his brother, growing up at Howenstow alone. He thought of Trenarrow. It was an effort to speak. "She doesn't know."

"Thank God." Trenarrow's hand slithered in and then out of the drawer. A dull glint upon metal. He held a revolver. "Thank God," he said again and levelled it at St. James.

"Roderick." Lynley stared at the gun. Wild thoughts—disconnected —darted through his brain. A black market purchase, a wartime antique, the gun room at Howenstow. Of course he'd have prepared for this moment. They'd been signalling to him that it was coming for days. Their questions, their interviews, their telephone calls. "Roderick, for God's sake."

"Yes," Trenarrow said. "I suppose that's right."

Lynley quickly shifted his eyes. St. James' face hadn't changed; it didn't show even a shadow of emotion. A movement at the edge of his vision and Lynley looked back to the gun. Trenarrow's finger was easing towards the trigger.

And suddenly before him was the possibility again, a thematic repetition he could not avoid. It was every foul wish in absolute spades.

There was only a split second to make a decision. Choose, he told himself fiercely. And he did so.

"Roderick, you can't hope—"

Lynley's words were cut off by the bellow of the gun.

Deborah pressed her fists against the small of her back to ease her tired muscles. The room was warm, and in spite of the window that was cracked open against the rain, the smoke from Harry Cambrey's cigarettes made the air malodorous, eye-stinging, and stuffy.

In the office, everyone had continued with his work. Telephones rang intermittently, word processor keys tapped, drawers opened and shut, footsteps creaked across the floor. Deborah had explored the contents of one entire filing cabinet, achieving nothing more than three paper cuts between her fingers and print stains across the palms of her hands. From the sounds Harry Cambrey was making—a groan, a sigh, a muttered oath—it didn't seem that he was having any better luck.

She stifled a yawn, feeling completely drained. She'd slept only an hour or two after dawn, and even then the fractured dreams she'd experienced had left her physically depleted and emotionally worn. The effort not to think about last night had taken its toll. Now she only wanted sleep, partly as succour but mostly as escape. Even as she thought about it, her eyelids grew heavy. The rain on the roof was wonderfully soporific, the room was warm, the murmur of voices so soothing . . .

A howl of sirens on the street below slapped her fully awake. First one, then a second. A moment later, a third. Julianna Vendale left her desk and went to the window. Deborah joined her as Harry Cambrey pushed himself to his feet.

An ambulance was just making the turn from the Penzance Road onto Paul Lane. Some distance ahead of it, where Paul Lane began the ascent into the hills, two police cars sped through the rain. Simultaneously, a telephone began to ring in the newsroom. Julianna took the call. The conversation was mostly one-sided. Her comments were terse, consisting only of, "When? . . . Where? . . . Fatal? . . . All right. Yes. Thanks."

She hung up and said to Cambrey, "There's been a shooting at Trenarrow's."

Deborah had time to feel only a frisson of danger, saying only, "Trenarrow?" before Harry Cambrey moved.

He bolted for the door, grabbing two cameras and a mackintosh on his way. He threw open the door and shouted over his shoulder to Julianna Vendale, "Stay by the phones!"

As he clattered down the stairs and into the street, another police car shot past. Oblivious of the rain, patrons of the Anchor and Rose as well as some of the inhabitants of Paul Lane began to stream out of buildings and take up the chase. Harry Cambrey was caught up in their midst, cameras banging against his thighs, struggling to make his way through the crush. From the window Deborah watched. She looked for them vainly, a blond head and a black one. Surely, they would be among the crowd. Having heard the name Trenarrow, they would be heading towards the villa.

A voice barked out from the street. "Don't know. Dead, we think."

The words were electrifying. Hearing them, Deborah saw Simon's face. She remembered the way he'd looked at Tommy—grim with decision—before he'd taken him from the office. With a rush of horror she thought: They went to see Trenarrow.

She dashed from the room and flew down the stairs. She shoved her way through the throng of people still gathered in the doorway of the pub and stumbled outside. Rain pelted her. A passing car honked its horn. Its tyres hit a puddle which sent up a spume of spray. But none of this existed. She knew only the need to find Trenarrow's home. She felt only the terror of a shooting.

In the past three years, Lynley had only alluded to the discord in his life. And even then, the allusion was made in actions, not in words. A preference for spending Christmas with her rather than with his family; a letter from his mother gone unopened for weeks; a telephone message never returned. But as they'd walked together to the cove this afternoon, he'd told her that he'd put all of it to rest—the enmity, the discord, the bitterness, the anger. To have something happen now was obscene. *Not dead. No.*

The words carried her towards the hillside. Rainwater shooting from an unguttered rooftop struck her cheeks and blinded her momentarily as she headed up the incline. She paused and cleared her vision, with the crowd surging round her, dashing towards the flash of blue lights in the distance. The air was alive with speculations on death. If there was a body to be seen or blood to be smelled, here existed the populace that would do the honours.

At the first intersection, she was pushed into the steamy windows of the Talisman Cafe by an angry matron who pulled a yowling little boy by the arm. "Watcher goin!" the woman shouted furiously at Deborah. She stood in odd Roman sandals that were laced to her knees. She tugged the child to her side. "Bleeding trippers. Think you own the village?"

Deborah didn't bother to answer. She elbowed past her.

Later, she would remember her headlong flight through the village and up the hill as an ever-changing collage: on the door of a shop, a rain-streaked sign on which the words *clotted cream* and *chocolate gateau* oozed into one another; a single sunflower, its enormous head bent; palm fronds lying in a pool of rainwater; munchlike open mouths shouting words at her which she did not hear; a bicycle wheel spinning in endless revolutions while the dazed rider sprawled in the street. But at the moment, she saw nothing but Tommy, in countless images, each one more vivid than the last, each one accusing her of betrayal. This would be her punishment for that moment of selfish weakness with Simon.

Please, she thought. If there were bargains and promises, she would make them. Without a second thought. Without a single regret.

As she reached the incline above the village proper, a final police car tore by her, sending up pebbles as well as spray from the street. There was no need for the horn to clear the road. Daunted by the downpour, the less hardy thrill-seekers had already started becoming discouraged by the climb. They had begun to seek refuge, some in shops, some in doorways, others flocking into the Methodist church. Not even the diversion of blood and a corpse seemed worth the potential ruin of fine summer clothes.

Only the most resolutely curious had completed the climb. Shaking her wet hair back from her face, Deborah saw them gathered in front of a drive where a police line was set up to keep them at a distance. There, the group had fallen into a speculative silence, one broken by the hot voice of Harry Cambrey who was arguing with an implacable constable, insisting upon entrance.

Behind them on the hill, rain assailed Trenarrow's villa. Its every window was lit. Uniformed men swarmed about it. Lights flashed from the police cars parked on its circular drive.

"Shot, I heard," someone muttered.

"Brought anyone out yet?"

"Nope."

Deborah scanned the front of the villa, working through the men, looking for a sign. He was all right, he was fine, he had to be among them. She couldn't find him. She pushed her way through the onlookers to the police line. Childhood prayers rose to her lips and died unsaid. She made bargains with God. She asked to be punished in any other way. She asked for understanding. She admitted her faults.

She ducked under the line.

"No you don't, miss!" The constable who had been arguing with Cambrey barked out the command from ten feet away.

"But it's—"

"Stay back!" he shouted. "This isn't a bloody sideshow."

Unmindful, Deborah started forward. The need to know and to be there overshadowed everything else.

"Here, you!" The constable moved towards her, readying himself to thrust her back into the crowd. As he did so, Harry Cambrey darted past him, scrambling up the drive. "Damn!" the constable shouted. "You! Cambrey!"

Having lost the one, he was not about to lose the other, and he gripped Deborah's arm, waving to a panda car that had pulled onto the verge. "Take this one," he called to the officers inside. "The other got past me."

"No!" Deborah struggled to free herself, feeling a rising sense of outrage at her own complete impotence. She couldn't even break the constable's grip. The more she fought him, the stronger he became.

"Miss Cotter?"

She swung around. No angel could have been more blessed a sight than the Reverend Mr. Sweeney. Garbed in black, he stood beneath a tentlike umbrella, blinking solemnly at her through the rain.

"Tommy's at the villa," she said. "Mr. Sweeney, *please*."

The cleric frowned. He squinted up the drive. "Oh, dear." His right hand flexed open and closed upon the handle of his umbrella as he appeared to consider his options. "Oh, dear. Yes. I see." This final statement seemed to indicate that an action had been decided upon. Mr. Sweeney drew himself up to his fullest height of not quite five and a half feet and spoke to the constable who still held Deborah in a determined grip. "You know Lord Asherton, of course," he said authoritatively. It was a tone that would have surprised any of his parishioners who had never seen him in blackface among the Nanrunnel players, ordering Cassio and Montano to put up their swords. "This is his fiancée. Let her by."

The constable eyed Deborah's bedraggled appearance. His expression made it perfectly clear that he could hardly give credence to a relationship between her and any one of the Lynleys.

"Let her by," Mr. Sweeney repeated. "I'll accompany her myself. Perhaps you ought to be more concerned with the newspaperman than with this young lady."

The constable gave Deborah another sceptical look. She waited in torment while he made his decision. "All right. Go on. Stay out of the way."

Deborah's lips formed the words thank you, but nothing came out. She took a few stumbling steps.

"It's all right, my dear," Mr. Sweeney said. "Let's go up. Take my arm. The drive's a bit slippery, isn't it?"

She did as he said, although only a part of her brain registered his words. The rest was caught up in speculation and fear. "Please not Tommy," she whispered. "Not like this. Please. I could bear anything else."

"Now, it will be all right," Mr. Sweeney murmured in a distracted fashion. "Indeed. You shall see."

They slipped and slid among the crushed corollas of fuchsias as they wound their way up the narrow drive towards the front of the villa. The rain was beginning to fall less heavily, but Deborah was already soaked, so the protection of Mr. Sweeney's umbrella meant very little. She shivered as she clung to his arm.

"It's a dreadful business, this," Mr. Sweeney said as if in response to her shudder. "But it shall be all right. You'll see in a moment."

Deborah heard the words but knew enough to dismiss them. There was no chance for all right any longer. A mocking form of justice always swept through life when one was least prepared to see justice meted out. Her time had come.

In spite of the number of men who were on the grounds, it was unnaturally quiet as they approached the villa. The crackle of a police radio was the only noise, a female dispatcher giving direction to police not far from the scene. On the circular drive beneath the hawthorn tree, three police cars sat at odd, hurried angles, as if their drivers had flung themselves out without bothering to worry about where or how they parked. In the rear seat of one of them, Harry Cambrey was engaged in a muffled shouting match with an angry constable who appeared to have handcuffed him to the interior of the car. When he saw Deborah, Cambrey forced his face to the officer's window.

"Dead!" he shouted before the constable pushed him back inside the car.

The worst was realised. Deborah saw the ambulance pulled near the front door, not as close as the police cars for there was no need of that. Wordlessly, she clutched at Mr. Sweeney's arm, but as if he read her fears, he pointed to the portico.

"Look," he urged her.

Deborah forced herself to look towards the front door. She saw him. Her eyes flew wildly over every part of his body, looking for wounds. But other than the fact that his jacket was wet, he was quite intact—although terribly pale—talking gravely to Inspector Boscowan.

"Thank God," she whispered.

The front door opened even as she spoke. Lynley and Boscowan stepped to one side to allow two men to carry a stretcher into the rain, a body upon it. Sheeting covered it from head to toe, strapped down as if to shield it from the rain and to protect it from the stares of the curious. Only when she saw it, only when she heard the front door close with a sound of hollow finality, did Deborah understand. Still, she looked frantically at the grounds of the villa, at the brightly lit windows, at the cars, at the door. Again and again—as if the action could change an immutable reality—she sought him.

Mr. Sweeney said something, but she didn't hear it. She only heard her own bargain: *I could bear anything else.*

Her childhood, her life, flashed before her in an instant, leaving behind for the very first time neither anger nor pain, but instead understanding, complete and too late. She bit her lip so hard that she could taste the blood, but it was not enough to quell her cry of anguish.

"Simon!" She threw herself towards the ambulance where already the body had been loaded inside.

Lynley spun around. He saw her plunging blindly through the cars. She slipped once on the slick pavement but pulled herself to her feet, screaming his name.

She threw herself on the ambulance, pulling on the handle that would open its rear door. A policeman tried to restrain her, a second did likewise. But she fought them off. She kicked, she scratched. And all the time, she kept screaming his name. High and shrieking, it was a two-syllable monody that Lynley knew he would hear—when he least wanted to hear it—for the rest of his life. A third policeman joined the attempt to subdue her, but she writhed away.

Sick at heart, Lynley turned from the sight. He felt for the villa door. "St. James," he said.

The other man was in the hall with Trenarrow's housekeeper who was sobbing into the turban she'd taken from her head. He looked Lynley's way and began to speak but hesitated, face clouded, as Deborah's cries grew more profound. He touched Dora's shoulder gently and joined Lynley at the door, stopping short at the sight of Deborah being dragged away from the ambulance and fighting every step that distanced her from it. He looked at Lynley.

Lynley looked away. "For Christ's sake, go to her. She thinks it's you." He couldn't face his friend. He didn't want to see him. He only hoped St. James would take matters into his own hands without another word being spoken between them. It was not to be.

"No. She's only—"

"Just go, damn you. Go."

Seconds ticked by before St. James moved, but when he finally walked into the drive, Lynley found the expiation he had searched for so long. He forced himself to watch.

St. James skirted the police cars and approached the group. He walked quite slowly. He couldn't move fast. His gait wouldn't allow it, crippled and ugly, and halted by pain. The gait that Lynley himself had given him.

St. James reached the ambulance. He shouted Deborah's name. He grabbed her, pulled her towards him. She fought back violently, weeping and shrieking, but only for a moment until she saw who it was. Then she was caught up in his arms, her body shaking with terrible sobs, his head bent to hers, his hands in her hair.

"It's all right, Deborah," Lynley heard St. James say. "I'm sorry you were frightened. I'm all right, my love." Then he murmured needlessly, "My love. My love."

The rain fell against them, the police began to move round them. But neither seemed cognizant of anything more than being held in the other's arms.

Lynley turned and went into the house.

A stirring awakened her. She opened her eyes. They focussed on the distant, barrel ceiling. She gazed up at it, confused. Turning her head, she saw the lace-covered dressing table, its silver hair brushes, its old cheval mirror. Great-Grandmama Asherton's bedroom, she thought. Recognition of the room brought almost everything back. Images of the cove, the newspaper office, the flight up the hill, the sight of the shrouded body all merged in her mind. At their centre was Tommy.

Another movement came from the other side of the room. The curtains were drawn, but a cord of daylight struck a chair by the fireplace. Lynley was sitting there, his legs stretched out in front of him. On the table next to him sat a tray of food. Breakfast, by the look of it. She could see the dim shape of a toast rack.

At first she didn't speak, trying instead to remember the events that followed those horrifying moments at Trenarrow's villa. She remembered a brandy being pressed upon her, the sound of voices, a telephone ringing, then a car. Somehow she'd got from Nanrunnel back to Howenstow where she'd made her way to a bed.

She wore a blue satin nightdress that she didn't recognise. A matching dressing gown lay at the foot of the bed. She pushed herself into a sitting position.

"Tommy?"

"You're awake." He went to the windows and pushed the curtains back a bit so that the room had more light. The casements were already open a few inches, but he opened them further so that the crying of the gulls and cormorants made a background of sound.

"What time is it?"

"Just after ten."

"Ten?"

"You've slept since yesterday afternoon. You don't remember?"

"Just bits. Have you been waiting long?"

"A while."

She saw then that he wore the same clothes he'd had on in Nanrunnel. His face was unshaven, and beneath his eyes his skin was dark and puckered with fatigue. "You've been with me all night."

He didn't reply. He remained at the window, far from the bed. Beyond his shoulder, she could see the sky. Against it, his hair was made gold by the sun.

"I thought I'd fly you back to London this morning. Whenever you're ready." He indicated the tray. "This has been sitting here since half past eight. Shall I see about getting you something else?"

"Tommy," she said. "Would you . . . is there . . ." She tried to search his face, but he kept it averted and it showed no response, so she let her words die.

He put his hands in his pockets and looked out the window again. "They've brought John Penellin home."

She followed his lead. "What about Mark?"

"Boscowan knows he took the *Daze*. As to the cocaine . . ." He sighed. "That's John's decision as far as I'm concerned. I won't make it for him. I don't know what he'll do. He may not be ready to draw the line on Mark yet. I just don't know."

"You could report him."

"I could."

"But you won't."

"I think it best that it come from John." He continued gazing out the window, his head lifted to the sky. "It's a beautiful day. A good day for flying."

"What about Peter?" she asked. "Is he cleared now? Is Sidney?"

"St. James thinks Brooke must have got the ergotamine from a chemist in Penzance. It's a prescription drug, but it wouldn't be the first time a chemist slipped something to a customer on the sly. It would have seemed harmless enough. A complaint about a migraine. Aspirin not working. No doctor's surgery open on Saturday."

"He doesn't think Justin took some of his own pills?"

"He can't think of a reason Brooke would have known he had them. I told him it doesn't really matter at this point, but he wants to clear Sidney thoroughly, Peter as well. He's gone to Penzance." His voice died off. His recitation was finished.

Deborah felt her throat aching. There was so much tension in his posture. "Tommy," she said, "I saw you on the porch. I knew you were safe. But when I saw the body—"

"The worst part was Mother," he cut in, "having to tell Mother. Watching her face and knowing every word I said was destroying her. But she wouldn't cry. Not in front of me. Because both of us know I'm at fault at the heart of this."

"No!"

"If they'd married years ago, if I'd allowed them to marry—"

"Tommy, no."

"So she won't grieve in front of me. She won't let me help."

"Tommy, darling—"

"It was horrible." He ran his fingers along the window's transom. "For a moment, I thought he might actually shoot St. James. But he put the gun in his mouth." He cleared his throat. "Why is it that nothing ever prepares one for a sight like that?"

"Tommy, I've known him all my life. He's like my family. When I thought he was dead—"

"The blood. The brain tissue splattered back against the windows. I think I'll see it for the rest of my life. That and everything else. Like a blasted motion picture, playing into eternity against the back of my eyelids whenever I close my eyes."

"Oh, Tommy, please," she said brokenly. "Please. Come here."

At that, his brown eyes met hers directly. "It's not enough, Deb."

He made the statement so carefully. She heard it, frightened. "What's not enough?"

"That I love you. That I want you. I used to think that St. James was thirty different ways a fool for not having married Helen in all these years. I could never understand it. I suppose I really knew why all along, but I didn't want to face it."

She ignored his words. "Shall we use the church in the village, Tommy? Or is London better? What do you think?"

"The church?"

"For the wedding, darling. What do you think?"

He shook his head. "Not on sufferance, Deborah. I won't have you that way."

"But I want you," she whispered. "I love you, Tommy."

"I know you want to believe that. God knows I want to believe it myself. Had you stayed in America, had you never come home, had I joined you there, we might have had a fighting chance. But as it is . . ."

Still he stayed across the room. She couldn't bear the distance. She held out her hand. "Tommy. Tommy. Please."

"Your whole life's with Simon. You know it. We both do."

"No, I . . ." She couldn't finished the sentence. She wanted to rail and fight against what he had said, but he had pierced through to a truth she had long avoided.

He watched her face for a moment before speaking again. "Shall I give you an hour until we leave?"

She opened her mouth to pledge, to deny, but at this final moment, she could not do so. "Yes. An hour," she said.

Part VII

AFTERWORD

28

Lady Helen sighed. "This moves the definition of tedium beyond my wildest dreams. Tell me again what it's going to prove?"

St. James made a third careful fold in the thin pyjama top, lining up the last point of the ice pick's entry. "The defendant claims he was assaulted as he slept. He had only one wound in his side but we've got three holes, each one stained with his blood. How do you suppose that happened?"

She bent over the garment. It was oddly folded to accommodate the three holes. "He was a contortionist in his sleep?"

St. James chuckled. "Better yet a liar awake. He stabbed himself and made the holes later." He caught her yawning. "Am I boring you, Helen?"

"Not at all."

"Late night in the company of a charming man?"

"If only that were true. I'm afraid it was the company of my grandparents, darling. Grandfather blissfully snoring away during the triumphal march in *Aida*. I should have joined him. No doubt he's quite spry this morning."

"An occasional bow to culture is good for the soul."

"I loathe opera. If they'd only sing in English. Is that too much to ask? But it's always Italian or French. Or German. German's the worst. And when they run about the stage in those funny helmets with the horns . . ."

"You're a Philistine, Helen."

"Card-carrying."

"Well, if you'll behave yourself for another half hour, I'll take you to lunch. There's a new brasserie I've found in the Brompton Road."

Her face came to life. "Darling Simon, the very thing! What shall I do next?" She looked round the lab as if seeking new employment, an intention that St. James ignored when the front door slammed and a voice called his name.

He shoved away from the worktable. "Sidney," he said and walked to the door as his sister came dashing up the stairs. "Where the hell have you been?"

She came into the lab. "Surrey first. Then Southampton," she replied as if they were the most logical destinations in the world. She dropped a mink jacket onto a stool. "They've got me doing *another* line of furs. If I don't get a different assignment soon I don't know what I'll do. Modelling the skins of dead animals lies somewhere between absolutely unsavoury and thoroughly disgusting. And they continue to insist I wear nothing underneath." Leaning over the table, she examined the pyjama top. "Blood again? How can you endure it so near to lunchtime? I haven't missed lunch, have I? It's hardly noon." She opened her shoulder bag and began to dig through it. "Now where is it? Of course, I understand why they insist on *some* naked skin, but I've hardly the bosom for it. It's the suggestion of sensuality, they tell me. The promise, the fantasy. What rubbish. Ah, here it is." She produced a tattered envelope which she handed to her brother.

"What is it?"

"What I've spent nearly ten days getting out of Mummy. I even had to trail along to David's for a week just so that she'd know I was determined to have it."

"You've been with Mother?" St. James asked incredulously. "Visiting David in Southampton? Helen, did you—"

"I phoned Surrey that once, but there was no reply. Then you said not to worry her. Remember?"

"Worry Mummy?" Sidney asked. "Worry Mummy about what?"

"About you."

"Why would Mummy worry about me?" She didn't wait for an answer. "Actually, she thought the idea was absurd, at first."

"What idea?"

"Now I know where you get your general poopiness, Simon. But I wore her down over time. I knew I should. Go on, open it. Read it aloud. Helen shall hear it as well."

"Damn it, Sidney. I want to know—"

She grabbed his wrist and shook his arm. "Read."

He opened the envelope with ill-concealed irritation and began to read aloud.

My dear Simon,
 It appears I shall have no rest from Sidney until I apologise, so let me do so at once. Not that a simple line of apology would ever satisfy your sister.

"What is this, Sid?"
She laughed. "Keep reading!"
He went back to his mother's heavily embossed stationery.

I always did think it was Sidney's idea to open the nursery windows, Simon. But when you said nothing upon being accused of having done so, I felt obliged to direct all the punishment towards you. Punishing one's children is the hardest part of being a parent. It's even worse if one has the nagging little fear that one is punishing the wrong child. Sidney has cleared all this up, as only Sidney could do, and although she had begun to insist that I beat her soundly for having let you take her punishment all those years ago, I do draw the line at paddling a twenty-five-year-old woman. So let me apologise to you for placing the blame on your little shoulders—were you ten years old? I've forgotten—and I shall henceforth direct it towards her in an appropriate fashion. We *have* had a rather nice visit, Sidney and I. We spent some time with David and the children as well. It's made me quite hopeful that I shall soon see you in Surrey. Bring Deborah with you if you come. Cotter telephoned cook with the word about her. Poor child. It would be good of you to take her under your wing until she's back on her feet.

Love to you,
Mother

Hands on her hips, Sidney threw back her head and laughed, clearly delighted with having brought off a coup. "Isn't she grand? What a time I had getting her to write it, though. Had she not already wanted to speak to you about seeing to Deborah—you know how she is, always concerned that we'll become social heathens and not do the proper thing in these situations—I doubt if anything could have made her write it."

St. James felt Lady Helen watching him. He knew what she expected him to ask. He didn't ask it. For the past ten days he had known something had happened between them. Cotter's behaviour alone would have told him as much, even if Deborah had not been gone from Howenstow when he'd returned from Penzance on the evening after Trenarrow's death. But other than saying he'd flown her back to London, Lynley said nothing more. And Cotter's grim restraint had not been a thing which St. James wanted to disturb. So even now he said nothing.

Lady Helen, however, did not have his scruples. "What's happened to Deborah?"

"Tommy broke their engagement," Sidney replied. "Cotter hasn't told you, Simon? From the way Mummy's cook tells it, he was practically breathing fire on the phone. Quite in a rage. I half expected to hear he'd duelled with Tommy for satisfaction. 'Guns or knives,' I can hear him shouting. 'Speaker's Corner at dawn.' Tommy hasn't told you either? How decidedly odd. Unless, of course, he thinks *you* may demand satisfaction, Simon." She laughed and then sobered thoughtfully. "You don't think this is a class thing, do you? Considering Peter's choice of Sasha, class can hardly be an issue with the Lynleys."

As she spoke, St. James realised that Sidney had no idea of anything that had happened since her bitter departure from Howenstow on that Sunday morning. He opened the bottom drawer beneath his worktable and removed her perfume bottle.

"You misplaced this," he said.

She grabbed it, delighted. "Where did you find it? Don't tell me it was in the Howenstow wardrobe. I can accept that for shoes but for nothing else."

"Justin took it from your room, Sid."

Such a simple statement, seven words, no more. Their effect upon his sister was immediate. Her smile faded. She tried to hold onto the edges of it, but her lips quivered with the effort. Liveliness left her. Her body seemed to shrink. The quick end to her insouciance told him how precarious a hold she had on her emotions. Her present madcap demeanour merely acted as a shield to fend off a mourning she had not begun.

"Justin?" she said. "Why?"

There was no easy way for him to tell her. He knew that the knowledge would only add to her sorrow. Yet telling her seemed to be the only way that she might start the process of burying her dead.

"To frame you for murder," he said.

"That's ridiculous."

"He wanted to murder Peter Lynley. He got Sasha Nifford instead."

"I don't understand." She rolled the perfume bottle over and over in her hand. She bent her head. She brushed at her cheeks.

"It was filled with a drug she mistook for heroin." At that she looked up. St. James saw the expression on her face. The use of a drug as a means of murder did indeed make the truth so unavoidable. "I'm sorry, love."

"But Peter. Justin told me Peter was at Cambrey's. He said they had a row. And then Mick Cambrey died. He said that Peter *wanted* to kill him. I don't understand. Peter must have known Justin told you and Tommy about it. He knew. He did know."

"Peter didn't kill Justin, Sid. He wasn't even at Howenstow when Justin died."

"Then why?"

"Peter heard something he wasn't supposed to hear. He could have used it against Justin eventually, especially once Mick Cambrey was killed. Justin got nervous. He knew Peter was desperate about money and cocaine. He knew he was unstable. He couldn't predict his behaviour, so he needed to be rid of him."

Together, St. James and Lady Helen told her the story. Islington, oncozyme, Trenarrow, Cambrey. The clinic and cancer. The substitution of a placebo that led to Mick's death.

"Brooke was in jeopardy," St. James said. "He took steps to eliminate it."

"What about me?" she asked. "It's my bottle. Didn't he know that people would think I was involved?" Still she clutched the bottle. Her fingers turned white round it.

"The day on the beach, Sidney," Lady Helen said. "He'd been humiliated rather badly."

"He wanted to punish you," St. James said.

Sidney's lips barely moved as she said, "He loved me. I know it. He loved me."

St. James felt the terrible burden of her words and with it the need to reassure his sister of her intrinsic worth. He wanted to say something but couldn't think of the words that might comfort her.

Lady Helen spoke. "What Justin Brooke was makes no statement about who you are, Sidney. You don't take your definition of self from him. Or from what he felt. Or didn't feel, for that matter."

Sidney gave a choked sob. St. James went to her. "I'm sorry, love," he said, putting his arm tightly round her. "I think I'd rather you hadn't known. But I can't lie to you, Sidney. I'm not sorry he's dead."

She coughed and looked up at him. She offered a shattered smile. "Lord, how hungry I am," she whispered. "Shall we have lunch?"

In Eaton Terrace, Lady Helen slammed the door of her Mini. She did it more to give herself courage—as if the action might attest to the fittingness of her behaviour—than to assure herself that the car door was securely locked. She looked up at the darkened front of Lynley's townhouse, then held up her wrist to the light of a streetlamp. It was nearly eleven, hardly the time for a social call. But the very unsuitability of the hour gave her an advantage which she wasn't willing to relinquish. She climbed the marble-tiled steps to his door.

For the past two weeks, she had been trying to contact him. Every effort had received a rebuff. Out on a job, working a double shift, caught at a meeting, testifying in court. From a series of unquestionably polite secretaries, assistants, and junior officers, she had heard every permutation of a job-related excuse. The implicit message was always the same: He was unavailable, alone, and preferring it so.

It would not be so tonight. She rang the bell. It sounded somewhere in the back of the house, resonating oddly towards the front door as if the building were empty. For a fleeting, mad moment, she actually harboured the thought that he had moved from London—running away from everything once and for all—but then the fanlight above the door showed a sudden illumination in the lower hallway. A bolt was drawn, the door opened, and Lynley's valet stood blinking owlishly out at her. He was wearing his bedroom slippers, Lady Helen noted, and a plaid flannel bathrobe over paisley pyjamas. Surprise and judgement played spontaneously across his face. He wiped them off quickly enough, but Lady Helen read their meaning. Well brought up daughters of peers were not supposed to go calling on gentlemen in the late of night, no matter which part of the twentieth century this was.

"Thank you, Denton," Lady Helen said decisively. She stepped into the hall every bit as if he'd asked her in with earnest protestations of welcome. "Please tell Lord Asherton that I must see him at once." She removed her light evening coat and placed it along with her bag on a chair in the foyer.

Still standing by the open door, Denton looked from her to the street as if trying to recall whether he had actually asked her in. He kept his hand on the doorknob and shifted from foot to foot, appearing caught between a need to protest the solecism of this visit and the fear of someone's wrath should he do so.

"His lordship's asked—"

"I know," Lady Helen said. She felt a brief flicker of guilt to be bullying Denton, knowing that his determination to protect Lynley was motivated by a loyalty that spanned nearly a decade. "I understand. He's asked not to be disturbed, not to be interrupted. He's not returned one of my calls these last two weeks, Denton, so I quite understand he wishes not to be bothered. Now that the issue is clear between us, please tell him I wish to see him."

"But—"

"I shall go directly up to his bedroom if I have to."

Denton signalled his surrender by closing the door. "He's in the library. I'll fetch him for you."

"No need. I know the way."

She left Denton gaping in the hallway and went quickly up the stairs to the first floor of the house, down a thickly carpeted corridor, past an impressive collection of antique pewter, winked at by half a dozen Asherton ancestors long since dead. She heard Lynley's valet not far behind her, murmuring, "My lady . . . Lady Helen . . . ."

The library door was closed. She knocked once, heard Lynley's voice, and entered.

He was sitting at his desk, his head resting in one hand and several folders spread out in front of him. Lady Helen's first thought—with some considerable surprise as he looked up—was that she had no idea he'd begun wearing spectacles to read. He took them off as he got to his feet. He said nothing, merely glanced behind her to where Denton stood, looking monumentally apologetic.

"Sorry," Denton said. "I tried."

"Don't blame him," Lady Helen said. "I bullied my way in." She saw that Denton had moved one step into the room. With another he would be close enough to put his hand on her arm and escort her back down the stairs and out into the street. She couldn't imagine him doing so without Lynley's direction, but just in case he was considering the idea, she headed him off. "Thank you, Denton. Leave us please. If you will."

Denton gawked at her. He looked at Lynley, who nodded sharply once. He left the room.

"Why haven't you returned my calls, Tommy?" Lady Helen asked the moment they were alone. "I've telephoned here and the Yard repeatedly. I've stopped by four times. I've been sick with worry about you."

"Sorry, old duck," he said easily. "There's been a mass of work lately. I'm up to my ears in it. Will you have a drink?" He walked to a rosewood table on which were arranged several decanters and a set of glasses.

"Thank you, no."

He poured himself a whisky but did not drink it at once. "Please sit down."

"I think not."

"Whatever you'd like." He offered her a lopsided smile and tossed back a large portion of his drink. And then, perhaps unwilling to keep up the pretence any longer, he looked away from her, saying, "I'm sorry, Helen. I wanted to return your calls. But I couldn't do it. Sheer cowardice, I suppose."

Her anger melted immediately. "I can't bear to see you like this. Walled up in your library. Incommunicado at work. I can't bear it, Tommy."

For a moment, the only response was his breathing. She could hear it, shallow and unevenly spaced. Then he said, "The only time I seem to be able to drive her from my mind is when I'm working. So that's what I've been doing, that's all I've been doing. And when I haven't been on a case, I've spent the time telling myself that I'll get over this eventually. A few more weeks, a few months." Shakily, he laughed. "It's a bit difficult to believe."

"I know. I understand."

"God, yes. Who on earth could know better than you?"

"Then why haven't you phoned me?"

He moved restlessly across the room to the fireplace. No fire demanded his attention there, so he gave it instead to a collection of Meissen porcelain plates on the overmantel. He took one from its stand, turning it in his hands. Lady Helen wanted to tell him to have a care, the plate might well shatter under the strength with which he gripped it, but she said nothing. He put the plate back. She repeated her question.

"You know I've wanted to talk to you. Why haven't you phoned me?"

"I haven't been able to. It hurts too much, Helen. I can't hide that from you."

"Why on earth should you want to?"

"I feel like a fool. I should be stronger than this. None of it should matter. I should be able just to slough it off and go on."

"Go on?" She felt all her anger return in a rush. Her blood heated in the presence of this stiff-upper-lip attitude which she'd always found so contemptible in the men she knew, as if schooling and breeding and generations of reserve condemned each of them to a life of feeling nothing. "Do you actually mean to tell me that you've no right to your sorrow because you're a man? I don't believe that. I *won't* believe that."

"It's nothing at all to do with sorrow. I've just been trying to find my way back to the man I was three years ago. Before Deborah. If I can reclaim him, I'll be fine."

"That man was no different from the man you are now."

"Three years ago, I'd not have taken this so hard. What were women to me then? Bed partners. Nothing more."

"And that's what you want to be? A man drifting through life in a sexual fugue? Only thinking about his next performance in bed? Is that what you want?"

"It's easier that way."

"Of course it's easy. That kind of life is always easy. People fade out of one another's bed with hardly a word of farewell, let alone one of commitment. And if by chance they wake up one morning with someone whose name escapes them, it's all right, isn't it? It's part of the game."

"There was no pain involved in relationships then. There was nothing involved. Never for me."

"That may be what you'd like to remember, Tommy, but that's not the way it was. Because if what you say is true, if life was nothing more than collecting and seducing a stable full of women, why did you never have me?"

He reflected on the question. He went back to the decanters and poured himself a second drink. "I don't know."

"Yes, you do. Tell me why."

"I don't know."

"What a conquest I would have been. Thrown over by Simon, my life in a shambles. The last thing I wanted was an involvement with anyone. How on earth did you resist a challenge like that? What a chance it was to prove yourself to yourself. What incredible fodder for your self-esteem."

He placed his glass on the table, turned it beneath his fingers. She watched his profile and saw how fragile a thing was his veneer of control.

"I expect you were different," he said.

"Not at all. I had the right equipment. I was just like the others, heat and pleasure, breasts and thighs."

"Don't be ridiculous."

"A woman, after all. Easily seduced, especially by an expert. But you never tried with me. Not even once. That sort of sexual reticence doesn't make sense in a man whose sole interest in women revolves round what they have to offer him in bed. And I had it to offer, didn't I, Tommy? Oh, I would have resisted at first. But I would have slept with you eventually, and you knew it. But you didn't try."

He turned to her. "How could I have done that to you after what you'd been through with Simon?"

"Compassion?" she demanded. "From the man bent on pleasure? What difference did it make whose body provided it? Weren't we all the same?"

He was quiet for so long that she wondered if he would answer. She could see the struggle for composure on his face. She willed him to speak, knowing only that he had to acknowledge his sorrow so that it could live and rage and then die.

"Not you," he said finally. She could tell the phrase cost him dearly. "Not Deborah."

"What was different?"

"I let things go further."

"Further?"

"To the heart."

She crossed the room to him. Her hand touched his arm. "Don't you see, Tommy? You weren't that man bent on pleasure. You want to think you were, but that wasn't the case. Not for anyone who bothered to take the time to know you. Not for me certainly, who was never your lover. And not for Deborah, who was."

"I wanted something different with her." His eyes were red-rimmed. "Roots, ties, a family. I was willing to be something more to have that. It was worth it. She was worth it."

"Yes. She was. And she was worth grieving over as well. She's still worth that."

"Oh, God," he whispered.

Her hand slid down his arm, closed over his wrist. "Tommy dear, it's all right. Really."

He shook his head blindly as if by that movement he could shake off his terrible desolation. "I think I shall die of loneliness, Helen." His voice broke horribly, the sound of a man who hadn't allowed himself to experience a single emotion in years. "I can't bear it."

He started to turn from her, to go back to his desk, but she stopped him and closed the remaining space between them. She took him into her arms.

"You're not alone, Tommy," she said quite gently.

He began to cry.

Deborah pushed open the gate just as the streetlamp on Lordship Place lit for the evening, sending delicate sprays of light through the mist that fell on the garden. She stood for a moment and gazed at the warm burnt sienna bricks of the house, at its fresh white plasterwork, at its old wrought iron handrail that forever rusted in spots that forever needed paint. In so many ways, it would always be home to her, no matter how long she managed to stay away—three years, three decades, or like this time, a month.

She'd managed avoidance through a string of fabrications which she knew her father didn't believe for a moment. *Setting myself up professionally, Dad. Working very hard. Appointments here and there. Showing my portfolio around. Shall we meet somewhere for dinner? No, I can't come to Chelsea.* He'd accepted the excuses rather than quarrel with her again.

No more than did she, her father didn't savour a repetition of their row in Paddington, a week after her return from Cornwall. He had wanted her to come home. She refused to consider it. He didn't understand. To him, it was simple. Pack your things, close the flat, come back to Cheyne Row. In effect, as far as he was concerned, return to the past. She couldn't do so. She tried to explain her need for a time that was solely her own. His response was a nasty castigation of Tommy—for changing her, destroying her, distorting her values—and from there the row grew, ending with her wresting from him a bitter promise not to speak of her relationship with Tommy ever again, to her or to anyone else. They had parted acrimoniously and had not seen each other since.

Nor had she seen Simon. Nor had she wanted to. Those few horrifying moments in Nanrunnel had exposed her to herself in an unforgiving light that she could no longer ignore, and for the month that followed, she'd had to examine and admit to the lie she'd been living for the last two and a half years. The lover of one man, bound in a thousand different ways to another. And yet bound forever to Tommy as well in ways she could never allow him to know.

She didn't know where to begin to undo the damage she had done to herself and to others. So she had stayed in Paddington, working as an apprentice photographer for a Mayfair studio, spending a long weekend in Wales and another in Brighton. And she had waited for her life to take on a semblance of peace. It had not done so.

So she had come on this visit to Chelsea, not exactly knowing what she could accomplish, only knowing that the longer she stayed away, the more difficult a reconciliation with her father would be. What she wanted from Simon, she could not have said.

Through the mist, she saw the kitchen lights come on. Her father passed the window. He went to the stove, then to the table where he disappeared from her view. She followed the flagstone path across the garden and descended the stairs.

Alaska met her at the door as if, with that preternatural sensitivity inherent to felines, he'd known she'd be arriving. He twitched one ear and began a stately crisscrossing through her legs, his tail waving majestically.

"Where's Peach?" she asked the cat as she rubbed his head. His back arched appreciatively. He began to purr.

Footsteps came out of the kitchen into the foyer. "Deb!"

She straightened. "Hello, Dad."

She saw him looking for signs that she'd come home—a suitcase, a carton, an easily movable item like a lamp. But he said nothing other than, "Had your dinner, girl?" and returned to the kitchen where the rich smell of roasting meat was scenting the air.

She followed him. "Yes. At the flat." She saw that he was working at the table, that he'd lined up four pairs of shoes to be polished. She noted the heaviness of their construction, necessary so that the crosspiece of his brace could fit through the left heel. For some reason, the sight effected a blackness in her. She looked away.

"How's work?" Cotter asked her.

"Fine. I've been using my old cameras, the Nikon and the Hasselblad. They're working for me well. They make me rely on myself more, on knowledge and technique. I find I like that."

Cotter nodded, applied two fingertips of polish to the top of a shoe. He was nobody's fool. "It's forgotten, Deb," he answered. "All of it, girl. You do what's best for you."

She felt a rush of gratitude. She looked round the room at the white brick walls, the old stove with three covered pots sitting on it, the worn work tops, the glass-fronted cabinets, the uneven tile floor. A small basket near the stove legs sat empty.

"Where's Peach?" she asked.

"Mr. St. James 's taken 'er out for a walk." Cotter gave a glance to the wall clock. "Absent-minded, 'e is. Dinner's been ready these last fifteen minutes."

"Where's he gone?"

"The embankment, I expect."

"Shall I fetch him?"

His reply was perfectly noncommittal. "If you fancy a walk. If you don't, it's fine. Dinner'll keep a bit."

She said, "I'll see if I can find him." She went back to the foyer but turned at the kitchen door. Her father was giving his complete attention to the shoes. "I've not come home, Dad. You know that, don't you?"

"I know what I know," was Cotter's answer as she left the house.

The mist was encircling each streetlamp with an amber corona, and a breeze was beginning to blow off the Thames. Deborah turned up the collar of her coat as she walked. Inside houses, people were sitting down to their evening meals while at the King's Head and Eight Bells at the corner of Cheyne Row, others gathered at the bar for conversation and refreshment. Deborah smiled fondly when she saw this latter group. She knew most of them by name. They'd been nightly patrons of the pub for years. The sight of them filled her with unaccountable nostalgia which she dismissed as nonsensical and pushed on to Cheyne Walk.

Traffic was light. She crossed quickly to the river and saw him some distance away, elbows resting on the embankment wall, studying the charming whimsicality of Albert Bridge. In the summers of her childhood they had frequently wandered across it to Battersea Park. She wondered if he remembered that. What a gawky little companion she'd been to him then. How patient and kind his friendship had been in return.

She stopped for a moment to observe him unnoticed. He scanned the bridge. A smile played on his lips. And all the while at his feet, Peach sat placidly chewing on her lead. As Deborah watched the two of them, Peach caught sight of her and began pulling away from St. James. She turned a quick circle, got tangled in the lead, fell in a heap, and gave a happy yelp.

Distracted from his admiration of one of London's most capricious structures, St. James looked down at the little dachshund and then back up as if to locate the cause of her desire for escape. When he saw Deborah, he released his grip on the lead and let the dog run to her, which Peach did, ears flopping wildly, rear legs nearly overtaking the rest of her body. She was a frenzy of joy. She threw herself upon Deborah, barking ecstatically, wagging her tail.

Deborah laughed, hugged the dog, allowed herself to be licked on the nose. She thought about how it was so simple with animals. They gave their hearts without question or fear. They had no expectations. They were so easy to love. If people could only be like that, no one would ever be hurt, she thought. No one would ever need to learn how to forgive.

St. James watched her walk towards him in the light of the embankment lamps with Peach dancing along at her side. She carried no umbrella against the mist that was creating a net of bright beads on her hair. Her only protection was a lambswool coat, its collar turned up so that it framed her face like an Elizabethan ruff. She looked lovely, like someone out of a sixteenth-century portrait. But there was a change to her face, something that hadn't been there six weeks ago, something aching and adult.

"Your dinner's ready," she said when she reached him. "You're out late for a walk, aren't you?" She joined him at the wall. It felt like a commonplace sort of meeting, as if nothing had happened between them, as if in the last month she hadn't faded in and out of his life without greeting or farewell.

"I wasn't thinking of the time. Sidney told me she went with you to Wales."

"We had a lovely weekend on the coast."

He nodded. He had been watching a family of swans on the water and would have pointed them out to her—their presence at this section of the river was certainly unusual—but he did not do so. Her manner was too distant.

Apparently, however, she saw the birds herself, caught in silhouette in the lights that sparkled from the opposite bank. "I've never seen swans in this part of the river before," she said. "And at night. D'you suppose they're all right?"

There were five of them—two adults and three nearly grown cygnets—floating peacefully near the pilings of Albert Bridge.

"They're all right," he said and saw how the birds gave him a small opening to speak. "I was sorry you broke the swan that day in Paddington."

"I can't come home," she said in reply. "I need to make peace with you somehow. Perhaps take a step towards being friends again someday. But I can't come home."

This was the difference then. She was maintaining that kind of careful emotion-sparing distance that people develop to protect themselves when things come to an end between them. It reminded him of himself three years ago, when she had come to say goodbye and he had listened, too afraid to speak lest saying one word might cause the floodgates to open and everything he felt to spill forth in a humiliating wave of entreaty that both time and circumstance would have forced her to deny. They had come full circle, it seemed, to goodbye again. How simple just to say it and get on with living.

He looked from her face to her hand resting on the embankment wall. It was bare of Lynley's ring. He lightly touched the finger that had worn it. She didn't pull away, and it was that absence of movement which prompted him to speak.

"Don't leave me again, Deborah."

He saw that she hadn't expected a response of that kind. She'd come without a line of defence. He pressed the advantage.

"You were seventeen. I was twenty-eight. Can you try to understand what it was like for me then? I'd cut myself off from caring about anyone for years. And all of a sudden, I was caring for you. Wanting you. Yet all the time believing that if we made love—"

She spoke quickly, lightly. "All that's passed, isn't it? It doesn't matter really. It's much better forgotten."

"I told myself that I couldn't make love to you, Deborah. I manufactured all sorts of mad reasons why. Duty to your father. A betrayal of his trust. The destruction of our friendship—yours and mine. Our souls couldn't bond together if we became lovers, and I wanted a soulmate, so we couldn't make love. I kept repeating your age over and over. How could I live with myself if I took a seventeen-year-old girl to bed?"

"What does it matter now? We're beyond that. After all that's happened, what does it matter that we didn't make love three years ago?" Her questions weren't so much cold as they were cautious, as if whatever careful reasoning she'd gone through in her decision to leave him were under attack.

"Because if you're going to make this leaving of yours a permanent arrangement, then at least you'll leave this time knowing the truth. I let you go because I wanted peace. I wanted you out of the house. I reasoned that if you were gone, I'd stop feeling torn. I'd stop wanting you. I'd stop feeling guilty for wanting you. I'd get the whole issue of sex driven out of my mind. You'd been gone less than a week when I saw the truth of the matter."

"It doesn't—"

He persisted. "I'd thought I could exist quite nicely without you, and my own hypocrisy slapped me right in the face. I wanted you back. I wanted you home. So I wrote to you."

As he was speaking, she'd kept her attention on the river, but now she turned to him. He didn't wait for her to ask the question.

"I didn't post the letters."

"Why?"

And now he had come to it. So easy to sit alone in the study and rehearse for a month all the things he had needed to say to her for years. But now that he had the opportunity to say them, he found himself faltering all over again and he wondered why it had always been so frightening that she should know the truth. He drew in air like resolution.

"For the same reason I wouldn't make love with you. I was afraid. I knew that you could have any man in the world."

"Any man?"

"All right. You could have Tommy. Given that choice, how could I expect that you might want me?"

"You?"

"A cripple."

"So there it is, isn't it? We end up at *cripple* no matter where we begin."

"We do. Because it's a fact of who I am and we can't ignore it. I've spent the last three years considering all the things I could never do at your side, things that any other man—Tommy—could do with ease."

"What's the point of that? Why keep torturing yourself?"

"Because I had to work through it. It had to stop mattering so much that I couldn't even hold you if I were unattached to this cursed brace. It had to stop mattering so much that I'm crippled. And that's what you need to know before you leave me. That it doesn't matter any longer. Crippled or not. Half a man. Three-quarters. It doesn't matter. I want you." And then he added unfairly but without a regret since there are no rules that govern affairs of the heart, "Once and for life."

It was done. In whatever fashion she would judge them, the words had been said. Three years too late, but said all the same. And even if she chose to leave him now, at least she chose knowing the worst he was and the best. He could live with that.

"What do you want of me?" she asked.

"You know the answer to that."

Peach moved restlessly at their feet. Someone shouted from the patch of green across Cheyne Walk. Deborah watched the river. He followed the direction of her gaze to see that the swans had cleared the final pilings of the bridge. They were floating unchanged as they had done before, as they always would do, seeking the safety of Battersea.

"Deborah," he said.

The birds gave her the answer. "Like the swans, Simon?"

It was more than enough. "My love, like the swans."